A BELLEVUE BULLIES Novel

BOARDED
by LOVE

TONI ALEO

Interior formatted and designed by E.M. Tippetts Book Designs

Books by Toni Aleo

Books in the Bellevue Bullies Series
Boarded by Love
Clipped by Love (early 2015)
Hooked by Love (late 2015)

The Assassins Series
Taking Shots
Trying to Score
Empty Net
Falling for the Backup
Blue Lines
Breaking Away
Laces and Lace (Due out November 2014)
A Very Merry Hockey Holiday (Due out December 2014)

Standalone
Let it be Me

Taking Risks Series
The Whiskey Prince
Becoming the Whiskey Princess (Due out 2015)

I couldn't have written this book without the beautiful sounds of Ed Sheeran.
I honestly listen to the + and x albums on repeat, when I am writing.
So Ed, this book is for you.
Thanks for the inspiration.

CHAPTER 1

 *Claire*

Something is off tonight.

I don't know what it is, and I don't know why I'm feeling like this tonight. But as I sit staring at myself in the mirror, I can't help but want more than what I'm doing right now. I mean, I have a good life and I am happy now, but something, something is missing. It honestly makes no sense; I'm actually loved and happy, so I have no clue what is wrong with me. I have everything I need and could ask for. But instead of being thankful and grateful, I question myself – my life – when I shouldn't because thankfully, I don't have to live the way I did four years ago.

I no longer have to worry constantly if my mom will be coming home with food instead of drugs or booze, that she wouldn't be alone. She was never alone. She always came home with some random sleazy guy that she would make me call "uncle," if he was around for more than five minutes. And soon the food she hopefully brought with her, usually cold, greasy KFC or burgers, would be forgotten. Instead, shit would get weird in our hundred square foot trailer; my heart would race, and I would be hiding underneath my bed from my new "uncle."

She had a tendency to pick the supershitty guys – it was like her superpower, one I hope she didn't pass down to me. She especially managed to pick the ones who liked to touch little girls, but thankfully, I was pretty good at getting away. I was always a kicker, a biter, and a nut-puncher. But that all changed when I turned fourteen – my mom brought home a guy that did get to me.

Because that time I didn't try to get away.

Wasn't my greatest decision, and I regret it now, but at the time I wanted to feel something. I wanted to feel what my mom felt, because obviously she was feeling something great, judging by the noises she made, but I felt absolutely nothing. I really wanted to eat that day. I hadn't eaten in four days, I was starving, and he worked at the grocery store, so I figured it was a good bet. I was empty in more ways than one, so I did it to get what I needed.

And because of that moment, for the next two years, I lived just like my mother. Drinking the Two-Buck Chuck she brought home, having sex with any guy who wanted me and promised me dinner. Disgusting, I know. I was basically what my mom was – a whore. And I was living the life I thought I was destined for, living the life I was dealt because no one gave a shit enough to tell me that there could have been anything else.

That all changed when my mom was brutally killed.

It was surreal, and for a long time I didn't believe it. I also blamed everyone, I think because I was so disgusted in myself that I wasn't sad. I didn't miss her. I was glad to be free of her, but I thought that made me a bad person. I was mostly mad at my real uncle for not saving me when he could. I'll never forget the moment that my uncle Phillip came into my life. I was sixteen, and I was angry that my mom was gone because of her own stupidity. I was scared that I was going to end up like her. For the first time, survival was not the most important option, and I was messed up. My great-aunt had been hell, putting me in religious rehab, calling me a whore and telling me I was just like my mother, and trying to "SAVE ME WITH THE JESUS." I just couldn't go back to her version of rehab with the orderlies that had grabby hands. That was *not* an option, so I did the most logical thing. I tore her house apart and packed what little shit I had and was gone.

I was walking down the street, getting ready to walk right out of town if I had to. But I knew I needed to stop and think, so I went to my favorite place, the Sculpture Garden in Minneapolis where I grew up. As I thought about my next move and what to do, Phillip was there to get me. He was driving from my aunt's house, trying to find me, and when he did, he wasn't going anywhere without me. He convinced me to go get waffles at this diner across the street, and it was there that he told me that he wasn't going to let me go the way he had let his sister go. Of course, I didn't believe him. I was used to men making promises they didn't keep just to use me. But now, three years later, I couldn't be more grateful for him.

At the time, I didn't understand how anyone thought a single, twenty-nine-year-old man would know how to take care of an angry sixteen-year-old, but obviously someone knew that he was what I needed. It wasn't easy. The first six months of being with him were complete hell. I drove him crazy; I tried to sleep with a couple of the guys from the Assassins, the team he played pro hockey for. I tried to push every button I could on him, but he never broke. He kept strong, told me he loved me, and would always be there for me, no matter what I did.

I'd never had that.

My mom only told me she loved me when she was strung out, wearing ripped up fishnets with makeup smeared on her face while she leaned back on some guy, his eyes locked on my small, fragile body. Or when she needed me to go to the store for cigarettes, or condoms, or something. And as I got older, she stopped saying it because I was competition for the attention of the men she brought home. I wanted to vomit when she would say it because I knew it wasn't true. If she really loved me, why was I living in a roach-infested house, hiding under my bed from the fourteenth "uncle" of the month? Why would I lock myself in the bathroom and cry because I was so hungry while she had lines of cocaine laid on every flat surface in the house, higher than a kite. Why wasn't I important enough?

I was destined to end up like her, and I probably would have ended up like her – beaten, raped, and found in a ditch – if Phillip hadn't come into my life.

It wasn't just Phillip, though; it was Reese too, his now soon-to-be wife. Before, I never had goals; I only wanted to get through the next day, wanting to feel anything enough to sleep with the next guy who wanted me. I used to think that I wasn't worth much, but Reese helped me to see that being a coked-out stripper like my mom wasn't what I was meant to be. I wasn't easy to talk to, but she found a way, and that was through dance. I've always loved to dance, not of the stripper variety like my mom, but more like the really awesome, choreographed stuff. I would spend hours watching music videos, when my mom would remember to pay the cable bill, and I would mimic the girls in the videos. I was amazing, and when Reese found me doing just that in her sister's house, the next thing I knew she had me in her studio learning routines with her.

And soon my dream was born.

Even looking at myself now, that dream still wants to be a reality. I feel it in my heart. I want to be a world-famous choreographer, teaching people like Justin Timberlake amazing routines to perform all over the world, or in Vegas, choreographing shows. The only problem is I'm not sure if it will to keep me safe, stable, and steady. I need that. After years of not knowing when my next meal was coming, I can't just throw caution to the wind and hope I make it. I need safety. I need stability. I've had that the last three years because of Phillip, but I can't depend on him my whole life. I can't depend on anyone. I have to work for me.

So while I would have loved to go to a dance school like Reese suggested, I decided to stay home near them and go for business. Maybe I'll take over Reese's dance studio, or maybe start my own. The possibilities are endless, and I think that maybe I'm working here just to have the option to go do something amazing later.

"Claire, you go on in thirty."

I nod without looking as I know the voice belongs to Ms. Prissy, before reaching back to French braid my bright red hair. Tucking it up in the back since my hair is so long, I reach for my black wig and slide it on my head. Pinning down the wig real tight, I start to put on my makeup in a rush. I'm running a tad bit behind since I stayed at the studio later, working on a routine for a duet that will compete in a couple weeks. As I apply my eye shadow in a dark, dramatic way, my hand pauses as the only advice my mom ever gave me rushes through my mind: *Never look back, baby. That's a real good way to get hit, head-on.*

Crap, why am I thinking of that? I can't sit here and think of her right now. I don't do it often, but when I do, I dwell, and right now is not the time to dwell. Ms. Prissy doesn't like when you're late, and I try never to be. I needed a job like this and got lucky when she wanted to hire me. I know that Phillip and Reese would give me the world if I asked, but I don't like to ask for things. I want to stand on my own two feet, be able to afford my next meal, and working here, I've managed to bank more than I ever thought, and I don't plan on stopping until I graduate. Then I'll have a down payment for a business of my own or to redo Reese's. I don't know. We will see.

"Oh my God, Claire!"

I look back at one of my friends, Ellen, with a puzzled look on my face. "What? What happened?

She didn't look like anything was wrong, but you never knew with her. Ellen reminds me a lot of my mom. She isn't an addict or anything, but she sure does love the men, and they *love* her. With her luscious blond hair, big breasts, blue eyes, and big, plump lips, the guys eat her up. She's sweet, but outside of work, we aren't friends. I don't need someone in my life who reminds me of my mom.

"That asshole I was sleeping with, he gave me crabs!"

I gasp, "What? One of your rockers?"

"Rockers" was what the girls who worked in the Rock Room called the guys who came in there. When the station beside me shakes, I look over to see my friend Tessi rushing to get ready. I shoot her a grin before turning back to Ellen.

"No! Heck no, but because I got the crabs, I can't fucking dance in there till I get rid of them. That's like a *WEEK!* I'm so fucking pissed."

I nod. I'd be pissed too if I actually worked in that room, but I don't, by choice. I don't have to grind on some forty-five-year-old for extra money. The girls in the club pay me extra to choreograph their routines – management does too for the group numbers – so I am pretty secure without the extra dough, plus my tips are fantastic. Some of the girls say they bring home thousands, but still, I can't do it. There is a difference between dancing onstage in only a bra and undies and dancing naked on some guy. I don't mind being looked at, but I do have a problem being touched. Hence the reason I haven't had sex in three years. I feel I did that enough in my younger teen years to suffice for the rest of my life.

"So who were you sleeping with?" I ask Ellen.

"Allen West, told ya he was a sleaze," Tessi says from beside me. I glance over at her before looking back at Ellen and then looking back at Tessi. I'm confused.

"Allen? My Allen? Tall Allen?"

"Yeah, didn't you go out with him a few times?" Ellen asks.

I blink a few times, confused. "I am still going out with him."

Tessi scoffs beside me as Ellen exclaims, "What?! That douche told me you broke up!"

"I mean, we weren't really together, but we were seeing each other. I never slept with him or anything," I say, but I still can't believe that not only has Ellen been sleeping with him, but he gave her crabs. *Small miracles... Small freaking miracles.*

"Damn girl, I'm so sorry," Ellen says with a worried look on her face.

I shake my head, waving her off. "Don't worry about it."

With a curt smile, Ellen runs off as I sit with my brush still held up to my face. I can't believe it. Allen West was a decent guy, solid, or at least I thought he was. I stayed clear of guys my freshman year and the beginning of this year, but somehow Allen talked me into a date and then another. The next thing I knew, we were walking across the quad holding hands. We had never officially put labels on each other, but he was fun to hang out with, and I thought that he would be a great guy to end my celibacy streak with, but I guess I was wrong.

"Wow. Just wow. Man, I can pick 'em, huh?" I say with a shake of my head.

"Yeah, I was gonna tell you about that today. Ellen called me last night, but I forgot to call you when I looked back down at my sociology work. I am going to fail that class," Tessi says as she brings her brown hair up into a high ponytail. Tessi, my friend Skylar, and I are the only girls from UB who work in the club. It's great money, easy hours, and they let you come and go as you please. Plus we have actual security so we won't get jumped in the parking lot. Girls who waitress at TGI Fridays have more problems than we do. And make less in tips.

"It's okay, and no, you won't fail. I'll help you," I say as I watch her for a moment. Tessi gives me a bright smile as I continue to watch her get ready. I'm zoning out a lot tonight, which is unusual. Usually I'm on top of things, helping the other girls who are behind. Tessi never needs my help, though. She's a lot like me, a go-getter, climbing out of her own issues. That's probably why we're such great friends. We both get it. We met at freshman orientation and became fast friends. I am the one who got her the job here. She is a great friend and one of the most beautiful girls I have ever seen.

She has beautiful, big brown eyes, with thick black lashes framing them, big breasts, and beautifully plump lips. She has dangerous curves and a really great attitude. Like me, she had lived a pretty rough life, and now is doing everything to make sure she never has to go back to the life she used to live. She's going to school to be a social worker; she wants to help kids who had shitty lives. She always tells me that she wishes someone had been there for her and me, and I do too, but then I think that maybe it was for the best. We learned from that shit and pulled ourselves together, and going to live with Phillip was probably the best thing ever. I know that it wasn't ideal for a kid to grow up like that, but I've accepted it. I figure it made me stronger. I learned from it and got my drive from it. I'm stronger than any of the silly girls I go to school with, and I like that. I wear my childhood like a badge of honor instead of being ashamed of it.

She turns to look at me and smiles. "You're not torn up by this, are you? Allen was a dick. You can get someone way better, girl. Don't sweat it."

She was right, obviously he didn't mean that much to me, because I'm not mad or even broken up about it. I don't even feel like I lost anything. I feel nothing. Surprise maybe because he was harboring an STD but nothing else. I nod. "Nope, not torn up at all. I'm not mad that he slept with someone else while talking to me, but I am mad that he could have gotten my vagina sick."

Tessi nods sagely as she moves some gloss along her bottom lip. "I would be too. Give him hell, girlfriend, but right now, you need to pop your contacts in and get onstage. Ms. Prissy hasn't been laid in weeks, and she is in full bitch mode, I can promise you that."

I laugh out loud as I turn to look back at myself. I still have a lot to do. I wish I could be like Tessi and not care if someone recognizes me in this place, but it always freaks me out that Phillip could come in here, or one of his friends. I'm not ashamed of what I do by any means, but I still don't like to advertise it. Plus, I'm not a hundred percent sure how Phillip would feel about this. Reese knows, but I've never brought it up to Phillip, and neither has she. But really, the thought of some guy coming up to me outside of the club is enough, so I do everything I can to change my appearance.

Reaching for my contact case, I open it quickly, popping in my dark brown contacts to cover my bright blue eyes. Positioning some fake lashes to make my eyes look fuller, I finish my eye makeup before applying some bright red lipstick. Pursing my lips at myself, satisfied with the way I look, I smile at my reflection before standing up to get ready. Reaching for my outfit for the night, I hurry to get ready because, like Tessi said, Ms. Prissy could be a major bitch when she wasn't getting laid regularly. After sliding the crystal-encrusted booty shorts up over my black fishnets, I slide my feet into a pair of black high heels as Tessi stands up to help me tie up the back of the crystal-studded corset.

"Claire! Let's go," Ms. Prissy yells.

Tessi laughs before swatting me on my butt. "Good luck."

I flash her a grin as I grab my fans and make my way to the curtain. Tonight, I'm doing an old-fashioned burlesque fan dance. I'd seen it on TV one night and then spent the next two weeks researching and rehearsing my set before I showed Ms. Prissy and management at the club. That was a year ago, and now I was the most popular act on the busiest night. I also do pole and regular burlesque dancing, but the fans are my favorite. I send Ms. Prissy an apologetic smile as I run to my mark, but all I receive back is an eye roll before she gets on the radio to let the tech guys know I'm ready. When "Diamonds" by Rihanna starts, I slowly pull the curtains back, revealing myself to the crowd as it erupts with catcalls and men hollering my name.

Showtime.

Oh, by the way, my name is Claire Anderson and I'm a nineteen-year-old sophomore at the University of Bellevue here in Tennessee. By night though, onstage and in this club, my name is Diamond, and I'm the best burlesque dancer at Ms. Prissy's Gentlemen's Club.

Nice to meet you.

CHAPTER 2

⚔ JUDE

My lungs are burning.

It has been a long practice and my lungs aren't the only things that are burning, my back is too. I'm gonna need a good rubdown after this, and it can't come fast enough. Ever since I took a hard hit into the boards a couple practices ago, my back has been tweaking. My dad told me this isn't a big deal, to push through the pain, and maybe he's right. This is my year. I have scouts looking at me from New York, Detroit, Minnesota, and Los Angeles. I was hoping for Detroit since it was my dream to wear the famous red and white jersey, playing for one of the first six teams in the NHL, but really, I'd go anywhere. As long as I'm playing hockey. Professionally.

I love the feeling I get when I step out onto the ice. The way the cool air fills my lungs, making me breathless. The smell of the ice tickling my senses before my heart begins to race from the adrenaline of dominating the ice. It has always been like that, and for as long as I can remember, I've loved it. I love everything about it. It is like a drug, my drug, and I wouldn't trade it for anything.

I knew from a very young age that I wanted to play pro, and even though the University of Bellevue wasn't my first-choice school, the scholarship they offered was top-notch, and soon they were my only choice. My dad told me that he would pay for the schooling wherever I wanted to go, but I didn't want to be indebted to my father. I knew that somehow he would hold that over my head, and I didn't want that. Plus, UB was going places and I wanted to help their hockey team, the Bullies, get there. I also didn't want to leave my family. I would never admit that to anyone; being the oldest boy of our family, I'm supposed to be the strong one – and I am – but still, I couldn't leave my family.

At first I didn't want to leave my mom since my older sister Lucy and I had moved out, and my dad was always leaving for work. Then at the end of my freshman year, Lucy moved back home after a failed marriage, and she was severely depressed. She was pregnant with Angie, my niece, and her deadbeat husband left her for someone else. It sucked and I wanted to kill him, but instead, we took her back like she never left.

My mom is a worrywart though, and sometimes she worries so much she makes herself sick, so I'm glad I'm close to home to help when I'm needed. She's doing better because Lucy is, but it was hard when my brother Jayden moved into the frat house as a freshman at UB. He also plays with me on the Bullies. He has scouts looking at him, but like they said to me, they wanted to see how we do in college.

My baby brother, Jace, is graduating high school this year. They say he will go straight into the draft; he's unbelievable and his talent is awe inspiring. While Jayden and I are jealous that we've had to go to college first, my whole family is proud of Jace. He's going to be a star. Hell, we all are going to be stars.

But first, I have to finish some college, and now that I'm here, I really couldn't think of a better school to go to. I love my team, and boy, do I love the girls at this school. I guess you could call me a ladies' man, and I wear the label proudly. I'm not one of those guys to be tied down. What is the point? There are too many girls wanting me, and I know the numbers will triple once I go pro.

Man, I can't wait.

Racing down the ice, I cut left and deke to the right before crashing the net, hoping for a rebound, but Shane, the best goalie I have ever played with, covers the puck and everyone backs away as the whistle blows. Flexing my back, hoping the tweak will go away, I look around as Coach Moss goes over the next play he wants us to carry out. Coach Moss is a great coach, but rumors are floating around that he's going to get replaced because he's going to move up to the NHL. I hope it happens after I'm gone because Coach Moss and I understand each other. He understands that I'm the best player on the ice, and I understand that as long as I do what he says, I could be one of the greats in the NHL. I have been playing for him for as long as I can remember, starting in the travel league alongside my brothers. He was the one who convinced the admissions committee to offer me a full scholarship.

When the whistle blows again, I move to the face-off circle by the boards, hoping we win the face-off. We do and I get the puck before passing it off to the right winger, but then he gets stuck with the puck behind the goal. I rush toward him, digging for it before winning it and taking it out toward the front of the goal. The play called for me to pass it to my right winger again because he was lined up with an opening, but I have one too. Kinda. So I shoot, getting past the two defensemen and going right over Shane's shoulder into the goal. My arms go up in the air as Coach Moss goes crazy, blowing his damn whistle.

"Sinclair! Sinclair!"

I ignore him, basking in my awesomeness as my teammates hit my shin with their sticks, celebrating an awesome goal.

"Jude fucking Sinclair! I know you hear me!"

I turn as Coach skates toward me, his face red with anger because, like usual, I didn't follow the play.

"I made it."

"Well, no shit, but that wasn't the play. West was open, completely open; you had to go through two defensemen to get it in. Yeah, you got it, but this isn't a one-man show. Go by the plays, or get off my fucking ice."

I hate when he gets like this.

"But I made it, and it isn't a one-man show if I'm winning for the team."

"Do you think some NHL team is going to keep you if you can't go by the plays?"

I think about that for a moment and then say, "I can go by the plays, but when I see an opening, I'm gonna shoot."

"There was no opening!"

I point at him with my gloved hand. "Um...actually, there was. I made it."

It surprises me that Moss's face becomes redder, but what doesn't surprise me is when he yells, "Laps! GO!"

I let out an aggravated sigh before skating off and doing my first of many laps.

Man, I love hockey. Even the laps.

Practice doesn't get any better after that. Coach is on me, and in a way, I understand where he's coming from – but at the same time, I fucking made it!

With a shake of my head, I dip under the hot water of my shower, and my body instantly relaxes as the scalding water runs over my tired muscles. With the season starting in a couple weeks, Coach has us practicing every single day except Sunday. And let me just say, a five o'clock practice isn't a joke. Especially when it is three hours long, and most the time, a lot of us have to go straight to class right afterward.

It sucks.

Since it's Saturday, Coach actually allowed us to sleep in. Practice was at one in the afternoon, but it didn't matter how late or early it was, I am still tired. All I want to do is fall into my bed and die, and that was sad because it's a Saturday. But even if I wanted to go out, I know I couldn't. I have homework, and if I want to keep my scholarship, I can't blow it off. I could always get someone to do it for me, but it kind of scares me that at any time I could get hurt and my career would be over. Then what would I do? I need to make sure I study and am ready for anything at all times. I figure if I do get hurt that I wouldn't want to leave hockey. So I'm going to UB for sports medicine, even if my father wants me to go into law like him. I don't want to be a lawyer. My dad is a workaholic, and I refuse to be like that.

Moving soap along my body, I close my eyes, going back under the water as the showers fill up. Since I have so much homework to do, I rush through my shower before going into the locker room to change. Even though the guys all like to socialize with each other during our showers, I don't. I mean, I live with these knuckleheads, why the hell would I want to talk to them while I'm washing my balls?

Reaching for my jeans, I pull them up before throwing on a tee and my Bullies sweatshirt. Shutting my locker and making sure it's secure, I make my way out into the harsh sunlight. After my eyes adjust, I look around and regret not riding my bike over to practice. It is such a pretty, sunny day, I figured the walk would do me good, but now I just want to go home. Letting out a breath, I start toward the Bullies' house. That's another cool thing about Bellevue, one of the board members was a huge hockey guy, and he had a house built for the Bullies team. We're a fraternity and it's pretty awesome.

Really, all of UB is awesome. It is only my sophomore year, but I'm convinced that this is the best private college in the US. We have everything a college kid needs. We have a food court with all the top fast-food chains in America, along with spots for those kids who don't eat meat. We have a little shopping mall, bookstores, and even a campus grocery store. The classrooms at UB really don't feel like classrooms. They are open, with big windows lining the walls and state-of-the-art technology throughout the whole campus. The sport facilities are top-of-the-line with everything an athlete would need. I don't know how the dorms are since I never lived in one, but for the fraternities and sororities, housing is downright awesome. It's like we're in our own little world; the only thing missing is a club on campus, but thankfully, there are a bunch of college clubs within walking distance from the Bullies' house.

"Hey, Jude."

I look up from checking my Facebook on my phone to see a group of girls waving at me. They are some of the Bullies' dancers, Amy, Rachael, and Maddie. I have slept with Maddie and Rachael, but Amy is untouchable since she's basically engaged to Shane Patrick, the Bullies' goalie. I flash them a lady-killing smile and am about to go over there to chat when my phone starts to go off with the familiar tone signaling that it's my mom. Looking down at my phone, I smile when I see my mom's face squished against the screen of my phone. I love taking pictures of people doing that. It makes it look they're trapped in my phone, and I always get a good laugh out of it.

Hitting talk, I say, "Hey, Mom."

"Hey, baby, bad time?"

"Nope, I just got out of practice, heading across campus to do homework,"

I say as I start walking again, despite the protests of Rachael, who is still yelling my name.

I wiggle my phone at her and continued to walk as my mom says, "Ah, the life of a college kid."

I smile. "It's a good life."

"I bet. Anyway, I was calling to see if you wanted to come to dinner tomorrow. Dad comes home tonight from Boston, and I think it would be good for Lucy."

Lucy is going through a lot right now. The divorce is finally done with, but now Rick, the bastard, still gets to see Angie once a week and it is killing Lucy. She doesn't want him anywhere near them, but it was court-ordered. Because of this, Lucy doesn't really go much of anywhere anymore. She really doesn't talk to anyone either, which is weird. She always used to call me – we're only three years apart and I love my sister, she's awesome – but lately she doesn't. I'm always worried about her, but there isn't anything I can do to help her but be there. I said I'd get the guys and we'd go kick Rick's ass, but she wouldn't let me. It was probably a good thing, since I don't want to do anything to jeopardize my scholarship.

I know with my dad coming in town, and because of Lucy, I can't say no even if I wanted to. Which I do. I want to sleep all day tomorrow and do laundry, maybe go to get a rubdown for my back, but my family means more than that.

"Yeah, Mom, I'll be there."

"Great! I'll make your favorite."

I smile at the gesture but say, "No, Mom, make Lucy's. Maybe it will help."

"You're such a good brother, Jude. I'll see you tomorrow at six. Love you."

"Love you too. Bye."

I hang up my phone, pushing my Facebook app as I climb the steps that lead me into the quad. I love the quad. Everyone gathers to hang out, do homework, listen to music, and just be together. We have a pit too, which was an area with steps going down into the ground where a big concert slab sits. Usually the band or dance team performs down there. The clear grassy area is full of people today, and I wave and nod at my friends, but suddenly, my eyes are drawn to a girl who is holding an armful of crumpled pink papers. She's pulling down the pink pieces of paper from various spots, but it isn't what she's doing that has my attention. No. It is her gorgeous, round ass. It has been a long time since a girl's ass caught my attention, but this girl's ass is a showstopper. Soon my feet change direction, and I'm heading toward her.

I haven't seen her face yet, but her curves and long red hair have me completely interested. I love a girl with some meat to her; skinny girls don't do it for me and this one…man. I could go on for days about how hot her body is. She is completely covered, no skin showing since she's wearing tight jeans with a pink Henley pulled over her fine ass. All I can do is cross my fingers she isn't a butterface. For those who don't know what that is, it's a girl who is hot everywhere, *but* her face. *Butterface.*

Moving around the tree where she was standing, I catch a glimpse of her face, and I am completely stunned. Big blue eyes, framed with big black lashes. She wears thick black frames, but I figure it is for style and not for sight purposes. Her skin is silky looking, her lips a delectable red that matches her fire-engine red hair, with a little nose that needs to be kissed. Hell, all of her needs to be kissed. Suddenly I'm not all that tired or even worried about my homework; my back doesn't even ache.

I want her.

I watch her for a moment as she moves from tree to tree, pulling down the papers with a scowl on her face. When I see that the flyers she's ripping down are "Lost Dog" flyers, I'm confused. We can't have pets on campus, but when I glance closer, I see that the picture isn't of a dog, but of one of my teammates, Allen West. According to the flyer, Allen has every STD known to man, and for some reason, I don't find that surprising. He gets around and is known not to wrap his shit up. Ever.

Dumbass.

Turning to look at her, I call out, "Do you have evidence to support this claim?"

She turns to look at me, her eyes locking with mine. Heat fills me from the top of my head to the tip of my toes. I could get lost in those eyes. I have never seen such a beautiful shade of blue before. They remind me of my mom's heart-shaped sapphire earrings she always wears.

Raising her brow, she says, "I don't, but then again, I wasn't sleeping with him. He gave my friend crabs. I'm pulling them down though. Nothing to see here, keep moving."

I watch her for a moment, a grin pulling at my lips as she pushes her glasses up with her middle finger. She reaches for another flyer just as another girl comes up and stops her.

"What the hell?!"

She must be the friend with the crabs. She's taller than the redhead by a foot with blond hair, blue eyes, and big plump lips. She's really skinny with a shirt that stops under a pair of fantastic tits and a skirt that is probably against the school code. She looks easy; I should be trying to talk to her, but one, the redhead has me in knots, and two, she has crabs. I watch as the redhead turns, her blue eyes blazing as she says, "Ellen, you can't do this. Allen could sue you, or worse, come after you. Let it go."

Ellen shakes her head. "Girls need to stay away from him. No reason for more vaginas to be infected by him."

"Why do you care? It wasn't like you two were dating! I was dating him, and look at me, I don't even care. Your vagina will heal, and all will be right in the world. No reason to slander this guy and make it worse on you."

Allen was dating her? I had never seen him with this girl or the Ellen girl, so really what did I know? I move my gaze from the redhead to Ellen, seeing that her eyes are filling with tears. I have to look away. I hate when girls cry.

"I can't work."

"It will be okay, I swear."

"If I can't work, I can't pay my bills." Ellen stresses, moving her hand along her cheek.

"But if you get caught doing this, boss lady could find out and fire you. Think, Ellen. Use your brain. I don't want anything to happen to you."

Ellen looks away, and for some reason, I find myself drawn into this drama. I want to ask who boss lady is and why the girl can't work, but I have no business knowing anything. I really should walk away, but I'm not done talking to the redhead. I basically know everyone, and the fact that I have never seen her before has me deciding I need to change that. I don't even know her name, and I find I desperately need to know it. I want them to work out their little issue so that the redhead can divert her attention back to me.

"Fine," Ellen says and then turns to walk away.

I watch as Ellen dumps the flyers she has in her hands, and the redhead lets out a sigh. When I turn to talk to her, she's already walking away, pulling flyers down as she walks. I rush to catch up to her, and when I do, I notice she's smiling, and then I see that she has sweet dimples. I like dimples. She has a very girl-next-door look to her, so *not* someone who Allen would hook up with.

That's probably why he was cheating on her; she wouldn't give it up. She is probably a virgin from the sticks of Tennessee. Her daddy is probably a preacher while her momma runs the bible school and focuses solely on making sure their beautiful, sweet little girl does something wonderful in this world. But then her eyes cut to mine, and something about the way her eyes darken has me thinking I'm completely wrong about her.

"Why are you following me?" she asks as she pulls down another flyer.

I shrug my shoulders. "I wasn't done talking to you."

She drops her hand from the tree and turns to look at me.

"Oh, really? What do you want to talk about?"

"The weather?" I ask.

"It's cold," she says with a look that tells me she's bored.

I smile. "Maybe you could tell me your name?"

"Why?"

"So I can call you something else other than the most gorgeous girl on campus."

It's cheesy, but hey, it works.

Her eyes widen as she shakes her head. "Does that actually work on girls?"

Or maybe it doesn't.

"Usually."

She smiles. "That's so sad. You might need to come up with something better. Anyway, see you around."

I watch as she turns her back to me and starts walking away once more. I watch as her ass sways back and forth, and I can't believe that my line or my charm wasn't working on her. This should be an easy bag, but I can tell she's a tough nut to crack. I think I should walk away, chalk this one up as a loss, but then again, I never lose.

So I do the next logical thing, I follow her.

Chasing after her, I fall into step with her once more. She's quick, but I'm quicker. Looking over at me, she rolls her eyes.

"Are you stalking me?"

I scoff. "Not at all. I just want to talk to you, know your name. I've never seen you before. Are you a transfer?"

"Sheesh, are you the CIA? Why so many questions?"

I smile as she stops, turning to look at me. A smile is pulling at her glossed-up lips, and it takes everything out of me to look from her lips to her eyes. "I told you I want to know you."

"Why?" she asks with her eyebrow arched as she put her hands on her hips.

I shrug. I could either lie or be brutally honest, and since I didn't like to lie to girls, I say, "You have a great ass, and much to my delight, your face is even better. So I think it's easy to say I'm pretty attracted to you."

She blinks a few times and then smiles. "Wow, you are something else."

I grin. "Is that a good thing or bad?"

She smiles back and then turns to walk away. Looking over her shoulder, she calls, "Good thing."

I couldn't stop smiling if I tried, but then I realize she's making a run for it, again. "Hey!"

She turns around, walking backward, her face bright as she looks back at me. "What?"

"Am I going to have to chase you all over campus just to find out your name?"

She laughs before bringing her bottom lip between her teeth. Very sexy. "Maybe?"

She continues to walk backward, her body calling to mine, and soon I'm nodding as I pick up the pace to meet up with her. "Are you in a rush, or are you trying to get rid of me?"

She looks over at me. "Both."

I laugh. "You haven't even given me a chance."

"Well, you see, I decided to start dating, and the guy I picked basically ruined the male gender for me. I have decided that I want nothing to do with guys till I graduate. Maybe then I can find a man worth dating."

I want to kill and kiss Allen West all in one. I want to kill him for ruining the male species, but then I want to kiss him since he let go of one of the most gorgeous girls I have ever seen.

I smile. "Maybe the man you're looking for is chasing you across campus."

"You?" she asks with her mouth pulling up at one side. She's spectacular, and I know that I have to have her. I don't know what it is, but I am completely smitten with one look into this girl's eyes. That has never happened to me before.

I shrug my shoulders as my face breaks into a wider grin. "Maybe."

She laughs. "So what, you gonna convince me you are the guy of my dreams?"

"I wouldn't have to do much convincing. I'm pretty much the greatest guy on campus."

She shakes her head, her eyes dancing with amusement as she says, "Wow, you are full of yourself."

I shrug. "Well, when you're this sexy, and have an amazing knack for pleasing women, you become very confident."

Her eyes darken as she holds my gaze. "I'm speechless."

"Don't worry, that happens a lot to girls. It's my sexiness."

She laughs again as she rolls her eyes, and I can't help but smile at her. She looks around us and then back at me. As we hold each other's gaze, lust washes over me. I want to wrap her up in my arms and hold her tight against my body as I kiss the hell out of her. Her lips are begging for me to kiss her, and I'm on the brink of doing it, but something is holding me back.

"So bringing back the question from earlier, are you new, a transfer?"

She shakes her head. "Nope, this is my second year."

"Mine too. I'm surprised I've never seen you before."

She shrugs. "I've kept to myself."

I nod. "Oh, what are you like a hermit or something?"

She smiles. "No, I work a lot. After that and school, I tend to sleep a lot."

"Me too," I say as I cross my arms across my chest. "I was actually about to go back to my house and go to sleep after I finished my homework, but I saw you first and had to talk to you."

Her cheeks fill with color as she looks away.

"I still don't know your name."

She looks up at me and says, "Claire. Claire Anderson."

I smile. She's beautiful, classy, and Claire fits her perfectly.

"What's yours?" she asks, crossing her own arms under her breasts. The top button of her Henley pops open, giving me a few glimpses of her delectable white skin and black lace bra. I promptly forget my name. When I don't answer, she looks down before glaring up at me, rebuttoning her shirt.

"Sorry, I think seeing the lace of your black bra just made me forget my name."

The glare she's pinning me with drops, and she shakes her head as she lets out a sigh.

"Anyway, what's your name?"

I smile, watching as her neck and cheeks turn red. Man, it is a great color on her. Looking deep into her blue eyes, I say, "My name is Jude Sinclair."

She blinks twice and then smiles. "Like, 'Hey Jude, don't be afraid'?"

Usually when people ask that, I get mad. Obviously my mom is a *huge* Beatles fan. I mean, not only am I Jude, but my sister is Lucy. As in "Lucy in the Sky with Diamonds"? My dad put his foot down for Jayden and Jace, but I'm not worried about them right now. For the first time, I'm not mad that she's teasing me. I only nod and say, "That's me."

What does that even mean?

CHAPTER 3

 Claire

J ude, or Hey Jude, as I'm going to call him, is not the guy you bring home to mother. Or in my case, Reese and Phillip. I can hear Phillip now, bitching that this guy is only out to get into my pants, that he is wild and not the right guy for me. I haven't dated since Phillip found me in bed with one of his teammates when I was sixteen. But that doesn't mean that boys didn't try to get with me, and Phillip always made a point to scare them away. Most of the time he is right; he was a wild boy himself until I came to live with him and Reese came into his life. I usually listen, but for some reason, Jude has me stopping, throwing Phillip out of my mind and focusing only on him.

When he said he was sexy, he wasn't lying. My heart still isn't beating right, hasn't been since the moment my eyes met his in the quad. He has dark brown hair that's shaved up on the sides of his head but is long on the top, falling into his eyes. It's fuller than a Mohawk, and I have to admit, it's super hot. His eyes are a dark green, his lips are thin and light red while his face is dusted with dark hair along his jawline. His shoulders are wide and his arms are thick; I could tell that even with him wearing a pullover, which meant this guy is toned. He's taller than me, and when he pins me with those green eyes, I feel like he's looking inside my soul. He has tattoos too, and that alone is a panty-dropper. I can't see them the way I want since he's covered up, but two are peeking out of the top of his pullover, and when he pulls his sweatshirt up to his elbows in a carefree way, I notice that his forearms are covered.

God, he is hot.

"So, your mom likes the Beatles?"

He nods, his eyes never leaving mine. It's weird; I'm used to guys looking at my body, but this guy is dead set on looking me in the eyes. It's nice.

"Yup, my sister's name is Lucy, but my dad wouldn't let her name my younger brothers."

I smile. I always wanted a sister, or hell, even a brother, and for a moment I wish that I'd had a mom and dad who thought it was a grand idea to name me after a popular song, so that when I was older, a guy would sing my name to me. It is a nice thought, but not what happened for me. I was probably named after some brand of cocaine or something.

"That's cool."

"Are you secretly laughing at me?" he asks, his eyes bright as his lips curve into a grin.

I shake my head. "Nope. I really do think it's a cool name, but believe me, whenever I see you next, I'll call you Hey Jude."

He doesn't smile or ever glare, he just holds me in a heated gaze. "When will that be?"

I'm confused. "When will what be?"

"The next time I see you."

"Oh, I don't know. Since you haven't seen me before this, it's probably the last time."

He shakes his head. "Nope, we will meet again."

I laugh. "Sure we will. So anyway, I'll see you around."

"You forgot two things," he says, stopping me by taking ahold of my hand.

I glance over at him, my hand burning in his. His hand swallows mine, and when our eyes meet, his eyes dance with mischief. It causes my heart to skip a beat.

Oh, this guy is sexy, with a capital S.

"And what might that be?" I ask.

"One–" he says, holding up one finger "–you forgot to tell me your major. I mean, come on, it's part of the script for college kids."

I have no clue what he's talking about, but I say, "Business."

"So you're one of those gung ho girls, one with a plan."

I laugh. "Yup, and nothing will stop it."

"Someone as beautiful as you, it's hard not to believe anything that comes out of that pretty mouth of yours."

My body catches on fire, and I can feel my blush creeping up my neck. With a grin, I say, "Okay then, Hey Jude."

"What?"

I look over at him, confused yet again. "Huh?"

"You said, hey, Jude."

Laughter bubbles in my throat. "I told you that was what I was going to call you from now on!" I explain, not holding in my laughter, but laughing so hard I can't breathe. He looks down, confused, but soon he's laughing with me. Catching my breath, I send him a grin before waving. "I'll see you, Hey Jude."

"Claire, I still have one more question."

I stop and turn again. Why do I keep stopping?

"And that is?"

"Can I have your number?"

I smile. I want to give it to him, but then again, I like this little cat-and-mouse chase we have going on. He looks like the kind of guy who likes a challenge, so maybe I'll give him one.

"What for?"

He gives me a deadpan look that causes me to cough to hide my laughter.

"So I can call you," he says slowly like I'm mentally challenged.

"Sorry–" I say, shaking my head "–I don't give my number out to strange men."

"I'm not a stranger. I just followed you all over campus," he informs me with a smile on his face.

"Oh, that's true. So I shouldn't give my number to stalkers either, right?"

I shoot his shocked face a grin and turn around. "See ya, Hey Jude."

"Oh! A challenge, I see," I hear him say. I turn to see that he has jumped on the stone wall and now is pointing at me. "I accept this challenge, Claire Anderson. If you think I'm a stalker now, you just wait! I will have your number, and I will get you to go on a date with me, and in the end, I will rock your world!"

"Sure, you will," I call at him as I continue to walk backward. "Good luck with that."

"I don't give up, Claire Anderson!"

I smile widely at him and then turn around, my smile growing. For some reason, I am really excited about this, and I hope like hell he does get my number and gets me on a date, rocking my world in the process. But I'll be damned if it is going to be easy. Looking behind me, I see that he's still watching me. A large smile is on his face, making his eyes shine. I roll my eyes and wave when he waves at me. I don't know what it is about him, but he excites me. No guy has done that, ever. I don't know what that means, but I'm sure it means something is bound to happen between us. I sort of hope it's of the naked variety, but then again, maybe it could be more. Maybe he could be what Phillip is to Reese, and I'd live happily ever after. And maybe I'll start choreographing for Justin Timberlake, and as I'm teaching him a routine, he'll tell me he's desperately in love with me and needs me for the rest of his life.

Letting out an aggravated sigh because my life is not a Disney movie – good guys don't go for girls like me – I cross my arms, hoping to shield my chest from the cold. It is a little nippy for the beginning of October, but I learned very quickly when I came to Tennessee that this weather has a mind of its own. As I round the corner to Fisher Hall, which is the building that houses my dorm, a crowd gathers around something. Since I'm nosy, I make my way to the crowd to see that a group of girls is dancing. Despite the cold, the girls wear little jumpers that are black and have a teal belt. The chest piece is covered with black mesh and crystals. When the girls do a turn, I see that in crystals on their backs it says "Bullies." I have to admit; they are really good. Not Reese Allen's Dance Company good, but good.

When the song ends, the girls stop with big cheesy smiles on their face. They are smiling so hard that I start to smile, which was probably their goal. As everyone claps, one of the girls picks up a megaphone and turns to the crowd.

"Hey, y'all! I'm Rachael Haynes, the captain of the Bullies Dance Girls. We hope you enjoyed our little dance routine, and want to invite all you sophomore girls to tryouts for the University of Bellevue Bullies. We dance at all the home games for the Bullies hockey team and any other event they sponsor. We're a tight-knit group of girls who love to dance and have fun. Do you feel you'll fit in? We have five spots open, and we're looking to fill them with amazing dancers! Tryouts are Tuesday at six at the meeting center in Bradshaw Hall. Grab a flyer, and I'll see you there!!"

Somehow I intercept a flyer. I don't know how, or why, for that matter, but soon I'm telling myself that maybe I could try out. It could be fun. Pulling my phone out of my pocket, I dial Reese's number, and she answers on the second ring.

"Hey!"

I smile. I love Reese. She's honestly one of the best people in my life. She was a little standoffish when I first met her, but we soon grew into friends, and now we have this amazing relationship where she's basically my mom.

"Hey! Quick question."

"I mean, shit, Claire, can't you tell me you miss me or anything?"

I laugh. "Ohemgeeeee! I miss you so, Reese's Pieces!"

She laughs along with me. "I miss you more, Claire. Summer flew by, in my opinion. But anyway, what's up?"

I know what she means. We spent the whole summer together. We went to Mexico, New York, and Florida for vacation. It was awesome. I lost out on some money, but at the same time, spending all that time with my family is much better than strutting my ass all over a stage.

Going back to the reason I called, I ask, "What do you think of my trying out for the dance team here at school?"

She pauses for a moment. "Hmm, it could be good. Do you have time?"

I think for a second. Do I?

"I think so. Keep me busy so I'll stay out of trouble, as Phillip says."

She laughs. "As if you've gotten in any trouble in years, but yeah, it will get you out there. Meet some people, make friends, and plus, it will keep you dancing for the future."

"Yeah. It's for the school's hockey team. I like hockey."

"Yeah, so really, there isn't a question. Do it. You'll love it. Do you have a routine in mind?"

I am always putting together dances in my head, and the next thing you know, I'm knocking crap over in my little bitty dorm room. My poor roommate and friend since I moved in with Phillip, Skylar, hates it. I think I have the perfect routine, and glancing at the flyer, I could throw all the required moves into it. Come to think of it, I'll make Skylar try out too.

I nod. "I think so."

"Are there required moves?"

"Yeah, nothing I can't handle, though."

"Cool, so do it."

I nod again, my lip between my teeth as I think it over. It could be fun. I like to dance, I like hockey, and sometimes I even like girls my age, so really it's a win/win for me.

"Can you meet me tomorrow at the studio and watch it?"

"Sure, can we do it early, though? I'm watching Dimitri for Piper so that she can fly out to New York to meet Erik for their ultrasound appointment."

Reese's sister Piper is five months pregnant with her second kid. We're all so excited and hoping for a girl this time around, even though Piper and her husband, Erik, want another boy. I guess if I had a kid as awesome as Dimitri, I would want another boy too. Dimitri is, I guess, my cousin? I don't know, Piper's son, who was Reese's nephew, and I have no clue what he is to me. I have been around him since he was a baby, and I love his little bitty butt. He's three years old and full of energy and basically the cutest little boy in the world.

But I was still stuck on why Piper had to go to New York for the ultrasound, especially when she lives in Nashville.

"Why are they going to New York for that?"

She laughed. "Erik is impatient, and he's so busy right now with the season and all. Phillip wanted me to come with them, but I offered to keep Dimitri. He doesn't need to be out in that cold New York air."

"Yeah, that's true, and that's fine. Can I come over afterward and help with him? I haven't seen him in weeks."

"You don't even need to ask," Reese says lovingly. "Have you talked to Phillip?"

"Not today. I talked to him yesterday."

"Okay, good," she says, and then she pauses before asking, "Did he tell you anything about our honeymoon?"

I laugh. He did, but I'm not saying anything. Phillip wants to surprise Reese with the most amazing honeymoon in Cabo. She's going to flip because she has wanted to go there for years.

"Nope," I lie with a smile on my face as I head down the hall to my room.

"You know I know you're lying, right?"

I continue to laugh. "I am not."

"Liar. Anyway, have you found a date for the wedding?"

That stops my laughter. I let out a groan, and she laughs as I fall onto the bench outside my door. She has been on me about bringing someone to their wedding, and I have tried everything to get out of it. I mean, she has only given me two months to find a guy who would sit through my, basically, parents' wedding. I don't even know why they have to get married so quickly! Yeah, Phillip has been asking Reese to marry him for the past three years, like every day, but Reese kept strong, saying she never wanted to get married. But then, all of a sudden, they're engaged. First they said they'll have the wedding one day, but then a couple months ago, Reese was like, "Now! We have to have it now!" Crazy thing. Crazy kids.

"Not yet."

"Come on, Claire, it can't be that hard. You're beautiful. There has to be a guy who would want to come with you."

Why does Jude Sinclair come to mind when she says that? Damn it!

"Reese, I have bigger things to worry about than finding someone to go to your impromptu wedding."

She laughs. "Whatever, bring someone. You're gonna be bored otherwise."

"I will not. I'll have you and Phillip."

"We will be making out the whole time. Bring someone," she says sternly.

"Whyyyyyy," I whine. "Guys are dumb. The last guy I was talking to had crabs."

"Ack!" she says in disgust. "That is gross."

"I know, so maybe I should just stop looking for guys. You know, my vagina could get sick."

She starts to laugh again. "You're dumb, hush. Bring a guy who isn't infested with bugs and have a good time at my wedding. Oh, by the way, we have dress fittings in a couple weeks! Aren't you so excited?"

I groan, causing her laughter to fill my ear.

CHAPTER 4

JUDE

Once I get back to the house, homework and even sleep are the last things on my mind. Pushing open the door that is never locked since someone is always home, I look around the main room for any sign of Allen West. Most of the freshmen hang out on the couches playing PS4; some are even studying, which surprises me since it is so loud. Passing through, I shake hands and greet my teammates before heading to the kitchen and then dining room to find that Allen isn't there. I peek out in the back where we have a huge fire pit and tables for beer pong, but he isn't there either.

He must be in his room.

Taking the stairs three at a time, I make it to the second floor. Our house has four stories. The main floor holds the living room, dining room, and kitchen, and the basement mirrors it but also has four bedrooms. It is usually where the seniors stay, as well as the captain. Since I'm the captain, I stay down there. I didn't want Jayden to have to room with some dirty ass, so he's rooming with me. It makes my mom happy to know that Jayden is looked after, when really it's Jayden doing the watching. Especially when I start partying. The second floor is for the freshmen and sophomores, while the top floor is for juniors. It's a huge house and a pain in the ass to keep clean, but it's home.

Taking the next flight of stairs, I finally reach Allen's door. I fling it open, not worrying about knocking, to find Allen on his bed with his computer in his lap.

"Sinclair. What's up?"

I find a chair and sit down, crossing my leg to let my ankle rest on my other knee. "Claire Anderson. Start talking."

His face scrunches up and he shrugs. "Why? You know I'm dating her, right?"

"Were dating her," I say, emphasizing the *were*. "Past tense since you were sleeping with some Ellen chick and gave her crabs."

"What!" he yells, visibly shocked.

"That's the rumor that Claire told me. It's easy to see that she doesn't want anything to do with you, and the next time you see her, you better apologize."

"Shit," he mutters before shutting his computer and reaching for his phone.

"No, not now, and not over the phone. Do that shit in person, but before that, tell me everything about her."

"Why should I? I don't want you going after someone I was with."

"I know you didn't sleep with her, so she wasn't technically yours. And also, if you don't, I'll make your life hell."

I add in a smile to make sure he knows I mean business, and it must have worked because he runs his hands through his shaggy blond hair before looking over at me.

"She's nineteen, hot as fuck, as you can tell. She kisses good but won't put out. She doesn't talk much about her family or anything. She really didn't talk about anything, and that's why I planned on breaking it off with her. I know she dances and enjoys it a lot. Teaches over at Reese Allen's Dance Academy. She's kind of boring, actually."

"Or maybe she was too good for your piece-of-shit ass," I say, giving him a dirty look. I don't like that he calls her boring. Claire is nowhere near boring; she's fucking interesting. "Where does she live?"

"Fisher Hall. She rooms with Skylar Preston."

I know Skylar; we have the same English class. She wanted to have sex with me, but I'm pretty sure that girl could kill me with her thighs. Since I like my girls a little squishy, Skylar is out of the question. She may be freaking gorgeous, but I want to have sex with a girl, not Zangief from *Wreck-It Ralph*.

"Okay, she's going for business?"

He nods. "She wants to open her own dance company."

"Do you know her schedule?"

He shakes his head. "Only that she has geometry and English in the morning on Monday, Tuesday, and Thursday. We always met for lunch at the pit since it was right beside the core class building."

I process all the info before standing up to head out. "Cool, thanks."

Before I can reach the door though, he says, "I'm telling you, dude, it's a waste of time. That girl has her shit locked up like a nun. She isn't going to just sleep with you."

I look back at him and shrug. "Who said anything about sleeping with her?"

Before he can say anything, because I know exactly what he's going to say, I open the door and shut it before heading down the three flights of stairs to my room. I know I shouldn't be surprised that Allen said that. I mean, I'm not shy with the ladies, and I make sure to please each one who wants my attention, but still, maybe I want something more. Okay, maybe I'm a complete liar. I haven't wanted someone as bad as I want Claire in a long time, and I can't wait to get in her pants, but a part of me wants to get to know her too. She interests me, and maybe she'll be the kind of girl to calm me down. Teach me a lesson about being with a woman. Make me a one-woman man.

Hey, miracles can happen.

When I open the door, Jayden is at his desk, his nose in his book. He looks up and nods before going back to reading. Like me, he has dark hair and light green eyes. We're both built the same way, strong and lean, but Jayden might be a tad bit bigger than me. Being a defenseman, it's expected for those hard hits. I'm a center, so I'm leaner for speed.

Ripping off my pullover, I throw it on the bed before throwing my wallet and keys on our bureau where pictures of our family sit. In the middle, surrounded by pictures of Angie, is a picture of me, Jayden, and Jace at the ages of six, seven, and eight. We're all wide-eyed and excited in our green jerseys for the rec league we played in. We always spoke of how we would all be in the NHL, on the same team, and how everyone would be scared of us because we were the best. I still believe that will happen, and I honestly can't wait. That's when life is going to be awesome.

I head to my own desk that holds my books and start my homework. I hate it, but it has to be done to keep my scholarship. We don't say anything as we both work, but when I'm done, I lean back in my seat and run my hands down my face. I want to call my mom and check in on her. My dad has been gone for almost a month, working on a big case in New York with one of his NHL clients who's divorcing his wife, and I know that Mom gets lonely. I know that Lucy, Jace, and Angie are there, but sometimes they make it worse. With Angie being so young, only a year, she gets into everything and Mom tries to take on so much. I made a promise a long time ago that when I got my first big check from the NHL, I was going to buy her a week at some ritzy spa. Somewhere she doesn't have to do anything but be pampered. I wish my dad would do that for her, but he's selfish. Don't get me wrong, he's a decent man, very well-respected, but that doesn't mean he's a good husband or father.

"Mom call you?"

I glance back to find Jayden in his bed, lying on his back. I nod before saying, "Yeah, dinner tomorrow?"

"Yeah, Dad is coming in, apparently."

"That's what I heard. How long you think he'll stay?"

"Maybe a day or two. He said something about coming to our opener, though."

I nod. "I'll believe it when I see it."

Jayden laughs. "Agreed.

My dad is somewhat of a workaholic, but like my mom says, he does everything to make sure she doesn't have to work and everyone's college is paid for. Not mine, though; I don't want to owe him anything. I want to know I did this myself if this is what I'm supposed to do. If I'm not supposed to play in the NHL, that's fine, I'll deal with that when it comes, but at least I'll know I did it myself. I'm not sure what my issue is with my dad, or if there is an issue, but I just can't have him pay for me. I have to make my own way.

"Talked to Jace today, too. He said that they are saying now that he might need to do a year in college, just to see how he'll adjust before they throw him in the NHL."

"Really? How's he taking it?"

"Pissed, of course. He doesn't want to go to school – he wants to play."

"Don't we all?"

"Yeah, but Mom is wondering where he will go. The scout said something about Wisconsin."

"Mom isn't happy, I take it?"

"No, she cried at the thought. I told her I'd talk to him, that maybe I can get him to come here."

"Yeah, it only makes sense that we all come through here before going into the draft."

"I think he wants to see what's going to happen to you."

I smile. "We know what's happening. I'm gonna play for a great team while y'all play school for another year."

"Ah, fuck you," Jayden says, sending me an envious look. "I'll be up there soon and hopefully on the team that kicks your ass."

"Whatever," I tease as I stand up, chucking my jeans off before settling into bed.

Silence fills the room as we both play on our phones, but then Jayden breaks it by asking, "How do you think Mom's gonna handle it when we all are playing all over the US?"

I shrug before glancing over at him. "I'm not sure. I don't like to think about it."

"Maybe Nashville will want you?"

I shake my head. "I don't think they're looking. Maybe they'll want you or Jace?"

"Jace has his heart set on New York, and I want Chicago."

I nod because I know this. While I don't want to leave my mom, I know Nashville isn't looking, but maybe they'll start once the season starts. I know it's not my responsibility to look after her, it's my dad's, but I can't help but want to be there for her. Make sure she's good. She's always done that for me.

"Who was the redhead you were talking to today?"

Meeting my brother's gaze, I smile. "Claire Anderson. My next conquest."

Jayden laughs. "Lord help us all."

"Oh, shut up. She's hot though, right?"

He nods. "Really hot. Too hot for you, to be honest."

I laugh at his smirk. "Please, she's just right for me."

"No girl is ever right for you, apparently."

"Maybe that was true, but I'm starting to reconsider it."

Jayden sits up, shaking his head. "I don't believe that for a second. I bet ya a hundred bucks that you won't get her and date her for more than a week. If she does give you the time of day, you'll get bored, like you always do."

Sitting up, I hold my hand out to him. He takes it earnestly, and I can see in his eyes that he thinks this is an easy bet. He couldn't be more wrong.

"You got yourself a deal."

CHAPTER 5

🩰 Claire

I throw open my dorm door, and Skylar looks up at me from her bed and then looks back down at her books that she has around her. "Hey, you."

"Hey, yourself," I say, throwing my bag on my bed. "What are you doing Tuesday around six?"

Before she can answer, I crawl into the bed with her, fitting myself in the little bitty space that doesn't have books and other crap on it. She sends me an impressive look, since it wasn't an easy feat fitting my long legs in the space she allowed, before saying, "Nothing." She thinks for a minute. "Yeah, nothing."

"Good, we're trying out for the Bullies' dance team."

She looks up and gives me a wary look. "Why on earth would we do that? We already have classes we do for Reese, and then we work all the time, and we have school."

Skylar works at Ms. Prissy's too, but instead of a dancer, she's a cocktail waitress. She did work onstage in the past, but her brother came in while she was dancing. Thankfully, he didn't notice her, but it ruined it for her, and she refuses to go onstage anymore. She's right that we work a lot, but we can talk to Ms. Prissy and fix our hours if needed. When I say that, she shrugs.

"Yeah, I guess, but I hate those dance chicks. They are such bitches."

I smile. "'Cause they are jealous of how beautifully gorgeous you are."

Skylar scoffs as she rolls her hazel eyes. She really is gorgeous, and I've always thought so. Wide hazel eyes with freckles along her nose and cheeks. Her brown hair cascades down her shoulders in a wavy, beachy look, and her smile is always unstoppable. She's beautiful and everyone thinks so. That's the main reason I have to go find places to study when she has guys over. She isn't a slut at all, but she doesn't hold back from the guys. She loves them. I wish I were like that again. Sometimes I feel weird for not being the least bit attracted to anyone… Well, no, I take that back. Allen was okay, and I would have slept with him eventually, but Jude, he has me feeling all kinds of feels that I'm totally not used to. My clothes basically evaporated under his intense green eyes.

Jesus, he was gorgeous. Shaking my head, I meet Skylar's eyes as she says, "Whatever. I really don't want to, and probably won't make it 'cause they're bitches, but yeah, I'll do it with ya."

"Of course you'll make it. We are amazing dancers."

She shrugs and I lean against her. I know she's stressing over her homework, and I want to help, but I have no clue about chemistry. She wants to be a vet, and while I support her and want her to succeed, I know it's going to be hard. Her classes are freaking challenging as hell.

"It will be fun," I promise, and she looks back at me.

"Yeah, I know. I'm just freaking out over this crap," she admits, giving me a sad smile as she points to her books and endless notes.

"I know. If you don't want to do it, I understand. You have a lot going on."

"Yeah, but I need a distraction when I'm not working on this shit. It will be good for me."

I smile, wrapping my arms around her. She has always been my friend, a real friend. Everyone hated me when Phillip started me at the school in his district. I was the new "rich" girl with a hotshot, hockey player uncle. I was kind of a standoffish bitch too, so that had a lot to do with why people didn't like me. Plus my hair was bright red, and people assumed I was an easy, emo chick. I wasn't emo for one, and maybe I might have been easy in the past, but once Phillip gave me stability, I was a completely different girl. I wanted things. I wanted to make him proud, I wanted him to love me, but he did no matter what I did, and I'm so thankful for that.

"You know that the hockey team is at the tryouts, right? And they judge the girls."

"Huh?" I ask, leaning up to look at her.

"Oh yeah, they have little paddles with numbers, and the captains take their opinions into consideration. It's kinda stupid 'cause the guys only judge you on your looks."

I smile. "We're in then. We're fucking hot."

She laughs like I wanted as I crawl out of my spot and go to my side of the room. Pictures of Phillip, Reese, and me are everywhere, along with pictures of Skylar and me. While I love my pictures, my favorite ones are the ones of the kids. I love my Dimitri and then Reese's sister Harper's kids, Ally and Journey. I spend so much time with them that they are almost like my sister and brothers. I even have pictures of my extended family, which is all of Phillip's teammates and their families. As I glance at all of them, like I always do, I can't help but think how I went from having no one to love me to now having so many that I am sometimes overwhelmed with love.

With a smile on my face, I reach for the pink flyers that Ellen was posting everywhere and chuck them in the trash as my smile grows.

Jude Sinclair.

Hmm. He was something, that's for sure, and I can't help but think of him. I told him that I'd probably never see him again, but I wish I could see him right now. I should have given him my number; I should have let him pursue me, instead of running the other way. I usually don't regret blowing guys off, but I am regretting it like crazy right now.

Glancing over at Skylar, I say, "Hey, do you know Jude Sinclair?"

Her head shoots up, and she gives me a Cheshire-cat smile, all her straight, white teeth showing as she slowly nods her head. "Everyone knows Jude Sinclair, Claire."

I give her a deadpan look. "Well, I didn't, until today."

"Did you sleep with him?" she demands, her eyes wide.

I laugh. "Jeez, Skylar, really? I wouldn't even sleep with Allen, which reminds me, he gave Ellen crabs. They were fucking. But anyway, you think I'm gonna sleep with some guy I just met? I'm not a slut, thank you!"

She makes a face. "Ew, he gave her crabs? While messing with you?"

"We weren't messing, just talking."

"Yeah, but still that's icky. You should kick his ass."

I shrug. "I guess if I cared, I would."

"True, 'cause if you'd cared you wouldn't be asking about the sex-on-legs Jude Sinclair," she says, waggling her eyebrows at me.

I laugh as I nod. "Yeah, you're right. He is really sexy."

"Oh, girl. I saw him go through his initiation last year at the frat, and let me say, it was mighty hard for him to keep his goodies in the boy shorts he was wearing. Not to leave out that the man is ripped, I think his abs have abs, but he's also covered in tattoos." She lets out a dreamy sigh. "He is… God, he is so fucking hot."

I snort with laughter as I fall back on my bed. My body is automatically hot at just the image that is running through my mind. "Yeah, I saw him fully clothed, and it took everything out of me to look the other way."

"Yeah, he has that effect on women."

"So he says," I add and she laughs.

"Oh yeah, he's cocky as hell too, but that comes with being the best player on the Bullies team."

I come up on my elbows, looking over at her. "He's a hockey player?"

She nods, a lusty look coming over her face as her eyes darken in color. "Oh yes… He knows exactly how to handle his stick. Great hands. Wonderful hand-eye coordination."

I can't believe how hard I'm laughing, and soon she's laughing with me.

Rolling onto my side, I shake my head at her mischievous smile and ask, "Is he seeing someone?"

Her lips curve even more as she shakes her head. "No, Jude doesn't date or see anyone. He sleeps with girls and lets them go."

My smile falls. "You haven't slept with him, have you?"

"In my dreams, yes, over and over again, but no, I haven't had the pleasure. He says I'm too nice – I think he's scared of my thighs."

Skylar does have some monstrous thighs, but it's muscle; she likes to ride bikes and dances, too. She's superfit and most guys are scared of her, which is stupid, in my opinion. I laugh as relief floods through me. Thank God, she didn't sleep with him. Girl code and all, I wouldn't try, but now that she hasn't touched him, I might consider it. Oh hell, who am I kidding? There was nothing to consider.

I want him.

"So he'll be there Tuesday?"

She nods as she marks in an answer on the paper she has in front of her. "He's the captain, of course he will be. His opinion matters a lot. He slept with Rachael at one point, and she does everything to make him happy in the hopes he'll come back. Which he won't."

"Interesting."

"That's for sure, but what's more interesting is that look in your eye. I usually only see it when you're determined to get a dance done. Never saw it concerning a guy."

I roll my eyes before lying on my stomach to place my head on the pillow. "It's nothing."

"Sure, it is," she says back with a grin. "Something big, and I can't wait to see what happens. Jude won't know what hit him when you come strolling into his life."

"Oh, hush," I say, but then we start laughing like banshees because we both know she's right.

The feeling that comes over me is somewhere between thrill and fear, but I like it.

CHAPTER 6

JUDE

'm not looking forward to this dinner at all.

Jayden drives us out to our family's home on the outskirts of Nashville. Dad wanted something secluded but also close enough to the city, and he got that in our huge country-style house. Growing up here was good, being only years apart, I grew up with two best friends instead of brothers. Yeah, we fought, and I'm pretty sure Jayden almost killed me once, but they are the two I would do anything for, after kicking their asses, of course. When we weren't rough, tough hockey players, we were soldiers, hunters, and ninjas getting lost in the nature that surrounded our house. There wasn't a time when my mom wasn't hollering for us and when we weren't constantly ganging up on Lucy. It was a great childhood, one with a great mom but an absent father.

Turning onto the driveway that leads us through the forest to our home, I pull out my phone to check my Facebook before I won't be able to. My mom has a basket by the door where our phones and keys go. All the people we care about are in one room, why do we need a phone, she always says. Pulling up my search bar, I type Claire's name and smile when her profile comes up. This isn't the first time I've done this since seeing her yesterday, and I can't help but feel the desire to look through her pictures. To know her. She has her stuff on private, so I'm only able to see tagged pictures and her profile pictures.

There are tons of pictures of her with kids and some of her in dance gear teaching little bitty kids. When I come to one of her wrapped up in a man's arms, I pause. They kinda look alike; he's huge with blond hair and blue eyes, but his nose is the same as Claire's. They are both grinning, obviously happy, and nothing but love comes from the picture. It must be her dad, but he doesn't look old enough to have a daughter her age. When I go to the second picture, it's her with the guy and then another woman. She's lean, but thick the way I like my women. She's stunning, long brown hair and brown eyes that shine off the screen. She looks nothing like Claire, but she looks at her like Claire is hers. It's weird, and I want to know who they are. I have a feeling I know the guy. I've seen him somewhere, but I can't place him, my thoughts are too flooded with Claire's gorgeous face.

When we finally reach the house, I turn off my phone and tuck it in my pocket, hopping out of the car just as Angie comes wobbling toward the car from my sister's arms. She's littler than most kids and just started walking a few weeks ago. Her brown hair is in spurts all over her sweet head. Her green eyes are shiny and wide as she screeches when she reaches me. She looks just like Lucy, which is good. We don't want anything reminding us of that jerk-off, Rick.

"Angie!" I exclaim, picking her up and kissing her face as loudly as I can. Her giggles envelop me, instantly making me excited to be here. Kissing me on my face, she hugs me tightly, her little head tucked under my chin, tickling my neck. I kiss her head, squeezing her tightly before Jayden takes her from me and she screeches for him. A grin sits on my lips because I know that kid is loved more than ever, and that will never stop.

When my sister's arms come around my waist, I hug her tight. She's my height, her brown hair long, reaching the middle of her back. She looks just like me; we all look like my mom with only my dad's green eyes. But her face is softer than the sharp angles that I have. Her eyes are also slanted a tad like my mom's, while my brothers' and mine are wide. When she looks up at me, I can tell she's struggling. We're two years apart, and before Jayden came, we were superclose. We still are but not nearly the way I would like us to be. She pulled away once she met Rick. Rick changed her. Fucking jerk.

"Hey, how are you?" I ask and she shrugs.

"All right, working and just trying to make it, I guess. I told Mom I want to get my own place, but she's dead set on me and Angie living here for the rest of our lives."

I smile. "It's what's best, especially with her babysitting and everything. Gives you time to save money."

"I know," she says but then her shoulders fall in such a defeated way that I want to do everything to make it better. I just don't know how. "I just hate that it's been over a year and I'm still heartbroken, you know? Like, he's already moved on, Jude. Getting married again, and it kills me because I'm living with my parents with our daughter, just trying to get by."

"It takes time," I stress. "You'll be fine. Maybe when I move, you can come out with me. Start a new life in wherever the hell I go. LA, New York? The possibilities are endless."

She laughs as she hugs me tight. "You don't want you older sister crowding your bachelor pad and you know it."

I smile. "Maybe not, but if it made you and Angie happy, I'd do it."

Her eyes lock with mine and she cups my cheek. "I know you would, but I'd never ask you to."

We share a long look, and I can't help how my chest aches for her. She used to be so happy, thought Rick was the only man to make her happy, and then it just went to shit. No one wants to watch anyone they love go through pain, and it honestly kills a piece of you when you have to.

"My boys are home!"

I look up to see my mom coming down the stairs, her grin unstoppable as she pulls me from Lucy's embrace into her own. Her brown hair falls in curls over her shoulders while her hazel eyes shine with love for me. My mom has always been a tad bit overweight, and while some people would frown on it, I love it. Her arms always feel warm and like home. I completely relax as I hug her tight. She kisses my temple before wrapping me tighter in her arms and whispering, "I've miss you, my Jude. I love you so much, honey. You're my favorite, you know."

She says that to all of us. One time I asked how all of us are her favorite, and she went into these elaborate reasons why. I was her favorite because I'm considerate and loving. Lucy is her favorite because of her quick mind and sweet heart. Jayden, because he always has a smile on his face, always waiting for a challenge, and then Jace is her favorite because he's the baby, and she can still snuggle him without his trying to get away. There has never been a moment that I didn't know my mom loves me. She went out of her way to guarantee to each of us that we were special. I smile against her neck as I squeeze her, picking her up off the ground, which causes her to squeal. We all laugh as I place her on her feet, kissing her on her cheek. "I love you too, Mom."

Pulling back from me, she cups my face before asking, "Please tell me you've found a girlfriend?"

I laugh as I shake my head, ignoring the fact that Claire comes to mind. "Too many girls, too little time, Mom."

She shakes her head before letting me go, shooting me a disgusted look before she reaches for Jayden, hugging him just as tightly. When someone jumps on my back, I hold their weight and smile when Jace's arm comes around my neck, choking me.

"Hey, bro," he says, squeezing my neck harder. I grab him by the back of his head and flip him off me, causing him to land hard on his back. He looks up at me with a glare, his green eyes flashing with anger, ready for a fight, but before I can kick him in the side or drop an elbow in his gut, playfully, of course... Okay, not really, but still, my mom is yelling at me.

"Jude Marshall Sinclair! Be care! He's fragile!" Mom scolds me as I reach out to help Jace.

He shoots me a grin before nodding his head as he stands. He's taller than me but lean like I am. Everyone says we could pass for twins except I'm covered in tattoos while his little girl skin is bare. Come to think of it, I'm the only one with tattoos. My siblings are sissies.

"Yeah, Jude, I could break," he says, batting his eyelashes at me before leaning against my mom for protection.

"Oh no, then you won't go into the draft, freaking girl."

He glares as I smile, wrapping my arm around his neck and hugging him close to my chest. I haven't seen him since I started school, and I've missed the little jerk.

"You heard I won't be going in for another year, right?"

"Yup, I guess I'll have to play for all three of us since Jayden probably won't go till next year."

"You think they'll draft both of us?" Jace asks and I shrug.

"Sure, why not? We're the best."

"Ralph wants me to go to Wisconsin," he says. I drop my phone into the basket as he does the same. Ralph is our agent and a longtime family friend.

"What do you want to do?"

"I guess go to Bellevue. I don't want to leave yet, but I want to be noticed."

I nod. "I get that, but remember I have four teams looking at me, and I go to Bellevue. We're gonna kick ass this year."

"Hell, yeah, we are," Jayden adds as he carries Angie on his shoulders toward the living room.

"You gotta do what you feel is right, Jace," I say, cupping his shoulder before turning just in time to see my dad standing up from his chair. He's around my height, but he's thick like Jayden. His dark black hair is cut short, his green eyes hard as emeralds. His mouth is in a straight line, and he doesn't look too pleased to see me, really. It's crazy because when I was outside, I was relaxed and free, but under my dad's gaze, I feel panicky, like I need to run back out. This is how it's always been. My whole life.

"He should go straight into the draft. No need to wait," he says, passing by me with no greeting at all. "You all should. You obviously haven't been working hard enough."

"Like he would know," Jayden says under his breath behind me. I want to laugh but I know better. My dad has never put his hands on us, probably because he isn't around, but when he is, it's easy to say that not all abuse is physical. I used to sit back and take it, but lately, I really don't give a fuck. I don't live here. I don't need him. Haven't needed him, so I'm usually the first one not to whisper under my breath. I let him know exactly what I'm thinking at all times.

"You're completely right, Dad," I say, and my mom sends me a look as Lucy shakes her head. "I obviously don't have a full ride to college or am the captain of a team when I'm only a sophomore or have the respect of my whole team. And Jayden must not push himself to the point of exhaustion every day and must not play rather than study, but he does both. Poor Jace obviously isn't the leading scorer in the high school league for the whole damn United States. Nope, that's not us. Must be some other Sinclair kids."

Dad glares back at me and places his hands on his hips. "Must be."

"Fucking jerk," Jace whispers and I nod in agreement.

"Did you come all this way to ruin the dinner your mother cooked?" he asks me and I shake my head.

"No, I came here to spend time with my family, but of course, you're here and have to make everything tense and forced."

"I can leave if you'd like, you know. We all have to make Jude happy."

"Dad, Jude, please," Lucy says, cuddling Angie in her arms. "Don't fight."

I set my father with a look as he slowly nods. "No fighting, sweetie. He knows he hasn't worked hard. That's why he's so defensive."

Before I can say anything else, Jace cups my shoulder, shaking his head as my mom says, "Okay, let's eat! I know y'all gotta head back early for classes."

I want to say more, but with one look in my mom's eyes, I know this isn't the time. I should have ignored his words, but like always, I let him get to me. I really don't understand it. Why do I care? He doesn't give two shits about me. I could be in the NHL, the leading scorer, and he will find something to bitch about. He will find something that I'm doing wrong, or that he thinks I'm doing wrong, and ride my ass about it. I know my mom loves me and is proud of me, along with my siblings, so really, I don't need anything else. Or at least, I try to say I don't. The truth is that I crave his attention, his love, and most of all, I want him to be proud of me. Crazy, I know. No one should have to fight for the love of their father, but, unfortunately, it happens every day.

Especially in the Sinclair residence.

CHAPTER 7

 *Claire*

I hate Mondays. They are dumb, in my opinion. I mean, why is there a day that is bound to be horrible? Every Monday is like this for me. For some reason, I can never remember to set my alarm before I pass out on Sunday, and so I wake up with only time to brush my teeth before running full speed out of my dorm toward my English class. It's sad and ridiculous, and as I look down at myself, I can't even muster up enough energy to be embarrassed that I'm wearing Pink! sleeping shorts and a large, purple Nashville Assassins hockey team shirt. Or that my hair is so large that it could give a southern belle from the eighties a run for her money.

I look busted, and usually I wouldn't care, but when I come out of my English class to find Jude Sinclair leaning against the wall, I curse the heavens. I try to walk by him, hoping he doesn't see me. But of course, no such luck.

"Lookie here, Claire Anderson, we meet again."

I hide my smile as I say, "Do I know you?"

He laughs as he falls into step with me. "Of course you do. Remember I'm the hottest guy on campus, the same guy you want to meet for dinner tonight."

I scoff as I pause to look at him. Of course, he looks devilishly gorgeous in a black tank and red athletic shorts. His arms are covered in tattoos, and I want to get closer to dissect each one, but since I'm playing that I don't know him, that wouldn't be a good idea.

"Sorry, I don't date."

His grin doesn't falter. "Why is that?"

"'Cause I did that not even a week ago and the guy had crabs."

I turn to leave but his hand wraps around my wrist, and instantly my arm catches on fire. As I look back into his hooded green eyes, he says, "First, I can give you a copy of my physical that says I'm completely clean, and second, don't make me pay for some jerk-off's mistakes."

I smile as my eyes lock with his. I want nothing more than to lean into him and brush my lips against his. I bet his lips are soft. They look so plump, so inviting. I want to get lost in his eyes, his arms, his body. God, I haven't ever felt like this. What is wrong with me? Oh my God, am I actually leaning into him? Oh shit. I am, and he is wanting it. His eyes are darker and he's leaning toward me. *Ack! Stop, Claire!*

Stopping myself, I take a step back, putting a good arm's length distance between us. Setting him with a look, I say, "You're trouble, Hey Jude."

He smiles one of those smiles that makes girls go out their mind and says, "And you are the most gorgeous girl I've ever seen."

"I highly doubt that, especially with the just-out-of-bed look I'm sporting, but thanks."

Leaning into me, his lips by my ear, he says, "If this is what you look like out of bed, I can only imagine how you'd look in it."

My mouth parts as my heart speeds up in my chest, banging hard against my ribcage as he pulls away, his eyes playfully on mine as I gasp for breath. "You'll never find out," I mutter as I take another step back.

"Maybe not today, but one day I will, and believe me, you'll like what you see…and feel, of course."

His voice is thick with lust and everything bad. I eye him cautiously before backing away from him. "Complete trouble."

His mouth pulls up at the side, and he's about to say something, but I run smack-dab into someone. Turning, I go to apologize, but it's Allen.

"Claire, I was looking for you."

"Ugh, why?" I whine as I let my shoulders fall and my head too. I don't want to do this right now. My Monday was looking good for a second there, but of course, Allen would ruin that.

"He has something to say to you, don't you, Allen?"

I look over to find that Jude is standing beside me. "Why are you still here?"

He flashes me a quick grin, but when he looks back at Allen, his look could kill. "'Cause I want to make sure he does what he needs to."

"Are you his dad?" I ask, my face all scrunched up.

Looking back at me, his grin is back. "Nope, his captain."

He says it like that explains it all, but it doesn't. Confused, I look back at Allen as he says, "I'm sorry, Claire. I was wrong for messing around on you behind your back."

My brow comes up before I glance back to Jude. "Did you threaten to beat him up or something?"

He's still grinning as he shrugs. "If that's what you want, I will, but no, I didn't. Laps are my punishment for hurting you."

Why does that make me giddy?

"It seems like he doesn't mean it," I say and Jude laughs.

"Yeah, I agree. Want me to beat him up?"

I glance over at Allen, who is glaring, and I shrug. "He has crabs, that's punishment enough. But now I wish I wouldn't have taken down those signs since I'm pretty sure you're not sorry you cheated on me, but rather sorry you got caught. Don't worry, I'm not the least bit upset about it. I might even move on pretty quickly, so don't worry about me," I say, then to show him he means nothing to me, I reach for Jude and place my lips against his.

It was supposed to be a quick kiss, but soon my lips are moving with his in a very, very slow and sexy way. His lips are soft and full, and God, he tastes good. Donuts. He must be carbing up. When his hands slide down my back, resting against my hips, I arch into him, deepening the kiss. People holler and the catcalls are ridiculous, but I don't care. I'm too lost in his lips and the feel of his chest under my hands to care. He's so hard and thick, oh sweet Lord, his body is a wonderland that I want to discover. When his fingers trail up my neck, that's when something snaps inside me, reminding me that I shouldn't be doing this. I pull away but he follows me, his teeth nibbling on my bottom lip before his lips assault me once more. You know, everyone always talks about sparks and fireworks when they kiss a guy – I hadn't ever felt that before, but I do now. But sparks and fireworks really don't do the way he kisses justice. It's more like a bomb, a nuclear one, because when I pull back, I'm actually dizzy.

What the hell did he do to me?

Setting him with a look, I back away, smacking away his grabby hands that are trying to pull me back in.

"Hey, come here. I'm nowhere near done with that sweet mouth of yours," he says, but I continue to smack his hands away before pointing at him.

"Trouble, pure freaking trouble is what you are!" Then I turn to look at Allen, and I wonder why he stayed to watch that, but whatever. "And you are an asshole. But no need to apologize, 'cause I want nothing to do with you."

Glaring at both of them, I stomp away, mad that I considered having sex with a cheating bastard, a crab-infested asshole, and then mad that I allowed Hey Jude to kiss the living stuffing out of me and make me want to have sex with him in the middle of the courtyard. There is something dangerous about him, and if I'm not careful, Hey Jude will have me naked and on top of him within seconds. The only thing is I'm not sure I want that. I mean, yeah, I want him, but I'm not sure if I only want him once. I may not know him, but I like him a little too much, and that scares me. I've never been in love, never felt those so-called butterflies, but as I'm walking away, those butterflies are going insane in my stomach. Which means one thing:

Jude Sinclair is undeniably trouble.

So when Skylar said that the dance girls were bitches, she wasn't kidding.

Before we even did the group choreographed part, Rachael, the captain, cut nine girls based on their body type and looks. It was rude and disgusting. I felt horrible for this one girl who started crying, and I was two seconds from walking out, but then I saw Reese was in the bleachers, watching. I couldn't walk out when she had come to watch, so I decided to stay in. After learning the dance, which I'm sure my nine-year-olds from the dance studio came up with, Skylar and I murdered it and were passed through to the second round. We started with forty girls and now were at twelve. They were only taking five, though. I was confident in us, but still nerves settled in my stomach.

"Okay, so we have to wait for the guys to get here. They'll be here in like two–" Before Rachael could even finish her sentence, the door was thrown open and in came a group of hot hockey guys. All of them were thick and big, and goodness, where the hell have I been? I have gone to the Bullies' games, but I never noticed how sexy the team was. I looked for Jude, hating how excited I am to see him, but I don't actually see him. Finally though, he brings up the rear, looking down at his phone and not really paying attention.

"So nice of y'all to be on time," Rachael says and Jude laughs.

"You're lucky we graced you with our presences, Rachael," Jude says, looking up from his phone.

"I can do without it."

"That's not what you said last night," he teases, and my stomach recoils at the thought of him with her as everyone laughs, causing Rachael's face to turn red.

"Whatever."

He rolls his eyes and I know he's lying. He wasn't with her. He doesn't even like her. "But really, I apologize, ladies. I told Rachael we'd be late. We had practice."

Everyone smiles and giggles as he flashes them a lady-killing smile before tucking his phone in his pocket. Rachael then snaps, "Whatever, come on, hurry up."

He sticks his tongue out at her before looking out at us, and it seems everyone stands a bit taller, even I do the same. When his eyes lock with mine, he grins, and I swear I'm on fire. My belly does a weird flip-floppy thing, and suddenly the day before, the feel of his lips on mine, washes over me, and I want nothing more than to have a repeat show. I know he's feeling the same thing because his eyes darken and are hooded as he holds my gaze. His mouth turns up at the side as he slowly lowers himself onto the bleachers, his eyes still not leaving mine as he grabs the paddle from someone, probably Rachael.

"Okay, so," Rachael says, and I cringe as I move my eyes from his. She has a nasally, annoying voice that makes me was to claw out my eardrums. "I'm gonna go through everyone's apps, and then we will decide the order for the solos. Everyone has two minutes to impress us and the guys. We take the guys' scores and what we think, and then tomorrow we will post the five new members. You are lucky you made it this far. Bring your A game or get the hell out."

"Gosh, she's a breath of fresh air."

I glance back to see Reese grinning at me. "I thought she was to the point, like you."

She gives me a deadpan look before smacking my ass playfully. Looking back at Rachael, I feel Jude's eyes on me, and when I look, I'm right. His eyes are doing a lazy stroll down my body, his mouth curving as he drinks me in. I'm usually very confident in my sports bra and booty shorts since this is my uniform most the time. Not to brag, but I have a great body, toned and lean, but my thighs are a little thick and my ass could stand my not eating those late-night bags of Cheetos. But under his gaze it doesn't seem like he cares. He wants me. And damn it, I want him.

"Claire Anderson?"

I look back at Rachael and raise my hand. "That's me."

I walk to the center of the floor and cross my leg behind my ankle, holding my hands behind me. She looks me over and she says, "How long have you been dancing?"

"My whole life," I answer.

"With, oh, Reese Allen's Dance Company? Your whole life?"

I nod. "Yup."

The whole dance team sizes me up and then looks back down at the paper in front of them, marking with their red pens. I figure that means I'm done, so I head back to where Reese and Skylar stand. When I feel Reese's hand slide into mine, I glance back as she says, "I hope you don't get in trouble for lying."

I shake my head. "I'm not lying."

"Claire, you've only danced with me for three years."

I smile. "Yeah, but my life didn't start until I came to you and Phillip."

I expected that to please her. I don't think I've told them enough how much they changed me, but what I don't expect is for her eyes to well up before she wraps me up tightly in her arms, kissing my cheek.

"I love you so much, Claire," she cries into my neck, and I hold her as she cries. I'm frozen because Reese doesn't cry. She's a hide your emotions kind of girl, and I am completely stunned.

When she pulls back, I say, "I love you too, but why are you crying?"

"'Cause I'm just so freaking proud of you."

My heart warms and I'm about to say how much she means to me when Rachael calls, "Claire Anderson, you're up."

Reese smiles. "Knock 'em dead, baby girl."

I shoot her a cocky grin as I back away and say, "Don't I always?"

CHAPTER 8

⚒ JUDE

I can still taste her on my lips.

I swear. The taste hasn't left me since I kissed her less than twenty-four hours ago, neither has the hard-on. She has me completely wound-up tight, whacking off till my dick is raw and wishing like hell to get in her pants. When I walked in to find her in only a sports bra and shorts that should be illegal… Well, I'm surprised I'm still vertical.

God, she is fucking hot.

Her long red hair is in a mess on top of her head with a cute little black bow at the base. She stands with such amazing confidence while the other girls cover their stomachs with their arms or slouch to the side, but not Claire. No, she stands proud, beautiful, and man, I just want to rush over there and touch her again. I still can't believe she kissed me senseless then ran off without a second glance. While I don't mind being used, I wasn't done.

I need her. On me. Beneath me. Anywhere on me. Now.

I can't take my eyes off her. I'm supposed to be watching some girl dance, but there is no way. Not with Claire in the room. She stands with the brunette from her Facebook. She's even prettier in person, but she holds no candle to Claire. Hell, no one does. I watch as they talk, and the love just shines out of the brunette's body for her. It's crazy to watch. It reminds me of my mom's love, and I figure it's her mom. I need to ask because I have to know. I don't know what it is about this feisty little redhead, but I want to know her ins and outs. Then I want to sleep with her. Continually. And then some more.

When Rachael calls for the numbers, I look over at Jayden and he shakes his head. "Were you even watching?" he asks in a hushed tone.

"Nope."

"She was eh, I'm giving her a six."

I nod and do the same, holding up my paddle. I see the girl's face fall and then I notice that it's April. I've slept with her. Well shit, guess I've burned that easy bridge, which really, I never planned on crossing again anyway. Looking over at my grinning brother, I say, "You couldn't tell me it was April? I was with her like two weeks ago."

Jayden laughs. "Dude, I can't keep up with who you sleep with, and I actually plan to judge these girls on their talent."

Rolling my eyes, I look back toward Claire. She's hugging the brunette, but then her name is called, and she slowly backs away, saying something, and I want to know what it is. I'm sorta disgusted with myself. I mean, why do I care? Why am I so hung up on this girl? She won't even give me the time of day. She's playing this hard to get shit, and I don't play those games. If I want attention, all I gotta do is stand up and snap my fingers, and three girls will be on me quick. So I should do that. I should ignore this attraction, this stalkerish tendency, and fuck someone who will give it to me easy.

The only problem is that I don't want them.

I want her, and when she struts to the middle of the floor, I know that I'll play whatever game she wants just for another taste of that delectable, red glossed-up mouth. When she purses those lips like she's about to give me a kiss that will shatter my world, I hold on to the end of the bleachers as "I Wanna Dance with Somebody" by Whitney Houston blares over the audio system.

And as soon as the music starts, time stands still for me.

She's shockingly amazing. I've watched girls dance, and then I've watched girls murder the dance floor, and Claire is murdering the hell out of the gym floor. Her body moves with such attention to the music – as if it *is* the music – and it's breathtaking to watch. The music is fun and she's grinning and having a good time, but like me, everyone is stunned. Each move is on point, no fumbles, no second-guessing; she knows what she's doing, and I can't help but admire her. When she goes into a series of turns that seem to go on forever, I want to stand and applaud her, but before I can, she stops, running her hands up her body and then she winks at me.

Fucking winks.

It is probably the fucking hottest thing I've ever seen in my life, but then she drops into the splits, and I swear I just came in my pants. She ends the dance with a leg stretch while doing a turn. It looks painful, but it seems like second nature to her. When the music ends, the girls to the side all clap and cheer, and I notice that Rachael and her clan are all impressed. That pleases me, and before I'm even asked for my paddle, I stand, holding up my ten.

Because Claire Anderson just blew away everyone around her with that dance.

Looking around, I see that everyone else thought what I did, because all I see are tens. When Rachael looks back at us, she glares before writing down the numbers. She then clears her throat and everyone quiets down, and she sets Claire with a look. "That was very impressive."

Placing her hands on her hips, Claire smiles before nodding. "Thank you."

"Watching you dance, I remember you from the competition circuit. You won everything."

"Well, when you train with the best, you tend to be the best."

"Touché, and let me just say that you are the first girl in my dance team history to get all tens from the hockey team."

Her eyes meet mine again, and she smiles before she says in a very low, sexy voice, "Well, thanks, boys."

Yup, my mind is mush. I can't speak, hell, none of us can. She is just so damn hot.

Claire then looks back at Rachael and says, "Thank you for allowing me to try out. I hope I get the opportunity to dance with y'all."

"I'm sure you will," Rachael says, and then she calls Skylar's name. I watch Claire walk back to the brunette, hugging her tightly and smiling so big her face is as bright as the sun. She is so beautiful.

"Jude Sinclair, you better give me a ten," Skylar then calls at me and I laugh.

"We will see," I say and she grins before her music starts, but like with everyone else, I can't watch her, and when she's done, I have to copy Jayden's score, which is a nine. Skylar seems to be pleased, which is good, but I just couldn't watch her.

I can't do anything when Claire is the room. She's the only thing I see.

⁂

Once Rachael announces that the tryouts are over, I hightail it toward Claire, reaching for her wrist to get her attention. She looks back at me and grins as she pulls a sweatshirt over her head, much to my dismay.

"So I heard you want to dance with somebody," I say teasingly.

She laughs. "Maybe. You the man for the job?"

I find myself nodding like a fool. "I could be the heat you're looking for."

Shaking her head, she looks away. "Didn't I say you were trouble?"

"You did," I say and I take a step closer. "But I think you are going to ignore that and take advantage of me."

Before she can respond, the brunette is beside us and asking, "Claire, who's your friend?"

Taking a step back, Claire swallows as her cheeks fill with color. "Reese, this is Jude Sinclair. The current trouble in my life."

Reese smiles as she holds her hand out for me. I take it, flashing the smile my mom says is my moneymaker before I say, "It's wonderful to meet you."

"You too," she says and I know she's eyeing my arms. Most moms don't like my tattoos, my mom included, but I love them.

"This is my mo– Holy crap, Reese, I almost called you my mom! My bad!" Claire laughs, but I can see that Reese doesn't mind at all.

Wrapping her arm around Claire's shoulders, she says, "It's fine. I would love nothing more than to be your mom, Claire. You know that."

"I know, but you're too young to have a nineteen-year-old hellion."

"Maybe, but you're mine nonetheless."

Claire beams at her before looking over at me. "Reese is my soon-to-be aunt/mom/dance teacher/best friend."

I smile over at Reese. "That's some title."

"It's one I wear proudly," she says before placing a kiss to Claire's head. "Okay, I gotta run before I start crying again."

Claire laughs. "What is up with all the crying?"

"Leave me be. Jude, nice meeting you. By the way, I love your name, very old-school."

I grin. "Thank you."

"Hope to see you again," she says, her eyes leaving mine to send a direct look to Claire, but all she does is glare before shaking her head.

"Hush, Reese," she says and Reese laughs.

"You'll see me soon, with Claire. I'm trying to convince her to date me."

They both look at me and then Reese says, "Oh Claire, I like him. He reminds me ever so much of someone I love very much."

Claire is still glaring as she says, "No, he doesn't, plus, don't let him fool ya, he only wants to sleep with me."

"That's how it started with me and my man," she teases.

"Ew, don't talk about my uncle like that."

She laughs but then sets me with a look. "Don't hurt her, or I will send my fiancé after you. He is scary."

"Not sure who we're talking about, but I have no plans of hurting her," I say quickly and Reese's grin is back.

"Good. Later, kids."

And then she's gone.

When I look back over at Claire, she's pulling up a pair of sweats. When she meets my gaze, color fills her cheeks again before she looks away. "She's sorta crazy. I love her, though."

"I think she's awesome. Reminds me of my mom."

She smiles, her top teeth sinking into her bottom lip. Taking a step toward her, I want to do the same, but before I can, she says, "You know that you don't want to date me."

I shrug. "That's up for debate. I thought I only wanted to have sex with you, but for some reason I just can't get you out of my head. I still taste you, Claire, and I know that has to mean something."

Her eyes darken with color as her breath hitches, and I know this is the time to go in for the kill. Closing the distance between us, I wrap my arms around her, taking her mouth with mine in a hot assault. Any protest is lost as my lips move against hers. Her body is so soft and feels so damn good against mine. The taste of her is intoxicating, and as our lips move in a way that makes it hard to breathe, I run my fingers up her arms, cupping her sweet face in my hands. As she bites into my bottom lip, I moan against her lips before deepening the kiss. Our tongues move in such a sweet, sexy dance, and everything inside me is on fire.

When I pull away, it's only to catch my breath, and I refuse to give her any space to breathe or decide this is a bad idea. "Let me take you to dinner."

Her eyes dance with lust and everything naughty. I've never been so turned on in my life. When her lips part to speak, I can't take it and crash my lips to her again. Pushing her against the wall, I press my body into hers, and I know that I should take it easy, but I can't. I need her. I can feel her heart beating in her chest, and I know it matches the fast beat of mine. Pulling back once more, I open my eyes, meeting her sweet, blue gaze.

"Say yes," I demand, moving my thumb along her jaw.

She shakes her head. "Why don't I just let you take me to bed?"

Oh sweet God, say yes, say yes, you dumb lug. Don't get lost in those eyes; say yes, and fuck her brains out.

But for some crazy, fucked-up reason, I can't listen to my dick. I shake my head slowly. "My momma brought me up to wine and dine a lady first."

Her mouth pulls up at the side as she slowly nods. "Maybe I'm no lady."

"See, that's where you're wrong, Claire. You are a lady. The only lady who has my full attention. I'm not sure what I'm doing, or even who I am right now, but I want to do right by you. And if after dinner, you still want to take me to bed, believe me, I will not stop you."

Her brows crowd in but then she's fully smiling at me, and soon my mouth curves into a matching grin. "Why is it every time I see you, you surprise me?"

Leaning my forehead against hers, I move my nose slowly along hers, my lips teasing hers before I whisper, "Because I'm trouble."

CHAPTER 9

Claire

Trouble indeed, but it didn't matter. He's pushing and pulling me straight to him, and I'm sure he isn't going to let me go. Not that I want him to. There is something about him that has me completely and utterly drawn to him, no pulling needed. While I want to sleep with him, I also want to get to know him. Really, I have no clue what I want. I just want Jude. All of him and I'm glad he turned down my offer to go to bed. While I want it, I don't think I would have gone through with it, but then with the way he's looking at me, his hooded green eyes flaring with lust, I'm thinking that previous statement was a total lie.

I damn well want him more than my next breath.

Swallowing hard, I suck in a breath as he runs his lips along mine in a very sexy, slow way. He isn't kissing me, his lips are only grazing mine, teasing me in such a hypnotic manner. I want so much more, but I like this game. I love the teasing. Nipping at his bottom lip, my teeth sink into it and his minty breath comes out in a gust against my mouth. Releasing his lip, I take his mouth with mine, moving my tongue along his as his hands fall from my face to my hips, holding me tight in his large hands. Pulling away, only a breath, I look into his eyes as my mouth pulls up at the side.

"If we keep on, dinner will not happen."

"I'm reconsidering my earlier proposition."

I smile fully as I run my nose along his. "You want me?"

He groans softly against my lips as he nods his head, his nose moving along mine. We're basically one, we're so close, and I don't think I ever want him to go anywhere else. The air around us is sizzling, and I find myself fighting for my next breath.

"I want you so bad I can't see straight."

I smile, loving that I'm affecting him the same way he's affecting me. Fuck it, I can't take this. I've been good too long. It's time to go back to my naughty side, and if for some crazy reason – because I know darn well Jude doesn't want anything more from this – he comes to think he does, then we'll cross that bridge at that point, but now…now I want to ride him like a horse and never look back.

"Let's go back to my dorm."

I can see the struggle in his eyes. He wants to be a gentleman and that pleases me. I know he hasn't ever treated a girl like that. He uses them and lets them go. I've heard the rumors and seen the way girls act around him, but with me…I affect him differently. I've never felt so powerful in my life, and it's my job to make guys hard with lust, but with Jude, it's a whole new ball game. His eyes have yet to leave mine, his hands haven't left my body since he started touching me, and I just feel so amazing under his gaze. I've never wanted to completely please a guy, but I'm shaking to please Jude.

His lips move, but nothing comes out, and I take that as a go. Reaching for his hand, I lace my fingers with his and pull out my phone to see that Reese texted me.

> *He's hot. Bring him to the wedding. I'll tell Phillip to be on his best behavior. I promise.*

Ignoring her message, I text Skylar.

> *Vacate now. Need room.*

She replies with a *10-4 good buddy,* and I know I'm solid. I know later I'll have to explain what happened, but now I get to enjoy Jude with no interruptions, and my body shakes in anticipation. Looking over at him, a grin sits on his plump lips, and damn it, I don't know if I'm gonna make it to the room. Stopping, I wrap my arms around his neck, kissing him deeply as his fingers come up under my sweatshirt, massaging my lower back as we kiss. Everything is on fire and I can't believe these feelings. It's deep in my stomach, tightening and scaring the shit out of me, but I don't care. For the first time in years, I actually feel something for the opposite sex. While before it was only to get off, to make myself feel alive, or to piss someone off, now – while I would love to get off too, and by the look in Jude's eyes, I know I will – I also want to enjoy him, and I want to please him.

I respect him.

Lacing my fingers with his, he looks deep in my eyes as his mouth curves in one of those devilish grins. "We can go get dinner, Claire, just say the word. I hope you don't, though."

"I'm not going to. Come on," I say before dragging him across the quad. I feel people looking at us but I ignore them. When I glance over at him, his eyes are on me, ignoring everyone too, and it's so elating. When my building comes into view, I almost squeal in delight before pulling him up the four flights of stairs to my dorm.

Throwing open the door, I go through, reaching for the hem of my sweatshirt before pulling it over my head and tossing it to the side. When I turn, Jude kicks the door shut and locks it before taking me in his arms, his mouth meeting mine in a magnetic kind of way. I get lost in the kiss, my head cloudy with lust as I press my chest against his. When his hands go to my hips and quickly lift me, I automatically wrap my legs around his trim waist before he turns, pressing me hard into the door.

I can feel him. Every single inch and my legs shake at the thought of him inside me. Tearing his mouth from mine, he kisses down my jaw, my throat, and dips his tongue between my breasts before pulling down my sports bra and taking my nipple in his mouth. The sensation warms me everywhere, and when he swirls his tongue around it, I cry out, my nails biting into his shoulders. Holding me up with his body, he runs his hand down my hips and takes ahold of my pants and shorts before pulling them down my thighs as far as they'll go. Placing his hands on my bare ass, he squeezes it before snaking one of his hands up to my dripping wet center. He then moves his fingers inside me. I cry out, my legs squeezing him as he slowly fucks me with his long, thick fingers.

Remembering that the walls are very thin and Skylar has warned me countless times to make sure music is playing, I say, "Oh God, Jude, give me a second."

He stops, looking at me questioningly before I search for my phone in the pocket of my bundled up sweatpants. When I finally find it, my hands are shaking, but somehow I link it to my Bluetooth speakers and push play on the first playlist I have. It's one of my covers' playlists, which is fine; it's mostly acoustic music. Total sex music. Or at least I hope it is. Really, who gives a shit? I doubt either of us will actually be listening. Turning it up to where I think we're safe, I toss my phone to the side and wrap my arms around his neck, bringing him in close. I kiss him slowly before parting and running my tongue along his lips.

"I usually don't do it with music," he says roughly against my lips, his fingers still playing with my naked ass.

"I don't want the RA called on me."

"See, no one can say anything at my house. I'm the captain," he says, giving me a grin. "Next time we'll go there."

Next time. Why am I hoping there is a next time when we haven't even gotten to the main event? Before anything else can be said, Jude carries me to the bed, laying me softly on it before pulling his shirt up and over his head. I sit up, pushing my pants, shorts, and panties down and off before reaching up to run my hand along his chest, down his abs, to the button of his jeans. When I glance up, his eyes are hooded, full of lust as he watches me. I want to admire all the tattoos along his chest and arms, but I am too far gone to care. I want him. Need him. Now.

I smile and he smiles back before reaching under my arms to help remove my bra and covering my body with his. He's so much bigger than me. Stronger and more defined. And God, he feels amazing against my naked skin. I'm used to being close to naked in front of guys, but being fully naked, all my imperfections out for Jude to see… I should be nervous, but I'm not. Looking into his eyes, I see nothing but pure admiration for me and it's so unreal. Never have I had this.

Sitting up, Jude drinks me in, his hands exploring my body. When he pauses, I cringe because I know he found it.

"That's hot," he says, running his finger along my brown mole that is under my boob.

"Sure it is," I say, smacking his hand away.

He smiles, bringing my hand up and biting my fingertip. I take in a deep breath as he says, "It is."

Before I can answer or tell him he's crazy, he's kissing down my throat, my breasts, my stomach, and when his mouth settles between my legs, I almost come off the bed. Biting down on my lip, I scream internally as he assaults my pussy like he owns it, and at that moment, he does. My whole body is blistering hot; sweat drips down my temple into my hair, and I try not to scream, but I'm not doing a very good job of it. When my body seizes, he doesn't let up. He ruthlessly licks my clit until I'm crying out so loud, I'm sure that people across campus hear me.

"Fuck, you're so loud. It's making me so fucking hard," he says, standing and chucking his pants off and to the side. When his huge, hard dick springs out toward me, I can see why all the girls on campus love Jude Sinclair.

"Holy huge penis, batman."

He laughs and my face turns red. I can't believe I just said that, but my filter is clouded with lust. Reaching out, I take his huge dick and cover it with my mouth, stopping his laughter. Taking a step toward me, he pushes his dick farther in my mouth. I suck him in and out of my mouth quickly. All of a sudden, though, my hair falls along my shoulders from where he undid my clip as I lick and tease him like he did me. I'm a little rusty since I haven't given head in a really long time, but the noises he's making are promising and fuel me to go faster as his fingers tangle in my hair. I can feel him about to come and I'm excited for it, but before he can, he pulls himself from my mouth and shakes his head.

"I want to be in you."

"Condom though, right?" I ask with my brows brought in.

He nods as he reaches for his jeans, pulling his wallet out. "Of course, baby."

Why did I just swoon? Lying back on the bed, I watch as he sheathes himself before covering my body with his. Cupping me behind my knees, he brings my legs back before directing himself toward my wet center. Before he can go in though, I say, "I haven't been with anyone in three years."

I'm not 100% sure why I said that, but something possessive burns in his eyes and he nods slowly. "I'll take it easy, but I'm not gonna lie, Claire. I've been around, but that stops after this."

Then he enters me and lights go off behind my eyes. He's too big or I'm too small, and I want to say stop from the burning sensation between my legs, but then he pulls out slowly, going back in again, and it starts to feel good with each thrust. Soon he's causing another orgasm within me and I'm thrashing beneath him. Pressing down on my legs, he drops his mouth to mine, kissing the stuffing out of me as he thrusts into me so gently but at the same time hard. It's insane and feels oh so great.

When my body tightens around him, he groans, dropping his head to mine as he continues to thrust inside me. "Fuck, you are so damn tight, baby," he whispers against my lips.

My nails dig into his ass as he picks up speed, our bodies slapping together, and then he slams into me one last time, a guttural sound leaving his lips as he falls on top of me, going completely limp. Closing my eyes, I take in a deep breath, our hearts both beating out of control but together at the same time. Turning his face, he smiles at me before pressing his lips to the side of my mouth.

"I knew you were a game changer, Claire Anderson."

I grin as I look over at him, meeting his lazy gaze. "And I knew you were trouble."

Kissing me again, he says, "The good kind of trouble, the kind that gives you multiple orgasms and feeds you."

I giggle. "True, and I am kinda hungry."

"Good, me too. Let's go get Waffle House."

I eye him and ask, "Why Waffle House?"

"'Cause it's my favorite. Do you not like it?"

I'm breathless. It's not every day you find someone whose favorite restaurant is Waffle House. It's more of a drunk spot to eat at, but I love everything about it.

And so does Jude.

I just slept with Jude.

And we both love Waffle House and have just had unbelievable sex.

As I look into his eyes, he waits for my answer, and I can't help but think that if he doesn't want to see me after we eat, I could be a little heartbroken.

Somehow, somewhere, sometime, I kinda developed some kind of hard-core, stupid crush on this guy who is nothing but trouble. A womanizing hockey player with a one-way ticket out of here. While I want to regret this, I can't muster up the feeling.

All I feel is amazing.

And I want so much more.

Swallowing loudly at the realization that Jude has completely rocked my world, I bite into my lip before saying, "It's my favorite, too."

With a wink, he kisses my nose before slowly removing himself from my body. "Good, let's get dressed and go, unless you want to cuddle or something."

I smile as I sit up. "Do you cuddle, Hey Jude?"

He shoots me a grin. "No, but I will if you want to."

I eye him as I ask, "Do you say that to all the girls you mess with?"

Disposing of the condom in the trash can by my desk, he shakes his head, looking back at me. "Nope, not a single one."

He then comes to me and I watch his sexy, naked body move and flex with each step he takes. His legs are a thing of beauty, hockey legs, and the rest of his body is beautiful too. I've always been attracted to hot legs and abs. I love abs and Jude has abs on top of abs, just like Skylar said.

Reaching out, he takes my chin in his hand, tipping my head back to look at him. "Didn't I tell you that you were a game changer?"

"You did, but I don't know what that means," I say, covering his hand with my own, while my other comes out to rest against his hip.

Grinning, he leans down, running his nose along mine before whispering, "Then I'll have to show you."

CHAPTER 10

JUDE

My body is still humming.

And as soon as my lips touch hers again, leaving isn't an option. I have to have her again. Dragging my mouth from hers, I nibble down her jaw, her neck, before sucking and biting on her sweet, full tits. Her body is perfect. She has a sexy hourglass shape to her and it's mouthwatering, causing me to hope my time with her never runs out. While she thinks her mole is ugly, I think it complements her body and turns me on as I run my nose along it, kissing each of her ribs before nibbling on her hip bone. Her fingers tangle in my hair, and I suck in a deep breath from the sensation.

"I thought we were gonna eat?"

"Well, I'm gonna eat you, and then we can go," I say before running my tongue up the slit of her perfect, glistening pussy. "That is, if you can walk."

"So cocky," she teases, and I grin as I run my tongue along her thigh. I've seen many girls naked, had a lot of them in my mouth, but there is something very pristine about Claire's pussy. It's beautiful, sweet, and bare. She has freckles that dust along the inside of her thighs and along her sweet folds. I want to trace each one with my tongue and get lost between her legs for the rest of my life.

I don't know what happened in this dorm room, but I know I'll never have enough of her.

Dipping my tongue inside her, I finger her entrance as I swirl my tongue around her clit. She squeals underneath me, her breathing so quick and fast as she digs her nails into my shoulders. Usually that's a turnoff, but I love it when Claire does it. Sometimes, I think girls do it to mark me, but with Claire, I know she's doing it out of pure ecstasy. Opening her folds, I suck her clit into my mouth, making her squirm before I start to fuck her ruthlessly with my tongue.

I look at her, her hands gripping her sweet tits, her back arching as she bites into her lip to keep from screaming. I can't wait to get her back to my place; there she can scream all she wants and no one can say anything.

Going faster, I quickly ignore the fact that I've never slept with a girl twice. The anticipation to do this all over again, to feel her sweet, tight pussy wrapped around my cock has my eyes crossing. I can't wait, and I have no remorse in knowing that I'm giving up my lifestyle for this girl without even knowing what her favorite color is. I don't care. I just want to be with her. When she suddenly screams out, her nails biting into my skin, I watch as she seizes up, my name falling from her lips as she shatters under my mouth.

It is the hottest thing I've ever seen.

And everything I was just thinking is set in stone.

Claire Anderson is the girl for me.

Forty minutes later, I fall into the booth beside Claire, my arm coming up and around her shoulders to hold her closer. Her lips are swollen, her face pink, and she looks so damn good in her hoodie and leggings that she put on quickly so I wouldn't have to wait. Not that I mind waiting. Her hair is in a mess on her head, and I want her to put it down. She's so gorgeous when it's framing her face and she's coming, screaming my name.

Man, I'm in deep.

Running my nose along her temple, I tease her ear as she tries to look at the menu. She giggles, trying to pull away, but she isn't trying hard enough. She likes it. She likes me. I know she does.

"You don't know what you're getting?"

She grins as she flips the menu over and then back. "Can't seem to find a big serving of Hey Jude Sinclair – they must not carry it."

I grin, nipping at her earlobe as I whisper, "I'm sure we can arrange some for dessert."

Turning her head, she brushes her nose along mine, kissing my bottom lip before whispering, "What about after dessert?"

I pull back some, meeting her shy gaze. "I mean, if you want me for another go, I'm down, baby."

She smiles as her face warms with color. "While, yes I do, I actually meant like tomorrow, or the next day, or the day after that."

"Oh," I say as I nod slowly, but before I can answer, she shakes her head.

"Ack, I sound like one of those needy girls who need some kind of reassurance that you'll do me later. Ew. Sorry, that's so not me or how I act. Can we start over? I meant to say I hope we can do it again… No, I didn't mean that 'cause that means I expect it, and that's not… Well, maybe, but shit, oh my God, I'm rambling, stop me," she says quickly, and I oblige by taking her sweet mouth with mine.

She melts against me as I hold her close with my arm. Pulling back, I smile before kissing the side of her mouth. "Rambling Claire is cute."

"She's annoying, hence why she doesn't come out much. You bring out weird things in me."

"Good," I say just as the waitress comes up. We order the same All-Star Meal and then fall lower in the booth, cuddling into each other. While sometimes sex leads to cuddling with girls, I usually find an out. But here, wrapped in the warmth that Claire is giving me, I don't want an out. I love the feel of her. My hand lazily plays along her arm and her hair smells so damn good. Something girlie and expensive I think because I usually don't smell something so alluring. Then again, maybe it's just Claire.

When she glances up at me, I grin and she smiles back as her face warms. "Shit, Jude, I'm all girlie around you. It's disgusting."

I chuckle as I hug her tighter against me. "I think it's adorable. Please continue. I love the color on your face. It matches your hair, which, by the way," I say as I lower my voice, "I was curious on your real hair color, but I got no clue, still. Care to fill me in?"

She laughs as she shakes her head. "It's blond."

I try to picture her as a blonde, but it doesn't fit. "I can't see it."

"Maybe I'll show ya a picture one day. It's more of a strawberry blond, but I've been dyeing my hair this color for years. Sometimes I'll do black tips or something else crazy."

"I love your hair. Don't get me wrong, but why do you dye it?"

"To be different. I want to people to see me."

"You don't come off as an attention whore, though."

She smiles as she nods. "I'm not now, but I didn't have the best childhood, and because of it, I wanted people to see me, notice me, so I did everything I could to make people look at me. Wore dirty, naughty clothes, shaved my head up one side at one point and... Oh my God, why am I telling you this?"

She tries to hide her face but I don't allow her, holding her where I can see her. "Because you trust me. Don't hide from me."

She bites into her lip and takes in a deep breath. "I wasn't the person I am now but I still love this look. I think I look very Little Mermaid-punky."

"Well, I guess I can say I've seen what's behind Ariel's shells, and I like what I found very much."

She laughs, smacking me playfully before shaking her head. "You're crazy."

"About you? I know. And, by the way," I say, capturing her lips with mine. I kiss her, slow and deliberate before pulling way to whisper, "I want to see you again and again. Game changer, remember?"

She nods slowly, her lips moving up and down mine as her eyes lock with mine. Her mouth is turned up in a cute little naughty grin as she says, "So I guess since you want to see me, we have to do that whole get to know you stuff, huh? I've never really dated anyone. Well no, I take that back. I was with this guy named Brian once, but he was more a friend than anything."

"Yeah, you said you hadn't been with anyone in a long time. Reason why you've been celibate?"

"Bad childhood. I slept around real bad when I was younger. When my uncle took custody of me, I still tried to ruin his life, but then decided to give him a chance. So I cleaned myself up and became me."

I nod, processing the information. "Can I ask why your uncle took custody?"

"Sure," she says before sipping a little of the iced tea she ordered. Clearing her throat, she looks back up at me. "My mom was a strung-out stripper who got herself killed over her next fix."

"Oh shit, I'm sorry," I say, sucking in a quick breath.

But Claire shrugs. "You know, I miss her, but I miss the her before the drugs took over. I am glad that the person who cared more about drugs than me is gone because going to Phillip and Reese really changed my life. I'm happy now and I'm healthy, and yeah, I broke my celibacy, but I think I chose a good person to break it with."

I grin, taking her lips with mine, drawing the kisses out of her slowly. I love kissing her – I can't get enough – and when we part, I follow her mouth again, going in for another kiss that turns into another.

"Jeez, Sinclair! Get a room!"

Claire smiles against my lips, and unlike any other girl, she deepens the kiss, running her hand up my face to tangle in my hair. My body hardens and I want to take her on the table, but I know that the good employees of Waffle House would not appreciate that.

"Damn, get it, Sinclair!"

I am going to kill my brother and our teammates, but it's like she doesn't even hear them. Claire continues to kiss me until finally I pull away. Getting lost in the depths of her beautiful blue eyes, I whisper, "You are so fucking hot."

She giggles as she smacks my face lightly. "You're not so bad yourself, hot stuff."

I smile but then turn to find my brother and some of the guys laughing at the corner booth. "I'm gonna make y'all pay tomorrow, assholes."

They all shut up when they hear that as Claire just giggles beside me. Turning to look at her, I love what I see. A little wisp of her hair is falling in her face, her cheeks are bright, her eyes shining, and her lips so swollen and delectable.

"Teammates?"

"Yeah, and my brother," I answer.

She eyes my brother, and when Jayden gives her a wink, I almost come out of the booth, but Claire's hand is resting on my thigh and I don't dare move, but I'll make sure to kick his ass later. "I can see the resemblance."

I shrug. "I'm hotter."

"Oh yes, by far."

She shoots me a grin just as our food is laid down in front of us and we both dig in. We eat in silence for a few but then she asks, "Is that your only brother?"

I shake my head, swallowing the piece of bacon I just threw in my mouth. "Nope, I have a younger one, Jace, and then an older sister, Lucy."

"Oh, that's right, Lucy in the Sky with Diamonds."

I nod then ask, "Do you have siblings?"

"Nope, only me, but I have a really huge extended family. Lots of kids for me to love on."

"That's cool. I have a niece, Angie. She's one."

"That's nice," she says. "What do your parents do?"

"Dad is a lawyer and my mom is a stay-at-home mom."

"That must have been nice growing up."

"Yeah, she spoiled us," I say with a chuckle. "And I'm her favorite."

"I wouldn't doubt that," she teases with a wink, and I smile.

"What about Reese and your uncle, Phillip, right?"

She nods. "Yeah, Reese owns the dance studio, Reese Allen's Dance Company, and Phillip plays for the Nashville Assassins."

I stop eating and look over at her as I process what she just said. Surely, he's not the Phillip Anderson I think he is. "You have his last name?"

"Yup, Anderson."

"Phillip Anderson, as in, leading scorer in the NHL, Phillip Anderson?"

She smiles. "That's the one."

I am speechless. I admire Phillip's game. We go to watch the Assassins play all the time as a team unity exercise, and Phillip has always been my favorite player, along with Erik Titov because of his speed and stickhandling. I knew that he looked familiar! How did I not place him?

"Wow, he's a great player."

"Yup, he's the best. Really wonderful uncle, too."

I take a swig of my orange juice as I continue to think on this. It's just so mind-blowing! Glancing over at her, I smile and decide I need to talk about something else before I start asking questions about her uncle.

"You've always danced?"

"Yeah, it's been a passion of mine, but I really didn't get to dance the way I wanted until I got to Reese. Have you always played hockey?"

"Yup, since I could walk. My dad played when he was younger, and put me and Jayden and Jace in it as soon as he could."

"That's really cool. You're really good from what I've heard. I haven't gotten to watch you yet."

"You will since you'll be shaking that fine ass for me at the opener."

She laughs. "I don't know. I think Rachael is threatened by me."

"Or jealous, or both, but who cares, they all need to be. You're the best. I've never given a girl a ten."

"I feel so special," she says, batting her eyes at me.

I catch her chin, holding her in place as her eyes meet mine. I love how her eyes settle on mine. It just seems so right, getting lost in the depths of her sparkling blue eyes. What I was about to say was supposed to be just something to say because it was nice, but as the two words sit lodged in my throat, I can't help but know they're the truth.

Bringing my lips so close to hers, I whisper, "You are."

CHAPTER 11

 *Claire*

Oh, Jude is laying it on thick, and I'm just eating it up.

While I want to think he's just laying game on me, I can't help but feel his words are genuine. That I am special. How after only a couple hours of being together does he think that, I'm not sure, but man, I hope he really thinks so. I think he's fabulous, amazing, perfect, and I can't believe how girlie I turn when he sets those sharp green eyes on me. But still, in the back of my mind, I hear everyone telling me that he's a player. That he doesn't do a girl more than once, but it just doesn't seem right.

This seems real.

When his lips press against mine, I'm breathless as he kisses me slowly, cupping my neck with his large hand. I love kissing him. Since the first time our lips touched, I've craved them, and as much as I don't understand, I can't help but love every second his lips are on mine. I mean, don't get me wrong, I really like having sex with him, but kissing him is probably my favorite so far. His lips are so plump, and it feels so sexy and naughty when our lips touch. Like it's illegal or something because we're so hot when we touch. I don't know, but man, I love it.

Pulling away, Jude smiles before kissing my nose and asking, "You ready?"

I nod. "Yeah."

"Cool."

He then reaches into his pocket to pull out some money. I watch as he lays a twenty on the table and then gets out of the booth, bringing me with him.

"Later, guys," he calls, and the guys in the booth all wave.

Looking up at him, I ask, "I don't get to meet your brother?"

He cuts a look at me and then shakes his head. "No way, I'm not sharing you yet. You're all mine tonight."

Man, I hate the doubt that settles in my stomach, because while I should be pleased by that statement, I can't help but think he didn't want to introduce me because he doesn't plan on seeing me after this. Refusing to let that bother me, I smile as his fingers lace with mine. The night is quiet and so is the quad. Only a few people are walking around, and some even sit in the grass, lying with someone or making out, while others look at the stars through their telescopes. I love the Bellevue campus. It's so remote, so amazing. It's almost like we have our own world, and I like that. Everything I want is here.

Especially now that I've met Jude.

"So what do you want to be when you grow up?" he asks suddenly, and I laugh as I smile at him.

Grinning, I say, "A princess."

"You're already Princess Ariel, so what do you want to be after that?"

I laugh as my heart skips a beat. "I would like to choreograph concerts for big-name stars, like Justin Timberlake or someone like that. Or maybe come up with amazing Vegas shows, or maybe even own my own studio."

"I can see it happening, and when you make it, make sure not to forget us little people."

I laugh out loud at that as I cup our hands in my other hand. "Please, you'll be some hotshot hockey player with babes throwing themselves all over you. So really, who will forget whom?"

He scoffs as he shakes his head. "I could never forget the most gorgeous girl in the world."

He turns me then, taking me in his arms before crashing his lips to mine. As I kiss him, I snake my arms around his waist, holding him tightly as our lips move together in such an erotic way. I love how we fit. I'm only tad bit shorter than him, so he doesn't have to bend to kiss me, and when we hug, we fit. As much as I want to say that it is meant to be, I'm not sure what is going to happen when Jude drops me off. I could always make sure that I see him again, but I refuse to beg for someone's love. Been there, done that, never doing it again.

Cupping my jaw, he runs his thumb up and down my chin, searching my eyes for something. I'm not sure what it is, but before I can ask, my phone buzzes in my pocket, signaling a call.

"Oops, hold on," I say, pulling away to pull my phone out. Jude doesn't go far, his arms are still around my waist and his lips rest at my temple as I look at the display to see it's Phillip. "I'm sorry, I have to answer this."

"That's cool, baby."

Swooning. Ugh. Hitting answer, I say, "Hey!"

"Hey, you. Heard you killed at your audition today. I'm proud of you. Reese recorded it and, boy, you smoked that dance."

I smile broadly as I look down at the ground. "Thanks, I'll send you a text tomorrow and let you know if I make it or not."

"There's no question. They'll be dumb not to take you."

I laugh as I rock back on my heels, but Jude doesn't let me get far. "I hope so. Are you home?"

"Yeah, got in about an hour go. I leave out again Friday, though."

"Crap, I probably won't get to see ya then."

"Probably not. I miss you."

"I miss you more."

My heart explodes in my chest as I grin. "So tell me why Reese is crying at, like, everything. It's scary."

"Well, you did say some really great things that could even bring tears to my eyes, but really, I don't know, she's weird… Oopphmm, damn, Reese! That hurt!"

I laugh as I ask, "What happened?"

"She kicked me in the gut. Damn it, she's crazy, I'm telling you."

I hear Reese in the background and then she's on the phone. "Hey, did you ask Jude to the wedding?"

"Ugh Reese, please," I say and I hear Phillip start asking who Jude is. "We're only friends."

But when I chance a glance at him to see he's watching me, his eyes tell me we're way more than friends…but for how long?

As he takes my phone from me, I shriek in shock as he puts the phone to his ear and says, "Reese? Hey, it's Jude Sinclair. Yeah, it was wonderful meeting you, but I want to say, Claire and I are way more than friends. Yup…okay… yeah."

I try to take the phone from him, but he's stronger than I am, holding me out from him as he continues to talk to my family!

"Mr. Anderson, yes, it's wonderful to speak with you."

I stop struggling then, my eyes going wide. He's talking to Phillip! Fuck!

"As I was telling your fiancée, this thing between me and Claire is special, and oh, you don't care? Oh. Okay. Well, I hope to prove to you that that is unnecessary. Yes, sir, thank you."

When he hands me my phone, his lips are in a grim line. I put the phone to my ear just as Phillip yells, "What the hell do you mean she's dating someone? And why put me on the phone with the guy? I don't want to talk to him!"

Deciding that I do not want to speak to my uncle, I hang up the phone and then shyly glance up at Jude. "Sorry?"

He laughs as he wraps his arm around my shoulders. "I think it's sweet he threatened to break my kneecaps and throw my body in the Red River. He cares for you."

"Oh, sweet baby Jesus, I'm so sorry. He is sorta overprotective of me."

Jude continues to chuckle as we start to walk toward my dorm. "Again, I think it's endearing. To kill for someone means you love them more than you love yourself, and that's special. You're special, Claire."

"So you've said," I flirt as I lean into him.

"And you know I don't lie."

I smile as I hide my face in his shoulder, and when I see my building, my heart falls into my stomach. I don't want this to be over, but I know Skylar is back in the room. She texted me during dinner asking if it was safe to return, and I gave her the green light since I knew I couldn't keep her from her own room. Still holding my hand, he walks me up the stairs and then all the way to my room before he pauses in front of my door.

Reaching for my phone, he takes it and does something and then his phone rings.

"Now we have each other's phone numbers. I should have done that the first time I met you."

"I would have kicked ya in the balls."

He laughs and I smile as he brings me in close for a long, toe-curling kiss. Threading my fingers through the short hair on the side of his head, I lose myself in the kiss. This could very well be the last time I see him, feel him like this, and I have to enjoy it. I just have to. As much as I believe he won't ever call me or see me again, I can't help but feel he will. I don't know if it is my stupid hopeful need, but I trust him. Again, not sure that is a good idea, but I do.

Parting, he nibbles on my bottom lip before he whispers, "I've never had such a great first date."

"It was the best."

"I'll see you soon?"

"You have my number."

"And you have mine."

I bite into my lip and he smiles before crashing his lips to mine again. Moving in unison, we kiss for what seems like ever. I could never get tired of the way he feels against me, and when he pulls away, I actually feel lonely without him.

"Goodnight, Claire."

"Night, Hey Jude," I say as his face brightens. I grin as my hand finds the handle and then I push it open, almost falling into my room, but to my delight, I catch myself before crashing to the ground. I send him one last grin before waving and shutting the door. Leaning against it, I lay my head against the coolness of my door and let out a long breath.

Did that just happen?

"So?" I turn to find Skylar watching me. "The room smells like sex and mint, and I am so freaking jealous that you banged Jude. So jealous. Was it good, at least?"

A dreamy look comes over my face as I basically float to her bed, falling on top of it, not caring one bit for her books or notes. "Oh Skylar, good is not the word. Perfect is more like it."

"Oh man, I bet it was. Is he hung?!"

Breathless, I say, "Like a Clydesdale!"

"Mother of God," she whispers and I nod quickly.

"It was amazing and perfect and ugh, as much as I want to believe there will be a second time, the doubt is there."

"Yeah, I get what you're saying. Jude isn't a one-woman man, babe. I hope you remembered that going in."

I nod as I sit up, letting out a breath. "I did, but Skylar, the way he looked at me, the way he treated me and talked to me, it just seems different."

"You're hot, babe, believe me, I know this. But Jude just isn't take home to Phillip material. He more than likely won't even text ya, which is shitty 'cause you're amazing."

My heart sinks because I think deep down I know that is the truth.

"Yeah, you're probably right."

"Don't be sad. He popped your celibate cherry. Now time to find Mr. Right!"

I shrug as I let out a very unhappy sigh. "I guess."

When a text signals, I look down at my display and my heart skips a beat at what I see.

>*Hey Jude: I didn't even make it out of the quad before I craved ur touch. I can't wait to see u again, baby, I'm counting the hours.*

"Is that from him?"

I nod my head as I reread his words. "Maybe it is different?" I ask, and my God, I sound so fucking hopeful.

"Are you sure that's Jude?" she asks and I nod, pointing to the top where it says *Hey Jude*.

"Ugh, I'm a little speechless," she admits and I couldn't agree more.

"Me too," I whisper but then quickly type him back.

>*Me: I can't wait to see u, when will I?*
>*Hey Jude: Sooner than u think. I'll be thinking of u all night.*

"Holy crap! Jude Sinclair does not talk to girls like this."

I shrug as I bite into my lip still staring at the screen. "He does with me."

CHAPTER 12

☒ JUDE

"First, you ever wink at Claire again, I'll gouge your eyes out," I say to my brother once I open the door to our room.

He looks up at me and laughs. "Whatever, dude. I was playing around."

"Don't do it again," I say sternly and he rolls his eyes. "But hey, you've done the girlfriend shit, right?"

Jayden looks back up at me and raises an eyebrow. "Yeah, why?"

"'Cause I think I might want to do that," I say, shutting the door and throwing my keys and phone down.

"I'm sorry, I misheard you," he teases and I glare.

"Shut up and tell me what I need to do to have a girlfriend."

He laughs as he shakes his head. "First ya gotta find a girl who wants that, which considering it's you, that shouldn't be a problem."

"Check, got that. Next thing."

He eyes me and then goes on, "You can't sleep with anyone else but her. She is it, that's all. You do everything with her, you call her, you walk her to class, you listen when she talks, and you treat her like a fucking princess 'cause she deserves it."

My face scrunches up, not because I can't do that, I can, no big deal, especially if it's for Claire, but because how the hell does Jayden know this? So I ask, "How the hell do you know this shit?"

"One, I've had a girlfriend successfully until she turned dumb, and two, I do everything Dad doesn't and it seems to work."

Jayden has always been the smarter Sinclair. "Good plan. Okay, good, I got this. So do I ask her now? Like, I don't want anyone else having her and shit, so do I just come out and be like, 'Hey, we're together'?"

Jayden is looking at me like I've grown three more heads. "What the fuck, dude? Who are you?"

I laugh as I shrug. "She's a game changer dude. I'm into her, big-time, and I don't want anyone else to scoop her up."

He still doesn't look convinced, or maybe he just doesn't understand how his brother who has never had a girlfriend wants one now. "The redhead?"

"Claire."

"I mean, she's smoking, but I still don't get it. You don't do this kind of thing. This isn't the Jude Sinclair I know, and I've known you since I was born."

I nod. "I get it, but sometimes you meet the one who changes it all, and she's it, man, hard-core."

"More power to ya, man, just don't rush it. See how it goes 'cause you may feel like this now, but what if someone comes up with a hotter pussy, and you're after them?"

I'm shaking my head before he's done. The great thing about talking to Jayden about this is that I can be the real me and he won't laugh. So I say the truth.

"Won't happen. I'm telling you, she's changed me. I've never chased after a girl, and I chased her. And I sure as hell never second-guessed having sex with one because I didn't want to rush it. This is real, man, and it's scary as fuck, but I can't see myself without her."

His face is a thing of horror, and then suddenly, he's reaching for his phone.

I ask, "What the hell are you doing?"

"Calling Mom. You're sick or something."

⁂

Knowing that Rachael works out in the morning, I head to the gym after practice looking for her. When I spot her on the treadmill, I lean against the front of it and she sets me with a look. "Funny seeing you here, but sorry, I'm not in the mood. It's that time of the month."

I scoff. "That's not why I'm here."

Her brow comes up. "Then why?"

"I want to know if Claire Anderson made the dance team."

Her brows come together as her nose lifts in the air. "Why would I tell you?"

"'Cause if you don't, I'll make sure that none of the guys from the team ever look your way again. I think herpes will keep them away." Her face fills with shock and I say, "Now come on, did she?"

She sticks her tongue out at me, and I wonder what I ever saw in her. Yeah, her ass is great, but she isn't very pretty most the time because of the bitchy face she always wears. "Of course she did. She was the best one who tried out, and she'll probably be the best on the damn team. Why? You trying to hit that?"

I shrug. "That's not any of your business. When are you posting the list?"

Still glaring, she says, "Four."

"Cool, have a good workout."

I hear her call my name, but I ignore her and head out of the building toward my first class. Talking to her has made me late, but I had to make sure Claire made the team. Checking my watch, I know I only have two more hours till I can meet her after her class and convince her to have lunch with me. I'm sure she won't say no, but still, it makes me nervous. Like Jayden said, this isn't me, and while I'm scared shitless of this, I can't wait for the next moment I see her, the next time I can touch her and feel her underneath me.

Speaking of Jayden, I could kick his ass. He really did call my mom, and of course, my mom fussed and begged me to bring Claire to dinner, but I quickly squashed that. There is no way I'm doing that yet. While I want her to be my girlfriend, I don't want to scare her off. Jayden told me to cool it, wait for her to say that she wants to be exclusive before I start slamming my chest with my fists and claiming her as mine. So I guess I'll chill even if I don't want to. I've always been the compulsive type on the ice, taking the shot when I know I have it, but in life, I calculate and make sure that everything I do is a good idea. Like which school to go to, what classes to take, who to be friends with, and who to trust.

Especially with females.

I never lie. I tell them upfront that our time together is a one-time thing and that's it. If they can't handle that, then sorry for them; I don't have time for crazy. I'm a busy, hotshot hockey player. There are too many girls who want one night with me, and the crazy thing is, I never uttered those words to Claire. They weren't even there. The only thing that was there was lust and need. When she touched me, everything went hot. She left her mark on me, and I am honestly A-OK with that. I like her. A lot. And I want her to see her, over and over again.

Thankfully the next two hours pass quickly, and while I have no clue what happened in my classes, I don't care as I run across campus to where her class is letting out. I left a little early to make sure I'm on time, and when I see her coming out of the building in a pair of sweats and a large purple Assassins sweatshirt, her hair down in waves along her shoulders, everything inside me stops. I don't even know who I am as I stalk toward her, and when she sees me, she grins, but I don't say anything. I take her face in my hands, kissing her hard against her sweet lips. Deepening the kiss, I feel her books fall to the ground as her arms come up to wrap around my neck, her thumbs playing with the back of my neck, curling my toes and making me hard in every place possible.

Parting, I kiss her bottom lip, running my thumb along her jaw as our eyes meet.

"Hi," I whisper and she grins.

"Well, hello to you," she says, her cheeks warming in such a lovely face.

"I've waited all morning to do that."

Her lips curve up even more, her teeth gleaming, and I see that one of her bottom teeth is a little crooked. For some reason, I find that incredibly sexy, and I can't help but kiss her again. Her tongue comes out, licking my bottom lip, and I groan before deepening the kiss more, moving my tongue with hers. I want to rip her clothes off and then mine and slam her against a wall, but I know we don't have time for that. We'll be lucky if we have time for lunch. Parting so slowly, I grin against her lips as her hand comes up to cup my face.

"Tell me you don't have anything planned for the next hour."

She laughs. "Skylar is studying, so we can't go back there."

I give her a playful scolding look before saying, "Who said anything about that? I want to sit on the quad and eat lunch with ya."

Her face warms even more as she nods slowly. "I think I have time for that," she says with a wink, lacing her fingers with mine.

Reaching down, I get her books for her, and we start toward the food court for some sandwiches before finding a nice spot in the sun. There is a chilly wind, but with the sun, it feels amazing. Crossing her legs, she sits down with her sandwich in her lap, taking a sip of her Coke as I do the same, opening my sandwich and taking a huge bite.

"How's your day been so far?"

I shrug. "It's better now."

She giggles before taking a bite of her sandwich, causing me to grin.

"Yours?" I ask.

She shrugs too. "It's been okay. Phillip has been calling me all day, and I'm ignoring him. Thanks for that, by the way. I was in a sex daze yesterday and really didn't care what you did, but today, I'm a little mad at you."

I send her one of my sweet smiles that I use to get me out of trouble with my mom and she caves quickly. She knows it too because she throws a chip at me as I laugh.

Going up on my knees, I crawl to her, my hands on either side of her hips and my face right in front of hers as I press my lips to her nose before whispering, "Sorry about that."

She pushes me away playfully but as I go to sit, she grabs my shirt, pressing her lips to mine again before releasing me for her sandwich. "Apology accepted, but you best believe there will be repercussions. I wouldn't be surprised if he comes down here looking for you. He'll probably threaten you some more, so be ready… I mean, if we still see each other and shit, which, by the way, what are we doing here? This isn't Jude Sinclair behavior according to the vast majority of our peers." Leaning toward me, she whispers, "Word on the street is you've been seen multiple times with a fiery redhead. Some say you've been taken off the market. This redhead must be something."

I laugh as I shake my head. "She is."

Her mouth curves in a grin as she picks at the lettuce on her sandwich. "So really, Jude, are we just having fun? Or what?"

I watch her as I ask, "What do you want?"

She laughs as she looks up at me. "I mean, what I want might not be what you want."

"So tell me anyway," I say, taking a drink of my Coke. "You never know."

"I wouldn't mind this going somewhere. It wouldn't be horrible to be with the hottest guy on campus."

I scoff as I grab her by her ankles, pulling her to me. She shrieks as I pull her between my legs, her legs sliding inside my hips and mine resting around hers. Meeting her gaze, I say, "I wouldn't mind that either."

"I find that hard to believe, but hell, people change."

"You're right…when there is someone to change for."

Her grin grows as she nods slowly. "Absolutely, but I've been warned not to rush this."

"Funny, so have I," I say and we share a grin.

"So, let's do this. We're dating and after, what, ten dates? We'll decide if we want to become Facebook official?"

I eye her. "Do these dates include sex?"

She shakes her head. "Heck no, we jumped the gun last night. I think we should draw it out. Get to know each other and then see if this is what you want."

"You mean what we want."

"I know what I want," she says, her eyes boring into mine. "I just don't want to put my heart out there for you to decide that this isn't what you want."

"Wow, this is some heavy shit," I say, running my hands through my hair. When I glance back up, her lips are in a straight line, her eyes a little sad, and I don't like that one bit. "But it's nothing I can't handle. I know what I want, Claire, and it's you."

She giggles as she leans toward me, kissing my lips softly before backing away to look in my eyes. "I want you too."

"Good, but can I request something?"

She smiles as her thumb moves lazily along my bottom lip. "Yeah?"

"Can we do these ten dates in ten days because I've been constantly thinking of your sweet body all night and day. I don't think I'll last weeks without having another taste of you."

Her face brightens with color as she looks down, biting into her lip. When she glances back up at me, she shakes her head. "You make me so shy and giggly. I've never been like this."

"That's a good thing, I think."

"Me too, and why don't we wait two weeks, instead? I'm pretty sure I'm not gonna see you every day, and with our schedules, we're both so busy. So we'll wait two weeks and see how we feel at the end."

"You'll be with no one else, right?"

She eyes me as her head nods slowly. "Of course, but neither will you."

"No problem." With a wide grin, I gather her in my arms and whisper against her lips, "I like that, and I'm pretty sure nothing will change."

Moving her nose with mine, she says, "I hope so."

As I get lost in her eyes, her kisses, I know that nothing will change this.

This girl is it, and I'm gonna prove that to not only her, but to the world.

CHAPTER 13

Claire

Holy shit. Did I just set up a trial period with Jude Sinclair in the hopes that he'll be my boyfriend at the end of two weeks? I must have because I'm kissing him like I just did. Our bodies have molded together and our lips move in tandem in a playful assault. I know that eyes are on us, but I don't give two shits. To say that people have been warning me left and right about Jude would be an understatement.

Apparently, Jude Sinclair is the whore of the campus.

I was in the shower this morning and three girls came up to warn me about him. Then in my first class, two said something and then four more did in my second. I assured everyone that I wasn't a dumbass and knew that he's led the life of the player and don't intend to give my heart to someone who doesn't want it. But that all changed when I saw him basically running across the quad toward me. It was breathtaking; he's so agile and beautifully athletic. Then he took me in his hands and kissed me as if he hadn't seen me in years. I felt missed, special. It was perfect, and I was certain that my heart would be his before I knew it.

While that does freak me out a bit, I'm happy with our plan. I think it is solid and I hope to God he doesn't screw me over, but I also know to keep my heart completely locked tight until the end of the two weeks. I trust him, I do, but I trust the guy who chased me across campus, who made sweet love to me and then took me to breakfast. The guy before that, I've heard, is not the greatest, and as long as he stays like this guy, I'm good.

Pulling back, he moves his thumb along my jaw as his eyes bore into mine. "I want to know what you're thinking."

I smile. "I'm thinking I hope that you don't hurt me."

"I don't plan to. You know what I did last night after I left you?"

"What?"

"I went back and asked Jayden how to have a girlfriend because I've never had one."

I scoff. "Oh, shut up! You did too, in high school, at least!"

But he shakes his head. "No, never. I was too focused on hockey and used girls for one thing. I didn't want to have to answer to anyone, but with you, it's different." Moving his hand up my face, he rakes his fingers through my hair, wrapping it slowly around his fingers as he holds my gaze. "I was told to treat you like a princess, so that's what I'm gonna do."

My chest warms, and I know my heart is banging against the box I've trapped it in. "Phillip and Reese are the only ones who have ever done that."

He nods. "So I have competition… I like competition."

I laugh as I lean my forehead against his. "Why, Jude? Why me?"

Looking in my eyes for a long time, I think he isn't going to answer, but then he says, "I prided myself on my game. I knew what I wanted from girls. I thought I only wanted sex from you, but then I second-guessed myself and thought maybe I should wait because I wanted to get to know you. I want to know everything, and then I want to know more. I don't know. It's crazy, I know, but it's different. You're different. You've changed my game completely."

I love what he's said, and I know he's being truthful. I can see it down in the depths of his green eyes. He means every word; he cares for me. "The same can be said for you. I was fine before you, but the moment I saw you, I wanted more. I never had that happen to me before."

His grin is unstoppable as laces his fingers with mine. "So I guess we're both doing something new and scary."

"Yeah," I agree, leaning my head toward his, my nose moving ever so lightly against his. "And I couldn't be more excited about it."

"Me either," he whispers and then he takes my lips with his. As I get lost in Jude's kisses and soft touches, I know that Jude is the one I could fall for and love. It would be so easy because his innocence on the matter is endearing, and I want nothing more than to be his first love.

And maybe his last.

❦

"So what are your plans for the rest of the day?"

Leaning against Jude, we walk toward my building after a nice lunch on the quad. "I have to go study for the quiz I have next in marketing – that's in two hours – then I have to go to the rink to see if I made the dance team. If I did, I have practice tonight."

"Cool, I'm sure you made it."

I shrug. "We will see."

"Yeah, so do you work?"

"I do. I work at the dance studio for Reese on Tuesday, Thursdays, and Saturdays, but once I get the dance schedule, if I make it, then no telling when I'll work," I say, knowing that I left my other job out. "You?"

"Nope, I play hockey and study and get ready for the draft."

"Oh, so you're going in for sure? I assumed, but wasn't a 100%."

He nods, a proud grin on his face. "Yup, next year as long as everything goes well."

I smack his arm playfully, puckering out my lip and say, "You jerk, you're gonna start something with me and then leave?"

He stops, wrapping his arms around me, holding me so close that thinking isn't an option. I'm completely intoxicated by his woodsy smell, his bedroom eyes, him, all of him. "By then you'll be so in love with me that you'll go anywhere with me."

I laugh, trying to get away, but Jude's biceps have biceps and they hold me close to him. "Whatever. I'm not going to follow you. I am an independent woman with a plan!"

He grins, pressing his lips to mine, and I melt in his arms, all past struggling disappears as I get lost in his kiss. Parting, he looks in my eyes as he smiles, but I can see that he is serious as a heart attack. "And I like that about you, but when the time comes, we'll discuss it and decide what's best for us."

I scoff. "Jeez, Jude, I was kidding. We might not even be together then."

"Oh, we will be, and you'll be right beside me at the draft and then at everything after that. You got me now, Claire, there is no getting rid of me."

Oh, heart be still and stay in the box!

I can say that all I want, but I'm pretty sure that my heart and my brain both know that there is no way my heart is gonna stay locked up when a guy like Jude Sinclair is after it.

"Ooowee, trouble you are, I knew it," I say with a shake of my head, moving my hands up his shoulders and then into his hair. "And I can't help but like it."

His grin is killer as he moves his hands in and down the back of my sweats. I giggle as he cups my ass and then his eyes go wide. "Dirty girl, are you wearing no panties?"

"A thong and I'm pretty sure this is not allowed."

His brows come together in such a perplexed way that I'm giggling even harder. "Whoa, we said no sex. Maybe we need to define that 'cause when I want to get me a handful of your sexy ass I'm going to, and if I want to bury my face deep between your legs, I'm going to do that, too."

Heat floods between my legs as my knees buckle. "Jesus H. Christ, you can't say shit like that during our two-week dating mode! That will lead to sex!"

"Sorry." He chuckles and I know he isn't sorry one bit. "Why don't we start this tomorrow and go up to your room now, and I'll do what I just suggested."

I shake my head, trying to take a step back, but his grip on my ass is ironclad. "No, sir, not only is my roommate up there, but I don't want this to be about sex. We both know we're sexually attracted to each other, like intensely, so let's make sure there's more to it 'cause I don't want to fall for you while you're busy just fucking me."

He eyes me, and then nods. "I get that, but I can fall for you and rock your world at the same time."

I laugh. "After the two weeks. Come on."

"Okay," he says slowly. "But please don't tell me I have to remove my hands."

I think it over and then nod. "Fine, hands are fine but no other places, and watch what you say before I forget this mess and hump your face."

"Yes, please do that," he says and then we both start laughing. Wrapping my arms around his neck, I grin up at him as I take in his beautiful face. He has a little scar along his jaw and then one on his lip. I point to them and ask, "What happened?"

"I busted my lip last year in a fight after a drunken night out, and then I fell when I was a kid off my four-wheeler and a branch went through my face."

I make a face. "Shit, that had to hurt."

"Like hell, but my mom says it brings character to my face."

"It does, makes you hotter in a rugged, mean way."

His face breaks into a huge grin before wrapping me up tighter in his arms and dropping his mouth to mine. We kiss for what seems like hours, but I know it's only seconds. His kisses are so damn intoxicating, and I feel like an addict needing another hit of his mouth. And as I watch him walk away with a promise that he'll see me later, all I can think is that I don't know when that will be, but I can't freaking wait.

After my last class, I meet up with Skylar and we head to the rink. We're both carrying our dance bags with the hopes we made it. I'm sure we did – we're both fantastic and Skylar did get some tens from the guys – but still, I'm a little nervous I won't. I would be so embarrassed if I didn't. Not only would telling Reese and Phillip that I didn't make it suck ass, but telling Jude would too. Oh my heart, anytime I think of him, it goes crazy in my chest, and my stomach does some weird flip thing that makes me breathless. I'm falling for him, even though I told myself I wouldn't, which is bad, very damn bad.

"Heard you and Jude were making out in the quad."

I smile as I glance over at Skylar, shrugging my shoulders. "Making out is a little overdramatic, we kissed and touched some but talked mostly."

"About?"

"About taking two weeks without sex to see if there is something there."

She stops mid-step and gives me a look. "And he agreed?"

"Yeah," I say with a grin. "And I trust him."

"Wow, I'm completely floored. Jude? A one-woman man? I've known him for the last two years and this has never happened."

"Yeah, he says he's never had a girlfriend."

"And look, didn't I say you were gonna rock his world. Once everyone finds out that it took one day with you in the sack, guys are gonna come out of the woodwork trying to get you to leave him."

"Whatever," I say, waving her off. "It wasn't even the sex that got him. It was me, he said. He just likes me."

"Aw, that's so sugar sweet. Jeez, I have a toothache, get out of here with that mess. Jude does not say things like that!"

"He does to me!"

"Whatever, I feel like I'm in *The Twilight Zone*. There are men made for just sex and some who are meant for relationships, and Jude was thrown in the other category a long time ago. I don't know how to adjust my categories in my head now. When I see him, I always see manwhore, not a one-woman, Claire-loving dude."

"We're not in love," I stress. "We're dating."

"Weird," she says with a shake of her head, and I laugh as we head toward the rink. Once inside, a group of girls from the day before is standing around a bulletin board, and slowly each one peels away, either happy or disappointed or crying.

"Ack, more Nos than Yesses, it seems," Skylar says as we make our way to the list.

I see my name at the top, and while excitement envelops me, I quickly search the list for Skylar's, and I let out a breath when I find it at the bottom. "Oh, thank God," I say and she laughs.

"Preston is gonna be at the bottom! We all can't be As!"

I smile and we embrace. I didn't think I wanted this as much as I do. I'm so happy, especially to be doing it with my best friend. Pulling away, I say, "I'm proud of you."

"Well, I'm proud of you. Now come on, let's go rock this first practice."

I agree and then turn, running smack-dab into Jude. "Oh hey!" I say with a grin, giving him a quick kiss.

He grins down at me and then pulls a rose out from behind his back. "Congratulations."

"Oh, come on! You don't give girls flowers!" Skylar whines, and I giggle as I take the rose, smelling its sweet scent.

"Sure I do, for the right ones," he says before winking at me.

I'm turning into a giggler because that's exactly what I do before saying,

"Thank you."

"You're welcome. Wanna meet up tonight? Or do you need to study?"

"Study, sorry, rain check? Lunch tomorrow?"

"Of course, text me when you're done with practice to let me know how it goes. Good luck and congrats again," he says and then kisses me so deeply that I'm a tad bit shy when he pulls away, kissing my nose. "See ya, gorgeous."

"I made the team too, Jude. Do I get a hug, kiss, or anything? Shit!" Skylar jokes, and I laugh as he kisses my nose again.

Holding up his hand, Skylar high-fives him as he says, "Congrats, Skylar, I knew you would make it."

"A high five? Before you'd at least smack my ass!"

He laughs and I do too. I know she's playing around. Skylar loves me too much; she wouldn't hurt me.

"Yeah, that was before I started dating Claire."

He sends me one last grin before walking away as both of us watch.

Beside me, Skylar says, "I have no clue who that is."

"That's my man, Jude Sinclair," I say with a little wiggle.

When I glance over at her, she isn't laughing or smiling; her face is contorted in a perplexed matter. "Why did you lie to him? Maybe you'll study between sets, but still, you will be at work."

My face burns with color and so does my throat as I avoid eye contact. "I don't want to tell him about that. It isn't who I am; it's a quick dollar so that I can have a steady life when I graduate."

"I get that, but you probably need to tell him."

"I will, come on. Let's go to practice before we're late."

Thankfully she agrees with not another word on the subject. While I know I need to tell him, I also think that maybe it doesn't matter. I work midnight to three in the morning, and I wear a disguise.

No one knows it's me. Hell, it's not really me, so why does it matter?

As much as I want to think it doesn't matter, I know it might matter to Jude, and that makes me more nervous than falling for him. I can't quit; I need that money to make sure I never have to depend on anyone for the rest of my life. It's gonna help me get my business. It's gonna be the start to my new life, but I have a feeling that Jude won't see it that way.

CHAPTER 14

 JUDE

Falling into my bed, a smile is on my lips as I dig my phone out of my pocket. It has been signaling a text for the last thirty minutes, but I really don't care. My thoughts are solely on a certain fiery redhead who I can't seem to get enough of. Glancing at the display, I see that I have twelve texts. Groaning, I scan through them all, seeing they all have the same thing in common.

> *Mandy: Jude, are you dating Claire Anderson? I thought you don't date! I didn't really like you.*
> *Julie: what the hell Jude, you told me you don't date but everyone is talking about how you're with that redhead! Yeah, I said that so you'd suck me off.*
> *Marianne: Why is that redhead good enough and I'm not. Answer me that Jude! Have you been around Claire? Touched her? No? Yeah, you wouldn't understand.*
> *Stacey: Jude, you are a dick and a half. How dare you date someone when you said you'd date me when you decided to start dating? Yeah, I lied.*
> *Jamie: I hate you Jude. You're a liar. That redhead isn't even pretty. Bullshit, she's gorgeous.*

And it goes and goes and goes. Everyone that I've ever fucked saying the same damn thing.

"Fuck, what is wrong with girls these days?"

Jayden looks up from his bed. "Huh?"

"Everyone is freaking out 'cause I'm dating Claire."

He scoffs. "Well, when you leave a girl's bed with the promise, 'When I'm ready to settle down, baby, you'll be the first one I call,' that tends to happen."

I glare. "Shut the fuck up. While I can see your point, I don't want to hear it. I want these girls to leave me the hell alone."

He laughs as he rolls his eyes. "Why don't you just change your number? It's gonna keep on and you know it."

"I swear you are the smartest out of all of us."

"This is true," Jayden says with a nod before opening his laptop. When another text comes through, I go to ignore it but then I see it's from Claire.

> *Claire: So, practice was canceled. People couldn't stay, so yeah, sucks, I guess I'm gonna go study.*

Quickly, I type back.

> *Me: Wanna hang with me for a bit? I gotta go change my phone number.*
> *Claire: Why?*
> *Me: Cause everyone won't leave me alone.*
> *Claire: Oh. Okay. Yeah. Do I want to ask why?*
> *Me: I'll tell ya when I get there. I'll be over in a bit.*
> *Claire: Okay. I'll be waiting outside.*
> *Me: Great.*

Standing up, I tuck my phone in my pocket and reach for my helmet then Jayden's. "I'm taking your helmet."

"Why?"

"For Claire. I'll order her one, but right now I need yours."

"Whatevs."

"Hey, I'm gonna text ya in a bit and then make yourself disappear."

"No way!" he complains but I settle him with a look.

"Would you like to share a room with another freshman instead?"

"You're an asshole, dude. I got homework."

"Go upstairs. You'll be fine. See ya."

I don't want to be an ass and kick my brother out of his room, but I also don't want to be feeling Claire up in front of him. Do I even get to feel her up? Hmm. That's something I need to ask about. Going out to where my bike is parked, I put my helmet on and slowly mount my black with silver chrome Star Bolt that my dad got me when I graduated. Jayden got a car, and usually we trade off whenever we feel the need to. I love riding my bike, though. It's probably my third favorite thing to do after hockey and sex. Putting Claire's helmet under the bungee cables that are on the back, I start the bike up, the roar of it vibrating underneath me before I slowly back up and then hit the gas to go.

I see her after taking the turn on her street. She's sitting on the bench, and when she sees me, her eyebrow comes up. She stands when I reach her, throwing my helmet up.

"Hey there, gorgeous, wanna go for a ride?"

With a wide grin on her face, she shakes her head. "Oooowwweeee, my uncle would say you are big trouble with a capital B and T."

I laugh, climbing off my bike. "Good thing I'm not trying to date your uncle then."

"I know you are big trouble, though," she says with a grin, stopping in front of me.

Raising my brow, I smile as I nod my head back to the bike. "Does that mean you're not gonna go for a ride with me?"

"Oh, hell no, it doesn't. I'm riding."

"Awesome," I say as I grin widely before taking the helmet off the back. I wait as she ties her hair at the back of her head, and then I slowly put the helmet on her head. It goes on easy since Jayden's head is massive compared to Claire's. "I'll order you a helmet tonight when I get back."

"Sounds good to me," she says before mounting the bike, and I decide she looks damn good on the back of my bike. Unlike other girls, she doesn't dress up. She's wearing Bellevue sweatpants and a large, purple Assassins sweatshirt. I'm beginning to think that's all the girl owns, and I don't care one bit. I love it. I like that she's comfortable around me in barely anything and naked.

I get on in front of her, and she waits till the bike roars to put her hands around my waist. "Have you ridden on the back of a bike before?"

"Nope, this is my first time."

"Awesome, get ready then," I say and we're off. It's a beautiful night. Clear and cool, and as I drive toward the Verizon store, I'm glad to have Claire on the back, holding me tight. Once we're there, I park the bike and get off, helping her next. She removes the helmet, and when she looks at me, she's grinning.

"That was amazing."

"Yeah, it's a wonderful night," I say, really pleased that she loved it. Usually it scares girls.

"Yeah, it is," she agrees as she hands me her helmet. "Why are we here?"

"'Cause my phone won't stop blowing up. I'm gonna change my number to get away from it. The people I want to call me will have my number, and that's it."

She smiles as I thread my fingers with hers. "So what you're saying is you're changing your number to get away from all the girls who are contacting you?"

"Exactly. Of course, except for you, my mom, and my sister."

"Aw, how sweet," she says, leaning against me, and I like the glow that's on her face.

Kissing her nose, I smile before saying, "Remind me to call my mom, though. She'll be here in two point three seconds if she can't get ahold of me."

"Will do," she promises and then we head inside.

After changing my number, I call my mom right away and then hurry off the call before she has me on the phone all damn night. Once we're on the bike and heading down the streets of Bellevue, I decide that I don't want to go back to the house. It's too nice out, and knowing my luck, Jayden won't have left the room. So instead, I head toward the park outside of the college. Usually I go running there, but today I just want to sit on my bike with the prettiest girl ever.

Parking near the pond, I shut the bike off then pull my helmet off before standing up and looking back at her. "Figured we can enjoy the night."

"Sounds good to me, but the grass is wet, isn't it?"

Going over to the grass, I find it is. "Shit, yeah, and I didn't bring a blanket. We can head back."

She shakes her head. "No, we're good, come sit down but face me."

"I love the way you think," I admit, heading toward her and doing what she asks.

She grins as she hands me the helmet and I lay it on the ground before folding my arms on her knees, laying my head on my arms, looking up at her. "So why did they cancel practice?"

She rolls her eyes. "'Cause they're dumb. Apparently half the damn team couldn't practice. But all us new girls were there, so why not start on us so we can be up to date, ya know? I told Skylar I have a bad feeling about this. I hate when people are all kinds of screwed up."

I smile. "I agree. I like things to be in order, that's why I'm captain."

"Yeah, I don't think Rachael will allow me to dethrone her."

"Too bad, you'd make a hot captain."

She laughs. "I'm pretty sure in your eyes I'd make a hot anything."

I act like I'm thinking for a second and then nod. "Yup, pretty much."

She giggles before running her hands along my neck and up into my hair, brushing it to the side. It feels so amazing that soon my eyes fall shut as she moves her hands through my hair. When her fingers slowly graze along the hair on my jaw, I open one eye to find her working her lip as if she's nervous, or thinking way too damn hard.

"What are you thinking about?"

She shrugs. "Crap."

I smile. "Wanna share your crap and see if I can help?"

She works her lips a little more, and then lets out a long breath. "So people are looking at me like I'm the dumbest bitch in the world for dating you, and it's superirritating. They are blowing your phone up, but they are coming at me, saying all these crazy things to me, like, don't I know you've been around and shit like that. It's annoying as hell." I sit up and her hands fall into her lap as she watches me. "I didn't say it to piss you off," she says quickly and I shrug.

"I know that, but I still don't like that it's happening to you. It's stupid," I say, my heart pounding in my chest. I have a feeling she's going to tell me she can't handle it and wants to cut things off with me. I can't blame her, though; I wouldn't want people in my face either telling me the person I'm dating is basically a manwhore. I mean, I know I was, but I don't want to be that anymore.

"Yeah, it's dumb, and I'm hoping it dies down."

"I hope so too. I mean, you can say I've seen more ass than a toilet seat, but am I proud of it? I was before I met you, not so much now. I'm more embarrassed than anything. But the big question is, is it gonna be a problem?"

She shakes her head. "I don't think so. I think the biggest thing that bothers me is that they say you're gonna cheat on me. The way I see it is, I'm with you, and I trust you until you give me a reason not to, and then I'm gone."

"I don't think that will happen."

Ignoring my comment, she goes on, "Plus, who am I to judge you? My past is way worse than yours. I slept with grown men at fourteen, so who the hell am I to judge anyone? I'm good with us. I just wish everyone would leave me the hell alone."

I try to keep my jaw from dropping, but it doesn't work. "Whoa, what?"

"Huh? I want people to leave me alone."

"No, the fourteen-year-old with grown men stuff."

She nods. "Oh, yeah, told ya, I had a bad, bad childhood."

Still a little shocked, I ask, "Care to elaborate?"

"Nope," she says, looking deep in my eyes. "But I will once I know you aren't going to run from my scary, horrible childhood."

Reaching out, I tuck a stray piece of her hair behind her ear and smile. "I don't think that's gonna happen."

"That's 'cause we're in the lusty phase, where we can't get enough. Plus, you want to see my ass again."

I laugh as I nod. "This is very true, but honestly, I really do like you, like, a lot."

"Like, a lot, a lot?"

She leans into me, running her nose along mine, her eyes pulling me in and making my heart beat faster. "A whole fucking lot."

Biting into her lip, she grazes her lips against mine, our breaths mingling, our hearts in time as my hands come up her thighs to the small of her back, resting under her shirt. She takes in a soft breath as our eyes lock, and everything inside me goes hot.

Then she says, "I think I might like you a little more than that."

She honestly just made my life with those eleven little words.

CHAPTER 15

🩰 Claire

"And because of that, I don't care what anyone says. I'm good, Jude, as long as you don't hurt me," I say, and I mean every word.

I've thought about this all day. Ever since the first girl came at me, I've been thinking about it, and I've decided that I've never cared what people thought about me before, and I'm not going to start now. Yes, it's only day one of dating Jude, and yes, a billion people have told me it's a bad idea, but I don't care.

I like him.

"I won't," he promises and I believe him.

I smile as he pulls me down from the bike and into his lap. I wrap my arms around his neck, and he smashes his lips to mine. Slowly we kiss, both of our mouths teasing the other's as his fingers stroke my back. Parting, I smile against his lips before leaning back and asking, "Take your shirt off."

He waggles his eyebrows, and I laugh as he says, "Why, yes, ma'am."

"Dork, I want to see your tattoos. I haven't gotten a good look at them, and they intrigue me."

He smiles before pulling his Bullies shirt over his head and into his lap. Leaning in close, I run my fingers on his chest where an anatomical heart with hockey sticks crossed through it is inked above where his real heart lies. I look at him questioningly, and he says, "Hockey is in my heart, my soul."

I nod before trailing my eyes up to his left arm where the measures for "Hey Jude" by the Beatles run along his whole arm, stopping at his wrist, the lyrics to the song under each note. It is beautiful, stunning even, with splashes of watercolor all throughout the tattoo.

"For your mom?" I ask, and he smiles as he nods.

"It's actually my favorite song. It's one of those songs that hits you in the heart."

"Agreed."

He flashes me a grin as I notice that along his bicep are five names: Mom, Lucy, Jayden, Jace, and Angie in beautiful script.

"Where is your dad's name?"

He shrugs. "I don't get along with my dad much."

I can tell that's a sensitive subject, so I just nod as I inspect the rest of his arm. He hadn't pushed for my deep dark secrets, and I wouldn't do that to him. There will be a time when we bare our souls to each other, but today is not that day. I take in the other things he has which are more abstract objects in watercolor. They're beautiful and everything ties together perfectly. Lacing my fingers with his, I notice that he doesn't have anything on top of his right arm, so I turn it over and decide that this one is probably my favorite besides the lyrics. It's a hockey puck coming out of his skin, blood dripping from the wound with little ice shards around it. Above, it has laces that look as if they're stitched into his skin to close the wound, and on them it reads "No Fear, No Pain, No Gain." It is completely badass, and nothing less than I would expect Jude to get.

"Totally badass."

"Thanks, it's probably my favorite piece."

"Which one was your first tattoo?"

"My heart one. I got it the day I turned eighteen."

"Supercool," I say and then add, "You can put your shirt back on."

"Are you sure?" he asks, waggling his brow at me.

"Yes," I laugh.

"Thanks," he says with a laugh. "It is getting chilly."

He throws his shirt back on and then sets me with a look. "Got any ink? And please let it be in a naughty spot."

I laugh, pulling up my shirt and my bra where my little bitty anchor sits. Around it are the words, "A smooth sea never made a skillful sailor."

"For your rough childhood?"

I smile as I nod. "Yup, Reese and Phillip took me to get it on my eighteenth birthday. They both got the same thing. Phillip's is bigger on his calf, while Reese's is on her thigh. It's special to us."

"It's nice," he says, tracing his fingers along it. "Any more?"

I shake my head. "Nope, I don't live in a tattoo parlor like you."

He laughs. "I'm due for a new one. I try to go every three months. You should come with me. I need one on the top of my arm."

"Okay, just let me know when," I say, letting my shirt fall.

Snaking his arms around my waist, he tickles my lower back as he looks up at me. "So what's your schedule like during the week?"

"Well, I find out tomorrow the schedule for dance team, and Reese is waiting for that so she can move Skylar's and my classes around with hers. I might be teaching all weekend only, which is fine. I love working with my little bits, and then my solos can come in on my downtime. I go to school every day. Classes are usually in the morning with free afternoons so I can study before going to work or whatever else I have that night. You?"

"Hockey in the morning, school in the morning and afternoon, and free weekends except when games start."

I nod, knowing that this was how it was going to be. I'm so busy. I work two jobs, I'm doing the dance team now, and I'm going to school. Why did I think having a boyfriend would be a good idea?

"Told ya we won't be seeing much of each other."

He shrugs. "We'll make it work. Lots of texting plus it will get us ready for the future when I'm rocking the NHL and you're creating dances for famous artists."

I laugh at that as I nod. "You kill me the way you do that. We've been doing this a day, Jude, one day, and you're convinced you have my forever without even knowing my deep, dark past. You could hate everything about me at the end of this two weeks, but yet, you see a future with me. This isn't a Disney movie, you know."

"Of course it isn't. We aren't singing."

That has me sputtering with laughter as I smack his chest, shaking my head. "You know what I mean!"

"I know. I just wanted to make you laugh," he says, rubbing his thumb along my lip. "But really, I feel something about you, and you forgave my shitty past. I'm sure I can forgive yours."

Biting into my lip, I shrug. "It's easy to forgive because I believe that people change. We grow and become better people because of the influences around us."

"You're right, and for me, it's you."

I grin widely as I let out the deep breath I took. He makes me breathless. While I say that this isn't a Disney movie, I feel like it is. I feel so wrapped up in him. I want to burst out in song, saying how much I really like him and how I want to believe that there will be a day that I'll be at home, making up killer dances while he's out scoring goals. I want to believe it, but I feel like I'm waiting for the other shoe to drop. This is all so magical, so perfect, but what's going to happen when he decides I'm not good enough for him? When he hears my past will I be able to pick up the pieces while I watch him walk away?

It scares me, it does, but I can't help but want to believe his words.

"So I know you're big into music, right?"

I smile, ignoring my thoughts and focusing solely on him, which is really easy. "I am."

"Are you one of those people who love everything?"

I nod with a grin growing on my face. "I am – total music whore. I can listen to anything and enjoy the hell out of it."

"What's your all-time favorite, though?"

I think for a minute as one of his hands leaves my back and comes up to trace along my jaw. "I'm a huge Justin Timberlake fan, so anything by him, but I also love old stuff. Like classic Etta James, it's so smooth and inspiring. Beatles, anything really," I say then start laughing. "I'm really easy to please."

With a wink he says, "I know you are."

My face flushes as I push him away, but he brings me back toward him, lacing our fingers together. "You?"

"I love rap and heavy metal, anything that can pump me up for a game."

"Phillip does that! Funny story," I say, basically jumping in his lap. "One time, Phillip grabbed my iPod instead of his, and when he went to get ready for the game, all my music starts playing, which is like a lot of covers of songs – don't look at me like that, I love that – but anyway, he calls me from the locker room, yelling, and makes me bring him his iPod because he can't play without hearing his songs. Are you like that?"

He laughs as he nods his head. "Yup, I have a certain playlist and listen to the whole thing before I lace up my skates."

"That's so weird!" I gush as I laugh. "But I think it's cool too 'cause I like the before-game traditions. I think it's neat."

"Yeah, I also have to have a bowl of grapes and Mango Frost Gatorade."

I giggle at him and he smiles. I know we've been here for a while, and of course, I am loving every second, but I know I need to get going soon. Pulling my phone out of my pocket, I see it's almost time for me to go, but I really don't want to leave. I'd rather stay here, locked in the gaze of this stunningly gorgeous man, than dance on a stage for men I don't care one bit for.

"I need to head back. I have to study and I'm tired," I say and my insides clench since I'm lying. I actually need to get home and shower and shave before heading to the club for my shift.

"Can you give me five more minutes?"

I eye him before asking, "Why?"

"'Cause I want to kiss you like this, and I think five minutes will sustain me until the next time I have you like this."

Before I can deny or agree, his mouth is moving against mine. His breath is minty, his lips so soft against mine. I think he knew I would say yes because I crave his kisses. I think about them constantly, about him, and I can't wait till the next second his lips are moving against mine. Running my fingers up the back of his neck, I press into him as his finger bites into the middle of my back. Nibbling down my jaw, he comes back to my lips, both of us teasing and nipping before he says, "Can I feel you up when we're dating?"

"No, that will lead to sex."

"So, I can't grab your boob?"

I laugh, pulling back. "No, Jude! We have to keep this PG-13 at least for two weeks."

He eyes me and then shrugs. "Okay, but come back here, I have at least two more minutes."

I comply and grin against his lips before our kisses turn hungry. I'm pretty sure rubbing up against each other is not PG-13, but I can't help it. He's so hard, so delicious, and when he pulls back, our heavy breathing is the only sound in the quiet park. I'm glad he's the one to pull away because I don't think I could have. Placing a kiss to my nose, he reaches down for the helmet before placing it over my head.

"Let's get you back before I bend you over this bike and have my way with you."

I scoff. "How very considerate of you."

"I thought so," he says with a wink as he gets up to put his on helmet on. Looking back at me, he adds, "I don't want to interfere with your studies."

My studies. Yeah...

CHAPTER 16

 JUDE

"So let me get this straight," Max Rivers says as he lounges against the boards, leaning on his hockey stick. Coach is running plays with the defense, so that leaves my line to hang for a minute, get a breather, and get some water.

"You're dating one girl. Just one, 'cause I heard it was one and that you were dating her. Something you don't do."

I nod as Jayden rolls his eyes. I think he's as annoyed as I am. "Yeah, dude, one chick."

"Why? You've never done that. I've known you since like fourth grade, and you've never had one girlfriend."

"Yeah, things changed."

"So you're giving up all the pussy in the world for one chick? At twenty years old?"

"He's dating her, not marrying her," Jayden says before I can answer. "And why the hell does it matter what he does?"

Max looks at me before looking back at Jayden. "Jude is the king of getting ass. It's shocking to us mere mortals that have to beg girls to date us." Jayden and I both just blink at Max before I shake my head. Before I can say anything, though, Max says, "I mean, does she have a golden snatch or something? What made you only want one?"

"For fuck's sake," Jayden says as I glare.

"Don't talk about her like that, and it's none of your fucking business," I sneer as Jayden pushes me back.

"Whoa, calm down, killer. Max is an idiot."

"I don't get what the big deal is. It's pissing me off. Not only are they are coming at me, but they're talking about Claire and shit. They're even coming up to her and telling her I'm a manwhore."

"You are a manwhore," he says, and when I flash him a dark look, he adds, "Reformed, manwhore, but what do you expect? You showboated yourself all over this campus as the biggest cock in Bellevue, so of course, there are going to be repercussions from it. The question you need to ask yourself is, is it true? Are you a manwhore?"

I shrug. "I don't think so. At least not anymore. I know, it's only been a week, but Jay, I haven't even wanted anyone else but her. I'm completely infatuated with her. It's kind of scary."

"And weird," Jayden adds as he shakes his head. "So be you, Jude. You didn't give a shit what people thought before, don't start now."

"Yeah," I agree before letting out a breath. "I just don't want her to start agreeing with them."

"From what you've told me, dude, I think she's the kind of girl who thinks for herself. Don't worry about it, just be you, okay?"

I nod. "Sure."

"Sinclairs! Get your asses over here and get to work! This isn't teatime! It's working time!"

Sharing a look, we smirk at each other before heading to the goal to get our plays. I can always depend on my brother, no matter what, and I'm lucky for that. Above all, though, he's completely right. I've never cared when girls talked shit about me because they always ended up in my bed. Didn't care that dudes were jealous of me because I got the most ass and play the best game. No, I did me, and I'm going to continue that.

I just now have sexy redhead beside me as I do it.

After a grueling practice, I stand within the circle of my teammates as Coach goes over more plays. "I'm pushing you so that we can be the best. All of you have been handpicked for this team by me, and I pick winners. So in two weeks when we face Nashville Tech, we will win, we will dominate, and we will make everyone proud to be a Bellevue Bully. I am proud of this team already and will be even more when we bring the championship home. Now make sure you study, focus on your classes, and above all, stay away from girls, and stop partying."

We all yell "Yup" together before all coming in, yelling, "Bellevue Bullies." Skating beside Matt and Trevor, I ask, "Doesn't he know that we still fool with the girls and party?"

They laugh then Trevor goes, "Well, you are only fooling with one now. Does that mean you're not gonna party anymore too?"

"Ah, fuck off. Of course I'm going to party."

"Sure, you are, she'll have you whipped into shape in no time. No more partying, no more anything except if you're with her, and while we're out having a blast, you'll be at home knitting a sweater. You wait," Matt says as he skates by me.

"What the hell ever, no girl will control me or have me knitting."

"I think you said you'd never have a girlfriend too," he says, looking back at me. "Funny how things change, huh?"

Glaring, I don't say anything as I watch him head into the locker room. I want to tell him he's an asshole, but it doesn't come out before he disappears behind the door. His words hit me in the gut, and I feel like I can't breathe. While I don't want to believe his words, I can't help but think this is the reason why I didn't want a girlfriend. I didn't want someone controlling me the way my dad controls my mom. That's why I've been solo my whole life; I don't want to depend on someone and then have them fail me. But for some reason, with Claire, I forget everything.

Finally finding my footing, I head off the ice and then to the locker room with Matt's words replaying in my head. Maybe I rushed into this, but as soon as I think it, I want to take it back. It isn't like that with Claire. She's a cool chick, relaxed and fun. She wouldn't do what my dad does to my mom, and I know that when I've only known her for maybe a week.

Be you, Jude.

Right. Jayden is right. That's all I need to do. Stop worrying about what other people say and just be me.

After my first class...

> *Me: Did you know that apparently since I'm dating one girl I've stopped partying?*
> *Claire: It happens like that?*
> *Me: Apparently. Stupid, huh?*
> *Claire: Not as stupid as what this girl just said to me.*
> *Me: What did she say?*
> *Claire: She said that I'm a witch and I've obviously hexed you. I told her actually I was a bitch and that you like that about me.*
> *Me: LOL! My God, where do these people get this shit at?*
> *Claire: No clue, total weirdos.*
> *Me: Couldn't agree more. Am I going to see you today?*
> *Claire: I have classes until 4 and then I have practice and then I have to go to work with one of my solos then I have to study, so unless you can meet me somewhere, I don't think so.*
> *Me: I'll meet ya at the rink for a quick kiss so you don't forget the feel of my lips, you being busy and all.*
> *Claire: I could be the president of the US and still would never forget the taste of your lips, Jude Sinclair. I'm counting down the hours till I see you.*
> *Me: I can't wait.*

After my second class…

> Claire: So did u know that u have a 19 inch dick?
> Me: WTF?! I mean I'm hung but not like that
> Claire: Yeah, that's why u wouldn't stay with anyone cause u broke all the poor vaginas on campus.
> Me: Are u fucking kidding me?
> Claire: I'm as serious as a heart attack. I hope ur laughing though cause I was laughing so hard she flipped me off and walked away.
> Me: LOL, ur nuts.
> Claire: I'm here all week.
> Me: Oh no, I get you way longer than that.
> Claire: We will see.
> Me: No need to see baby, I know it.
> Claire: ☺

During my third class while my teacher was grading tests, I texted Claire again.

> Me: Did u know I get to see u in approximately an hour and 23 minutes?
> Claire: Did u know that I am very excited about that?
> Me: I didn't know that.
> Claire: Well I am.
> Me: Good.

It was easy to say I was grinning the rest of the period. As I started toward the rink, my phone sounded, and I pulled it out to find another text from Claire.

> Claire: So guess what I've decided?
> Me: What? U want to have sex today instead of waiting 13 more days?
> Claire: LOL! No…Jesus, get ur head out of the gutter.
> Me: Hard to do when it comes to u.
> Claire: Haha. Anyway, I've decided that when people say ur name to me, I'm gonna ignore them. Act like I don't even hear them.
> Me: Let me know how that goes.
> Claire: Will do, but in the meantime, check out "Don't Matter" by Akon. It's our jam right now, I've decided.
> Me: I'm downloading it now, are u on your way here?
> Claire: Yeah, changing now.

Me: Which means you're naked? ☺
Claire: Bye, Jude.

Laughing, I tuck my phone in my pocket and open the door to the rink before heading to the gym where the girls usually practice. As I walk, I listen to the song and find myself grinning that she sent me a song about how we're gonna ignore the haters and enjoy each other. It's sweet and I decide that I'm going to look for a song to send her. I first find a spot outside the gym and drop down onto a bench before doing that. When I find a good one, I save it and decide to wait till later to send it to her since I know she's on her way here. With nothing to do, I check my Facebook. I'm deleting messages from, you guessed it, girls who want to yell at me since I won't answer their phone calls, when a shadow appears in front of me. Looking up, I find that Rachael is looking down at me, her hands on her hips.

"Can't answer my text?"

I shrug. "Phone isn't in service."

"Forgot to pay your bill?" she asks sarcastically.

"Yeah and decided not to hook it back up," I answer, matching her tone.

"You're such an ass. What's up with you? And what's this crap about you dating Claire Anderson?"

I shrug again and decide to do what Claire said she's gonna do. "I have no clue what you're talking about."

She glares and then shakes her head. "Fine, be an asshole."

She walks away and I look back down at my phone to continue deleting messages. Just as I'm finishing, a text comes in from Jayden.

Bro: Wanna play some pickup at the tennis courts?
Me: Yeah, I answer back. Give me 10.
Bro: I'll grab your bag.

"Texting someone special?"

I look up to find Claire grinning down at me. Her hair is in a braid down her shoulder with a black bow clip thing holding her bangs out of her face. She's wearing short black shorts, her legs so long and delicious. She also wears a thin white Beatles tee that hangs off her shoulder; underneath it I can see her black sports bra, and my fingers itch to be on her. Standing, I tuck my phone in my pocket, wrapping my arms around her waist, pulling her in close. Without answering her, I capture her mouth with mine, kissing her slowly and seductively, showing her how much I've missed the feel of her lips against mine.

Running her hands up my arms, she snakes them behind my neck, taking a step forward, molding her body to mine. Texting her all day has been freaking awesome, but feeling her, touching her, and just breathing the same air as her is the ultimate high. Everything Matt said before is completely gone. Nothing matters but her and me, and I know that I am in a good place. That I made the right choice. She's the girl I'm supposed to give up everything for, and I'm fine with that.

Parting, I kiss her lips again softly before pulling back to look at her. "I'm holding my someone special."

"Such a smooth talker," she says with a wink, and I smile.

Not letting her go, I say, "It was my brother. We're playing pickup."

"Sounds like fun."

"You should come play one time."

Her mouth pulls up at the side. "I'll smoke your ass."

I laugh out, leaning against her, running my nose along hers. "Do you know how unbelievably hot it is that you just said that?"

She wiggles against me and my fingers bite into her back. Leaning in, I think she's going to kiss me, but instead, against my lips, she whispers, "Judging by the thickness of you, I'd say pretty hot."

"You're right," I mutter before kissing her again.

Pulling back, she grins as she says, "Did you like the song?"

"Yup, fits our situation very well, I think."

"I think so too," she says, leaning into me. "I need to go in."

"I know," I say, holding her closer, wanting to mold her into me and become one. "I don't want to let go yet."

She gives me a sad nod as she runs her thumbs up my jaw. "I don't want you to either, but unless you are gonna come in there and dance, I gotta go."

"It may surprise you to know that I am a badass dancer, so maybe I should."

She giggles, and it's such a beautiful sound. One that curls my toes and makes me tight everywhere. "I'd pay to see you in a Bullies' dancer outfit. I hear you're hot in a pair of ladies' panties."

I laugh out loud and nod, thinking back to the night I pledged at the house. "Yeah, great night, but I'll pass and leave the dancing to you. But one night, I'll have you in my arms, grinding against me, and all I'll be thinking about is…"

"Sex?" she asks with a grin.

"No, how fucking hot you are and how lucky I am."

Her cheeks darken with color and soon my lips are against hers. As our mouths move together, I can feel someone staring at us, but I can't bring myself to pull away. I need this kiss to last me until I see her again, and I'm not sure when that will be, so I deepen the kiss. Hoping to take every single bit of her with me. When we part, she smiles up as me as she tenderly kisses me on the side of the mouth.

"Wanna know what I'm thinking about?" she asks as she breaks free of me and starts to walk backward toward the door.

"How lucky you are to kiss me?"

"Nope, I already know that," she says, flashing me a bigger grin.

"Then what?" I ask.

"About how I don't know how I'm gonna last twelve more days without you inside me."

Holding on to the bench for support, I say, "Oh, that's dirty, Claire Anderson!"

Biting her bottom lip, she does that hot thing where she winks at me, leaving me utterly speechless before saying, "No one said I play nice. Bye, Jude."

She blows me a kiss, and I stand there, willing my dick to stop growing. I can't play hockey with a hard-on, but as I watch her walk away, her hips swaying side to side, her ass crying my name, I know that's exactly how I'm gonna play.

And how I'm gonna be for the next twelve days.

CHAPTER 17

Claire

"Reese, I don't think I'm gonna make it."

Reese's laughter rings in my ear. "Why? It can't be that bad."

"The dance we're learning… We're learning from a video from 1999! I swear!"

Her laughter continues as I let out a frustrated breath, rushing across campus so I can get my homework done before heading to work.

"Well, tell them, Claire. I mean, you are an award-winning choreographer. Tell them to let you work something up. They'd be lucky to dance your choreography."

I let out another breath. I had been thinking the same thing since they started teaching us the dance my seven-year-old kids from the studio could do, but I don't think that Rachael would allow it.

"I have something," I say but then sigh. "But I swear the captain hates me."

"Why do you think that?"

"She just looks at me in such a horrible way. She's either suffering from Resting Bitchface or she hates me."

"Again, what reason does she have to hate you? You're amazing."

Ah, the unconditional love I get from this woman makes me so happy, but I'm unable to smile from the problem that lies before me. "There are a couple."

"Like?"

"For one, I'm a better dancer than she is," I say.

"Well, of course you are," she says so matter-of-factly, it makes me grin.

"And two, I may be dating the guy she wants to date."

She squeals so loudly that I have to pull the phone away from my ear. "You're dating!"

Rolling my eyes, I say, "It's nothing to get excited about." But as soon as the words leave my mouth, I know they're a lie.

"Yeah right, you haven't dated since starting school! He must be something! Oh, is it Jude?!"

Groaning, I say, "Yeah, you know it is."

"Yeah, I did, just wanted you to confirm," she says before snickering. "Did you invite him to the wedding?"

"For gosh darn sakes! No! We're dating, not getting married!"

"Well, duh, you dork! Y'all are dating, and you need a date for the wedding."

"Oh my God, can we please go back to what I called you for?" I ask, pushing the door to my dorm open.

"Fine, tell them that you would love the chance to give them more options for dances. If they say no, flip them the bird, and start your own dance team."

"So mature."

"I try," she says while laughing and I laugh. "Don't worry, as soon as they see your stuff, you'll be golden, baby."

"I guess I'll try that."

"Good, now, can you promise me something?"

I feel like she's about to trap me, and I'm not sure why I say yeah, but I regret it as soon as she asks the next question.

"Ask Jude to the wedding. Phillip will be nice. I promise."

"The hell I'll be," I hear my uncle say and I smile.

"You don't even know what I'm talking about! Or who for that matter," she yells back.

"You are trying to get her to invite that douche bag to the wedding. I swear I'll be a complete asshole."

"Then you won't get laid."

"Ew! Niece on the phone!" I complain and she laughs.

"Like you don't know what sex is, but anyway, I'll stop him. And also, remember we have a dress fitting Friday."

I fall face-first on the bed and then roll over before saying, "Yeah, I'll be there. Make sure the dress you pick for me isn't whack."

"I'll let you pick it."

Thank sweet baby Jesus. "I love you."

"I love you more. See you Friday."

"Awesome, tell Phillip I love him too."

"I will, sweetheart. He's leaving in a bit for Colorado."

Before I can say anything, Phillip comes on the line. "Hey, I'll be back in a week. Be good, okay?"

"Aren't I always?"

"You have been, but I don't trust this Jude guy. What kind of name is that?"

"A classic one and he's supernice. I really like him. I think you would too if you gave him a chance."

He makes a disgruntled noise. "I don't think so."

I snicker. "I love you, Phillip."

"Love you, Claire-bear. Text me if you need anything."

"I will. Have a safe trip and score a goal for me."

He promises me he will, and with a grin, I hang up and then dial Jude's number. I'm not sure if he's done playing hockey, but I'll leave a message if he isn't. I just want him to know I'm thinking of him. He was so sweet to meet up with me for a few minutes. Okay, let me be honest; I just miss the guy.

To my surprise, he answers on the second ring. "Hey, beautiful, how was practice?"

"Completely horrible," I say with a grin, butterflies doing crazy flips in my belly. "Are you busy?"

"Still playing some pickup but I'm never too busy to talk to you. What's up? What happened at practice?"

"I think Rachael hates me and those dances are whack. I swear they're from 1999."

He laughs. "Yeah, they've been doing the same routines for years, and she probably does. You're dating me. Everyone wants me, remember?"

I roll my eyes at his cockiness, trying to ignore how much it turns me on. I don't have much luck with that. "Yes, you cocky thing, you, and that reminds me to really wonder if I should trust you."

He laughs. "Baby, I'm all yours, I promise. People can want me, but I only want you."

I smile, I don't need the reassurance because I do trust him, but still, it's nice to hear. "I know, but it's not smart to tell the girl you're dating that everyone wants you."

I can hear his smile in his voice. "You're right, but in my defense, I'm saying it just for the chance to remind you that I only want you."

I hate that I'm grinning. I should be mad but I'm not. "Okay, fine."

"Did we just have our first fight?"

"Hardly," I laugh and he chuckles.

"I think we did which means we need to have makeup sex or kiss or something."

"You just want a reason to touch me inappropriately."

"Of course I do," he says like it's general knowledge, when really, it is. I was dumb to assume otherwise.

"Anyway, but yeah, back to dance issues. Reese told me to say something to them."

"You should. You're the girl to bring life back into the team."

That makes me smile a little harder than it should. "Thanks. I'll let you get back to hockey. I was gonna leave you a message. Didn't mean to stress you out and be a bitch."

He laughs. "You didn't, and I want to know what this message was gonna say."

I think for only a second and know exactly what it was gonna say. "It was gonna say that I hope you kiss me really hard when I see you next."

"That would be a really hot message to get. Let's hang up and you do it for me, okay?"

I bite into my lip to stop from grinning harder. "Okay."

"And another thing."

"Yeah?"

"I promise to do just that when I see you, baby. Gotta make up for being an asshole."

I blush, covering my face with my hands. "You weren't an asshole, and I can't wait," I say breathlessly.

"Me neither. I'll text ya when I'm done."

"Okay, bye."

"Bye, babe."

When the phone goes dead, I dial his number again and it goes straight to voice mail. Smiling extremely hard, I say, "I hope you kiss me really hard when I see you next. Which I hope is very soon. Have fun, text me later."

Before I can say anything more, I hang up the phone and sit with a contented grin on my face. I like him. A lot. Way more than I've ever liked a guy. It scares me how strongly I feel about him. I may be rushing into this, and it may be insane of me, but I feel good about it.

I just hope he doesn't prove me wrong.

⊱❧⊰

"So heard you're dating Jude Sinclair."

I look up into my mirror to see Tessi standing behind me. She's wearing only a pair of panties, her brown hair in curls down her chest, covering her boobs. I lift an eyebrow before coming closer to the mirror to fix my eyelash. "Yeah, I am."

"You know he's been around, like, everywhere, right?"

My lips go in a straight line as I nod. I know this isn't the last time I'll hear this, but coming from my friend kinda makes it worse. "Yeah, I know."

"Okay, but you know, like, everyone, right? I mean, I think a good 70% of the girls in the school have been with him."

"That's a little exaggerated, don't you think?"

She thinks for a second. "No, I don't. Girls love him, and we all know Jude loves the ladies."

"Have you slept with him?" I ask, and while I wait for her to answer, I try to figure out if I'm gonna care.

Her face twists in disgust. "Hell no. I don't sleep with anyone, remember?"

Relief floods me as I nod. "Yeah, I forgot."

"Yeah, I mean, he's cool. Super good-looking and he's real nice. I had to do a project with him, and he was the sweetest even after I told him he wasn't getting any."

"He tried to have sex with you?"

She nods. "Of course he did. He loves it. I even accused him of being addicted to it."

I laugh with her, but it's empty. I don't know why I'm letting this bother me. I haven't before, but now as I sit here putting gloss on my lips, I can't help but be jealous of all these girls. What if they come back, or what if he meets someone better than me? No. It won't happen. He won't hurt me.

But if he's addicted to sex, maybe he will?

"I know that look, and don't let what I say bother you. I'm just surprised that he's settling down, but that's wonderful. All guys grow up, and you're the one who's gonna make him 'cause we all know you won't deal with being cheated on."

I bite into my lip. "We're only dating. He could do what he wants."

"But he won't. I've heard all about the way he looks at you. Everyone who isn't being a jealous bitch is saying that it's like he's a different person. Embrace it, babe. Enjoy it. He's a fine, fine man."

She's right. "Yeah, I like him a lot."

"Good," she says, throwing a tee on before reapplying the makeup that could have come off. When I reach for my brush, I see that my phone is blinking with a text message. It's two in the morning, who would be texting me? Maybe Skylar, but when I read the display, it's from Jude.

Hey Jude: I know it's late but I just wanted you to know I'm thinking of you.

My heart feels like it's coming out of my chest, and I know there is no stopping the grin on my face. As I glance over at Tessi, she's oblivious to my happiness and doing her makeup, and I hate how much I want to show her the text message to prove that Jude is amazing and sweet and now a one-woman guy. I shouldn't have to prove that to anyone; I shouldn't care, but something inside me wants everyone to know that he's a good guy. I don't know why he's slept around so much, but I do plan on finding out. The only thing is I know when I ask that, I'm gonna have to tell him about my past, and I'm not sure I can do that.

"Does he know you work here?"

I glance over to see that Tessi is watching me, a small smile sitting on her lips. Shaking my head slowly, I say, "No, I don't want to tell him. I haven't told anyone. Only Reese knows and then, of course, the girls who work here."

"Yeah, I don't know if I'd tell him either. He might not like that."

"What guy would?"

"True, but it's good money."

"Damn good money."

"Claire, honey."

Tessi sits up, and I turn to see Ms. Prissy coming toward me in a leopard-print bodysuit. Her bright red hair is up in a high ponytail, with her plump, red lips bright and shiny. Her breasts are huge and her ass is even bigger, filling out her bodysuit nicely; the older men go crazy for her. Smiling up at her since I know she's still mad about the fact that I gave her a schedule for the dance team and what days I need off, I say, "Hey Ms. Prissy."

"Listen I need three new numbers, two group and one solo for Tessi. Something hot for her and burlesque for the groups, but still sexy. Also, I need a new pole routine for you and Ellen. I need it in a month, the third of November."

"For? It's not time for new routines yet."

"I know, but I have some investors coming from Vegas, Florida, and New York, so I need to impress them."

I nod. "I'll get it done."

"Fabulous, thank you."

"No problem," I say, and she smiles before walking off. I say I want to quit, but I'm comfortable here and I love my job offstage. I mean, being onstage doesn't bother me much, but still some days I wish I were strictly backstage. No one looking at me, no one judging me, or getting hard from me. Sometimes I feel like a piece of meat, but then other times I feel incredibly special. I love the audience when it's full of classy men – not the drunks that come in after a night of drinking to try to convince me to sleep with them – but the ones who appreciate a beautiful woman moving in a sensual way. Thankfully, we have more of the latter, and that's why I stay. But now that I have Jude in my life, I don't want anyone looking at me because I don't want anyone looking at him.

But how do I quit? I need the money, the security, because I might not have the blanket of support and love I have now forever. It could all end, and then I'll find myself at rock bottom, a strung-out stripper like my mother.

I can't let that happen.

I won't let that happen.

CHAPTER 18

 *Claire*

I'm dragging ass this morning.

Something fierce.

I was supposed to get off at three, but we had a group of owners of some sports teams come in, and Ms. Prissy wasn't letting me leave until I gave them a show. Which I did, and yes, I walked away with more money than I make in a week, but still I'm beyond tired. But when I see Jude strutting toward me from the vocational building, my mood picks up a bit. His face is bright, a big grin on his lips with his hair falling in his eyes. He's wearing jeans and a Henley, and when I glance down to see I'm wearing the same old sweats, I suddenly wish I was dressed a little better.

"Have you seen me in anything but sweats?" I ask when he stops in front of me.

He smiles. "I've seen you naked."

I laugh as I smack his chest, but before I can take my hand back, he grabs it, pulling me into his arms. Pressing his lips to mine for a quick kiss, he pulls back, his grin still on his lips as he says, "And it was a wonderful day, the heavens parted, and God released one of his angels for me to turn into a dirty little demon."

I roll my eyes as I wrap my arms around his neck. "You're impossible."

"True, but really, I like the way you look. Jeans, booty shorts, sweats, naked, I'm not picky as long as it's you, looking at me with those eyes and grinning at me with those lips. All I need is you."

Biting into my lip, I lean into him, pressing my lips to his. His arms come around me tightly, squeezing me as I deepen the kiss, our tongues playing in a slow, teasing way. When we part, I dust his jaw with small kisses, the hair on his jawline tickling my lips and tongue. When I reach his lips again, his fingers bite into my back before he takes over the kiss. With his body enveloping mine, his mouth is dangerous, and I am a willing victim to his assault. I can't get enough.

Pulling away slowly, his mouth follows mine, causing me to smile as I stop, his own smile crashing against mine, leaving me breathless. I love this. I love how playful but sexy we are together. I've never ever been so turned on in my life but at the same time so happy. It's crazy and ridiculous, but Jude Sinclair makes me giddy.

As we part, his hands come up to my face, holding me tenderly as his green eyes bore into mine. "Told ya I'd kiss ya hard," he says and I smile.

"Best kiss ever."

"Oh, you just wait, I have way more in my arsenal."

I giggle as I hug his chest, resting my chin on it as I look up at him. "Promise?"

"Swear."

We share a smile, and he lowers his head to kiss my nose before asking, "Are you still mad at me?"

"I was never mad, more annoyed."

"Okay," he says, giving me a look. "Are you annoyed?"

My mouth turns up at the side as I slowly shake my head. "I can't be annoyed when I'm looking at you."

He smiles before leaning down to kiss me softly. As he pulls away, his arms tighten around me as he asks, "What do you have next?"

"Nothing, I'm going home and sleeping."

"Want some company?"

"If we sleep, yes. If you want more, you know the answer."

He gives me his best innocent look, and it does nothing but make me laugh out loud. "I promise to be on my best behavior," he vows, and for some reason, I believe him. Or maybe I hope he won't so I can get another delicious piece of Jude pie. Either way, I lace my fingers with his and we head toward my dorm.

"Is Skylar there?"

"Nope, she has classes the rest of the day. I'm supposed to meet her at practice."

"Okay," he says, flashing me a grin, but when I set him with a glare, he holds his two fingers up. "Scout's honor, I'll be good."

"Were you even a Boy Scout?"

He laughs and then winks at me. "Nope."

I shake my head laughing and he pulls me in against his chest as we head toward my dorm. My conversation with Tessi comes to mind, but I can't bring myself to ask him. It will bring us to a whole other level, and I'm not sure if I'm ready to share that kind of stuff with him yet. I'm not sure I'll ever be ready to share that with him. It was such a dark time in my life; only certain people know about it – only because they have to love me – but Jude doesn't. He could run the other way and never look back. That scares me, and I think I'll leave both our issues to rest for a bit.

Reaching my dorm, we climb the stairs and then drop our bags by the door before Jude shuts it.

"I have good memories in this room," he says as he leans against the door, looking all long and lean and sexy.

"Yes, but no repeats. I'm so tired. I stayed up way too late studying."

"Me too, I texted you at two."

Smiling, I say, "I know, thank you, it was sweet."

"I guess you can say I missed ya," he says, coming toward me, and guilt eats at my chest.

"I missed you too. I must have fallen asleep before that," I say, wrapping my arms around him before he captures my mouth with his. Holding me tight to him, he lowers us to the bed, lying on top of me as we kiss and tease each other. When his hand cups my breast, I pull away, setting him with a look. "What happen to Scout's honor?"

He pauses, breathing hard while his eyes shine with lust. "I wasn't ever a Scout?"

I laugh as I push him off me. He falls willingly to my side and smiles at me. I smile back before standing and removing my sweatpants and sweatshirt, leaving me in panties and a sports bra. When I go to get back in bed, I notice that Jude's eyes are wide and his lips are parted.

"What?" I ask, climbing under the blankets.

"You want me to sleep by you when you're wearing only that?"

I shrug. "Yes, I sleep like this. I hate clothes. You're the one who wanted to sleep with me."

His eyes blazing with lust, he nods slowly. "I still do."

Sitting up, he rips off his shirt and throws it on the floor before coming under the blankets with me. As he hugs me close to his strong, warm chest, I nuzzle into him, closing my eyes and settling in, but his pants are rough on my skin.

"Take your pants off," I whisper against his chest.

He doesn't say anything for a moment, and then he says roughly, "If I take them off, I can't be responsible for what happens."

I giggle. "Nothing is gonna happen. Take 'em off."

He complies then comes back to me, wrapping me up in his arms. I feel so warm, so safe in his thick, toned arms. My body molds to his, and I'm so comfortable that sleep is not far away. Before I can fall though, he asks, "What are you doing tonight?"

Opening my eyes, I look up to find him watching me. He moves his hand up to move a piece of my hair out of my face and then kisses my nose. Flashing him a grin, I say, "I have practice, I have to go teach my eight-year-olds, and then I'm free."

"Cool. Do you like to sing karaoke?"

My smile widens as I nod. "I'm a girl, of course I do."

He returns the grin and then says, "Me and the guys go out every Thursday for karaoke night. They have dollar drafts and it's a good time. Wanna come?"

I eye him. "Won't I interfere with your guy time?"

He runs his nose along mine, his eyes locked on mine as we share the same air. "No, everyone brings their girls. It's fun."

"So I'm your girl?"

Giving me a look that tells me that was a dumb question, he says, "Of course you are."

That makes me giddy as I slowly nod my head. "Then yes, I'd love to come."

"Good," he says then kisses my nose before closing his eyes.

"Just to let you know, though, I'm gonna kick your ass at karaoke."

A smile comes across his lips as his eyes close and he says, "I accept that challenge."

Grinning, I lay my head on his chest and then close my eyes. Within his warmth, it doesn't take long until I'm out like a light.

⁂

Walking with Jude Sinclair across the quad with our hands locked has people stopping and whispering. It's bothersome as hell, but then I glance up at him and think, who the hell cares? Not only do I get to hold his hand, I just had the most unbelievable nap wrapped in the warmth of his gorgeous arms. I feel so refreshed, and I have him to thank for that. Usually it takes me a while to fall asleep in the middle of the day, but with Jude, it was instant. I'm not sure what that means, but it has to be good.

"So, what are you doing next Saturday night? I hope you don't have to work."

"Why, what's going on?"

"We have our annual Latin night at the frat house. Cesar's mom makes rice, beans, and tacos, and we drink margaritas. It's a blast," he says then he smacks himself in the head. "What am I doing? Of course you'll be there. We hire you guys to come and do a cute little Latin dance."

"What? We dance for y'all?"

"Yeah, for the whole party. It's fun. You'll have a blast."

Okay, first, I need to make sure I have that off. Ms. Prissy will probably murder me, but oh well. And second, there is no way in hell I'm doing one of those 1999 videos for the Bellevue hockey team party. No fucking way. "I'm not dancing. I'll come, but I'm not dancing if we're doing those crappy-ass dances. I bet they'll do the Macarena. No way in hell."

He laughs. "They did that last year."

"Of course they did. Fucking hell, no way. I'm saying something."

"Good, get it done, baby. Do something supersexy. Shake that ass for me."

He winks and I laugh as he wraps his arms around my shoulders, pulling me in close. He then asks, "So you'll be my date, right?"

"Date? Hmm, let's see if my schedule is clear."

He stops, glaring at me, and I can't hold in my laughter, especially when he starts tickling me relentlessly. When I fall to the ground, he falls on top of me, tickling and kissing me as I shriek and giggle. Settling between my thighs, his eyes meet mine and something inside me shifts.

I superlike this guy.

"Be my date," he demands, moving his hand up my cheek and into my hair.

"Don't tell me what to do," I say back and he smiles.

"Please be my date?"

As I wrap my leg around his hip, his eyes fall shut from how close I allowed him to get. Moving my thumb along his bottom lip, I whisper, "You know by then our fourteen days will be up."

He nips at my thumb as his eyes lock with mine. "So you'll be my girlfriend?"

My heart completely comes out of my chest at that point, and it takes everything out of me to hold in my smile as I shrug. "If you ask nicely, maybe."

He nods, and then hops up, and I miss his warmth immediately as he reaches down to help me up. "Good, then you'll have to go since boyfriends and girlfriends do everything together."

I don't move when he starts to walk. Mulling his words over, I ask, "So what you're saying is that you're not going to be all romantic and ask me sweetly to be your date to Latin night?"

He flashes me a grin and says, "Of course I am, when I'm good and ready. Don't rush me, woman."

He wraps his arm across my shoulder, and we continue toward the rink. When we're almost there, I look up at him and ask, "So you think at the end of our fourteen days, you'll want to be my boyfriend?"

He glances at me and says, "If I could ask you now to be my girlfriend and know you'd say yes without question, I would."

His eyes are so tender and full of admiration for me. I've never felt so gorgeous in my life than I do now under his gaze in a ratty pair of sweats and a tank. My hair looks like a bird's nest, but it doesn't matter with his eyes on me. As much as I want to enjoy what he just said, something bothers me about his statement.

"What makes you think I wouldn't say yes?"

His mouth pulls up at the side as he shrugs. "I think you need the reassurance that I don't only want you for sex, that I'm in this for the long haul, so I'm gonna wait it out. Make sure you're happy with us before I ask to make you mine."

My eyes are locked with his because he hit that nail right on the head. "You're completely right."

"I know. I usually am," he says with a goofy grin, his seriousness long gone and replaced with a grin. He then leans toward me, pressing his lips to my cheek before hugging me tight to his side, and I know right then that it's gonna be completely easy to fall for this guy.

When we reach the rink, he kisses me long and sweetly before making me promise to text him once I'm done. As I watch him walk away, my heart feels like it's coming out of my chest, and everything inside me is so warm and fuzzy. I don't want to go anywhere; I want to stay here and watch him walk away. Knowing that can't happen, I turn and head inside. Once inside the gym, I drop my bag against the wall and throw off my sweats and tank, watching as some girls stretch and others talk. When Rachael sees me, she gives me a look – not a welcoming one – before turning back to talk with her minions.

Rolling my eyes, I head to where Skylar is stretching and grin as I drop down. "Saw you had a visitor this afternoon. In your bed. With no clothes on."

I smile as I nod. "Yeah, we took a nap. We had underwear on."

She waggles her eyebrows at me, and I giggle as she asks, "Did ya get some action?"

Shaking my head, I smack her thigh as I stand to stretch my quads. "No, I told you we're waiting two weeks before doing that again."

"And I told you, you are completely insane. If I had Jude Sinclair naked and willing in my bed, I'd be on that like a fat kid on cake."

"You're nuts," I say, laughing as I pull my leg up by my head. She rolls her eyes and continues to stretch until Rachael comes to the middle of the group.

"All right, so glad to see everyone. We're gonna go over the video some more for our main dances and then learn a new dance that we'll be doing for the Bullies' Latin night that's next Saturday. Old team, it's the same from last year. New girls, it's not hard, so you'll catch on easily."

"'Cause a five-year-old could do it," I say under my breath, and Skylar smacks my arm.

"Shh," she mouths and I roll my eyes.

"Everyone good?" Rachael asks.

Her eyes settle on me, almost challenging me, and I decide that I can't do this anymore.

"Nope, not at all," I say, and I hear Skylar groan beside me.

Everyone turns to look at me and Rachael's hand comes on her hip, her eyes sharp as razors. "Problem, Claire?"

"Just a small one," I say, holding my finger and thumb a tad bit apart.

"Shut up, Claire," Skylar whispers, but I ignore her. She agrees with me; she thinks these dances are dumb! Why is she trying to stop me?

"And that is?" Rachael asks.

"That the dances are whack. I swear they were made in 1999, and I refuse to look stupid in front of our campus and peers doing something so easy that the seven-year-olds at my studio could master it in a day's time."

Puckering her lips, she says, "I don't see anything wrong with our dances, and I refuse to use our money to pay for a choreographer just to make you happy. I don't know how things are done for you at your studio, but you aren't going to be spoiled here."

I take a step forward, my blood pressure rising a bit. Oh, the desire to flip the girl the bird and start my own dance team is so tempting, but I'm going to keep my cool. I'm going to make this team better. For what? I have no clue. I don't even know why I care, but I feel like I need to do this. "For one, I'm not asking to be spoiled, and two, no one said anything about hiring anyone. I am an award-winning choreographer. I can come up with kick-ass dances that will make us look spectacular. We're all so beautiful, with amazing bodies and talent that is being wasted on crap-ass video dances. This dance team can be more."

I can see on everyone's faces that they are all for it, but Rachael's is twisted in disgust. "So you want to take over my team."

I shake my head. "No, that's not what I want. I'm too busy with work and school to do your job, but coming up with dances is second nature to me. I can do it."

"How surprising since it seems all your time is spent on your boyfriend?"

I glare as everyone looks down at the ground. "I have no clue what that has to do with anything. I want to help make the team better, not talk about my personal life."

I don't even think she heard me, because she says, "Do you know how stupid you look with him? We all know it's a joke. He's a player. He's slept with all of us, and he's probably screwing some dumb freshman behind your back while you stand here right now."

Taking in a deep breath, I try to count to three as I hear Skylar say, "I told you to shut up."

Looking back at Rachael, I let out the breath and ask, "Is this the part where I get mad and break up with Jude 'cause of what you've said? Because apparently I look so stupid to be with such a player, when in reality, he has been the sweetest, most amazing person I've even met. He changed his phone number so people like you can't get ahold of him. When he looks at me, he's looking at me and only me. So I should throw that away because you said so? Have you slept with him in the last week? Have any of you?"

No one will meet my quizzical gaze; even Rachael looks away.

"No? Okay, now let's get one thing straight," I say as her gaze meets mine. "When we're in this room, don't come at me with anything but dance. My personal life is my business, not yours. If Jude hurts me then it's my fault 'cause everyone told me over and over again what a player he is, but it's not your concern." Rachael doesn't say anything and I continue, "Now, as I was saying, can I please choreograph us some kick-ass dances because I do not want to look like an idiot in front of my man and the whole campus, not to mention my family. So are there any objections to that?"

CHAPTER 19

JUDE

ittler Bro: *I think something's up with Mom.*

Instead of replying back to Jace's text, I decide to call him. He answers on the second ring.

"The whole reason I texted it was 'cause I didn't want to say it out loud, asshole."

"Shut up, go outside. What's going on?"

I hear him shuffling through the house and then my mom yell, "Stop shuffling your ever-loving feet, Jace Ryan!"

I smile as he apologizes before I hear the door shut. "Okay, so I heard her crying, like, all morning."

"Why?"

"I don't know, Jude, or I would be telling you why she was crying."

Duh. As my heart speeds up in my chest, I ask, "Did you ask her?"

"No, as soon as I came in, she dried her face and left the kitchen. I asked Lucy and she doesn't know either. She said she would ask her, but when she did, Mom started fussing over Angie and completely ignored her."

Something inside me twists. My mom only cries when she's stressed or if my dad has done something to her. I know that Lucy, Angie, and Jace are good; Jayden and I are golden, so I know she isn't stressed about us. I talked to her yesterday too, and she said everything was fine, so I don't know what's going on. Spinning my chair around, I think as I spin and then ask, "Was Dad supposed to come home?"

"Not from what I know."

"Yeah, I don't know either. Hmm, okay, I'll call her."

"Don't tell her I said anything!"

"I won't, promise. Thanks, Jace."

"Thanks, Jude."

Nothing else is said and I hang up. Stopping my chair, I lean on my legs trying to figure out what I'm going to say to her. I'm not sure, but I have to speak to her. I'm even tempted to drive out to the house to see her face-to-face, but I have a date with Claire in a bit, and I don't want to miss that if nothing is wrong. If I'm not happy with the phone call, then I'll drive out there.

I dial her number and she answers right away. "Hey, honey!"

"Hey, Mom," I say. "What's up?"

"Nothing much, just making some dinner. You?"

"Nothing, just checking in. I was thinking about you."

"Always so caring and thoughtful. I love you so much, Jude."

I smile, my chest warming a bit. My mom is the best thing in my life. "I love you too, Mom. Everything okay?"

"Yes, honey, why wouldn't it be? I am blessed with four beautiful, smart children and a gorgeous granddaughter."

So my dad pissed her off; she usually includes him in that blessing, even though he doesn't deserve it. "I think Jayden got all the smarts, but we all are beautiful."

That makes her laugh and I ask, "When is Dad coming home?"

"I don't know," she basically snaps and then quickly says, "Excuse me, honey, that was rude. I'm really tired."

Whoa, yeah, something is really wrong. "Are you sure? Did Dad do something?"

"Honey, I don't want to talk about your father right now."

"Okay," I say, and I'm not sure what to say after that. Suddenly the words leave my mouth before I can stop them. "Can I fix whatever it is?"

When I hear her take in a deep breath, I know she is fighting back tears. "My Jude, always the fixer."

"Mom, what is it?"

"Don't worry, honey, it's all okay."

"Can I fix it?" I ask again.

"No, honey, but don't worry, okay? I'm going to be fine."

"I'm coming out there," I say, standing up to get my keys.

"No, Jude, I promise I'm fine."

"I don't believe you, Mom."

"I know, but I promise, everything is going to work out fine. No worries. How are you? How is the girl I keep hearing about? What's her name?"

"Claire," I say even though I know she's just trying to change the subject. Maybe I need to let it go for today, but I'll call again tomorrow and the next day just to make sure my mom is okay. I might even call my dad, but the thought of doing that makes my stomach hurt.

"You should bring her to dinner. How about next week sometime?"

"Yeah, Mom, sure, I'll ask her," I say, and I'm not sure why I said that. Maybe because I know she's upset and I want to make her happy. I don't know what's going on, but I'll find out and then I'll fix it.

"Great, baby. I'll talk to you tomorrow okay?"

"All right, Mom," I say and then I hang up, telling her I love her. I know that she said everything is going to work out, but a feeling in my stomach tells me that something is really wrong.

Thoughts of my mom have played heavy on my heart all evening, but when I see Claire coming toward me, I welcome the distraction. She looks unbelievable. Her legs are encased in black tights with boots coming up to her knees, and she wears a large green sweater that goes to mid-thigh. Her hair is in a braid down her shoulder, and she's wearing makeup along with the geeky glasses from when I first met her. Stopping in front of me, she grins, her lips so glossy and sexy.

"Hi, I'm looking for this über hot guy named Jude. Do you know him? We have a battle to get to," she says in a high-pitched, Valley-girl voice.

I smile as my arm snakes around her, my gaze meeting hers. "I'm right here, baby. Come here, let me mess up that lip gloss."

And then I kiss her. Hard. All the stress in my body just releases the moment our lips touch, and when her tongue moves along mine, everything inside me is hard. Moving my hands down her hips and then over her sweet ass, I pull her closer to me, deepening the kiss, not able to get enough. Parting only to breathe, I go in for another kiss, but she stops me, pressing her finger into my lips.

"What's wrong?"

Confused, I ask, "Huh? Nothing, I'm kissing you."

"Yeah, I know, but something is off. Are you okay?"

How does she know this? "Yeah," I lie.

"Don't lie to me. What's wrong?"

"How do you know I'm lying?" I ask incredulously.

"I don't know, but I know you are. What's wrong?"

"Just worried about my mom. It's nothing."

She eyes me for a second and then asks, "Anything I can do to help?"

I shrug. "I don't even know what's going on, but when I know, I'll tell you."

"Okay," she says and then she goes up on her toes, kissing my lips softly. Wrapping my arms so tight around her, I take over the kiss, lacing my fingers behind her back, holding her as close as I can.

When she smiles against my lips, I smile too, pulling away to say, "It's so good to see you."

"You too," she whispers against my lips. But then she backs away quickly, her eyes bright as she says, "Guess what!"

"You look superhot in those leggings? I know. Come here, I'm not done kissing you."

She giggles as she tries to stop me, but soon she's kissing me, taking over the kiss I initiated. Moving her fingers through my hair, she cups my chin before pulling her mouth away. I try to chase her for another kiss, but she presses her finger to my lips again. After she sets me with a look that tells me I better listen, I smile and say, "Sorry, I can't get enough of those lips."

"You're lucky you're cute."

I shoot her a cheeky grin and she rolls her eyes. "But really, guess what!"

"What, baby?" I ask, pulling her into my arms, cupping her ass as I meet her gaze.

"I'm going to choreograph for the dance team!"

Pride explodes in my chest as hug her closer, my face breaking into a grin. "I'm so proud of you!"

"Thanks," she says before pressing her lips to mine for a quick kiss.

"That's amazing. How did that happen?"

She shakes her head. "Wasn't easy. Rachael called me dumb for trusting you, and then I told her that what I do outside of dance team is none of her business, and then I said that I can make this team better. The team was on board and voted my way. Rachael was the only one who didn't vote for me – even her minions voted for me."

"Wow," I say, surprised that Ally and Mia went against Rachael. They have all been best friends since birth. "That's 'cause they know you're the best."

"Aw thanks," she says, leaning into me playfully. "I'm pretty excited."

"I am too," I say, wrapping my arm around her shoulders. "I can't wait for my baby to blow people away."

She grins up at me, her cheeks flushing with color. It leaves me breathless when she looks at me like that. Like I'm the most amazing guy in the world, as if I'm worth it, when I know I'm not. I know I haven't led the life a girl like Claire deserves, but for some reason she believes in me and trusts me. When I look in her eyes, I feel like I am the guy she deserves.

Clearing my throat, I say, "I know you're used to winning, but I'm about to murder you in this karaoke war."

She looks up at me, a gleam in her eyes that tells me to watch out. "We will see."

I don't say anything back because it's too loud once we're in the bar. It's a little college pub called The Gilroy. The owner knows the team and usually lets the underage kids drink when we bring in our fake IDs. He doesn't question us, which means we come only here to spend all our money. When I see some of the guys from the team, including my brother, I head toward them, pulling Claire with me. When I glance back, she's looking around, taking it in, and I wonder if she's ever been here.

Once we reach the group, I lean in and ask her just that. She shakes her head and says, "Nope, first time."

I smile as I nod, and then thankfully, there's a break in the music. Pointing the guys, I say, "Claire, this is my brother Jayden, Bryan, Matt, Caleb, and his girlfriend, Hannah. Everyone, this is Claire."

Claire gives an awkward wave while everyone just grins at her as she says, "Nice to meet you guys."

I sit in the open chair beside Jayden and then pull Claire into my lap. She leans back into my chest and smiles at me before giving me a kiss on the cheek.

"So you're the girl to change my brother?"

We both look over at Jayden, and I love the grin that sits on Claire's face. It's a playful one. "Yup, he apparently likes me."

"I know. He talks about you all the time."

I glare at my brother, but Claire seems to like that. Looking over at me, she runs her thumb along my jaw. "He's pretty great."

"Yeah, my mom is excited to meet you," he says and then takes a swig of his beer with no cares in the world. Acting as if he's saying it's a beautiful night. Damn asshole.

Claire glances at me, surprised, and I set Jayden with a look that could kill. "Thanks, asshole."

"Oh, you hadn't told her yet that you promised to take her to dinner with our family?"

"Oh wow," she mutters, and I swear my brother is going to be sleeping in the tub for the next couple weeks.

Meeting Claire's surprised gaze, I say, "Yeah, is that okay? Sorry, my mom asked, and I said I'd ask you."

"When?"

"Next week. She's excited to meet you, but I get it if you don't want to come."

"No, it's not that, it's just, wow, your mom."

"And family," Jayden adds, and I flip him the bird.

He laughs before taking a swig of his beer. Ignoring him, I look back at Claire. She works her lip and then meets my gaze again. "Sure, I'd love to."

I smile as my heart beats loudly in my chest. I don't know why I thought she would say no, but I did. I'm usually so confident with girls, but with her, I'm nervous and unsure of myself. It's a new feeling, one that I'm learning means I actually care for this girl. I hug her tightly in my arms as she leans back into me, and I can feel everyone staring at us. I know it's new and weird for me to be so into a girl, but people are going to have to get used to it. Claire is someone special.

My game changer.

Kissing her ear, I nibble on her lobe before saying in her ear, "You don't have to come."

Why did I say that?

She looks back at me and smiles. "I want to."

"Promise?"

"Swear it."

We share a smile before she leans over and gives me a soft, sweet kiss on my lips.

"Who's ready for some singing?" Matt yells as he throws a twenty on the table. I fish my money out and throw two down for Claire and me.

"What's that for?"

"The buy-in. We sing three songs from each category. Last week's winner picks, and you can't look at the screen once or you're out. You get extra points if people cheer for you. Hannah is the judge."

She makes a face. "Extreme karaoke."

"Yeah, that's how we roll," Jayden says. "Extreme karaoke, beer pong, roller hockey, we're extreme kinda guys."

"Sounds like my kind of fun," she says with a grin before looking over at me. "I'm superexcited."

"Good, so I guess I'll be a gentlemen and let you go second so I can show you the ropes of how to sing a good karaoke song."

She laughs, her body vibrating against mine. "How sweet of you. But get ready to be schooled."

"Uh-oh! I think Jude has been challenged," Jayden says and I roll my eyes.

"I think you can take him, Claire," Matt says. "I mean, you did get him to sleep with only one girl."

Claire laughs as she rolls her eyes. "He isn't sleeping with anyone, for your information, especially not me."

That stuns my friends, and to my surprise, doesn't embarrass me at all. I'm proud that I've only slept with one girl in two weeks. That's a record for me. Knowing that it's a good time for me to exit, I tap her butt to get up. I stand up behind her and then kiss the back of her head before walking around her. Looking at me, she asks, "Where are you going?"

"Off to pick the categories."

"Why?"

"'Cause I'm the winner from the last week."

I flash her a grin before leaning over for a quick kiss and then head off to get my songs. I should feel bad that I'm about to kick her ass in karaoke, but I guess the competitor in me can't muster up any guilt. Too bad, too, because Claire is going down.

CHAPTER 20

JUDE

"Okay, categories are as follows," I say once I come back to the table. Claire has a water in front of her that Jayden must have gotten her when he went to get a beer. They're sitting close; probably so they could hear each other over the music because I know my brother would never cross me. We're too close. And he knows how much she means to me. He's probably the only person I trust at this table. Caleb probably wouldn't do anything, but Bryan and Matt are horn dogs out for a little tail, and if I see them give my girl anything but a friendly smile, I might knock out their teeth.

With everyone's attention, I say, "Pop, love songs, and rap."

"Love songs!" Matt says with his face twisted.

"What the hell?" Bryan asks.

"He's got a girlfriend now," Jayden says with a grin. "He's all about that mushy shit now."

"Shut up," I sneer before flipping him the bird. Looking over at Claire, I see that her cheeks are a little darker in color, and she's grinning wide. Leaning over to her, I brace my hands on the chair arms, bringing my mouth so close to hers that it wouldn't take much move moment to feel her lips against mine. "I hope you're ready because I'm about to dominate here."

She scoffs, rolling her eyes. "You ain't about to dominate anything. I'm a master at this."

"We will see," I say before standing up.

"Oh, we will," she says, pursing her lips up at me.

I want to give her a kiss, but she's my competitor now, and I'm about to whoop her ass. Heading toward the stage, I take the mic and put it on the stand. I hear my name screamed by some of the girls, and when I look out to where

I know Claire is, her eyes are on mine, a challenge in her eyes. She doesn't care about the girls; she doesn't care about anything but me. That's freaking awesome, but I'm not going to let that distract me. She's going down.

I know I have all three categories. I know my music, but I know she does too. She might get me on the pop one, but I'll have one over on her in the rap and love song categories. When the music to "Say it, Just Say It" by The Mowgli's starts, everyone in the pub goes crazy. I sing like I'm going for a Grammy, working the room, getting people to clap and scream, while knowing all the words. It's fun; I love singing. It's always been a passion of mine but hockey always won over it. My mom always says I could be the next Michael Buble, but I would rather be the next Wayne Gretzky.

Soon the song is over and the crowd goes nuts, even the bartender is clapping. Putting the mic back on the stand, I head over to where Claire is coming toward me, a grin on her face.

"Impressive," she says, stopping in front of me. "But I'm better."

With only a wink, she passes by me and I swear I'm so hard I can't breathe. This girl gets me on so many levels, and knowing that she is as big a competitor as I am turns me on so much I'm not sure I can move. Somehow my legs start to move and I head back to the table to drop down into the seat beside Jayden. Claire is still setting up her song, so I reach for the beer that Jayden has for me and take a long pull.

"I like her."

I glance over to see my brother's eyes on me. "Me too," I answer.

"She's great. She likes you too."

"Good, that's what I want."

He nods and then turns as the music to "Dark Horse" by Katy Perry starts. Oh, smart move. It's the hottest song out and everyone in the pub is up, dancing and singing along. Claire's voice is nice too. She wasn't lying when she said she liked to karaoke. She can carry a tune, and damn, she looks good doing it. But when she starts to move her body to the music in a sexy way, the guys in the pub start to holler and my body tightens with jealously. I don't want to share her with anyone in this pub; I wish it were only us two, but I know that's silly. She isn't dancing for anyone but me. Her eyes haven't left mine, and soon I'm wound tighter than a clock.

Jesus, she is beautiful.

"She got you on this round."

I scoff at Jayden. "No way!"

"Yes, way," Matt says, his eyes all over Claire's body.

"Hey, asshole, watch it!" I say sternly, and he laughs, waving me off.

"I'm not dumb, Jude. I don't want your girl."

"That's right," I say just as she stops singing and the pub cheers loudly for her as she puts the mic on the stand.

When she starts down the stage, I watch as Jimmy Tavins, a guy who plays for the football team, stops her, and she smiles up at him as he talks to her. I want to get up and go tell him to get away from my girl, but before I can even move, she's waving him off before heading toward me. Dropping down into the seat that Jayden left empty since he went to sing, I look over at her.

"What did Jimmy have to say?"

She eyes me, and then rolls her eyes. "I know you aren't jealous."

"No way, I'm just asking," I say and she laughs.

"Oh gosh, nothing. He asked me if I wanted to dance, and I said no, that I'm with someone. Is that a problem?"

Yes. "No, not at all. You can dance all you want."

She laughs as she wraps her arms around mine and leans her face on my shoulder. "Do you know how cute it is when you pout being all jealous?"

I don't answer and she giggles as she rubs her nose along my jaw. "Have I told you that I'm glad I'm here with you?"

I give her a sideways glance and shrug. "No."

Her giggles continue but then her hands slide down my thigh and I jump in surprise. Looking at her, I say, "Wow, getting a little frisky, aren't you?"

"I'm trying to cheer you up," she says innocently and I laugh, bringing her in for a kiss, but she dodges it. "I don't kiss my competition."

"But you'll feel them up?"

She looks at me all wide-eyed and like I'm an idiot. "Of course. It weakens you."

All I can do is shake my head. "Well played, Ms. Anderson."

"Thank you," she says and turns her attention to the stage where my brother is doing a horrible rendition of NSYNC's "Bye, Bye, Bye." We watch as Matt, Bryan, and Caleb have their turns, and in my opinion, my only competition is Claire. Going up next, I grab the mic as Justin Timberlake's "Summer Love" starts. Looking out toward Claire, I smile as I sing and she moves in the chair, singing along with me. Moving my body to the beat, the girls all scream, and my girl looks at me like I'm a big piece of cake and she is the fattest kid in America craving me.

Hell, if I'd known singing Justin Timberlake would get her all hot and bothered I would have done this four days ago.

Finishing the song, the place goes wild and I know I've taken this category. There is no way she can beat that response or the fact that I didn't miss a lyric at all. Jumping off the stage with a little more pep in my step since I know she won't beat me in the rap category, I head toward her and she meets me in the middle again.

"Was that for me?"

I shrug. "Maybe."

"Good choice, but my beloved JT won't distract me from kicking your ass.

Now if you'll excuse me, I have extreme karaoke to beat you in," she says with a look, and then she passes by me as I fight the smile that wants to come out.

This girl is nothing but fire.

When I get to my seat, I turn to see that she's handing the DJ her phone and then she goes onstage. I don't know what she's doing, but then the soft medley to a song starts and her voice is like an angel's, filling the quiet pub. I know the lyrics though; it's a remake of Drake's "Hold on, We're Going Home." It's soft and beautiful, and as I watch her sing, I know my chances of winning this round have just been blown out of the water. Not only that, but good God, she is amazing and the words…I know they're for me. Because she's a good girl and I know it, and everyone knows I act so different around her. While I had done the same, it was playful and to throw her off her game, but this feels way different. When her eyes meet mine, everything inside me sizzles.

When she ends the song with a grin, the crowd isn't as loud as they were for me, but still, she won that round, in my opinion. Coming offstage, she exchanges a grin with Jayden before coming toward me as I stand.

"I have to admit, that may have thrown me off my game," I say and she smiles up at me.

"That's our song," she says as she takes a step toward me. "At least for now."

"So that means you'll be taking me home?"

Her smile grows. "Or maybe you'll take me home? For sleeping purposes, of course."

"But of course," I agree, and she laughs as I wrap my arms around her, kissing the top of her head.

She turns in my arms and I hold her as we watch as the rest of our group go. They all suck and I really don't know why I come here to steal their money. It sort of makes me an asshole, but it's fun nonetheless, and if they want to donate to the "Jude likes food" fund, that's on them. As I hold Claire, I can't help but want to steal her and take her back to my house, hold her body and feel her against me as we sleep. As soon as that thought enters my head, I can't help but wonder who I'm becoming. There was a time when I wanted to get a girl home to fuck her, but I just want to cuddle with Claire. This girl has completely taken over my brain, and I don't mind one bit.

When it comes to my turn again, she turns in my arms and gives me this little puppy dog look that has me weak in the knees. Batting her eyelashes as me, her hands slide down my back to my ass where she grips it, causing me to groan, my eyes locked with hers.

"I hope you don't mess up," she says with a big innocent grin that I know is crap.

Removing her hands, I playfully push her away and set her with a look, totally surprised by her antics to win. I can't help but admire them, but still! I don't like being the victim of them.

"You play superdirty!" I accuse.

"Dirty is the only way to win," she says with a grin.

I eye her some more, and I know that I'm in trouble with this girl. Heading toward the stage, I know I am going to win, even with her ruthless playing. I know this song like I know the back of my hand. It's one of my warm-up songs and also a favorite. When the beat drops and "Talk Dirty" by Jason Derulo comes over the speakers, the girls lose it. I know everyone likes this song; I've sung it before and cleaned house against everyone. I start to work the crowd, acting as if I'm singing to everyone. Before I would have been, but now, I'm just trying to win. When I catch her gaze, she's glaring, but there is a grin on her face, so surely I'm not in trouble.

If I am, I'll worry about that after this. Right now, I gotta win.

When I finish the song, everyone is so loud that I think I'm playing hockey and not trying to kick my girl's ass in some karaoke. High-fiving people and receiving hugs and even numbers from girls, I head toward Claire and she's still giving me that glare. Reaching for her hand, I place the numbers in it and she rips them up before throwing them in the trash beside her.

"I was gonna do that," I say and she rolls her eyes.

"I'm sure you were. I'm just making sure it's done right."

Laughing, I say, "Aw, are you jealous, baby? That's so cute."

With her eyes in slits, she flips me the bird and walks past me. I smack her ass, and her hands go to cover her ass as she looks back at me, a beautiful, happy grin on her face. Sticking her tongue out at me, she goes to the DJ and I laugh all the way back to my seat.

"You are a completely different person when you're with her," Jayden says when I reach him.

I shrug. "Maybe."

"It's good, Jude, real good."

Looking away a tad bit embarrassed, I watch as Claire goes to the middle of the floor. When the music for "Drop it Low" by Ester Dean starts, I know I'm in trouble. Like I knew she would, as soon as she starts singing, her ass is wiggling and moving along with the beat, sending the guys in the pub into a frenzy. Holding on to the chair, I watch as my girl basically works her ass like a stripper would. Everyone in the pub is on their feet in no time, hollering and cheering her on as she not only sings well but works that ass like she wants the gold. Or better yet the hundred and twenty bucks that sits in the middle of the table. Dropping it down, she moves with the music, and while yes, it turns me on, I have to applaud her drive to win.

Bowing as everyone cheers and hollers, she stands back up and then looks over at me with a look that tells me she knows she just won. When she comes to the table and Hannah hands her the money, she grins at me as she steps over to me.

"Guess there's a new winner in town," she says, fanning the hundred dollars out and cooling herself with it.

"You cheated."

She laughs. "How?"

"Working that stage like a stripper! That's not fair, all that ass is memorizing!"

Something flashes in her eyes, but it's gone immediately, and she's laughing while looking away. "Good thing, huh?"

"How is that a good thing?!"

Looking up at me, she says, "'Cause all this ass is yours."

Something hot lights up her eyes and I reach for her, pulling her against me as I nod slowly. "Yeah, you're right, that is a good thing. A really good thing."

I may have lost, but really, with that last statement, I think I just won.

CHAPTER 21

JUDE

I love walking with Claire like this.

My arm is around her shoulders, her arm comes across her body and her fingers are laced with mine. She's tucked into my side, so close and it feels as if she's molded into me. Like a part of me, almost.

It's comfortable. It's right to me.

"I have to admit," she starts and I look down to meet her blazing blue gaze. "I didn't expect you to sing so well."

"Ah, underestimating me. How shitty of you." She laughs, and I smile before saying, "Yeah, my mom always says when I don't want to play hockey anymore that I need to sing, but I won't ever not want to play hockey."

"I haven't seen you play yet, but I know how hockey players are, and that's usually how it is. All-in or nothing."

I nod. "Yup, very true. You have a nice voice."

"Thanks," she says with a grin. "I have a karaoke voice but not a stage voice. I'm more of a dancer, I think."

"Yeah, I have to agree with you on that. I've seen you dance, which, by the way, what do you mean you haven't seen me play? That's just sad. We've been dating for almost a week, and you haven't seen me murder the ice yet. I'm so appalled."

She laughs, turning out of my arms and then dropping her hand from mine to wrap around my waist. Looking up into my eyes, she grins and I'm lost in her gaze. It's heart-stopping, honestly.

"I promise to come to your next practice. When is it?"

"Saturday, 5:30 a.m."

"Good God! Why?"

I laugh. "'Cause my coach is evil."

"Agreed. Jeez, yeah, I'll be there."

"Awesome," I say and she wraps her arms around me a little more firmly. My heart warms as she tucks back into my side and we begin walking again. I feel so right with her like this. I feel as if this is what I'm supposed to do all the time. Close to my girl, her body pressed to mine and walking, silently, with no cares in the world because I have her to myself. It's perfect.

When we reach the Bullies' house, I stop and look down at her. "So where are we going? Am I taking you back to your dorm, or are you staying here?"

She grins up at me. "Can you keep your hands to yourself?"

I smirk. "I can try, but more than likely, I won't."

"Should I go home then?"

"No, you should come in," I say, kissing her temple. We start for the door and she says, "I have to leave early though. I have to go dress shopping with Reese."

"Do you need a ride?"

"No, I'll go get my car and head out."

"Want to go get it now?"

She shrugs. "It doesn't matter."

"Yeah, let's go. We'll ride my bike."

It only takes a few minutes to get on the bike and head to her car. She points out her car and when I see that it's a BMW Z4 Roadster, I'm floored.

"Damn, you drive that?"

She laughs as she gets off the bike, handing me her helmet. "It's old. Don't get hard off it."

I scoff. "It doesn't matter how old it is, that sucker is beautiful."

"Yeah, funny thing is I used to think this car was ugly. I was wrong, obviously. I love her and her old ass – she's my girl. Anyway, I'll meet you over there."

"Cool," I say, still checking out her car and then checking her out as she gets in it. It's extremely sexy having a hot girl in a hot car. I have to adjust in my seat just to relieve some of the pressure my dick is causing in my jeans. Letting out a long breath, I can't help but think that it's gonna be hard, literally, sleeping beside a hot girl who drives a hot car. I'll manage, though.

Pulling away, I drive toward the house and wait out in the parking lot for her. She pulls up a few minutes after I do, and I laugh as she gets out of the car.

"With all the power that car has, you drive like an old lady?"

She glares. "For your information, I don't like getting tickets, and having this kind of car, campus police are on me like white on rice."

"Always so responsible," I tease, but when the heat flashes in her eyes, I am swallowing loudly.

"Let's go inside and I'll show you how irresponsible I can be," she says as she comes up to me, taking my face in her hands and pressing her mouth to mine. Wrapping my arms around her, I kiss her hard, holding her so close I'm sure she can't breathe, but I can't help it. Heat rolls off her body, and my dick is so hard against the zipper of my jeans that it hurts, but I just can't stop. I need to feel her, and the more we kiss, the more I know my earlier thought of not being able to sleep beside her and not be buried inside her rings true. But when she pulls away, her eyes blazing with lust, I know that I'll wait forever as long as I get to see that look after each kiss.

"That's against the rules," I point out, and she smiles a little minx-type grin.

"Maybe we can bend them a bit?"

I eye her, wondering if this is a trick. She could be testing me, but the lust in her eyes says she isn't, and I don't know how I feel about that. While I want nothing more than to lose myself completely in her, I know that I want her to know this is for real.

"Let's go in," I say roughly and she nods, looking so damn good it hurts.

Dragging my gaze away from her, I head inside, and as soon as the door shuts, all the guys who are on the couch look back at us. One by one, they grin, and I glare as they all shout out catcalls.

"Get it, Sinclair."

"Yeah, buddy, back on the horse."

"Damn, she's fine."

In my head, I'm planning Matt's funeral as I flip them off before heading downstairs to my room. "They're idiots."

"Most guys are."

I flash her a mock hurt look, and she laughs a little harder. "Except for you, babe."

"That's right," I say, wrapping my arms around her and then pushing her against the door, intending to go in for a long, lusty kiss, but before I can, it slams open and Jayden looks up from his computer, raising an eyebrow.

"Hey, guys," he says cautiously.

"Hey, leave," I say.

He glares and Claire smacks me.

"That's rude!" she scolds me and I laugh.

"Do you want him seeing you in panties and a bra?" I ask and her look says it all. No, she doesn't. Looking back at Jayden, I say, "'Cause I sure don't, so leave, Jay."

"No way. I was here first."

"I don't care, this room is off-limits for the night," I say, detangling myself from Claire and throwing my keys down.

"That's fucked up. You never cared before!" he says, grabbing his computer and then his pillow before standing up.

"You had sex with girls in front of your brother?" she gasps, bringing my attention back to her. "And you watched?"

I shrug. "They didn't matter."

"I didn't watch. I'm not a freak," Jayden says.

Shaking her head, she says, "That's so not okay."

"Yeah, probably wasn't. Bye, Jayden," I say as he passes by us.

"Fuck off!"

"Thanks," Claire calls.

"You're lucky she's nice!" Jayden yells as he stomps up the stairs.

I shut the door and then glance down at her.

"I think he might be upset."

Laughing, she says, "I think so. Can't blame him."

"Ah, he can room with a freshman if he's that mad. I need privacy with my girl," I say, wrapping my arms around her and pulling her in close, nuzzling her neck.

"Isn't he a freshman? Why is he sharing with you?"

Pulling away, I kiss her jaw before letting her go to remove my shirt. "'Cause my mom wanted to make sure he was safe, and plus freshmen are dirty. I'm not."

She looks around my room and nods. "Yeah, I can see that."

I flash her a grin before pulling off my pants and then locking the door. Running toward the bed, I jump onto the small trampoline I use for cardio when I'm bored and bounce up onto the bed. Feeling like a badass, I send her a grin.

"Impressive," she says, but I don't think she thinks I'm as cool as I do.

"Thanks," I say with a wink. "Care to join me in my love bed in the sky?"

Giving me a look that tells me she's not impressed with my love bed in the sky, she says, "Have you washed the sheets lately?"

That came off a little sharp. "Of course," I say slowly, eyeing her. "Wait, are you mad 'cause girls have been in my bed?"

"I'm not mad," she says as she removes her shirt and then leggings, leaving her in a delicious pink push-up bra and matching thong. "I don't care. Just don't call it some stupid love bed in the stupid sky."

Yup, she's mad.

"You're such a liar," I say as she climbs the ladder to my bed.

"Whatever. And what grown man sleeps in a bunk bed!"

I chuckle as I shrug. "It's not really a bunk bed 'cause Jayden's bed is over there instead of under mine."

"Still, it's weird," she says with a snotty little look as she lies beside me.

Laughing, I look over at her. "Stop."

"Stop what? I'm doing nothing," she says, cuddling up with my blanket, but I pull it away and cover her body with mine.

She looks up at me, stunned and maybe a little turned on, but soon her snotty look is back, and it only makes me harder. I know she feels every inch of me, and I'm going to make her wetter than a pool in a second, but first I need to nip this in the bud.

"Stop," I say, meeting her defiant gaze. "What did I say to Jayden? Those girls didn't matter. You matter. I don't want anyone looking at your body but me."

She looks away as she shrugs. "I don't know why it bothers me, I really don't. I just don't get it. Why did you think it was okay to have no respect for those girls?"

Leaning on my elbows, I let my weight fall on her as I meet her gaze again. "Because it was no challenge. They gave it to me like you give a kid candy. It was easy and fast and I didn't have to put any emotion into it. You're right that I had no respect for them, but it's different with you."

"Why, though? It doesn't make sense to me."

"You made me work for it the first time I met you. You didn't just fall in bed with me, and then when you did, I wondered if I should. I actually questioned my motives with you, and I knew that it meant something, you know?"

She brings her lip between her teeth and then lets out a breath. "So what happens when it's not a challenge anymore?"

"It isn't a challenge now, Claire," I say slowly.

"Yes, it is! I won't give it up."

I nod. "Maybe, but I don't need it. I need you. I need this."

She reaches up and cups my cheek, her thumb slowly moving through the scruff on my jaw. I need to shave but I have no real urge to. Looking deep in my eyes, she asks, "So you aren't addicted to sex or anything?"

I laugh, breaking our intense stare-off, and shake my head. "I'm addicted to you, Claire. I don't want anyone but you."

Meeting her gaze again, I see hers is full of heat, and I swear I see her whole heart. My chest constricts while everything inside me goes hot. This girl is going to be the death of me with only a full-of-heart look. It's intense. We are intense.

"This isn't about sex, is it?"

"It isn't for me," I answer. "Is it for you?"

She shakes her head before I get the whole sentence out. "Not at all," she says. Then she asks, "You like me, don't you?"

I nod slowly, leaning down, my lips only a breath from hers. "Oh yeah, I do. A whole fucking lot, too."

"I feel the same," she whispers.

Getting lost in her eyes, feeling her heart bang against mine, feeling the heat between her legs... It's too much to handle and soon the words are out of my mouth before I can even process them.

"I think I'm falling for you."

Her thumb pauses on my cheek as her eyes go wide. "Seriously?"

My heart is in my throat. Fuck. She doesn't feel the same. Looking down at her nose, I take in a deep breath, embarrassed, feeling so dumb. Why would I say something so fucking stupid? So soon?

Before I can even say anything, she brings her face down some so she can meet my gaze. "I feel the same, Jude. Don't hide. I just thought that I was crazy for thinking that. I mean, it's only been a week, and I'm convinced you are the guy I could fall completely for."

My heart falls out of my throat and hits my stomach hard, leaving me breathless. "I know I can, with you and only you."

"I've never trusted anyone, Jude. It took Reese and Phillip forever for me to fall for them and trust them. I don't know why it's so easy with you. This world is full of empty promises and false hope, but when I look at you, I don't feel that. I feel all these crazy butterflies and shit. They scare the hell out of me because I've been hurt so many times, but I just have this urge to jump with you. To trust you, completely, no matter what."

Cupping her face, I feel like I can't breathe because that's everything I feel. I feel like this is real. Like it's forever-type shit, as insane as it is. "I know you've been hurt, and I know that people have not been the greatest to you, but I want to change that. I want to be good for you. Worthy of you. I want to make you proud."

Closing her eyes, she brings me down, our lips touching ever so softly. Parting, I kiss her gently again, enjoying the sweet tenderness of our kisses. Pulling back, I look down at her, and she is just so beautiful. Her eyes are heavy-lidded, her lips parted and swollen from my kisses. Her breasts are pushed up against my chest, her hands at my sides holding me close while stray pieces of her hair fall from her braid.

"You're so beautiful. So amazing, Claire."

She cups me behind my neck and brings me down to her lips for a long heart-pounding kiss. My whole body catches on fire, moving against her, rubbing myself to the point that I'm sure I'm going to come in my boxers. Our limbs are tangled, our mouths moving together in such a perfect way. I'm humming with awareness of her, our breaths coming so harshly while we continue to tease and drive each other crazy. I know I should stop this. I already can't see straight and I'm harder than a board, but I can't seem to pull my mouth from hers.

Finally, she does and I thank the Lord above, but then she whispers, "Make love to me."

Everything stops. I'm frozen, and oh God, how I want to. My dick jumps to life, pointing right to her heavenly center, but my brain is screaming that it isn't time yet. We have to wait. No matter how much we both want it, it's better this way. This way I know she'll never doubt me, doubt us, because if I can hold out from being inside this beautiful woman, I have to love her. That's all there is to it. Maybe I need it too. Maybe this is the real test to show me that I don't need anything or anyone but her.

Shaking my head slowly, my lips dust against hers as her breath comes out in a whoosh. "We have eight days left."

"Bending the rules, remember?"

I shake my head. "No rule bending, you naughty girl. We're in this together."

Moving her hands into my boxers, she cups my ass, pressing her center against my raging hard-on, and fuck, I go cross-eyed. Letting out a ragged breath, I take in another deep one as she says, "I want you, though."

"Oh baby, you have no idea how much I want you," I basically whimper. "But it's better if we wait. Remember, guarantees and showing you you're the one and all that jazz. Please, don't make this any harder than it already is," I say, pleading. "I don't think I can keep saying no."

A grin crosses her lips as her hands leave my body and come between us. I think she's going to touch my dick and ignore my plea. If she does do that, fuck it, put a fork in me, I'm done. But to my surprise, her hand goes into her panties.

Meeting her gaze, I know my eyes are wide as she says, "I'm so fucking turned on, Jude. I have to get off, and if you won't do it for me, I have to. I just do."

She moans as her fingers touch her center, and I can't speak. I can't even think. Somehow, I push myself up, giving her room to touch herself. With her eyes locked on mine, she starts to finger herself and I can't breathe. Falling back on my haunches, I reach for her thong and pull it off her, throwing it over my shoulder so I can watch her fingers slowly move in her wet pussy. I've never had a girl finger herself in front of me like this; my dick is rock hard. I can't see straight but somehow I continue to watch her, my heart pounding in my chest as I watch her fingers glisten with her wetness, teasing me in the most unfair way. I want my mouth on her, I want to lick her pussy dry, but I know if I touch her, I'm going to lose it. I'm going to fuck her so hard that both of us won't be moving for the next twelve hours.

Closing her eyes, her hand pulls her bra up, catching her nipple between her fingers as she slowly fucks herself with her beautiful fingers. The thought that she must do this often turns me on even more, and I'm not sure how I'm still sitting here without touching her.

I must fucking care. A whole hell of a lot because soon she's panting, moaning sweetly as she plays with her clit, her eyes meeting mine again, and my body is so tight, I don't dare move. I'm scared even the littlest move and I'll fall dick-first inside her, intentionally. Holding my gaze in her hot, lusty, dirty one, she runs her tongue along her lip and then her whole body seizes up. She moans out loudly, hitting her climax, and fucking hell, my balls draw up and I'm fucking coming in my boxers.

Bracing my hands on my knees, I take in a deep breath and let it out in a whoosh. I don't, can't move for what seems like hours. I've never done that. I always have to touch my dick to come. I've never just come from just watching a girl get off. Fuck, that was hot. When her hands come up to my face and her mouth presses against mine, I melt against her, wrapping my arms around her.

Parting slowly, I kiss her bottom lip, then her chin before meeting her satisfied gaze. "I wish you would have done it for me. I was hoping you would take over."

"Yeah, I wanted to, baby, but I couldn't trust myself," I admit.

A sneaky grin comes over her lips as her arms hang loosely around my neck. "So eight more days of this?"

"Yes, eight fucking days."

She giggles as I unhook her arms before climbing down the ladder. When I throw my boxers off and into the hamper, she asks, "What are you doing?"

"Well, while you were getting off, I got off, in my boxers."

"You came in your boxers?" she asks, her face red and laughter playing in her wide eyes.

"Yes, Claire, see what you do to me?"

"Sorry?"

I flash her a dark look. "Don't be sorry, that was the hottest fucking thing I've ever seen."

Her sneaky grin is back, and I try to ignore it as I pick up her thong, handing it back to her. Hitting the light, I climb the ladder and then get under the covers with her, pulling her body close against mine. After I kiss her temple, she nuzzles into my neck and soon sleep takes over.

⁂

The next morning, I feel her moving and I wake up reaching for her, but she's already getting dressed. When I see Jayden in bed, I glare but then look back at Claire as she comes up to the side. Why the hell is he in here? Asshole.

"He's asleep. Don't worry, he didn't see anything."

"I'm still gonna kick his ass," I say, glaring.

"Don't, Jude, he just wants to sleep in his bed."

Meeting her sweet gaze, I shrug, deciding I won't kick my brother's ass, or maybe I will and not tell her. Cupping her face, I ask, "Are you heading out?"

With a grin, she leans into my hand and says, "Yeah, I gotta meet Reese in five. I'm running late," she says with a guilty grin. "I'll call you when I'm done. Thanks for last night."

Leaning over the rail, I kiss her lips and smile as she pulls away. "Anytime. Have fun."

"I will," she says with a little wave and then she's gone. I thought it would be hard for me to go back to sleep but soon I knock back out. When the dinging of my phone wakes me up not even an hour later, I want to be mad, but when I open the text to find my girl in a floor-length, backless blue dress, I couldn't be mad if I tried. She's gorgeous, and I love the way the blue looks on her skin. The dress hugs every inch of her, and it's a mouthwatering sight.

Then I see the text underneath, and as I read, there is no wiping the grin off my face.

> *Claire: Will you be my date to my uncle and aunt's wedding if I wear this? And it's in two weeks so you'll more than likely get laid afterward.*

As I quickly type back, I can't help but wonder how does she not know that I'd do basically anything for her?

CHAPTER 22

 Claire

know I look dumb sitting in a floor-length gown with my phone glued to my hands waiting for a text from Jude, but I have to know if he will go. While I know it's superearly to ask him to go to a wedding for my overprotective, crazy uncle and my beautiful aunt, he invited me to meet his mom, and also we basically declared that we're falling in love with each other. And then I fingered myself in front of him. And he came in his boxers. So, I figure asking him to go to a wedding isn't that weird. Right? Ah! I don't know; he isn't answering me!

Letting my arms fall on my legs against the silky fabric of the royal blue bridesmaid dress, I let out a frustrated breath. I do love this dress, though. I wasn't sure when Reese pulled it out, but now that it's on me, I love it. It's very formfitting all the way to my knees then it goes out in beautiful layers of fabric in a mermaid style. The back goes down to right above my butt, but then the top has this beautiful lace that comes along my shoulders and chest, giving a peekaboo of my chest, but in a very classy and beautiful way. I thought when I came here today that I was going to be wearing some crap dress, but Reese had other plans. It's a gorgeous dress and I know I should be admiring it, but I can't help but wonder what the hell is taking so long to answer my text! He can't be asleep! Or crap, maybe he is?

Ugh! I'm about to toss my damn phone and figure this is his way of saying no when a text comes through.

> *Hey Jude: I would go with u if all that wasn't in play. All u have to do is ask. But btw, u look crazy hot in that dress.*

Smiling like a complete dork, I type:

Me: Fine, will u, Jude Sinclair, be my date to my crazy uncle and aunt's impromptu wedding? And btw, thanks. I thought u might like it.

Hey Jude: Yes. I would love to. Crazy uncle and all.

Before I can type back, another text comes through.

Hey Jude: And btw, I can't wait to peel that dress off ur sexy body.

Feeling all hot, I type back: Thank u. We'll talk details later.

Then I send another one. And btw, I can't wait for u to do just that.

Hey Jude: btw...I miss u.

Me: btw... I miss u more.

A dreamy grin comes across my face as I lean on my hand, staring at his words. I've never been one to daydream, but staring at the simple words, I find myself imagining our life together in the future. Him playing in the NHL while I cheer him on after getting done at the studio that I'll have, maybe being pregnant and being a big, happy family...

"What are you doing?"

I look up to find Reese coming toward me, and my mouth promptly drops to the ground.

"Oh, Reese," I gasp, holding back the tears as she walks up on the little platform. She's gorgeous. That's all I can say. Simply stunning. When she told me her dress was amazing, she wasn't lying. With a bright, happy grin on her face, she stands tall in a sheer lace dress with a silk underlay. It's long-sleeved with the lace coming along her arms to her fingers in a royal, classy way. The front dips all the way down to the middle of her chest, showing a beautiful but elegant view of her breasts. I know that will be Phillip's favorite part, but then I see the back. Breathtaking. Unlike my plain back, her gorgeous black tree tattoo covers her whole back and is on display since the dress is completely backless. The lace molds to her skin like it was meant to be there and then splays along the floor, making her look like a beautiful princess.

A lady walks behind her, laying the back of the dress out, and I take in every single, beautiful detail. The diamond studded belt, the birdcage veil, the sheer elegance of the dress. It's stunning. She's stunning.

"God, Reese, you're gorgeous," I breathe as tears well up in my eyes. "So gorgeous."

Standing, I let my hand fall to my side and she grins at me, holding in her own tears. "Thank you, Claire. I was hoping you'd love it as much as I do."

"I do."

"Good, I love your dress too. We're getting it."

"Okay," I say, knowing that she's right, but I can't take my eyes off her. I've seen her every way, from dolled up to the nines to looking like bear crap with the flu, and she's always been gorgeous. But seeing her like this, a bride, is mind-blowing. She never wanted this. She never wanted to be tied down to a guy, but she is, and she loves him. And she loves me, the troubled teen who was hell-bent on ruining them all. She never stopped loving me too. I think it was always love at first sight for the both of us. She was my person and I am hers. I may tease her about this wedding, but I'm so excited I can't contain it.

My two favorite people are becoming one. It gives me hope, really, that not all people are shit. They show me the meaning of love, that people stick things out even when they don't want to, and I'm so grateful to be there every step of the way. I'm scared shitless of doing this with Jude. Completely trusting him… But I don't think there is another way. If he breaks my heart, cheats on me, and leaves me, then at least I'll know I tried. Phillip and Reese tried, and look, now she's in a wedding dress. You just have to try.

I look back at Reese and her hands come up to her stomach as she takes in a deep breath, meeting my gaze in the mirror. "Do you think Phillip will love it?"

I nod slowly. "He's gonna be floored. That dress was made for you, Reese. It's amazing."

She smiles and my heart comes out of my chest when a tear slowly rolls down her cheek. Coming up on the platform with her, I wrap my arms around her and she hugs me back tightly, kissing my temple before I nuzzle my face in her neck. As I hold her, I can't believe how much everything has changed. How did I go from having such a crappy life, where I basically didn't care if I lived or died, to now having all this?

An uncle and aunt who love me.

And now a guy who's falling for me.

I sorta want to pinch myself to make sure it's all real.

⁂

After getting the dresses packaged up and carried to the car for Reese to take home, we head down the road to our favorite sushi place. Sitting in the booth, we order before settling into easy conversation that comes naturally to us. Everyone always assumes we're sisters, and while I don't mind that, I consider her more my mom than anything. She's stern when she needs to be and loves me unconditionally. It's a great balance, and I love her for it. My mom was never that way. All she cared about was the men, drugs, and the booze; I was always a ninth thought. It sucked, but I learned from it, and I feel like it's made me stronger. I thought I didn't need anyone back then, I thought I was fine on my own, but now I know I was so wrong.

I could have lived without love, but I learned I thrive with it. And now that I've have it, I can't be without it.

"Remember you have that pole class next week," Reese reminds me as I stuff my face with a piece of sushi.

Nodding while covering my mouth, I chew up the piece and then wash it down with water before saying, "Yeah, Wednesday, is everyone coming?"

She smiles. "Well, Piper is bitching 'cause she's pregnant and doesn't know why I'm making her continue the class when she's getting bigger, but I told her to shut up. We started as a group, we'll finish as a group."

"Awesome, I can't wait to see everyone," I say, speaking of my Assassins family.

"Yeah, they are excited. I heard Fallon is getting a pole installed in the bedroom," she laughs and I laugh along.

"I bet Uncle Lucas loves that."

"You know he does," she says, shaking her head. "They are crazy, but it's fun."

"Agreed. I'm using that dance for one at Ms. Prissy's. Do you think that's bad? Like recycling dances?"

"No, not at all. It's a private class. We're just testing the waters, no big deal."

"Okay, cool," I say. "Ms. Prissy was telling me some investors are coming."

"Wow," Reese says, looking up at me. "That's huge. When I was there, we had some come from Florida and Texas – opened up two new Prissy's and I even went to train the staff. It's a lot of fun and lots of money to be made. I actually had the chance to run one of the Prissy's, but I had just been accepted to the dance company. Make sure those are the best dances you've ever come up with for the club. This could be good for your career."

"Yeah," I say as my stomach drops. "Do you think it could be a career? Burlesque?"

She nods as she meets my gaze. "Claire, you could be the best burlesque choreographer I've ever seen. You have amazing talent. That's why Ms. Prissy pays you way more than she ever paid me. You're doing well for yourself. Not everyone can say they make two grand for a two-minute piece at the age of nineteen. Lord knows, I couldn't. You could own your own club and succeed, so make sure you impress those investors."

"I will. I really want this. I think that it would be good not only for Ms. Prissy but for me."

"It can be. Believe me. Big things can happen, babe."

I smile, excited about it all. I've been thinking about it a lot and hoping that maybe this is my break to get into the world of dance. Choreographing amazing dances for Las Vegas shows would be amazing, and I love burlesque. It's so sexy and fun, and I know I'm good at it.

"Can I come and show you what I've got so far?" I ask, needing her support.

"Of course."

"Thanks," I say and then I chew on my lip for a moment, mulling over the words in my head before I ask what I've been wanting to ask for a while. Reese had worked for Ms. Prissy all summer long for four years when she was home from college. She would also sell pieces to Ms. Prissy by videotaping them and sending them to her when she was gone. Like she'd said, Ms. Prissy paid her well, but she pays me better. Which works great for me – I'm making a lot of money and doing something I love. Not many people can say that.

But that's not what's bothering me. I'm good with my money and my work, but I'm not good with hiding it from Jude or even Phillip.

Looking across the table, I ask, "So did anyone know you worked there?"

She shakes her head. "Nope. Not even Piper knew until my third year there. Then she started working there," she says with a laugh.

I smile as I pick up a piece of sushi before throwing it in my mouth. When my phone starts to sound with a text, I chew my piece as I dig my phone out of my pocket to see that it's a text from Jude.

> Hey Jude: Wanna eat some food on a blanket outside?
> I laugh. Like a picnic.
> Hey Jude: saying do u want to have a picnic makes me sound like a girl, so wanna eat on a blanket outside?
> Me: Weirdo. Will there be waffles?
> Hey Jude: there will be now.
> Me: Then yes, I'll love to have a picnic with you.
> Hey Jude: haha. 7ish?
> Me: sounds good.
> Hey Jude: btw…I miss u.
> Me. Btw…I miss u way, way more.
> Hey Jude: I doubt that.

"Jude?"

I glance up from my phone to meet Reese's knowing gaze. Tucking my phone in my pocket, I shrug. "Yeah, how did you know?"

A grin pulls at the side of her mouth before she takes a drink of her water. "Only a guy can put that grin on your face. You're basically glowing, Claire."

"It's no big deal," I say even though I know I'm lying my ass off. I look away shyly. I don't know why I'm shy about him, but I am, especially in front of Reese. I don't get why, because with anyone else I'm loud and proud, but she knows me. She can see through me in a heartbeat and will know that he means more to me then I'll let on.

"Don't lie to me. He means something to you and that's good," she says and then pauses. When I look up, I see that she's watching me. "Is he the reason you asked who knew about me in the club?"

"Yeah," I say, picking up a napkin and tearing it apart. "I haven't told him and I feel like I'm lying to him. I don't want to do that because this is new and perfect, and oh God, Reese, I'm falling for him. He means so much to me in such a short amount of time, and honestly, I don't think I could lose him."

She nods, a smile playing on her lips. "That's wonderful, Claire. I'm so happy for you and can't wait to see this blossom for you. I didn't have a boyfriend back then, so it was different for me, but I'm assuming that you think Jude won't like his girlfriend dancing for a group of men. Even if it is in a classy way like burlesque dancing."

"I don't think so," I say. "But I can't quit. I need the security of that money."

Her face scrunches up, and I regret the words I say as soon as they leave my lips. I just got myself in a world of trouble.

"We've been through this, Claire. You don't need money – we will take care of you."

"I know you guys will, but I don't want to depend on you my whole life. I have to stand on my own two feet."

"I understand that, but you don't have to do something you are ashamed of to make ends meet. We will take care of you."

"I'm not ashamed," I say, but that's not the whole truth. I love doing this, but I know that Phillip and Jude won't like it, and because of that, I'm ashamed. Shaking my head, I whisper, "I have to take care of myself."

"I wish I could slap your mother. God rest her soul, but I mean, shit, Claire. How much do we have to do to reassure you that we aren't going anywhere? All these years have passed. Have we left? No, we're here for the long haul. Beside you, loving you, you know we love you, right?"

I nod, meeting her gaze. "Of course I do, but–"

"That's all that matters," she says, "We love you. Nothing will ever stop that. You have to quit with this. I know people have come and gone in your life, but sweetheart, we aren't going anywhere."

I want to trust and believe that, I do, but it's hard. But I grew up with my mom saying, "No one stays forever," and I believed her. Reese and Phillip could decide they are done with me in an instant. Hell, Jude could too, but while I pick up the pieces of my heart, I have to have something to fall back on. I have to have that security. Money is that. I will always have food and shelter as long as I have money.

Reaching for my hand, she squeezes my fingers and I look up at her. "Answer me this: do you like dancing onstage?"

I bite the inside of my cheek so hard I taste blood so I let up. I don't want to answer her because I know what she's going to say. But I also know I can't lie to her. "I don't like the attention sometimes. I don't like dancing as someone else, and I don't like when we get the drunks who try to grab me and shit, but I love the idea of burlesque."

"Then you quit. Right now."

I'm shaking my head before she finishes the sentence. I ignore her irritated look and say, "Reese, I need another twenty grand and I'll quit. I'll have enough for a studio and a decent life after I graduate. Not much longer, a month or two at the most. I want to do this investors thing too."

Eyeing me, she doesn't say anything for a long time, and then she asks, "I can't talk you out of this, can I? You're gonna do it no matter what? You know you can do the investors thing offstage."

I nod. "Yeah, I know, but I make so much money onstage. I can't walk away from that, plus Ms. Prissy would freak if I quit. I'm her best dancer."

"I know, honey, but if you don't like it, you don't have to do it."

"I know, but I do like it…sometimes, and I think in my heart I know y'all will never leave me, but I'm scared. I need this security. Please just let me get it and then I'll quit. I promise."

"Two months, that's it."

"Two months. Then I'll quit. But what should I do about Jude?"

Shaking her head, she says, "Quit, or tell him."

"I'm afraid if I tell him he'll leave. I know it hasn't been that long, but I don't want to lose him."

"If he leaves, then he doesn't deserve you. But you need to be honest or this will blow up in your face. This is a respectable business; it's not like being a stripper. You aren't that."

I know she's right, but maybe I can just keep it quiet for another two months. Though, that just doesn't seem right. I feel as if I'm not giving him all of me and I hate that. I know he's an all-in kind of guy, and I feel like he deserves the same from me, but I don't know how to share this with him.

Looking across the table, I know she's frustrated with me. Maybe even a little hurt. "Are you mad?"

Looking at me, she says, "No. I'm hurt. I thought we'd done everything we could to make you feel secure in our love, but I guess not."

"No, you have, I promise. I'm just scared, Reese. I love you guys. I couldn't be the person I am without you."

"Then quit."

"In two months, please. Two months, Reese."

Shaking her head, she takes in a deep breath and then lets it go. "Fine, but you need to tell Phillip too while you're at it. Especially if this becomes something you're going to do forever. I know that you may be scared that he'll be mad, but I bet you he won't. He wants whatever is going to make you happy."

"I know that, but he still isn't going to like that I'm onstage."

"No, but he'll get over it as soon as you tell him this is something you want to make into a career. You're good at it, beautiful at it. Phillip is all about what makes us happy, and that's all that matters. He always says as long as his girls are happy, life is good. That's what a good man does. He loves you for all of you and supports you in what you want to do. I bet if you tell Jude the same thing, he'll understand. You just have to believe that."

"I love making dances and I love the sexiness of burlesque," I admit and she smiles. "But I'm worried they won't see it that way, they'll think it's stripping or something degrading. No one has ever seen my tits or vagina."

"I agree, and I'm sure they will too."

"I just want to be happy."

"Then do it, baby. But be honest. Don't hide what you are proud of. You just have to be honest. Honest about everything, Claire. Don't hold back. I'm sure he'll understand and support you."

I sure do hope so.

But something tells me that, while Phillip might do as Reese says, Jude is a whole other situation.

One that scares the hell out of me.

CHAPTER 23

 *Claire*

When I'm not dancing with the dance team, I'm at the studio, and when I'm not at the studio, I'm dancing at Ms. Prissy's. Somehow, between all this, I'm also going to school, studying, and falling for Jude Sinclair a little more each day.

It's magical, really.

I should be overwhelmed and stressed out, but for the last six days, I've felt amazing. Perfect even. He makes everything so easy. It's not hard to be with him and I enjoy that. I don't want to work to like someone, and I feel like it shouldn't be like that. It should be easy, and with him, it is. He's honestly my favorite person right now, and that's saying a lot because I love Phillip and Reese something crazy. But there is something about Jude that makes me breathless and excited for every second I get to be with him.

I just enjoy him.

I love learning things about him, discovering his likes and dislikes. I mean, he loves candy but only fruity stuff. No chocolate! I told him he was nuts, but when he told me he wasn't a big fan of cake, I told him I didn't think this relationship would work. He proved otherwise by kissing the hell out of me and letting me know I'm not going anywhere without him. It's little things like that that just make me all ooey and gooey inside. He's so fun to talk to especially when he talks about all the trouble he and his brothers got into, which was a lot. He has so many stories, and while I love his versions, I bet his mom's versions of everything will be more entertaining. I am nervous about meeting her and the rest of his family, but in a way, I'm good with it. I know that he respects his mom and loves her more than anything, but I figure if after all this time he hadn't been with anyone, and now he's bringing me home, Mrs. Sinclair is bound to love me or hate me. Hoping for the first option!

While this week has been amazing getting know him even more, my favorite part besides cuddling with him has been watching him play hockey. Don't get me wrong, I'm not a fan of early mornings, especially when I'm out till four in the morning dancing, but I would honestly get up every single morning to watch Jude play. And I have for the last three days. I used to think that Phillip was the best player I'd ever seen, and maybe I'm being biased because I like the guy, but my God, he is phenomenal. He's so quick, knows the game like the back of his hand, and makes the plays that need to be made. He's a little selfish with the puck, but it's because he knows he can score, and I admire that. He told me he's learning to be a better team player, but he can't resist making the big plays, and I love watching him do it.

It's almost like he is the whole package to me. He's sweet, romantic, and so damn honest. If he doesn't like something, he tells me, and he makes it known when he does like something. Again, it's just so damn easy. I can lie on him and read a book and not worry about a damn thing. It's all just so comfortable. We fit together when we sleep, we like the same foods, and the boy can kiss my socks off. I'm falling for him. That's all there is to it, and I can't figure out how that makes me feel. On one hand, I am all for it – hell yeah, let's do this! But, on the other hand, what if I give him all of me and he decides that some other girl is more worth his time? I know that every person has that fear, but unlike other people, I can't just stop. I have to be with him – I have to see him, talk to him, and kiss him. I need him. I can't turn around and run like I want to; I'm rooted to this guy.

Knowing that I'm going to see him in a matter of hours to head out to his family's house makes me extremely excited. To my surprise, I'm more excited about seeing him than seeing my Assassins family, and I kinda feel like an asshole for that. These are my favorite women ever. I shouldn't be counting down the minutes to the end of this class to see Jude, but…I am. That makes me an asshole, huh? I just can't help it!

Taking off my shirt and sweatpants, I fold them before hitting the floor to stretch. I'm wearing my bra that Reese got me. It says "Get Sexy" on it, and on the ass of my booty shorts, it says "One pole at a time." To say that Phillip didn't like the outfit at all is an understatement and further supports my claim that he's probably going to lock me up when I finally get the balls to tell him about Ms. Prissy's. He knows that Reese used to work there, but it's different with me. I'm his niece, basically his daughter, and I don't think he's going to support me. No matter how excited I am about the investors.

Just the other night, I performed and started teaching the choreographed numbers I had come up with, and Ms. Prissy was blown away. She joked that I was going to be taking over the business, and it pleased me beyond belief. I called Reese at two in the morning just to tell her. I'm excited, and a part of me can see the bright lights of Las Vegas. The only thing I hope is that Jude gets picked up by either the Ducks or the Kings… Oh, and that he stays with me when he finds out I dance for horny men.

My phone dings and I head to my bag to get it, and when I see the message is from Jude, I say, "Speak of the devil and he shall appear."

> Hey Jude: U want me to pick u back up at 5 right?
> Me: Yeah, I'll be ready, my class gets over at 4:15, I'll be down there by then.
> Hey Jude: Ok, awesome, see you soon.
> Me: Great.

I go to put my phone down, but before I can, another text comes through. Leaning against the pole, I click on it and smile as I read his text.

> Hey Jude: btw…I miss u a whole heck of a lot.

I smile as my heart soars. I didn't get to see him but for a few minutes yesterday since Tuesdays are insane for both of us. I have an afternoon class, dance, and then classes here at the studio, and he has an afternoon class and hockey that night. Because of that, we only had about ten minutes to see each other and it wasn't nearly enough, so I know exactly what he means.

> Me: btw…I miss u a whole heck of a lot…more.
> Hey Jude: ☺
> Me: <3 See you soon.

Pushing off the pole, I head to my bag and toss my phone in it. Standing up, I glance out at where ten dance poles are set up for the new class Reese and I are trying out. We already have tons of moms signing up for it, but I want to practice on my family first. The training for pole dancing was amazing, and I've been using a lot of what I learned from it, but mostly I use stuff from the club. My main goal is to make them feel sexy, and since that comes easily to me, this is fun. The great thing is that it encourages fitness too, and my aunt Elli has already lost ten pounds this month from doing it each week!

Holding on to the pole, I spin myself around as I wait, but I don't get all the way around before the door opens and in piles my adopted family. Rushing to Harper, I hug her tightly as she kisses my cheek. She helped raise me when Phillip would travel for hockey and I love her for it. She's Reese's older sister and treats me like I'm hers. When Elli Adler grabs me, I just relax against her. Her arms have always been home to me. Even being the owner of the Nashville Assassins doesn't keep her from coming to all my events and sending me loving texts. She has been a constant presence in my life, and it's refreshing having her in it. I hug Fallon Brooks and Audrey Odder next. They are sisters, and while I love them, I'm not as close to them as I am to Harper, Elli, and Piper. They trust me enough to watch their kids when they need me to, so that has to mean something. When Piper snags me, I grin as I hug her tightly before bending down to kiss her belly.

"So, tell me what it is," I demand, but she shakes her head. Unlike her twin sister, she's the light version to Reese's dark. They have the same face, but she's more petite, with blue eyes and light brown hair, while Reese is tall with brown eyes and hair. She's so beautiful pregnant, and I wish she wouldn't have waited as long as she has to have another one. Dimitri, her son, is probably my favorite kid in the whole wide world. I am beyond excited for this little baby. Sometimes I wish Reese and Phillip would have kids, but I know that won't happen. Reese doesn't want kids and has repeatedly said I'm enough.

"No, not telling. It's a surprise." Piper grins, rubbing her belly affectionately.

"Tease." I glare playfully, a grin pulling at my lips as I hold her little belly in my hands. She isn't showing much, but I know it's in there.

She smiles, but then her brows come together and she eyes me slowly. "Something is different about you."

"You losing weight?" Harper asks and then Elli nods.

"I was gonna ask the same. You look thin, Claire. Make sure you eat. I know it's stressful with school, but you have to eat."

I roll my eyes, dropping my hands from Piper's belly. "I'm eating guys, I promise."

"It's her glow that's throwing you guys off," Reese says, wrapping her arm around my waist. "She's dating."

All of them grin and make little noises of delight as I glare up at Reese. "Thanks."

"Anytime," she says with a wink.

"Who is he?" Harper asks.

"How old is he?" Audrey asks next.

"Is he hot?" Fallon asks with a wag of her eyebrows.

"Does he treat you right?" Piper asks.

"Does he play hockey?" Elli asks and I shake my head, even though I knew this was going to happen.

"His name is Jude, he's twenty, he's hot, he treats me like a princess, and, yes, he plays hockey," I answer, and they all seem pleased.

"As long as he plays hockey, he's good for ya," Elli says with a wink before standing by her pole and kicking off her shoes.

"You know there is more to life than hockey? Right?" Audrey asks her, but Elli shakes her head.

"No, hockey is life, and a guy who plays hockey is the best kind of guy.

Hockey players are the best, in my opinion, and all of you agree 'cause y'all are all with one," she says with a grin and I laugh.

"She's right. Hockey players are hot," Reese says and then takes her shirt off.

I agree completely, especially after seeing Jude kill the ice, but I don't say that because I notice my aunt has a gut. Something she doesn't have unless she stress eats, which happens a lot when Phillip is gone. Poking her in the stomach, I ask, "Stress eating before the wedding?"

Glaring at me, she pulls back and smacks my arm, hard. "Shut up, I am not."

"Ow!" I complain, holding my arm where it stings.

"You are looking pudgy, Reese, but I mean that with all the love in the world," Elli says when Reese sends her a dark look.

"I don't. You're getting fat. What's wrong with you? It's a wedding that you wanted, remember?" Harper says, always the blunt one out of the bunch.

"You did," Piper says. "I was there when you told Phillip that y'all are getting married as soon as possible."

Reese reaches for her shirt and throws it back on. "Screw you guys," she mumbles as she goes by her pole.

"I mean, you're still so hot," I say, feeling bad, but then she looks at me, fighting a grin, and I know she isn't mad.

"Don't suck up to me now."

I laugh along with everyone else and then walk to the stereo. I'm not a fan of the sound quality in this room, but Reese guarantees me that she's getting that fixed before we start real classes. The room used to be Reese's old apartment, but we turned it into a studio. I used to do solos up here, but now we've turned it into the "Get Sexy" room.

Turning around, I look at everyone and smile. All of them so different but the same. They are all extremely successful women and are all so beautiful, but each one of them is her own person. I love these women. They are my people – my family, my foundation – and I am thankful for that. As I stand here, I can't help but think what Reese said is true. I want to believe her, know that I don't need the security of money when I have all this love, but it's so hard to do. It's like I'm programmed to make sure I have a security blanket, and maybe it's smart but dumb at the same time because at any second, I could lose two people I care for. Phillip could turn his back on me like he did my mother and his sister and so could Jude.

I need to be honest.

Not now, but soon.

Right now I have a job to do.

Taking in a deep breath, I look out at my dancers and smile. "So does everyone remember the dance?"

A few shrugs and shy looks from everyone except for Reese. She nods with confidence as Piper says, "I know it, but I think I'm gonna look dumb with this big ol' gut!"

"Never! You aren't even that big!" I say with a shake of my head. "It's about being sexy, hot, just move with the confidence that you are the sexiest chick in the world and Erik is sitting in front of you, drooling."

"It works. I actually did this for Phillip before," Reese adds.

I make a sound of distress as a look of horror comes over my face. "Reese! Niece here!"

She laughs and waves me off. "Again, I know you're having sex, so hush."

I stick my tongue out at her and then say, "Okay, I'm gonna do it, and y'all just follow along on the first part, and then we'll work on the middle together."

I push play to Beyoncé's "Drunk in Love," filling the studio with the sexy, erotic beat, and then I'm off. I move up and down the pole, moving my body like I want a hundred-buck tip. The older guys are good for those. Holding on to the pole, I move my hips against it and drop to the ground, legs open before going back up. It's a very easy routine. I'm not trying to hurt anybody, and while I know the ladies are getting a great workout, I want it to make them feel like they are sexy as hell. When I reach the end of what we've rehearsed before, I hit pause and then turn to look at everyone.

"Good?"

Elli raises her hand and says, "I didn't do anything 'cause like always, I'm distracted at how good you are at this! It's insane! Y'all are gonna make a killing with this class. It's only been a month, and I want a pole. I bet Shea will love that!"

Everyone laughs and I just smile.

I am good at this.

Now I just hope that the two people I care most for will believe in me.

After a great class, I take a quick shower in Reese's old bathroom and then quickly get ready. I only have forty minutes to get ready, and to my surprise, I manage to make it on time. Wearing my favorite red skirt and black-and-white striped shirt, I top off the outfit with a pair of nude high heels that I stole from Reese and pull my hair in a high, messy bun since my hair is still a tad bit wet. I hope that Mrs. Sinclair likes how I look, but most all of all, I hope it makes Jude drool a bit. Packing my bag, I make sure I have everything because after we get back to Jude's, I have to go straight to the club for my shift tonight. Since I have asked for almost every weekend off, Ms. Prissy is making me work a lot of weeknights. Some would think that isn't good money, but it's surprising how many business guys come in after a long night at work and will drop a grand at a time on someone they like.

Heading downstairs, I step out and find that Reese and everyone haven't left yet. They are standing in a circle talking, and my heart immediately speeds up.

They are going to see Jude. And probably talk to him.

Fuck. Me.

Glancing at the clock, I see that I have three minutes to get rid of them.

"Aw, Claire, you look gorgeous," Elli says, and I smile.

"Thanks, why aren't you guys gone yet?"

Reese laughs as she snakes her arm around me. "We were waiting for Jude to get here."

"For the love of God," I mutter, and right on time, I hear the roar of Jude's bike and then see him as he pulls up next to Elli's SUV.

Shit, shit, shit.

Standing, he pulls off his helmet, brushing his hair out of his face and then he grins up at us.

"Sweet baby Jesus," Piper mutters.

"Good job, Claire," Audrey says.

"Really good job," Fallon adds.

"Well, hot damn," Harper laughs. "Claire got herself a hottie, huh?"

"If I were ten years younger and not married to the hottest man in the world, I would be hollering for sure," Elli says, and all I can do is turn beet red because I know Jude hears them.

"Ooooo, Phillip is going to hate him even more now. That motorcycle is trouble," Reese mutters as Jude heads toward us, looking confident as always and so freaking hot.

His eyes are locked on me and I freaking love that, but I know what Reese says is true. Phillip is going to hate every single thing about Jude.

The only problem is…I don't care.

CHAPTER 24

 JUDE

Man, Claire looks hot.

Even with the eyes of five beautiful ladies on me, I can't take my eyes off her. She's stunning, and I can't believe that I'm lucky enough to have her waiting for me. Placing my helmet down next to hers, I head toward her, my eyes locked with hers. She's all polished and glossed up, looking spectacular in a skirt that shows off those great legs she has. The same legs I want wrapped around my waist, and you better believe I'm counting down the seconds until that moment.

Don't get me wrong, I love being with this girl, and I know this is not solely about sex, but I'm really going to love it when I can bury myself deep inside her without any rules or restrictions. The last six days have wreaked havoc on my control. Ever since I watched her come undone without me doing anything to her but watching, I'm constantly thinking of doing just that to her. I want the chance to make her come, to make her whisper or scream my name, but most of all I want to hear her say she loves me.

It's crazy, but I think I love her.

The last six days I've been immersed in her. I've learned everything and enjoyed every second of it. I don't get bored with her. I don't wish I was anywhere else; I just want to be with her. I never thought I could miss someone every second of the day, but with her, I do. I miss her constantly and wonder what she's doing at all times. I keep my phone close just in the hope she'll text me. I've become one of those pathetic guys who live and breathe their girl, and I have no fucking problem with it.

I just want to hear those three words.

I need to hear them. I just don't want to rush things, but every time she locks me in that intense, lusty gaze of hers, I feel like I'm losing my balance and falling hard against the ice. She knocks me on my ass every time, and I can't help but enjoy it. She makes it hard to breathe, especially now as she heads down the stairs, a sneaky little grin on her face. When she stops in front of me, I take ahold of her waist and smile.

"You look really good, babe," I say, leaning in for a quick kiss. "Superhot."

She giggles against my lips before parting to say, "So do you."

She then turns to the ladies who are currently checking me out. I remember Reese, but everyone else I'm curious about. I feel like they are checking me out but also sizing me up the way Reese is. It makes me nervous, but thankfully, Claire introduces us.

"Okay, well, this is Jude. Jude, these are my aunts: Elli, you remember Reese, Piper, Fallon, Harper, and Audrey."

"Nice to meet you fine ladies," I say with my lady-killing smile and all of them blush a deeper red before saying the same.

"Okay, well, we're gonna go," Claire says, lacing her fingers with mine.

"Where to?" Reese asks.

"I'm meeting his family," she says and everyone looks as if they want to throw a party.

"That's wonderful!" One of them says, I think Elli, maybe? She looks superfamiliar. Not sure where I know her from, but I'm sure I know her from somewhere. "We should have you over for dinner with everyone, Jude. It will be fun!"

"Sure," I say. "That would be great."

I'm not sure how Claire feels about that, but soon I see that she does not agree.

"Hell no, I am not bringing him into a firing squad of hockey players. Knowing them, they'll tie him up and shoot pucks at him! No way!"

"Huh?" I ask.

"I told you Phillip plays for the Assassins. Elli's the owner and her husband is Shea Adler, and then the rest of them are all married to players, and no freaking way. I won't subject you to that."

That's where I know her from! Holy crap, now I'm starstruck.

"Don't listen to her. We'll make the guys play nice, Jude. But maybe we'll let Phillip at him before we bring in everyone else," Reese suggests. "Make sure he makes it through that first."

They all laugh and Claire lets out a sound of frustration. "I'm leaving, bye! Let's go," she says to me and I comply, walking with her to my bike.

"Nice meeting you all," I call at them, but when we are far enough away, I lean into Claire. "I wasn't the least bit scared to meet your family, but I'm rethinking that now."

She laughs as I hand her the helmet I had ordered for her. "Yeah, don't worry. I'll make sure you are good and in love with me before I do that to you. By then you won't run, hopefully."

I smile and then pull her to me, pressing my lips to hers for a longer kiss. I know her aunts are probably watching us, but I really don't care. I want to feel her lips against mine; I've missed them. When she pulls back, I smile against her lips and whisper, "I won't ever run."

"So you say, but that could change when the hockey sticks and tape come out."

I eye her. "That sounds superkinky."

"You freaking freak, hush. Get on the bike. Let's go meet your normal family," she says, her face turning redder with every passing second.

Laughing, I get on my bike and say, "Baby, my family is nowhere near normal."

"I don't doubt that, but mine is crazy!" she says loud enough for the five women to hear, but I don't think they care because they just laugh. "Nuts, I tell ya," she mutters as she pulls out a pair of sweats and slides them up her body, covering her legs.

I smile as she puts her helmet on and then ask, "Ready?"

"As I'll ever be," she says, climbing on the back of the bike.

With one last wave to the ladies, we're off, driving through downtown Nashville then onto the interstate to head to my family's home. Nerves are eating me alive and I really don't know why. I am confident my mom will love her. She is amazing. Even Lucy and Jace will like her, but knowing my dad will be there has my stomach in knots. The only reason I agreed to this was because he wasn't supposed to be home until tomorrow. For some fucked-up reason he came home early, and now I'm as nervous as I would be playing in the college finals. I'm not excited about this at all, but when Claire's arms hug me tightly and her thighs squeeze me, I can't help but feel a little better.

With her by my side, I'm pretty sure I can do anything.

It's a nice evening, and I hope that the temperature stays like this. I don't want her freezing her ass off on the way home, but if need be, I'll drive Jayden's car back, and he can drive the bike home. He should already be there by now. I kind of wish we would have all ridden together, but then I would have missed out on feeling my girl's body wrapped around mine.

Pulling into my family's driveway, I head down the gravel drive, kicking up rocks, and I know that my mom will probably tear me apart once I'm inside. Never stopped me before, though. Pulling in beside Lucy's car, I shut off the bike and then pull my helmet off, brushing my hair to the side with my fingers.

"Wow, this is a beautiful home," she says as I get off.

"Yeah, my dad had it built for my mom when I was two."

She smiles before handing me her helmet, and I help her off her bike. As I strap the helmets to the bike, she takes off her sweats and tucks them in her bag.

When she goes to put the bag on her shoulder, I take it from her, putting it on my own and then lacing my fingers with hers.

"Nervous?" I ask and she shakes her head.

"Nope, I'm actually excited."

I smile, but I know that it's fake because I'm nervous and not the least bit excited. Though, when the door opens and my mom comes out, throwing the screen door back, I put a huge grin on my face before leading Claire up the stairs.

"Hey, Mom," I say, kissing her cheek, and she hugs me tightly before kissing the side of my mouth.

"Hey, honey. Move, I want to see her," she says, pushing me to the side and then holding out her hands. Claire takes her hands and smiles as my mom takes her in. "Stunning. You did good, honey."

"She'll do," I say with a wink, and like I expect, Claire glares. But what I don't expect is for my mom to basically punch me in the chest, knocking the air out of me.

"I don't know where I got him from. You'd think he was raised in a barn," she scolds, wrapping her arms around Claire and leading her inside.

"I was joking!" I say, following in behind them. "Of course I did good. She's freaking hot."

Looking back at me, Claire sticks out her tongue playfully and I do the same, loving the laughter in her eyes. Setting her bag down, I go to catch up with them, but I'm attacked by a little monster who wraps her sweet little arms around me.

"Angie!" I say, kissing her cheeks and nuzzling her neck, which makes her laugh. She soon leads me to her dollhouse and has me playing with her before I know it. I don't mind. Angie is my little princess, and I'll do anything to make her happy. I'm a little worried about Claire, but then again, she can handle herself. She's quick on her feet and can adjust to any situation, which is something I admire about her.

"Hey, bubba," Lucy says as she comes up beside me. "Where is your lady?"

"Mom stole her," I say, standing up to give her a side hug and kiss her cheek. "I think they're in the kitchen."

"I gotta go check her out, make sure she's worthy of my brother."

I laugh. "She is, probably better."

Lucy sends me a grin, and I pick Angie up so we can follow. She complains a little bit, but soon she starts to inspect my nose and mouth and forgets that we aren't playing anymore. When I reach the kitchen, I find Claire leaning on the counter that Lucy, Jace, and Jayden are sitting at as my mom talks loudly with her arms flailing in the air.

"You would have thought he broke all the bones in his body. He was screaming and crying so bad. I mean, he only fell two feet," she says and everyone starts to laugh. I know she's talking about the time I fell ten feet out of a tree and broke my arm. It's one of her favorite stories. I'm not a fan of it.

Glaring, I say, "It was ten feet, and it hurt! What kind of mother makes fun of her kid breaking his arm?"

"A truthful one! You sprained it, and it was two feet. It didn't even knock the air out of you," she says, but I'm sure my mother must be losing her memory because that tree was a hundred feet in the air and I fell at least ten feet.

"Whatever," I say as Angie reaches for Lucy. Handing her off, I head toward Claire, wrapping her up in my arms. "Don't listen to her, she's losing her memory. I'm tough and strong. I don't ever cry."

"He was screaming, Claire, like a freaking girl, big tears rolling down his girlish face," Jace teases.

"How do you know? You were like five!" I counter.

"Nine," Jace corrects me, and I'm not sure if he's right or not, so I roll my eyes.

"Whatever," I say, which makes everyone laugh. Claire's body shakes my own, and I smile as I kiss her temple.

"He's right, Claire. Jude is the biggest baby," Jayden says, and I flip him off behind Claire's back so that Mom can't see me.

"I am not. Tell them, baby. Tell them I'm big and strong," I say and she giggles.

"Strongest guy I know, hottest too," she says, and my mother beams as Jace and Jayden roll their eyes.

"He is kinda cute, isn't he?" Mom asks with a grin, cupping my face before turning to take the chicken out of the oven.

"I think he's ugly," Jayden says.

"Looks like a goblin to me," Jace agrees.

"I was thinking an ogre," Lucy chimes in and I let Claire go to flip them all off while my mom's back is turned. Claire is laughing beside me, and I send her a mock glare before wrapping her up in my arms and kissing her hard against the lips.

Parting, she smiles as she says, "I think you're hot."

"That's all that matters then," I say and then smile at my mom when she turns to look at me. Her eyes are so full of love and happiness. I was so nervous about coming here, but now I feel good about it because I know Mom likes her. She has to. "So I see everyone is getting along? We like her?"

"Of course. She's delightful," Mom says with a grin before heading to the dining room.

"I think she's great," Lucy says. "Must be something amazing if she can pin you down."

Claire grins up at me, and I return the grin before saying, "Yeah, she is."

When my mom comes back into the room, she says, "Let's head into the dining room. I hope you're hungry, Claire. You are little skinny; I might need to fatten you up."

Claire laughs as she shakes her head. "I guess I need to. My aunts said I was skinny today too."

"I don't think you're too skinny," I say as I walk with her to the dining room. "I think you look great."

"That's 'cause you like me."

"Maybe," I say before we both share an intimate grin, but as soon as we enter the dining room and I see my father, my grin disappears. "Dad."

"Jude," he says, and immediately I don't like the way he's looking at Claire. "So this is the guest of honor?"

I nod. "Claire, this is my dad, Mark Sinclair."

My dad doesn't move as he says, "You can call me Mr. Sinclair."

"Of course. It's nice to meet you," she says and heads toward him to shake his hand. "You have a lovely home."

"Thank you," he says, still eyeing her, and I'm not sure if he's disgusted or he likes what he sees. Either way, I am sure I don't like the way he's staring at her.

"Let's eat," Mom says, and I pull out a chair for Claire. She falls into it and then I sit beside her, taking her hand in mine and then taking Jayden's. My mom blesses the food and then we dig in. "It's so wonderful having you, Claire. I hope you enjoy the dinner."

Claire's grin is genuine as she says, "Everything is wonderful. Thank you for having me and making me feel at home."

"Of course," Mom says with a grin, but when I look at my dad, he's still staring at Claire.

He then asks, "So you go to UB with Jude?"

Swallowing what's in her mouth, she nods. "Yes, I'm a sophomore."

"Scholarship or your family paying for it?"

Mom stops eating and looks at my dad. "Why does that matter?"

"'Cause only people with money go to UB."

"So it matters if she has money? I don't see how that makes a difference."

My dad glares as he says, "Because I would like to know. Can I ask a question without being questioned by you?"

I grit my teeth as I stare at my plate. I refuse to fight with him in front of Claire. I may have told her we weren't normal, but I don't want her to think we're insane.

"My uncle pays for my college," Claire answers suddenly. "He plays for the Nashville Assassins."

Looking up, I see my dad is interested. "Is that right? Who is he?"

"Phillip Anderson, number thirty-three."

"Wow, that's supercool!" Jace says. "Do you know the whole team?"

She nods. "Yeah, they are basically family."

"That's so cool!" Jace gushes as Jayden rolls his eyes. "I'm a huge Shea Adler fan."

"He's a supergreat guy, funny too. Maybe one day we can all go to a game. We can sit in my Aunt Elli's box. Does Angie like hockey yet?" she asks Lucy as she tickles Angie's neck.

She giggles as Lucy says, "You know it. She's a Sinclair. There is no other way but loving hockey."

"I approve going to the box. Please, Jude. Man, come on," Jace says, looking at me as I give him a dark glare.

"Shut up," I say, but Claire looks back at me.

"It's fine. I'll set something up, and I'd love for all of you to come."

Everyone smiles, nodding, and I like that they are getting along, but then my dad clears his throat and I wish he would just disappear.

"So what are you going to school for, Claire?"

Looking at my dad, she answers, "Business."

"So you want to start your own business?"

"Yeah, or take over my aunt's. She's the owner of Reese Allen's Dance Company."

He nods. "I know of that studio. I have colleagues who take their children there."

"Maybe I know them. I work there now."

"Hmm, so you're a dancer?"

"I am."

"Interesting," he says, and I want to scream. What the hell does that mean? And why the hell do I care if he doesn't like her! I fucking do, and that's all that matters.

"And I assume you are good at it since you want to run the business?" my mom asks.

"I am. Not to toot my own horn, but I'm a national champion. I have seven classes that I teach, and right now I'm doing the choreography for the Bullies' dance team," she says, her face glowing with pride.

"Thank God. They kinda suck," Jayden says, and Claire laughs.

"Used to suck," she says with a wink.

"She's spectacular, Mom, really good," I say, and Claire smiles back at me, making my heart pick up speed.

"That's wonderful. I can't wait to see you perform. At the opening, I assume?" she asks, and I nod.

"Yes, ma'am. We do the halftime show."

"I can't wait! How exciting, watching my babies kick some hockey butt, and then I get to watch you. It's going to be great," she says, and I love how excited she is. Everyone is grinning, happy, and I've never felt so completely whole in my life. I want to gather Claire in my arms and tell her that she makes me the happiest guy in the world. I mean, my family is eating her up. I knew they would, but still, it's comforting knowing that she fits in here. That everyone loves her.

"So is that your real hair color?" my dad asks, and everyone's smile falls as Claire glances over at him.

Okay, I take that back, everyone except my dad likes her. He seems to be hell-bent on ruining this evening.

"No, it's not. I'm a blonde, but I like to spice things up, and I think the red is more me than blond," she says.

"It's a little bold, but then again, Jude has some kind of fauxhawk, Mohawk, crazy crap going on on his head. I guess we should be thankful you're not covered in tattoos and piercings," he says, and I swear my blood pressure is through the roof.

Not able to take it anymore, I say, "Wouldn't have mattered if she was 'cause you've been dead set on not liking her from the moment she set foot in this house."

"Jude Marshall, please," my mom stresses. "Not in front of our guest."

"Tell him to stop talking to her like she is the shit on his shoes and I'll be fine, Mom. I'm not going to sit here and listen to this. We can leave."

"No, not at all," Mom says loudly and then looks at my dad. "Mark, that's enough. Be nice or you can leave."

Dad scoffs while all of us are wide-eyed, looking at my mother. She's never talked to my dad like that. "You aren't going to kick me out of my own house."

"The hell I won't," my mom sneers, and I swear you could hear a pin drop, it's so quiet. I watch as my parents stare into each other eyes, nothing but heat and anger in their gaze, and I know that something really wrong is going on.

Knowing that I'll have to wait to find out, I look over at Claire. "Told ya we aren't a normal, happy family."

⁂

Thankfully it's still warm enough to ride home on the bike since I need the ride to calm down. After a very tense dinner, I was ready to go, but Claire insisted on helping my mom clean up, and I'm glad she did. They bonded some more, and afterward, my mom hugged her tightly, saying she hoped Claire would come back. I thought she would say hell no, but when she looked into my mom's eyes and said, "I'd love to," I knew she was telling the truth. I saw it in her eyes, and I'd like to think she wouldn't lie to my mom.

When I get on the road to the Bullies' house, I see that it is packed with cars, making me remember that there's a party since we don't have practice tomorrow morning. Coach had to go out of town, so we're supposed to do a skate on our own. Because of that, the guys wanted to have some people over.

Pulling up beside her Roadster, I shut off the bike and get off, taking my helmet off as she does the same. When I hear loud music playing, I look at the house and can see the shadows of people in the backyard. They are loud and I know that soon campus police will be called if I don't go in there and shut them up.

"Party?"

I nod. "Yeah. Campus police will be here soon."

"Fun time," she says, laying her helmet by mine.

When I look back at her, she gives me a half-grin as she shrugs her shoulders. "Well, that was interesting." She pauses, her eyes searching mine. "I love your mom, Lucy, Angie, Jace, and Jayden, but I have to admit, your dad is an asshole."

I laugh as I nod. "Yeah, sorry about that."

"No biggie. He won't keep me from visiting with your mom again; she was awesome."

I wrap my arms around her waist and kiss her neck. "Thank you for going."

She threads her fingers through my hair, and I close my eyes as she says, "Thanks for inviting me. I guess my family is next. I can guarantee you that it will be worse than that."

I chuckle against her skin, nibbling up her jaw before saying, "As long as I'm with you, I'll endure it."

When I pull up to look into her eyes, she's grinning, her eyes bright and inviting. Leaning into her, I kiss her lips softly, but soon our kisses turn demanding. I crave this. Need it. Sliding my hands down her back, I cup her ass and press her closer into me, loving the feeling of her body against mine. Parting, I kiss her top lip before whispering, "Three more days."

"Till?"

I smile and then open my eyes to find her watching me. "Till I can take you to my room and devour you, woman!"

She laughs as she pushes me away playfully. "No way, not until you ask me to be your girlfriend in a totally cheesy romantic way that I can tell our grandchildren when we're old and gray."

I laugh as I nod. "I got you."

"You better," she says with a wink and then leans in for a quick kiss. "But I gotta go."

"What? Stay. Let's go to bed."

"With a party going?" she says with a laugh. "No way in hell. I'm dead on my feet."

"Yeah, I know," I say, and then I see Rachael with some of the girls from the team. I nod my head toward them. "Rachael and them are here. Wanna come hang out?"

She laughs. "No way. I have to deal with her tomorrow."

I smile as I kiss her again, and when her arms wrap around my neck, I deepen the kiss, holding her close. We kiss for a little longer until she pulls away. "I gotta go now, or I'll never go."

"I'm hoping for the latter," I say with a wink, and she laughs before kissing my cheek.

"Are you sure you're okay?"

I shrug. "I'm a little embarrassed, a little pissed," I admit.

"Don't be. He didn't scare me off. I love your family, and I've dealt with worse."

I smile, kissing the side of her mouth. "You shouldn't have to deal with anything like that."

"Ah, it's part of life. There are assholes everywhere. Thankfully, I found a good one."

She flashes me a grin and kisses me on the cheek before heading to her car. I watch as she throws her bag in and then as she waves at me. "Don't let it bother you."

"I'll try."

"I'll call you tomorrow?"

"All right, babe."

"Thanks again for taking me. I really like your family, minus your dad," she says with a grin.

I laugh as I nod. "I agree. Thanks for going, see you tomorrow."

"Bye," she says and then she's gone.

Letting out a long breath, I take our helmets and head inside.

Once I shut the door, Matt grabs me and says, "Dude, I need a beer pong partner. Let's go."

I'm not tired so I agree, but when I see that we're playing against Rachael and Mia, I wish I would have declined.

"No girlfriend tonight?" Rachael asks, and I have to admit that before I would have thought she was smoking in the barely-there skirt and shirt, but now I want nothing to do with her.

"Nope, she went home," I answer as I fill the cups with beer.

"So that means you're single tonight?"

Rolling my eyes, I let out a breath. "No, I'm not. I'm Claire's."

And after tonight, I know I'll always be hers.

CHAPTER 25

🩰 Claire

It hasn't been the best day. I'm supertired since I didn't get in till late, and I'm irritated because I failed my math pop quiz this morning. That's what I get for not studying when I should have. Instead, I went to dinner with Jude's family, but I don't regret that. Even if his dad is a Grade A asshole, I'd fail a billion tests just to hang with his mom again. She was an amazingly cool woman, and I'm glad I got to meet her, even if I did have to endure Mark Sinclair.

I really don't understand it. Mrs. Sinclair, Lucy, Angie, and Jace were amazing, good people and superfun, but Mr. Sinclair was rude and just angry from the moment I walked into the house. I spent all night trying to figure out if it was something I did, but I came up with nothing. I was polite, sweet, and all-around awesome, so really, I don't get it. I don't know what's up that dude's ass, nor do I know what's going on between Jude's parents, but it's obvious it's something major. They didn't seem like a loving couple, not in the least.

With all that on my mind, and the fact I'm tired, dealing with the dance team is not what I want to do right now. What I'd love to do is go to Jude's and take a nap. That's what he's doing since he's hungover from playing beer pong last night. While I don't condone drinking till you are passed out drunk, I understand why. His dad really gets to him, and Lord knows, I used to do the same thing. Drink myself numb so I didn't feel all the pain and hatred in my heart, but I'll be damned if I'm going to allow Jude to do that. He gets one time, and I plan on telling him that tonight when I see him. There are other ways to handle anger and hurt. I learned that in therapy.

I kinda wish I was in therapy right now. That's how bad I want to leave this rehearsal. While I love teaching dance, teaching to a group of jerks is really trying my nerves. I figure that this is practice to get me ready for the bigger assholes of dance, but my goodness, how can a group of eight girls bitch so much? I mean, we are dancers! We had to be able to do certain stuff to join! So I really don't understand why, when I add that stuff in the dance, people want to bitch. It's insane and annoying. I don't even want to be here, but I know I can't leave. We perform Saturday, and I love this piece. I worked hard on it, and it's going to be freaking fabulous as soon as these girls get it down. I don't want us looking stupid in front of the Bullies team.

Especially my man.

"I can't do a triple! I just can't!" Mia complains and I stop the music.

I take in a deep breath and head toward her. "Yes, you can. Pull up, strong back leg, and hold it out," I say, holding my arms out as I demonstrate it for her. "It's all in the back leg. You have to push off with it to get you around three times. You can do it."

She tries it a couple times, and finally the third time, she does it. "Feels good, right?" I ask as she grins at me.

"Yeah, I got it, thank you. You're really good at this."

"Thank you," I say, and we share a small smile before I look out at the rest of the group. "Any other problems?"

No one answers me, so I go get the remote and then head to my spot which is right beside Rachael. I didn't want to be by her, but I wanted to be in the middle so the team could see me. Since she's the captain, I put her in the center, but I kind of wish I had stuck her in the back, or maybe even in the hall. I hate the way she's watching me in the mirror, but I ignore her and hit play before calling out, "Five, six, seven, eight."

The music to Jennifer Lopez's "I Luh Ya Papi" starts and so do we. We all move in perfect unison, all attitude and great movement. I am so proud of this group in this moment. There are a few little wobbles here and there, but for the most part, it's outstanding. When we finish, I stop the music and turn to the girls. "Great job, ladies. That turn was great, Mia. Keep working on it. Great attitude, Skylar. Remember, we have to point toes and be strong. Now, we only have twenty seconds left, and I want to do a side stretch. Like this," I say then I throw my leg straight out to the side, my torso following the movement to where my body is completely horizontal, standing on one leg. Standing back up, I ask, "Who can do that? Or who wants to try?"

Only Skylar raises her hand as Rachael says, "No normal person can do that. I mean, how do you even do that and stay upright?"

Why does this girl test my patience? I have ten-year-olds who do that stretch beautifully. Swallowing loudly, I say, "I know a lot of people who can. It's all about the strength in your bottom leg. Let's all try it."

She doesn't say anything, and I demonstrate it a few times. Then I watch as some try it. It's too rough though, and I know I can't make everyone do it. When Rachael does it perfectly though, I clap in excitement.

"Great job, Rachael!"

When she gives me a shitty look, I want to punch her in the throat. But I ignore the need to do that because, as we're both in the middle, we can do it together while everyone else does heel stretches or something. I explain what we're going to do and everyone seems to be on board. I then run it over and over again, despite people bitching because I want this to be perfect. It isn't till Rachael calls practice that I stop.

Unhooking my iPod, I head to where Skylar is standing by our bags, chugging a water. Before I can get to her though, Mia stops me. "Can you show me that stretch again? I want to try it again."

"Sure," I say, laying my iPod down and then doing it for her. She tries to mimic me, but her bottom leg isn't strong enough. "It takes practice."

"Yeah, you're really flexible too."

"Yeah, I am, years of practice and stretching."

"I bet Jude loves that," Maddy says in a snotty little way.

I ignore her and send Mia a smile before heading to my bag.

"Obviously not, since he was single last night," I hear Rachael say.

Looking up, Skylar says, "Ignore her. She's looking to get a rise out of you."

I ignore Skylar though and say, "What does that mean?"

"Claire, ignore her," Skylar says again, but I wave her off.

Setting me with a bitchy look, her hands on her hips, Rachael says, "Exactly what it sounded like. Jude was single last night at the party."

"Oh no," Skylar says faintly.

Taking a step toward Rachael, I ask, "Oh really?"

"Oh yeah, but don't worry," she says, giving me a very condescending look. "No one expected y'all to work."

My face heats with anger as my heart pounds in my chest. It can't be true. It can't be. "How do you know this?"

With her eyes locked on mine, her chin up in the air in a defiant way, she says, "'Cause I slept with him."

I can hear the gasps but mostly all I hear is my own heartbeat in my ears. "Is that right?"

"Sure did, right, Mia?"

Mia looks away and shrugs as my eyes bore a hole in her head. "I don't know."

I don't necessarily trust Mia, but she's an all right person, unlike this cuntbag.

"You followed me downstairs. Don't act like you don't know what happened," Rachael says, and when Mia's eyes meet mine, I actually want to cry.

"She did go into his room. I don't know what happen though 'cause I went back upstairs," Mia says quickly.

"Yup, he got superdrunk and begged me for it. I was a little tipsy, but I couldn't say no. Though this morning when I woke up, I sorta felt bad since we're so close and all," she says, her eyes in slits. I want to reach up and claw them out of her face, but I know that won't do anything but get me kicked off campus since there is a no-fighting clause. She's lucky that I care about my education, or I'd beat the living crap out of her. I don't want to believe the words that are coming out of her mouth, but it just seems like too much of a coincidence. I mean, he was at the party, he was drunk, and now he's hung over. He told me it was a wild night. He was honest about everything, but did he leave some things out?

Turning before I do exactly what I want, which is beat this bitch's ass, I head out of the building, ignoring Skylar and forgetting my bag and the fact that I'm wearing only a bra and booty shorts. I don't even feel the cold air, though; I'm too mad. Thankfully the Bullies' house isn't too far though, because once I reach the door, my toes are frozen. Tears sting my eyes, but I refuse to let them fall. He didn't do this. I know he didn't, but just to be sure I'm going to ask him, and if he lies to me, I swear I will choke him.

The only problem is that somewhere deep inside me, I wonder if he did, and I honestly hate that.

Walking into the house instead of knocking, I head downstairs to his room and knock on the door. Jayden answers and gives me a weird look before I say, "I need to speak with Jude."

"Where are your clothes?"

"Don't worry about that. I need to see Jude," I say, my voice stern.

He shakes his head, concern on his face as he points upstairs. "He's upstairs eating."

"Thanks," I say and I rush back upstairs with Jayden on my heels.

"Everything okay, Claire?" he asks, trying to keep up with me. "Do you want a shirt or something?

"No, and it depends on if your brother cheated on me," I answer as I make my way to the kitchen.

"Oh hell," he mutters just as I reach it to find Jude with his head on the table, a bowl of cereal beside him. He looks like hell. His hair is all in disarray and he's not wearing a shirt, just athletic shorts. His face is pale and I almost feel bad, but then I remember that he might have slept with Rachael, and all my sympathy flies out the damn window.

He looks up at me and his brows come together. "Where are your clothes?"

"Don't worry about that," I say, waving him off. "Did you fuck Rachael last night?

His brows come together more and he sits up. "Huh?"

Letting out a long breath, I say it a little slower. "Did you–" I say, pointing to him "–have sex–" I say, and then take my finger and put it in the hole I'm making with my other hand "–with Rachael?"

"No way. Why would I do that?"

"I don't know. 'Cause you can't last two weeks without it? 'Cause I'm not enough? Be straight with me, Jude, because she's claiming it, and announced to the whole fucking dance team that y'all fucked last night at this party! You better not be lying to me!" I yell and he stands up slowly.

"What the hell? I'm not lying, and also, why the fuck would you entertain that shit? You know she's a liar and out to ruin us."

"It's just such a coincidence since I left and you were at the party that she was at and someone saw you walk into the room with her!"

His eyes go wide as he shakes his head. "Claire, I can't believe you are even coming at me with this. I did not sleep with Rachael. Not only do I have no freaking desire to ever touch that chick, but I'm with you. Totally with you."

I want to be mad, I want to scream, but I can't help but believe the words he says. "It just seems like you would."

"Why? That doesn't even make sense. Have I given you any sort of doubt in the last two weeks? No. I've been yours since the moment I saw you."

"It's just hard to believe, Jude. Everyone says you aren't the guy I'm falling for, and now this comes up, and I know the other shoe was bound to drop. This was too good to be true."

"It is true," he says, taking a step toward me. "I don't want anyone but you, and yeah, it's fast, and yeah, I did a one-eighty. But I did it for you. Because you matter. You have to believe that you are important, that you matter to me," he stresses, and I look away. "I may not know your story 'cause you haven't told me yet, Claire, but I want to do everything to make you feel important and loved. I don't want you to ever think of that life before. I want to make you forget it and show you a better life. I want your trust, baby, because you have all mine."

Oh, fuck me, I could have done without that last sentence. The tears well up in my eyes, and I look down at the ground, not knowing what to say. Cupping my chin, he brings my face up to look into my eyes. His green eyes are shining with all the love and trust in the world, and I know darn well he didn't cheat. I think I knew before I came over here; I was just so scared that I wasn't enough. I've never been enough before, so why would I be now? But then, that's not true either because I'm enough for Phillip and Reese and the rest of my family. I need to stop this way of thinking. I'm not that person anymore, I'm new and shiny and Jude sees that.

"I heard this song and the whole time I'm thinking of you because I only miss you when I'm breathing, baby. Even when you're here, in front of me, I miss you because I feel like I can't get enough of you. Do you think I'd fuck that up for some bitch who doesn't matter?"

Swallowing back my tears, I shake my head. "I don't think so."

"That's right. You are too damn important to me. So please don't ever entertain that bullshit, and believe in us, 'cause this is real."

I nod again and he presses his lips to mine. I melt into his lips, his arms, his body. Holding me up, he kisses the hell out of me, making me breathless and leaving me starting to feel dizzy. Parting, he leans his forehead against mine and I meet his gaze, my heart exploding and coming back together in my chest.

"I'm sorry. I'm an idiot."

He smiles as he nods. "Just a little bit, but it's okay, I like that about you."

A grin pulls at my lips and I lean in, about to kiss him, when someone says, "Since you two are done, I'd like to say I slept with Rachael last night, not Jude."

I look over to find that it's Matt who's standing beside Jayden with his arms crossed across his chest. "She came out of your room bitching that you wouldn't give it to her, so I gave it to her. She told me not to tell you guys, but it isn't like I care what she says, and plus I don't like when people start drama. So yeah, I hit it, and Jude didn't. He's all obsessed with you and shit," he says, and Jude scoffs.

"Obsessed is a little overkill. I just like you a lot," he says and I smile.

"Good, 'cause I like you a lot too."

And I do. So much.

I might even love him.

CHAPTER 26

Claire

"I'll come with you to get your stuff, and then we'll come back here to chill while I get over this hangover," he says once he's dressed.

I smile up at him, threading my fingers in his hair. "Stay here, I'll be back."

He shakes his head. "Fuck no. I don't even want to know how many guys hollered at you while you rushed over here in that, so I'm going to make sure no one else does on the way back."

I roll my eyes. "Jude, I made it just fine, and you're dead on your feet. Go to bed. I'll be back."

I don't even know why I wasted my breath, because he pulls me out of the house and we walk, our fingers tangled together, toward the Bullies' arena. I shiver once the cold air hits me and lean closer into Jude. Pulling off his own long-sleeved shirt, leaving him in a black tank, he hands it over to me, and I smile in thanks before putting it on as we continue to walk.

Wrapping his arm around my shoulders, he pulls me in, kissing my temple before saying, "That shirt looks good on you."

I look up at him with doubt in my eyes. "It's huge on me."

He smiles. "Yeah, but it's mine and it's on you. That's hot."

Giggling, I cuddle into him, loving the way he smells. It's a woodsy and spicy smell, and as I bring the collar of his shirt up over my mouth and under my nose, all I smell is him. Looking up at him, I say, "I'm stealing this shirt."

"That's fine," he says and it saddens me how sick he looks. Then again, I hope it teaches him not to be drinking his problems away.

"You look like crap," I say as he pulls the door open for me.

He nods. "I feel like it."

As I pass by, he grabs a handful of my butt and I roll my eyes. "Obviously not, since you're getting frisky."

He laughs, snaking his arm around my waist and pulling me so that my back is to his chest. Nuzzling his nose in my hair, he whispers, "I'm always up to get frisky when it involves you, baby."

Butterflies go nuts in my belly as we head toward the dancing room. Kissing my temple, he whispers, "I missed you last night. Did you sleep good?"

Ugh. Nodding, I say, "Just fine."

"That's good. Saturday you aren't getting away. You're staying to party and then sleeping with me."

I smile. While I love this side of him, the demanding one, the one that needs me so much he can't breathe, I love giving him a hard time even more. "Is that a demand or a request?"

He smiles in my hair, his teeth tickling my earlobe, and then he says, "Let me reword that."

"Good idea," I tease.

"Please, come party with me Saturday and sleep with me afterward."

"I think you keep forgetting I'm not one of your quick lays – you have to respect me."

"No way, I've never mistaken you for one," he says, kissing my neck. "You're too special."

Smiling a little too hard, I say, "Well, then good, I'll be there."

"That's right. You better say yes," he says roughly in my ear before nibbling on my neck and making me weak in the knees. I laugh out loud as we reach the door to the studio. I push it open, trying to get away, but he takes me in his arms, crashing his mouth against mine, slamming me against the door. Moving my hands, I wrap my arms around his neck, holding him tight as we kiss hungrily.

His hands slowly move up my waist and climb up my ribs, but before he can reach my breasts, someone says, "You two aren't alone."

Breaking apart, we both look to the side to see Skylar and Rachael sitting on the wall with their phones out in front of them. Rage fills me from the top of my head to the tip of my toes when my eyes meet Rachael's. She's wearing a hurt look, almost devastated, and I don't understand it. Why is she looking at us like that?

"What are you doing?" I ask as Skylar stands, grabbing my bag and clothes to hand to me.

"I wanted to make sure your stuff didn't get jacked, so I waited. And she wouldn't leave for some reason, so we've been waiting," she says, and then stretches her arms above her head. "I'm tired. I'm going back to the dorm for a nap."

"Thank you," I say as she walks out the door.

"No problem. Be good," she says, pointing a finger at me. "And you," she then says to Rachael, "don't be such a bitch all the time."

When I look back at Rachael, she's standing, her arms crossed across her chest, still wearing that look on her face. I ignore her, putting on my clothes because I don't trust myself to say anything to her. I am still so mad at her and don't trust her as far as I can throw her. Which wouldn't be far. It's just shitty what she did, what she claimed.

While I don't trust myself to speak to her, Jude must not care because he says, "That was superlow, Rach."

She shrugs as she looks down at the ground, wringing her fingers together. "I just don't get it. I don't know how you could lie to my face the way you did."

"The same way you just did," he says with a shrug. "I never promised you forever, and don't say I did. I said if I decided to start dating, I'd call you."

"But you didn't," she says, looking up at him, and I see her eyes swimming with tears. "You called her."

"I didn't call her. She took over my thoughts and my mind. I couldn't stop it," he admits and her shoulders drop. She takes in a deep breath, and it honestly pains me to see her like that. I know it doesn't make sense, but no one wants to see someone hurt, even if they are a raging bitch like Rachael. She obviously cares for him – a lot – and he doesn't realize it at all.

"You love him?" I ask suddenly and both of them look back at me.

"What? No," he says with a chuckle and then looks back at her. "What? Seriously, Rachael? We fucked like twice. It was nothing."

"Wow, jerk," I say, smacking his arm. "It might have been nothing to you, but it was something to her."

"Fuck off, Claire, you don't know anything," she sneers. She then starts to walk toward us, going for the door, but Jude stops her, taking her arm in his hand.

"Really?"

She doesn't look at him as she shrugs. "I've known you for like ever, Jude. How did you not know?"

She then shakes her arm from his grip and leaves, slamming the door behind her. Looking back at me, he asks, "Should I go after her?"

"If you want to, by all means," I say, but I'm not sure why. I don't want him to chase after her; I want it to be done, but maybe it can't be done without his saying whatever he has planned to say to her. "I didn't know y'all knew each other for a while."

Still looking at the door, he shrugs. "We went to school together, but I never knew. Not that I cared one way or another, or do now. I can't control what she feels, and I don't feel bad because I know I didn't give her any reason to fall for me."

He looks back at me like I have the answers, and I just shrug. "Jude, you don't have to give anyone a reason. It's you that they fall for."

What I've said about Rachael must not matter because his mouth curves at the side as he reaches for me. I guess it's good that he doesn't care that she loves him, that all he cares about is me, but still I kinda feel bad for her. It has to be hard to love someone and for them not to love you back. I can't imagine that kind of rejection.

"So you've fallen for me?" he says, waggling his eyebrows at me.

I laugh as I smack his hands away. "Whoa there, buddy, don't go jumping to conclusions."

"Oh, come on, you know you love me," he says, pinching my butt, making me jump.

"In your dreams," I say, moving out of his reach and heading out the door, but before I can open it, he slams it shut.

Turning me, he leans into my body, his mouth so close to mine as he whispers, "You're damn right, in my dreams. But I hope one day it will be a reality."

I can see it in his eyes. I think he may love me, but there is no way I'm going to say it without his saying it first. No way in freaking hell.

Reaching up, I cup his face, rubbing my thumb along his bottom lip. "This is some deep stuff. Let's go back to your house and lie around and be lazy instead."

He nods as he wraps his arms around me, picking me up off my feet. "I'll get you to admit it sooner or later," he says with a wink. "I know you do – I can feel it."

I laugh. "I have never told anyone I love them but my uncle and aunt, so keep that in mind, mister."

He smiles. "So I'll be your first?"

I look away, my cheeks warming. "Yeah."

"Good, 'cause you'll be my first too," he says, bringing me down so he can kiss me softly.

And I don't know why I think this as I kiss his sweet lips – because, for goodness' sake, this is freaking crazy and fast and could end in a fiery blaze – but I still think it. I still crave it. And as I close my eyes extra tight, I pray and hope that, maybe, I'll be his last.

Once we're back at the Bullies' house, we end up in Jude's bed watching *Wicked Tuna*. It's my favorite show but he doesn't seem entertained in the least. He seems more entertained by tangling his fingers in my hair than watching and I don't mind really. I'm comfortable, lying across his chest, our legs tangled together as I'm engrossed in the art of tuna fishing. Moving my hand under his shirt, I circle my finger along his abs out of habit. It's my favorite thing to do when we lie with each other.

It's intimate and special.

"Can we please watch something else?"

My body shakes with laughter as I sit up to look down at him. "Don't like tuna fishing?"

"No, not at all. Let's watch *Cops*," he says, taking the remote and changing it.

"You're lucky I like this show."

He flashes his teeth at me in a silly way and I settle back down on him. "So, guess what?"

Looking up at him, I smile. "What?"

"Tomorrow is our fourteenth day," he says with a big grin on his face.

With a mock shocked look on my face, I say, "No! Really? Man, time flies."

He laughs as his arm tightens around me. "Don't act like you haven't been counting down the time with me."

I shrug. "Maybe I have, maybe I haven't."

He kisses my temple and then we both turn to watch the show. "My favorite part is when someone gets tased," I say with a smile. "I always laugh so hard."

"Me too," he says, his body rumbling with his chuckle. "I also like the people who are like, 'No, I have no drugs,' and then they have a whole car full."

I nod as I laugh. "Classic, I tell ya."

"Yup," he says just as the person on the TV gets tased. We both burst out laughing as the person falls to the ground and the cops attack him. "Greatest show ever."

"Agreed," I say as my laughter subsides. Looking up at him, I watch as he watches TV, and I can't help but wonder how I got so lucky to lie in bed with someone so fantastic? Girls want him something crazy, and I was the lucky one to land him. He likes me. He wants me. How did that happen? I'm not sure, but I am so thankful. Now all I gotta do is make sure not to screw it up. I need to tell him my secret, but every time I look at him, I don't know how to say the words I know will make him mad or jealous.

When he looks up at me, he smiles, his eyes locked on mine as he cups my face. "What are you thinking, baby?"

I bring my lip between my teeth, the words right there. *Just say them, Claire. Be honest.*

"Are you going to talk to Rachael?" I ask, and as soon as I do, I hate myself even more.

"Probably. Don't think I want her or anything like that. It's not that. I just need to shut that down, you know? I can't have her coming at you with bullshit. I'll fix it and hopefully she'll understand that I never meant to hurt her."

I nod. "I'm sure she will, even though she doesn't deserve it," I say.

"True, but I want to fix it. For us. I don't want any more drama. I want to be drama-free, just happy, me and you."

"Me too," I admit as I let out a long breath. "But we're in college. College is drama."

He laughs. "This is true, but maybe things can be normal between us."

I want that more than I want my next breath. "Yeah, hopefully."

Smiling, he presses his lips to mine and then asks, "So what are you doing tomorrow around four?"

"Nothing," I say, nuzzling my nose along his. "Are we going to karaoke? Hope you're ready to lose again!"

"You cheated, and yes."

"I didn't cheat, and do you want me to come here at four?"

He shakes his head. "Yes, you did, and no, I'll text you when we're ready."

"You're insane, but okay. So what do you need me at four for?"

"You're delusional to think you can beat Jude motherfucking Sinclair fair and square at karaoke, and no reason at all."

We eye each other and then I sit up, pointing at him.

"Oh my God! You know I won, and you're also lying!" I accuse, but he just smiles.

"No, you didn't win, and I'm not lying at all."

"Yes, I did, and yes, you are."

Sending me an evil grin, he says, "Guess you'll have to wait, huh?" He then leans in, his mouth right by mine, and with a grin on his face, he whispers, "And you cheated."

Pushing him away, I yell, "You're impossible!"

He gathers me in his arms, pressing his lips to mine, and I can't help but love every moment with him. And when he pulls back, his eyes blazing with lust and everything hot, my heart does a little flip-flop in my chest.

He whispers, "You're such a beautiful, gorgeous, amazing cheater."

Closing my eyes, I laugh so hard that tears sting my eyes, and I know that I've fallen a little bit more for Jude motherfucking Sinclair.

❦

The next day I'm walking through the quad with a huge grin on my face.

After spending most of the night in Jude's bed, I went to work and it was a wonderful night. I made a ton of money, and the girls are catching on to my choreography perfectly. The investors will be here soon, and I'm confident in what I have. I know I'll land them, and I think Ms. Prissy knows too. When she told me how proud she was of me, I took my phone out to text Jude but then stopped myself. What was I going to say? It ruined my night, but then I woke up this morning to the sweetest text ever.

> Hey Jude: Today is going to be special.
> Hey Jude: Not cause I plan on banging you.
> Hey Jude: Which I do, but because I get to see you and be with

you.
Hey Jude: And ask you a very important question.

It was sweet and amazing, and I'm still grinning like a lovesick fool. I never thought I'd want this. I've never wanted someone as much as I want him, and while it's freaky stuff, I'm excited for our future. I know that he's going to ask me be his, and I plan on screaming yes. No matter what, I know I want to be with him, but I also want to share my accomplishments. I don't want to blow the investors away and then not being able to tell him because I'm hiding it. It's time to tell him. No matter how much that scares me.

"Claire."

I turn to find Jayden coming up toward me. "Hey Jayden," I say with a smile. "What's up?"

"I have been sent to find you."

Raising a brow, I ask, "Oh really? By who?"

"Jude," he says, rolling his eyes. "Come on."

"Where are we going?" I ask, but I don't expect him to tell me. Glancing down at my phone, I see that it's two minutes before four and a grin spreads across my face.

Thankfully, Jayden doesn't prove me wrong when he ignores my questions and says, "You've changed my brother, and I have to thank you for that."

A smile tugs at my mouth as I hug my books. "He's pretty amazing."

"Yeah, but only when he's with you. It's like he's a different person. You make him a better person."

I'm fully smiling now, and when I see that we're going into the hockey arena, I look over at him. "He wanted you to bring me to the rink? Am I going to watch him play?"

He laughs. "No, come on," he says, leading me up a back staircase that I didn't know existed. When we reach the top, he throws open the door and jerks his head to the side, telling me to go. I do as he asks and turn to wait for him, but he shakes his head. "Go to the edge."

Looking at the railing and then back at him, I ask, "Why? Are you going to push me off?" He gives me a look and I shrug. "I saw it on some killer show. Brother was jealous of brother, so he killed the other's girlfriend."

"Wow, yeah, you two are made for each other," he says, then mutters, "Weirdo."

"I am not!" I say and he laughs.

"No, I'm not going to push you. I'm not going to take away the person who makes my brother happy. So go," he demands, pointing to the railing.

I send him a grin. "That's incredibly sweet."

"Yeah, whatever, don't tell him I told you that or I'll push ya next time," he says and then he winks before going out the door, slamming it behind him.

When "Not a Bad Thing" by Justin Timberlake starts to blare through the arena, I start for the railing, curious. But when I get to the edge and look over, I don't expect to see what I see.

Standing in the middle of the rink on the ice is Jude, looking dashing in a pair of jeans and a Bullies sweatshirt, holding a big bouquet of roses, a grin on his beautiful face as he looks up at me. But that isn't what catches my gaze, surprisingly. It's that below him, spelled out in hockey pucks that take up most of the ice, it reads: **Claire, be my girlfriend?**

Tears rush to my eyes as my breath catches in my throat.

This. Can. Not. Be. Happening.

CHAPTER 27

 Claire

drop the books that are in my arms and hold my chest as a sob fights to come out. When he starts to sing along with the words to the song, my heart explodes in my chest, and it feels as if millions and millions of butterflies are going nuts in my stomach.

"Cheesy and romantic enough?" he calls up to me.

I smile as I nod, tears flooding my eyes, but I don't want to let them fall. I don't want this to affect me as much as it is, but soon I can't keep them in. Slowly they roll down my face and I know I love him.

I love Jude Sinclair with a fierceness that cannot be touched.

Yes, it's insane that it's only been two weeks, but this is different. We're different. We're special, and I can't get enough of him. As I slowly shake my head, I wonder if I'm dreaming, and if I am, I hope I never wake up. This is simply perfect. Amazing.

"Come on down here," he says then. "I want to dry those tears. They better be happy ones! And you better say yes!"

Laughter bubbles in my chest, but when it comes out, it sounds more like I'm choking than laughing. "You know damn well the answer is yes. Hold on, let me take a picture."

"No, come down here with me, pictures later."

Deciding that he's right because I want to kiss the stuffing out of him, I throw my bag down and rush down the stairs, wiping my face free of tears. Soon I'm in the cool rink and I rush to the ice to find my man, my *boyfriend*, standing there waiting for me. A grin curves his lips and his cheeks are warm with color. Taking my time, I go on the ice and he meets me halfway, the roses dropping to the ice as he takes me in his arms, meeting his lips to mine.

Wrapping my arms tightly around his neck, I move my tongue with his as he picks me up off the ice, holding me up and close against him.

There is something about kissing him that hits me right in the middle of my chest. It's like a feeling of falling, almost. It makes me breathless, and I know that I need to go slow and enjoy it, but I can't. I need him. My heart pounds hard against his chest, and I can feel his too. A strong, steady beat that has me smiling against his lips, I love that I affect him as much as he affects me. Pulling back, my head rests against his as we share the same breath, a little cloud appearing around our mouths. As he sets me down on my toes, I look up into his intoxicating green eyes and my heart comes into my throat.

Slowly his thumbs brush along my cheek, catching any stray tears before replacing them with soft kisses. He's so beautiful. So stunning. His hair is falling in his eyes, his eyes so intensely on mine and his lips puffy from our kiss. He brings his hands up from my waist to cup my face, running his thumbs along my jaw as his eyes search mine. The words are right there and I know I should say them, but they are lodged in my throat. I need to tell him about my job before I profess my love for him because that's not fair. I can't expect him to love me when he doesn't know everything about me.

"Okay, this is pretty amazing."

He squeezes me close, his nose brushing against mine as he says, "So what do you say? Wanna be mine?"

I grin as I lean into him, bringing my arms around his waist, holding him tight to me. "I'm pretty sure I've been yours since the moment I met you."

His mouth turns up at both sides, fully grinning at me as he nods. "I've been yours too."

"This is crazy," I say, and I want to believe that it is, but it seems so right. "How does this happen so fast between two people?"

"I don't know, but I wouldn't change a thing about us."

"Me neither. It's only been two weeks, but it feels so right, you know?"

"Yeah, I do. It's been the best two weeks of my life. I am finally alive being with you, and I didn't think that could happen off the ice."

Looking deep in his eyes, I fight off the tears and then very softly, I admit, "I never thought love was made for me." Moving my nose along his, I say, "But you changed my mind."

"You were made to be loved by me, and no one else can ever take that away," he says and then takes my mouth with his in a deep, toe-curling kiss. I'm not sure what he means with that statement. Is he saying he loves me? Does he love me? Surely he does! Who does something this amazing for someone? Well, someone who wants sex really bad would, but he isn't pushing for that. He's holding me, treasuring my lips as he kisses me slowly, so he has to love me. Right?

Pulling back, he grins against my lips before kissing me once more and then pulling completely away. Reaching down, he grabs the bouquet of roses and hands them to me. "So what do you think of everything?"

I smile as I lace my fingers with his, needing to touch him. "It's amazing, Jude, thank you."

"Anything for you," he answers. He then smiles back at me, bringing my hand up to kiss the back of it before looking up. I do the same to see Jayden leaning across the railing, a phone in his hand. "Smile."

He brings me up under his arm, close to his chest, and I smile up at Jayden as he takes the pictures of us. I can't wait to send these to Reese; she'll flip when she sees them. Turning me in his arms, he dusts my jaw with kisses before I say, "Wow, you had this all planned out, huh?"

He smiles up at me and says, "I wanted to make sure you never forget this moment."

"How could I? This is the most romantic thing anyone has ever done for me," I admit. "I kinda feel like I'm dreaming."

He shakes his head, cupping my face in his hand before dropping his mouth to mine. He doesn't kiss me though, instead he smiles, his lips lightly touching mine and then he says, "I know what you mean."

Then he kisses me, pressing our bodies together and smashing the roses between us, but I can't seem to muster up any energy to care. I'm so engrossed in him. I'm too much his to care about anything but kissing him with all the love and desire in my heart. As his mouth moves with mine, I want to ask if he loves me, but then I feel so selfish and wrong for hoping he does. In a way, I'm giving him a false claim of who I am. I mean, I'm not saying that burlesque is who I am, because I'm more than that, but it is a big part of me. If this works out with the investors, then it will be my career, and I'm not sure how he will feel about that.

He pulls back slowly, looking into my eyes, and I know it's time. "I have to tell you something," I whisper and he smiles, his finger moving along my jaw to my lips.

"What's that, baby?"

I get lost in his eyes as my heart pounds so loud I can hear it in my ears. I love the way he's looking at me. As if I'm it. I'm his, and I know in my heart that's true. He may have not said it, but his actions mean way more to me than words. This couldn't have been a quick setup. It takes time to line the pucks up perfectly, and he got me flowers and cleaned up, looking so damn hot it's mind-blowing. This took time. Time he could have used on anyone or anything else, but instead he used it on me. I mean something to him, and I know that I can't fuck that up for both of us.

"You make me so happy," I say and I close my eyes, leaning into him.

His arms come around me, holding me tightly as he whispers, "I feel the same way, baby."

If he's happy with me, he won't leave me, right? He'd stay; he would accept the job I love to do. But for some reason, I don't believe that. I think he'll run the other way, and I can't risk that. I can't. Melting against him, tears sting my eyes as we slowly sway back and forth to the music. Dusting kisses up my jaw and cheek, he pulls back, looking deep in my eyes as he says, "Wanna get out of here?"

I give him a cheeky grin. "For what?"

Eyeing me, he smiles as he says, "Anything you want."

"So, just hypothetically speaking, if I wanted to go back to your house and play chess, we could do that?"

He nods, his face straight as he says, "Hypothetically, we could do that."

"Or? I feel an *or* there," I say, a grin pulling at my lips.

"Or…" he says, dragging out the word. "I can take you back to my house and bend you and fuck you in every way possible," he says, stealing my breath and making it hard to breathe. "But that's hypothetical. It's whatever you want."

Leaning into him, I move my hands up his hard chest and around his neck, looking deep in his eyes. "I think I like the way you think. Being bent in every way possible is way more fun than chess."

"True," he agrees. "And way more challenging."

"Agreed."

"So…"

My face hurts from smiling so hard. "So I think you should get me home, Jude."

He doesn't nod or say anything; he just takes my hand and basically pulls me off the ice. Once our feet hit a hard surface, not a slippery one, we're hightailing it out of the place.

"Shit, I forgot my bag," I remember.

"Jayden will get it," is all he says as he pushes through the door. But instead of going out the front door, he goes to a side door and pulls me through, pushing me against it to slam it shut before pressing his mouth to mine. He sloppily kisses my mouth, knocking my world off its axis as he kisses the living hell out of me. Melting against him, I moan out as he nibbles at my neck, biting and sucking as his hands come up to grab my breasts.

Pulling away, he looks in my eyes and all I see is red-hot lust. He's going to take me against this door, and I have no damn problem with that at all.

"You can't wait," I say, reading his face. "You're going to fuck me right here."

Cupping my face, he slowly shakes his head, and I'm surprised that I misread him. Bringing his mouth close to mine, his eyes lock with mine as he says, "Yes, I can't wait. But no, I'm not going to fuck you, Claire. I'm going to make love to you. Probably superfast, but I promise when we get back to the house, I'll take my time."

"Oh," is all I can say before he takes my mouth with his.

Pressing me against the door, he holds me still by pressing his pelvis into mine and slowly removes my shirt, my bra following quickly behind it. Looking my chest over like a starved man would, he molds my breasts together before dropping his mouth to them, sucking and nibbling on my nipples, sending heat straight between my thighs. Tweaking my nipples, he devours me as I cry out, squeezing his shoulders. Letting go of my breasts, he nibbles up the middle of my chest, kissing my throat and then coming back to my mouth as he undoes his pants. I push my sweats down along with my panties, kicking them to the side as he breaks the kiss to do the same, pressing his long, raging hard-on against my stomach.

I know he thinks he's about to make love to me, but I have other plans.

Dropping to my knees, I take his dick in my hands and slowly move my hands up and down him, his eyelids falling in a hooded way, watching me intently. Pressing my back against the wall, I guide him into my mouth and to the back of my throat. He moves my hair out of my face before very slowly moving his dick in and out of my mouth. His hands move along my shoulders, my throat, and jaw as I suck him hard and take him as far as I can down my throat, which isn't as far as I'd like since he's so big. He seems to like it though, his breathing picking up as he whispers my name.

"That's perfect, baby," he moans, tangling his fingers in my hair. "Fuck, you are so hot. Yeah…Claire…mmm."

Picking up speed, I rake my teeth along his shaft as I cup his balls, molding them slowly as he quickly thrusts in my mouth. I know he's about to come, I mean, he's basically screaming my name, and I feel his dick seizing up. Like I suspected he would, his legs buckle and he's coming hard, my name falling off his lips as he squeezes my shoulders in his hand. I suck him dry, milking him until he can't take it anymore. Moving his limp dick out of my mouth, he picks me up and presses me into the wall. Closing the space between us, he takes my mouth with his, kissing me long and hard, curling my toes and making it hard to breathe. He then takes my legs, hooking them over his arms before pressing his hands into the wall, opening me wide for him.

I feel completely exposed and I want to be a little shy, but that look in his eyes tells me I have nothing to be shy about. Pressing his hands into the back of my knees, he holds me up before dropping to his knees and burying his face between my wet folds. I cry out, my nails digging into his shoulders as he makes love to me with his mouth. I tremble with need, my heart pounding, my legs shaking from my impending orgasm, and I'm not sure how much more I can take. I've been craving this for days, been dreaming about it, and now it's happening. In a hot, sexy way against a wall where anyone could find us. The thrill of that has me crying out louder, my hands squeezing his shoulders as he slowly moves his tongue in and out of me, his nose pressing against my clit. Moving up, he holds nothing back, flicking his tongue ruthlessly against my clit, and I come, my whole body coming undone beneath his talented mouth.

Standing, he presses my legs back, opening me back up, and enters me with one swift thrust. I moan as he fills me completely, and then I remember that he did not put a condom on.

"Whoa, whoa, condom."

"You're not on the pill?"

"Oh, I am. As you were, fingers crossed no babies are in our future," I mutter against his jaw. I trust him completely. He's clean. He's mine.

"At least not for now," he says.

And for some dumb reason that makes me really happy, but then I'm frowning because there could be no future for us if I don't grow some balls and be honest. Deciding to think about that later, I wrap my arms around his neck as he pounds into me, his dick completely filling me and making it hard to breathe.

"God, you feel so good," he mutters against my neck.

"Oh, Jude," I whisper as my body seizes up again, squeezing him tightly with another orgasm. He pushes through though, making my legs shake as he takes what he wants, and he can have it. His fingers bite into my thighs as he continues to move into me, taking my breath with each thrust. Sweat drips down my back, my heart is racing, and I've never felt this damn amazing in my life. When I feel the muscles in his shoulders tense up, I squeeze him and he stills inside me, his head leaning against mine. He then thrusts slowly once, then twice before stilling once more, gasping for breath.

Opening my eyes, I meet his and I smile. My heart is going insane in my chest, my stomach feels like it's dropped to the ground, and as I look into his beautiful green eyes, I know that everything inside me is his. There is no other way. I'm his.

"I love you," I whisper without really thinking it through. While I know I mean the words, I can't help but feel a little dumb for admitting them. I mean, for shit's sake! It's only been two damn weeks! As we stare into each other eyes, I'm internally freaking out, and he isn't saying anything. He's just staring at me, his eyes soft and locked on mine.

Dropping my legs, he cups my face in such a fierce way that it takes my breath away. Moving stray hairs out of my face, he says, "I love you a whole hell of a lot more."

It's like firecrackers and glitter fly in the air as my heart just sings for him. Shaking my head, I say, "If you say so, buddy."

"I know so," he says in such a way that tells me he does. Smiling, he takes my lips with his, and I know I can't tell him. I can't risk the way he makes me feel. I can't lose him. He loves me, but I don't know if he loves me enough to love my job. I'll quit. No biggie and I'll stay here and own a studio. Or wherever he goes, I'll go and we will be fine. I don't need Vegas; I don't need bright lights and stages with sexy burlesques dancers dancing to my stuff.

I just need Jude.

CHAPTER 28

⚔ JUDE

Rolling over, I wrap my arms around Claire's waist and pull her in tight against my chest, but before I can settle into her, she turns, cuddling into my chest, and I coil around her as if I'm shielding her from the world. I want to stay like this, never let her go, but I know she has to get up soon. I wasn't expecting her last night, but she texted me early in the morning saying she couldn't sleep, so I offered for her to come here and I'm glad I did.

Moving my lips along her temple, I inhale deeply, memorizing her scent as a smile settles on my face. "I love you," I say, and each time I utter those three simple words, my heart constricts because I know what she's going to say back.

"I love you more," she says, placing a kiss right on the tattoo on my chest. "Shh, I have at least an hour."

I smile, kissing her, and say, "Twenty minutes actually."

She groans as she nuzzles closer, draping her leg across my hip. If she didn't need the sleep, I would slowly slip it in her, but since I know she has to go to the studio soon to teach little girls, I leave her be. One would think that would annoy her, but when she talks about the girls, she gets a dreamy look in her eyes. It's sweet and I like that about her. She loves her job; she has such a passion for dance. It's beautiful and I enjoy watching her do something she believes in. I can't wait to see where we will be in a year's time. I wonder if she'll follow me wherever I go, and I wonder if it is selfish of me to expect her to. What if she wants to finish school? Or stay here? What will we do then?

I'm not sure, and even though it worries me, I know we'll make it. She's mine.

Closing my eyes, I'm about to fall asleep when her alarm sounds. Sitting up, she grabs her phone and turns it off before running her hands through her hair and then looking back at me. "Good morning."

I smile. "Morning."

Lying down on me, she frames my face with her hands, dusting my jaw and lips with hers. Looking down in my eyes, she smiles as she says, "Thanks again for letting me come over. I just couldn't sleep."

"Anytime, babe, you know that."

"I feel bad," she says with a sheepish grin. "Kicking Jayden out and all... Maybe next time I can drag you out of bed to come to my dorm?"

"But we can't kick Skylar out," I point out. "Jayden doesn't mind."

"The hell I don't," he says suddenly and Claire covers her mouth, holding in her laughter as I smile.

"Of course he doesn't 'cause he sneaks back in once we're asleep," I say and Jayden agrees.

"Yup, I need my bed."

"Sorry, Jayden," she says over her shoulder and I reach up, placing my lips to her bare neck. She giggles, leaning into me and then falling on top of me. Liking her position, I grin as I run my hands down her bare back to her sweet ass.

"You have to leave, huh?"

"Yeah," she says, letting her legs drop to either side of my hips, pressing her sweet center against my hard one.

"So no time to, you know?" I say, waggling my brows at her as I thrust up against her.

She laughs as she says, "No time to kick Jayden out of the room? Nope, no time."

"So disappointing," I say as she kisses my nose and then rolls off me.

"Agreed," she says with a wink. "Roll over and close your eyes, Jayden."

"Roger that," he says and then she goes down the ladder to get her clothes. I lean on the railing and watch as she gets dressed.

Once she's dressed in some Assassins sweats, she looks up at me expectantly. "Are you going to drive me to the studio?"

"Oh yeah," I say, getting up and out of bed. "I forgot, sorry, babe."

"You don't have to. I can drive, but you're the one who offered."

I shake my head, grabbing my jeans and then a tee. "You're right, I did 'cause I want to."

"Are you sure?" she asks, putting her bag on her shoulder. "You can go back to sleep."

"No, I'm good, come on."

Taking her hand in mine, I grab our helmets and then say bye to Jayden before heading out and up the stairs.

Once outside, the sun shining brightly on me, I bring her in closer to me. "Told ya it was going to be a perfect morning to ride."

Grinning up at me, she leans up, kissing my jaw before we reach my bike. Getting our helmets on and securing her bag, I'm about to start the bike when she says, "Can we stop at a gas station before we get there? I need some water and something to eat."

"Sure," I say before bringing the bike to life, and it roars beneath us.

Leaning forward, she wraps her arms around me and then we're off. It's a quiet morning, which is surprising since it's a Saturday. Usually it's nuts out and I'm thankful it's not. I don't want to concentrate on what I'm doing; I just want to enjoy it. I want to enjoy the feeling of her holding me, knowing that she loves me. It's only been two days since she uttered the words to me, and I've never felt so complete in my life. It's like I was waiting for that moment my whole existence, as if I was waiting for Claire. And now that I have her, I don't ever want to let her go.

Since that moment, making love to her against the wall in the arena, I've been that lovesick boyfriend, texting and calling and wanting to be near her every second of the day. And that's not an easy feat. We both have so much with schoolwork, dance, hockey, and life, it gets in the way. But somehow we're surviving it all, and I couldn't be more thankful for that. It's about to get worse though, I feel. My first game is Friday and then starts the morning and night practices, which means I'll see her even less than I do now. It worries me, but I believe in this.

In us.

When we're almost to the studio, I find a gas station and pull in, parking the bike before getting off and helping her. Setting our helmets down, she grabs her wallet and we head inside.

"I need to take a leak," I say, and she rolls her eyes at me.

"Good to know. I'll be ready once you are," she says, a little grin on her face before she heads off. Before she can get far though, I pinch her butt, giving her a grin before heading to the bathroom. After doing my business, I go out to find her and when I do, I don't like what I find. She's pulling out of a hug with some guy, a grin on her face as she greets him cheerfully. It doesn't take long for me to recognize him; it's Patrick Franklin from the Nashville Assassins. I used to like him, thought he was a great player, but the look in his eyes as he basically eye-fucks my girl has me wanting to rip him to shreds.

"Damn, Claire, I think you've gotten hotter," he says and she laughs.

"Oh please," she says, waving him off.

"How old are you now? Tell me the truth this time."

Still laughing, she says, "I'm nineteen now."

"Legal and ready to mingle," he sings, waggling his eyebrows. "What are you about to do? Let's go get some breakfast, catch up."

Instantly I want to rush out there and push the guy away, but only a psycho would do that. Claire can handle herself. She wouldn't cheat on me. She loves me. So as I act as if I'm trying to decide on some M&Ms, I listen as Claire says, "Sorry, can't. I have dance to get to."

And you have a boyfriend, I say in my head.

"Still at Reese's?"

Why didn't she say she has a boyfriend?!

"Yup, I'm getting my business major so I can take over one day or maybe open a studio somewhere else. Or do Vegas shows. You never know."

"That's good. I'm glad. I haven't seen you in a long time, and I'm not lying when I say you've gotten hotter. You're beautiful."

She smiles. "Thank you."

"Why don't I give you my number, and we can go somewhere after you get done?"

He pulls out his phone but she shakes her head. "Sorry, Patrick, but I'm with someone."

He eyes her. "Is it serious? Can I steal you away?" he asks with a cheeky smile.

She shakes her head, a warm grin coming over her face. "No, it's superserious. He's pretty amazing, makes me really happy."

"That's good. I'm glad you're happy, you deserve that," he says and then he smiles. "I should have snatched you up when you turned eighteen. I still think about our time together."

Her face burns with color as she pushes him away. "Oh, hush!"

He laughs and she giggles as she reaches for a bag of popcorn. "I gotta go. I don't know where my man is, must have fallen in the toilet or something. I'll see you around, Patrick," she says, and then gives him a sideways hug.

"It was great seeing you," he says, wrapping both his arms around her and hugging her tightly.

"You too, bye," she says, and when she turns, she sees me, a grin coming over her face but I can't enjoy it because fuck-a-doodle-doo is watching her ass as she walks away. I glare at him, and he meets my gaze and then grins. Chucking his chin at me, he turns and thankfully is gone as Claire wraps her arms around me. "What happened to you?"

"Nothing," I say, and it comes out sharper than I intended. She eyes me curiously and I say, "I heard your whole conversation with that guy. Past boyfriend?"

"Nope, I almost had sex with him to drive Phillip crazy, but it was nothing and I only see him at Assassins functions," she says, releasing me and going to the cooler for a water like it's no big deal. I know it shouldn't be, but it bothers me.

"So I shouldn't be mad, right? Or let this bother me?"

She looks up at me and shakes her head. "I promise it's not a big deal. It was the old me, the nasty one who had a bad childhood."

"That you still haven't shared with me, by the way."

She nods. "You're right. Maybe I should change that?"

As she looks up at me, I know that she's right. I shouldn't be mad or anything. She's mine. Completely and utterly mine. I was pretty confident about that earlier, but now that she wants to share her past with me when before she didn't has to mean something. Reaching out, I lace my fingers with hers, bringing her close to me before kissing her nose. "I'd like that," I say in a whisper against her nose. "I want to know everything about you."

"Okay, well, you have been warned. So no running, okay?"

I shake my head. "I couldn't run away from you if I tried."

She grins as she reaches up, cupping the back of my neck to bring me down for a long stomach-flipping kiss. When we part, I kiss her bottom lip and say, "Let's get out of here."

"Yeah, I'm gonna be late," she says as we rush to get out of the gas station. It doesn't take long to get to the studio as it's right down the road, and thankfully, we're not late. Hopping off the bike, she tucks her helmet under her arm and then grabs her bag. "You'll be here around three?"

I take ahold of her shirt, bringing her to me. "Yeah, I'll be here."

She smiles sweetly before bending down for a quick kiss, but that isn't enough for me. Deepening the kiss, I hold her face as my lips move against hers. Pulling back, she smiles as she kisses me one last time and whispers, "I love you."

Matching her grin, I run my thumb along her bottom lip as my whole body tingles for this girl. "I love you more."

"Hey, guys."

I look away from Claire to see her aunt Reese coming toward us. She matches Claire, wearing sweats with her hair pulled up in a high ponytail.

"Hey," we both say as Claire backs away some, but I snake my arm around her waist, pulling her back to me.

Smiling, Reese says, "So, how's it going?"

"Good, thank you. You?" I say.

"Good, thanks," she says and then meets Claire's eyes. They stare at each other for what seems like ever, and as I watch them, I wonder if they are telepathically talking to each other. It's weird, but finally, Reese looks at me and says, "How would you like to come to dinner Wednesday?"

"He's busy," Claire says, giving me a look that says I am very busy in fact, but I don't remember being busy.

Shrugging my shoulders, I say, "I'm pretty sure I'm supposed to say I'm busy, but I can't remember with what."

"Jerk," she mutters, pulling herself out of my arms and shrugging her shoulders. "It's your funeral."

I laugh as Reese rolls her eyes. "It's not a big deal. Phillip will be nice, I swear."

"You can't guarantee that," Claire says and then looks back at me. "She can't guarantee that."

"Oh, hush, it will be fine. I'll figure out the details with Claire. Excited to see you on Wednesday!"

"See you then," I say as she waves and then heads inside. I reach for Claire, pulling her to me as I hold the bike up. "Don't you want me to meet your uncle? You met my family."

"You've meet Reese. Believe me, that's good enough. He's gonna be an asshole, and I promise you're going to say I'm not worth all that trouble."

I smile as I nuzzle my nose against her ear, taking in her sweet scent. "Don't you know that you are worth all the trouble in the world and that I will never stop loving you?"

She doesn't say anything so I look at her, hoping she sees it in my eyes, but hers are suddenly so sad. With a melancholy smile, she says, "I wish you could guarantee me that."

Cupping her jaw, I bring her eyes up to mine and say, "I can."

"How?"

I smile as I stroke her jaw with my thumb. "Easy. As long as there are stars in the sky, I am yours. Forever and always."

"Some nights it's cloudy, though," she points out.

I nod. "You're right, but the stars are still there. And that means that I may be mad or upset with you, but I'll always love you. I mean, come on, Claire, it's taken me twenty years to find the person I'm meant to love. That doesn't ever stop."

"That was supercorny," she says, her eyes playful.

I laugh as I nod. "Sometimes you get supercorny when a person makes you feel like this."

"Feel like what?"

"Like they've taken over you. Flood your thoughts, make you so breathless and blown away by them. It's a crazy thing, love, and sometimes it brings out the crazy in you."

"Crazy in love? Like the song?" she says, her lips curving into an even bigger grin.

"Exactly."

Reaching up, she traces my lips with her finger before saying, "I love you, Jude."

I smile, nipping her finger and making her jump before crashing my lips to hers. As I kiss her, I hold her close and the love pours out of me for this girl. I mean every word I say. She is it. She is my forever. Is it too damn soon to know that? I don't think so. I think when you know, you know. Everyone wants that person, the one who they'll spend forever with, and thankfully I found mine and knew right away. Do people think we're nuts? Hell, do we think we're nuts? Yes. Do I fucking care? No, because I love her.

Pulling away much too soon, I say, "I love you. Now go before I steal you and take you back to my place."

She lets me go and grins. "I think I might like that."

"Oh, you would, believe me," I groan, my dick coming to life in my pants.

"I think I'd like it more on that bike though," she says and then she bites her lip playfully, her eyes full of lust.

Hot. Damn.

Breathing out slowly, I grip the handlebars as my whole body vibrates with want. "I will make sure that happens soon."

"Promise?" she asks, taking a step back, her eyes locked on mine.

"I swear."

CHAPTER 29

⚔ JUDE

After parking my bike beside Jayden's car, I hop off it and head inside. Before I can get to the door though, my phone rings. Pulling it out, I see that it's my agent, Ralph.

Answering it, I say, "Hello?"

"Hey, buddy! How's it going?"

I drop down on the steps and brace my elbow on my knees as I say, "Good, thanks. You? How're the kids? Your wife?"

"I'm breathing, wife and kiddos are good. Thanks for asking," he says, and I can hear the smile in his voice.

I've known Ralph as long as I can remember. He and my dad played hockey together when they were younger. He's in his late forties and just started a family a couple of years ago. Said life was too hectic to bring a family into, and my dad was always so jealous of him. He would always say that Ralph was living the life, traveling all over the world, not giving a damn about anyone. I don't know what changed, but now, Ralph seems like a different person, a little happier. While I feel that Ralph's family is a blessing and something that was good for him, I think that to my dad, we're a burden. I hate that I feel like that. I should know my dad loves me, but sometimes I don't think he does.

"So the reason why I'm calling, bud, is that we have four teams that want to meet with you throughout the season. The Kings, Hawks, Rangers, and Lightning."

"Good teams," I say even though the Wings aren't on the list. I really wanted the Wings, but I still have plenty of time to make them bite and consider me. I'd be an asset. I know that.

"Real good teams, especially since the Kings just traded one of their top players for a first-round pick. If the draft goes the way it should, you'll go first, I think, or at least, I hope."

"Sounds great to me."

"Me too. So main thing, stay healthy, focus, and kick some ass, kid. The NHL is right there, waiting for you. Only nine months till we're there."

"I'm ready."

"I know you are, and so am I. Then I'll get Jayden and Jace in there and have all the Sinclair boys kicking some NHL ass. I'm hoping maybe we'll get some bites and I can throw Jayden in this year, but I won't unless I'm confident. We'll see."

I nod, excited for my and my brothers' futures. We are going to rock the NHL. "Awesome. I'm excited."

"Good, that's what I want to hear. All right, bud, like I said, keeping kicking ass, please God stay healthy, and just do you. Be amazing."

"Will do, thanks for calling."

"Anytime, bud. I'll see you Friday. Me and the family will be there for opening night."

I smile. "See you then."

Leaning on my elbows, I hang up and let out a long breath. This is good. The teams are good. Los Angeles, Chicago, New York, or Tampa. They are far from home but doable. I can do this. This is what I've been hoping for my whole life. This is my dream, and I am making it a reality. I want to be happy, ecstatic even, because not everyone has more than one team looking at them, but I'm nervous. Will my mom be okay without me? And also, will I be able to convince Claire to go with me?

They are the two most important people in my life, and I'm not sure how this is going to work. I know my mom will be supportive; she has known from the beginning that this could happen, but Claire… She didn't sign up for this, but she knew. She had to know that I might leave Tennessee. Can we do long-distance? Will we? Or will she follow me? I know this is kinda crazy to think of now since I have nine months until the draft, but maybe I should find out before I fall even more for her. But then what? If she doesn't want to go, do I break it off? That seems impossible to me. I'm completely invested in this girl, so really there is no other option. I should just let it happen. Everything will work out. We will be together because we love each other and we're fighters. We'll fight for us. Yeah, we're good. And my mom, she'll be solid. Everything will be fine.

Letting out a breath, as if I'm letting that thought go, I feel better. I know it will be fine. Leaning back on my hands, I look up at the sky and take in another breath before letting it out. I should go inside but it really is a pretty day. I wish that Claire didn't have to work. It would have been a perfect day to lie around in the grass and be lazy. Deciding that I'll do that and just imagine she's here, I go and get a blanket before laying it on the grass and lying down. Closing my eyes, I let my breathing even out and relax. I let go of all my thoughts. The draft, my mom, Claire, everything, I just completely relax and before I know it, I'm out.

I wake to the sound of my phone ringing. Sitting up, I grab it to see that it's my dad. My brows come up as I lean on my knees, hitting answer.

"Hello?"

"Jude?"

"Yeah?"

"Hey, it's your dad," he says and his voice is short.

"Yeah, I know. I have caller ID. What's up?"

"Always the smartass, but I don't have time to scold you on that," he says and I roll my eyes. "Did you talk to Ralph today?"

"I did."

"Good, the teams are okay, I guess."

I hate the way he does that. Make everything sound like crap when this is the biggest opportunity in the world. The NHL is what every hockey player wants, and he says it like it's nothing. Like I'm playing for a rec league.

"Yeah, great teams even."

"They aren't the Wings though, or even the Bruins for that matter, but whatever. Maybe you'll get traded."

"I have time. They can still come for me."

"Doubt it."

Letting out a breath, I wonder why I even answer his calls. "Why did you call again?"

"To talk about the teams," he says. "But if you're busy, I'll let you go."

"It's not that. It just seems like you're being a jerk when your son is going into the NHL, and that seems a little insane to me."

"I don't see myself being a jerk, Jude Mitchell, I see it as pushing you. I want what is best for you, and the best is not those four teams."

"That's only your opinion. I think they are all Stanley Cup-winning teams. That's awesome."

"Maybe in your eyes, but I want more for you. Which reminds me–" he says before pausing "–are you still seeing that girl?"

My skin breaks out in gooseflesh. Why is he asking about Claire? "Claire," I say, reminding him of her name. "Yes, I am."

"Hmm. I don't know about her. I feel like I know her from somewhere."

"I don't know how, but it doesn't matter because she's great, amazing. I love her."

He scoffs. "What the hell do you know of love, Jude? Nothing. It's not even a real thing."

I pause, my heart clanking against my chest. "So you don't love me? Mom, Jayden, Lucy, Angie, or Jace?"

"Of course I do, but that's different. What you're feeling right now is lust, and enjoy that, but don't get all wrapped up in this girl to where your game starts to suffer. I'll be watching you, Jude Mitchell. Don't let her ruin you."

I don't know why I let him bother me, why I even care. But that pisses me off to the point of no return. Claire wouldn't do that. She loves me. "She won't ruin me. She's changed me. Made me a better person."

"You're still the same person – you're just trying to impress her for some ass, Jude. Don't lie to me or yourself. You're exactly like me. We aren't made for that stuff and I got stuck. Don't get stuck, and don't tell your mother I said that. It'll piss her off. I love your mother, but that took a long time for me to realize. Don't make my mistakes. Go into the NHL, enjoy life, and leave her behind. She'll hold you back."

I feel like he's kicked me in the gut. Who says this to their kid? Doesn't he want me to be happy? "I have changed, Dad. I'm nowhere near the kind of person you are, and I know that loving someone is not a mistake. Not when they lift you up instead of holding you back. Don't talk about Claire, my mother, or anyone I love like that. You are lucky to be loved by Mom 'cause God knows you don't deserve it. I'm going to go into the NHL, and I'm going to do it with Claire beside me. I'm going to be the best player in the world 'cause not only am I a badass player but I'm loved by her."

He laughs and it makes my skin crawl. "Keep dreaming, kid. You'll end up with kids and a wife and no NHL in no time."

I don't even know what to say. I'm so hurt, so fucking mad. Ending the call, I drop my phone before falling onto my back and squeezing my eyes shut. I don't know why I let him affect me. Why I even listen to him. He's a fucking jerk. He doesn't love me, or anyone but himself for that matter. When everyone realizes this – and leaves him – he'll die an old, sad man with no one, while all of us are happy and loved. That thought alone has me calming down. His words are like rocks and meant to shatter me, but I won't allow him that power. I know what I have. I know who I am and what I can accomplish. I can do anything I put my mind to, but with Claire encouraging and giving me her love, I can do it ten times better.

Somehow I think she knew I needed her because my phone dings with a message.

> *Claire: Just got done with my second class and I find myself watching the clock, hoping it tells me it's time to meet you downstairs. I miss you.*
> *Smiling, I text her back.*

> *Me: I miss you. I just took a nap, but was woken up by my dad*
> *calling. Jerk.*
> *Claire: Ew. Is he being a meanie?*
> *Me: He always is.*
> *Claire: Want to talk about it?*
> *Me: Ur busy, we can talk later.*

I wait for her reply but then a picture of her and me kissing comes up because she's calling me.

I answer with a grin, "Hey."

"Hey, I got time. What happened?"

"He's a dick."

"Yeah, I know that, but what happened?" she asks, and then I hear a door shut. She must have shut it to give us privacy.

I let out a breath and say, "Well, my agent called. I have four teams looking at me."

"That's amazing!" she squeals. "Which ones?"

I smile. "Kings, Rangers, Lightning, and Hawks."

"Oooo, go with the Rangers. I love New York. But then again, I love LA too, and LA is close to Vegas! Maybe I can get a job there! Hmm. Chicago is great. So is Florida, the ocean. I love the ocean."

I laugh, my heart hammering against my chest. "So you'll come with me?"

"Well, duh! I can teach or open a studio anywhere! But we'll worry about that in what, a couple months? When's the draft?"

"June."

She goes through the months out loud, and I assume she's counting because then she says, "So nine months, yeah, we'll worry about that then, but I *love* the ocean."

"I don't think you realize how happy you make me," I say, my heart in my throat.

"Aw, Jude, I love you, and you make me happy, but we both know that," she laughs. "What happened with your dad?"

My heart drops in my stomach, and I feel like I want to puke. I don't even want to talk about him, but I know I need to get the words out of me and for her to reassure me. I don't know why I need that. I've never needed reassurance before but with her, I do. "He first downplayed the fact that the teams want me."

"Okay, he's dumb, go on."

I want to laugh, but instead I say, "And then he went on this spiel about how I'm not made to be with anyone, that I'm him and all this other bullshit. That you're going to bring me down and hold me back. That being with you will ruin me."

The line goes silent, and I wonder if she hung up. But when I check my phone, it displays the call is still connected. Clearing my throat, I say, "Claire?"

"Yeah, I'm here. Listen, I would never ever do that. I promise you, I won't."

"I know you won't. That's what I told him," I say. "I just hate how he doesn't believe in me."

"He's just a sad dude, Jude. I'm sorry, he's a jerk. You don't deserve that. Maybe you should call your mom, talk to her?"

I shake my head, even though she can't see me. "I don't want to tell her what he said. It will hurt her feelings and she'll worry about me and she doesn't need that stress."

"See, I just don't get it. You're such a good dude. You love your mom something crazy, and you care about people's feelings, you know? Maybe that's why he's such a jerk 'cause he knows he can get to you. Ignore him. Just do you."

I nod. "Yeah, you're right."

"It happens often," she teases, and I smile. "So let's change the subject. I have two minutes." I laugh and she says, "Did you read Rachael's status on Facebook?"

"You two are friends?"

"We have to be, I'm on the dance team."

"Oh yeah. No, I've been napping."

"Lucky ass, anyway, she put this long-ass status about how it's hard to let go of someone and forget them when you have such great memories with them. And so some girl is like, girl, forget those people, if they don't want you, they don't deserve you. And she says, but he does deserve me, I just need him to realize that and get off the girl he's with. I wanted to comment, but I know she did it to bother me."

"Wow, that's crazy. Facebook is a cesspool of drama."

"Agreed. Crazy bitch. But really, you should talk to her. Get that all taken care of. You know? She's obviously hurting, and as much as I don't like her, I have to assume a broken heart hurts, and also I don't want her thinking she has a chance with you."

"She doesn't, and it shouldn't be broken. I never ever gave her any kind of hope of something happening between us."

"Jude. Don't lie to me. I've heard it from half the damn campus that you promised to get with them first if you ever started dating."

I laugh. "It was an empty promise."

"That people took seriously. When you want someone so bad, you don't hear things right. You hear what you want to believe, and they took your words to heart."

I never thought of it that way. I never really cared, though. It was just fun back then. Now that I'm in love and hang on every word she says, I can see what she means. I kinda sorta feel like a jerk for leading on so many people. Clearing my throat, I say, "Yeah, I guess you're right."

"Again, it happens often," she says and I scoff, my face breaking into a bigger grin. "I gotta go, babe. See you at four? I gotta go by my dorm to get my outfit for the dance."

"Is it hot?"

"You know it. I'm gonna be your little Mexican cutie."

I chuckle. "A pale, blue-eyed, redheaded Mexican? I think not."

"Hey, it could happen. See you soon."

"Bye, babe," I say and then hang up. Lying back on the blanket, my arm rests across my stomach as I take in a deep breath and let it out. I feel a hundred times better and my dad is a distant thought, all because of one phone call from my girl. Closing my eyes, I decide to sleep for a little longer but then my phone dings again.

Picking it up, I see it's a text from Claire.

> *Claire: btw…I love you.*

My heart feels as if it is blowing up in my chest, and I can't help but love the feeling. It's so breathtaking and special. Only she can make me feel like that too.

I write back quickly.

> *Me: Btw…I love u more than you'll ever know. Thanks for being there.*
> *Claire: I'll always be here for you.*
> *Good. That's really fucking good.*

CHAPTER 30

⚒ JUDE

"So, I have to admit something."

Claire looks back at me and grins. "What? Gosh, you look silly in that sombrero."

I send her a devilish grin as I run my fingers along the huge-ass sombrero hat I'm wearing. It goes great with my poncho and khaki shorts. "This sombrero is what makes me look silly? Not the big black mustache?" I ask, twirling the ends of my pasted-on mustache.

She laughs as she rolls her eyes. "You're right. That *is* what's making you look silly."

I pinch her butt as she walks by me, and she smacks my hand away as she goes to my mirror to put lipstick on. She's wearing tight red shorts with a frilly, black, Mexican-inspired top. Her hair is back in curls, held up by a big black rose.

In other words, she looks fucking hot.

Looking at me in the mirror, she says, "What did you have to admit? Hey, stop staring at my ass."

I chuckle as she pulls her shorts down some, trying to hide her assets, but there is no hiding that spectacular ass. "Hey, that's my ass to look at, thank you."

She sticks her tongue out before turning to look at me. "Whatever. Admit what you gotta admit."

I stand and walk toward her, wrapping my arms around her waist and picking her up off the ground. She squeals, wrapping her arms loosely around my neck as I say, "You, my love, are *muy caliente*."

Her face warms with color as she says, "Why, thank you. I didn't know you spoke Spanish."

"I do, thanks to four years of it in high school."

I basically learned it so I could talk girls out of their panties, but I don't think I should say that to my girlfriend. Might piss her off.

"Ooh, say more," she demands, a lusty grin playing on her sweet mouth.

Letting her slide down my body, I tuck my fingers inside her shorts as I bring my lips close to her shiny red ones. I then whisper, "*Tu estas muy caliente y demasiado bella, mujer. Te quiero acostar y hacerte cosas tan sucio.*"

Taking in a sharp breath, she grins at me. "Good God, that's hot. What does it mean?"

Nipping at her bottom lip, I say in a throaty, rough way, "You are so hot, my beautiful woman. I want to lay you down and do the nastiest things ever to you."

As the last word leaves my mouth, I press into her with my pelvis, letting her feel every hard inch of me. Her eyes darken with color before she goes up on her toes, her lips only a breath away from mine. Everything she does makes me hard, even just her breathing. She's so undeniably amazing and she drives me absolutely insane. Threading her fingers in my hair, she says, "I like when you talk dirty to me…especially in another language."

I smile but then her lips are moving against mine. Holding her close, I move my tongue into her mouth and then along her tongue, deepening the kiss. Curving my tongue up, I lick the roof of her mouth before moving it again with hers. Pulling back, she kisses my bottom lip, then the side of my mouth before my jaw and then chin. Looking up at me, she says, "Red is a good color on you."

She then turns my face so that I see myself in the mirror. Red lipstick is all over my face, and you can tell I just got done kissing the hottest girl in the world. She goes to wipe it off, but I stop her. "Don't, I like it."

"What? You like wearing lipstick? Weirdo! Let me wipe it off."

"No, I want everyone to know that the girl with hot red lipstick kissed the hell out of me."

Blushing, she pulls away as she reaches for her lipstick. "You're crazy."

I smack her ass playfully, making her jump, and her hand quickly replaces mine as she gives me a dirty look. "Ow! That hurt!"

"No, it didn't," I say, smacking her other cheek. "I'm gonna do that as I'm hitting you from behind later," I say, waggling my brows at her.

"Smack my ass again and you won't be hitting anything later but the bed to go to sleep," she warns, her eyes sparkling with lust. Her face tells me she doesn't like it, but those eyes, they love it. She turns to reapply her lipstick and I move behind her, rubbing my hands along her sweet cheeks.

"I'm sorry, baby. Here, let me rub them."

She tries to ignore me, but when my fingers dance along the edges of the shorts, her eyes catch mine in the mirror and she says, "What are you doing, *señor?"*

"Trying to get a little piece of this sweet ass," I say roughly against her cheek. "I've missed you all day."

My hand snakes around the front, cupping her center, and I watch her eyes fall shut as I squeeze her. Teasing her a bit, I slide my finger along her delectable pussy. When a little sound leaves her mouth, my dick comes to life, pushing against the shorts I wear. Pulling her into me, I move my finger inside her shorts, then her panties, and just as I'm heading for what I'm craving, the door flies open and my cock-blocking brother walks in.

Removing my hand, I turn to look at him. "What?"

"Everyone is looking for you, and Claire, Rachael is looking for you," he announces, and while I want to be mad that he interrupted us, I can't help but chuckle at his outfit. He's wearing khaki shorts with a white tank and a plaid shirt buttoned at the top. His hair is slicked to the side, and he's drawn a teardrop under his eye.

We take Mexican Night seriously around these parts. I can't wait till Cowboy Night.

"Thanks, Jayden," Claire says, doing one more run of lipstick before turning to head for the door. "I'll see you out there."

"Good luck."

She grins as she nods. "Thanks, babe."

Then she's gone, leaving me with my brother who is looking at me like I'm a science experiment gone wrong. "What?"

"You know you have lipstick all over your face, right?"

I nod. "Yeah, and did you know you just interrupted us?"

"Oh, my bad, I'll knock next time," he says, but I don't believe him one bit.

"You say that every time," I point out and he grins back at me, his green eyes flashing with mischief.

"Maybe one time I'll remember, too."

"Yeah, like you'll remember to bring me my money?"

His brows come in. "What money?"

"Um, I don't know if you remember, but two weeks ago you told me I'd get bored with Claire and I haven't – I love her – so you owe me hundred bucks."

He rolls his eyes and I'm about to say something, but then Claire is in the doorway, her hands on her hips as she eyes us both. "You bet your brother that you wouldn't get bored with me?"

I shake my head as I point to him. "No, he said I would get bored. I knew I wouldn't."

Smacking Jayden on the arm, she says, "That's rude! I'm not someone you get bored of!"

Holding his arm, he says, "I didn't know you then! He always gets bored."

"Whatever. Don't make bets about me anymore, got it?" she says, pointing at him, and he nods quickly. Then she turns to me, her little blue eyes blazing with annoyance. "You either."

"Yes, ma'am."

She then goes to her bag, grabbing her iPod, and looks back at me. "You coming?"

"Yup, I'll be out there in a minute."

"Okay," she says and then she's gone again.

As I look back at Jayden, he says, "She's freaking scary, dude."

"Yeah, and if I don't get my money, I'm gonna sic her on you."

"Your own brother? That's so messed up."

"It's okay. I have another one," I say with a grin.

He flips me off and then he heads out the door. Letting out a breath, I try to readjust my dick before following him upstairs. The whole house is decorated like a huge fiesta. Everything's so bright and colorful. Big cactus inflatables are all over the place along with huge bowls of ice filled with Coronas. After I point to one, a freshman pops the top before handing it to me, and I head out to the backyard where the festivities are being held. There is a huge floor that the girls will dance on and tables are around for everyone to hang out at when we aren't dancing. Food is everywhere – beer, margaritas, the works, and the place is packed with people.

This is one of the biggest parties of the fall, and we aim to please.

The party is in full swing, and I'm surprised at how much I just want to find Claire and take her back to my room. I usually love parties, but lately, lying in bed watching TV is way more fun than having to deal with partygoers, which basically consist of girls who chase me left and right. As I head to my seat, I'm bombarded by them and they ask where I've been and blah, blah, blah. Soon I'm doing a dance to get away from the girls, and it's not a dance I want to do. I just don't get it. I mean, hasn't anyone seen that I am "in a relationship" on Facebook? I thought if you put it on Facebook it was real. Is that not the case anymore? Must have missed the memo.

Heading toward the table that my friends are at, I grab a plate of food and then settle in the seat beside Max. Thankfully they chose the seats right by the dance floor so I can see my girl dance. I'm excited to see her do this. She has been talking about it for the last week and is so excited about it.

"Dude, the dance girls are fucking hot," Max says and I give him a look. He quickly adds, "Except for Claire. I did not look at her at all."

"He's lying. I saw him checking out her ass," Jayden says and Max glares.

"Asshole," he mutters and Jayden laughs.

"I'm pretty sure I've told you not to check my girl out," I say and Max shrugs.

"When a girl is that hot, it's hard not to look."

"Then I'd try harder," I say as I take a bite of my taco, ending the conversation. Thankfully, I don't have to wait too long for the girls to hit the floor. They are probably the only reason I'm out here, to be honest. Everyone is staring at me, looking and whispering, and it's bothering the shit out of me. Why am I still being talked about? It's been two weeks; shouldn't everyone accept that I've changed and move on?

Rolling my eyes, I watch as the girls head to the floor in a very formal, unified way. Front and center is my beautiful girlfriend and beside her is the chick who is in love with me. I don't get it, but I plan on fixing it later. Right now though, I'm gonna watch my baby kill this dance. She sends me a grin, and I smile back just as the music to a popular Jennifer Lopez song starts, then the dancers start. They are so together and actually look professional, and I bet altogether it's an amazing show, but my eyes can't leave Claire's body. She moves like the music is in her. It's amazing. Unlike the other girls though, she dances a little more sexually. Or maybe it's just my dirty mind, but it seems like when she dances, she's having sex. Her eyes are glazed over, her body so sexy and hard-hitting to each beat. She loves this. It's sexy, she's sexy, and boy, I'm lucky she's coming downstairs to my room when this thing is over.

When Rachael and Claire bend over, spreading their legs in splits but still standing up, the crowd loses it. It is pretty badass. As the song ends, the girls move quickly to the beat, shaking their asses and making the guys go nuts. Looking over her shoulder, Claire winks at me, and I stand with everyone else, cheering them on.

"Man, that was awesome. Thank you, Claire!" Jayden hollers, and she grins like a fool. The group then heads off the floor the way they came in, and I fall back in my chair, grabbing my beer.

"Dude, your girl is so fucking hot," one of the seniors, Justin, says.

"Yeah, thanks," I say offhandedly as I take a drink.

"I can see why you gave up all the ass you got. She's got a spectacular one."

"Yeah, I know. Keep your eyes off it," I say, meeting his gaze.

His eyes are challenging as he says, "What if I don't?"

"I'll rip them out of your ugly-ass head then, your choice."

"Jude," Jayden warns and I ignore him, my eyes telling Justin he better fuck the hell off.

Before anything else can be said, Claire falls into my lap, wrapping her arms around my neck.

Giving me a bright grin, she says, "What did you think?"

Wrapping my arms around her hips, I say, "Amazing. You were a showstopper, baby."

She grins happily as her cheeks warm. "Thanks."

Kissing me loudly on the lips, she leans against my chest and grabs my plate. "Can I eat this?"

"Sure," I say, moving my hand along her thigh. "Give me a bite of that taco first."

She smiles as she feeds me, and I can see Jayden making gagging faces, but I know he's just jealous. The hottest girl ever is feeding me, and he has to use a fork. I'd be jealous too. We eat together, and when we're done, I think we're gonna relax, but soon she's pulling me onto the floor to dance. I don't mind it, I like to dance, but I don't like the way people are looking at her. I know she's sexy, I get that, but I don't want people watching her all the damn time. It seems every time I turn my head someone is looking, and it is honestly driving me up the fucking wall. Jealously bubbles inside me and I hate that feeling. I shouldn't be insecure, but I am. I don't understand it, really. Wrapping my arms tighter around her waist, I pull her to me, hoping people know she is mine.

I mean, they have to know. Right?

Moving her fingers in my hair, she brings my face down so she can see me. "What's wrong?"

I shake my head. "Nothing," I answer.

I then turn her around, pressing her back to my chest, and she begins to move her ass against me. Bending over some, she puts her hands on her knees and starts to move her ass like a girl in a rap video. It's beyond hot, but I can't enjoy it because all I see are the guys staring at her, mouths parted and with wide eyes. It makes my blood boil, and I want nothing more than to take my poncho off to cover her up. I don't think it's what she's wearing though; I think it's just her. She's insanely sexy and everyone wants a piece of her. I don't like that. Not one fucking bit.

Thankfully the song turns to a slow one, and I turn her back around and wrap my arms around her as we slowly move to the music. Looking up at me, her fingers tickle my neck and a content little grin sits on her face. She really is so beautiful, and I should be flattered that everyone thinks my girl is hot, but for some reason I'm just jealous. Is it because I'm scared that she could leave me? I don't know, but I don't like the way I feel.

"Don't lie to me again, Jude. Tell me what's wrong," she says against my cheek, and I let out a breath as my arms tighten around her.

"Nothing, baby. Let's just dance."

She moves her tongue along my jaw to my ear, and I take in a deep breath as she whispers against my ear, "Why don't we take the party inside?" As she nibbles at my ear, my hands tighten at her waist and she says, "In your room, or maybe your bed, to be exact."

Pulling back, she grins at me and I ask, "You're done with the party already?"

"Yeah, I ate, I danced, I drank, now I want you to do nasty things to me."

Grinning, since I'm always down to worship her sexy body, I nod. "All right, baby, let's go."

I take her hand in mine, and we make our way through the party. Reaching my room, I open the door and she walks in before me. I shut it behind me and she turns and says, "Make sure it's locked."

"Check," I say, throwing off my poncho and locking the door. When I glance at her though, she's not naked. Her hands are on her hips, her gaze locked on me. "What are you doing? Get naked."

She shakes her head. "Not until you tell me what the hell is wrong with you."

"You tricked me!" I accuse and she doesn't move.

"Oh, I plan to let you do what you want, but first I want to know what is wrong."

Mimicking her stance, I say, "Nothing."

"Liar. You lie to me again and I'm gone."

I glare and she glares right back; she isn't going to budge. I let out a breath, running my hand through my hair. "Fine. I don't like people staring at you."

"Huh?" she asks, her face twisted in confusion.

"I don't like the way people stare at you, like they're having sex with you. It pisses me off."

"Why? That's dumb. They can look all they want, but I'm not touching them, and they sure as hell ain't touching me."

Letting out another breath, I roll my eyes. "I get that, but it makes me mad."

"Why, Jude? Do I get mad when girls stare at you, or better yet, when they hit on you? No, I saw it over and over again tonight, and all I did was sit back and trust that you're not going to fuck around on me."

I look away and nod. I know she's right, but it still doesn't ease my jealousy. "I'm jealous. That's all I can say."

She smiles as she comes toward me, stopping in front of me. "Okay, Jude, and that's fine, but you have nothing to worry about. I'm all yours."

Reaching up, she runs her fingers along my lips, in a intoxicating way. "I don't want to be needy and stupid, but for some reason, when it comes to you, I think I am."

"You're not, I promise. This is new. We're both learning how to do this, but we have to remember and trust that neither of us is going to screw the other over."

"You're right."

"I know, now stop all this and remember that I love you and would never ever get with anyone else but you…and Justin Timberlake."

I laugh as I grip her hips, bringing her against me. "Sorry, babe, no JT. You are all mine."

When she grins and reaches for my face, I think she's going to cup my face or something but instead, she quickly pulls off my mustache. It feels as if she ripped off my real mustache, and I holler out as she laughs. "Sorry, can't kiss you with that damn thing on your face. It's itchy."

"You took my face with it!"

"Oh, I did not, you drama queen. Come here," she says, pulling my mouth down to hers. Kissing her, my heart pounds against my chest, and I find it hard to form a coherent thought. This girl is so fucking hot, and my God, I can't get enough of those succulent lips.

Parting, our breathing is labored as beautiful lust swirls in her blue eyes. Leaning against me, she whispers against my lips, "Make love to me, Jude."

"Your wish is my command, sweetheart."

Grinning at me, she presses her lips to mine again. I hold her tight as our mouths almost dance together. She moves one way, I go the other, our mouths in perfect unison. Her body then molds to mine, and I know that I have nothing to worry about. She isn't going anywhere. She loves me.

She's mine.

CHAPTER 31

⚒ JUDE

Moving her back, I slowly drop my hands to her ass, pressing her against my growing erection. Parting, we hastily rip our shirts off, our mouths coming back together as we push off our bottoms. It's sloppy and kind of hectic, but it's us and I love it. Unhooking her bra, I deepen the kiss as the cups fall away, her breasts pressing against my chest. When her hands slide into my boxers, I take in a sharp breath, letting it out just as fast against her swollen lips before she pushes them down. Then she does hers, and thank God, we're both completely naked for each other. Running my finger down the middle of her chest to her belly, I swirl my finger slowly around her belly button, admiring her beautiful body. She's so toned but also curvy; it's sexy as hell.

I lift her up, and her arms and legs wrap around me as I walk toward my bed. I'm not sure how I'm going to carry her up to the bed, but I'm going to figure it out while still kissing her amazing mouth. Reaching my ladder, I lean her against it, holding on to it as I press into her, deepening the kiss as my heart beats out of control in my chest. I feel like a raging furnace. My whole body is on fire for this hot-as-sin girl. Threading her fingers in my hair, she goes up on a higher step and then slowly moves her wet pussy along my dick. My toes curl against the hardwood as a harsh breath leaves my mouth.

"My God, you are so hot," I basically moan.

"Right back atcha," she gasps before taking my dick and moving it up and down her pussy, her wetness covering my dick. Breathlessly, I grip her hips as she moves the tip of my dick against her clit. Her breathing is erratic and her eyes are glazed with lust as she pleases herself with my dick. I want to do it for her, but I am enjoying the view of this a little more. There is something about this girl pleasing herself that gets me off. As her legs shake with her orgasm, I hold on to her, not allowing her to fall as she yells my name, her hand squeezing my dick as she comes.

I want to be inside her.

Deep inside her, like, right now.

Taking her by the back of her knee, I part her legs and then thrust up inside her tight pussy in one swift movement. Groaning, I grasp her knee as she squeezes me tighter than a vise grip. It feels so damn good; she's so tight, so fucking hot, ah, fuck. My hand grips the ladder as I pound up into her, losing my mind with lust and all things hot. When her hands cup my face, I look up from where I am watching myself disappear in her to meet her blazing blue eyes. She takes my lips with hers in a harsh assault, blowing my mind and making everything inside me blow the hell up. When I thrust up into her hard, she cries out, her nails digging into my shoulders, and I do it again and again until my legs are shaking and I can't hold back anymore. Letting out a yell of my own against her swollen lips, I fill her up as my legs buckle underneath me, shattering my world.

Gasping for breath, I slowly kiss her neck, her jaw, before meeting my lips to hers. She lets out a little sigh before kissing my bottom lip, then top, running her tongue lazily behind each kiss as my eyes slowly drift shut. I feel so unbelievable and spent. Opening my eyes, I meet her loving gaze and a lazy smile curves my lips.

"I've never had ladder sex," she says, the red blush creeping up her neck to her cheeks.

"First time for everything," I say, letting out a long breath.

"Yeah, and with us, there are a lot of them."

I nod, squeezing her ass as I nip at her bottom lip. "And to think, we have the rest of our lives for more of them."

With a shy grin on her face, she says, "Exciting thought, huh?"

"Sure is," I admit. "Now let's get cleaned up."

After cleaning up, we find ourselves in bed, her body lying across my chest lazily, her fingers dancing along my chest. The sounds of the party are still in full swing and I hear people running down the hall, but here in my love nest, I don't hear anything but Claire's breathing and her soft words. Moving my fingers in her hair, I smile as she glances up at me, her face warm with color.

"Tell me something," she says, and I clear my throat.

"What?"

"Why do you think you feel jealous?"

I shrug. "I don't know... Why does anyone feel jealous?"

She eyes me. "I understand what you're saying, but I don't get it. You are a superconfident man. You have to know I'm not going anywhere, that I know where I'm at is good."

A grin curves my face as I meet her gaze. "I think I do know that. I think it's deeper than that."

Her brow comes up. "What does that mean?"

She sits up and I do the same, stretching my arms above my head before looking back at her. "It's just that I've watched my mom for years basically have the phone glued to her hand twenty-four seven and hang on every word my dad says. She does everything for him and waits on him hand and foot. She loves him, like a lot, and sometimes when I look at you, I see myself being like that. I love you so much, so hard, and it has been so fast that I feel it everywhere. And it scares me that you could just leave me or find someone better or something."

"I don't want anyone else," she promises and I nod. "Have I made you feel like I do?"

I shake my head. "No, not at all, it's just that sometimes I think my mom is living in a loveless marriage. I'm not saying he's cheating on her, or he's going to leave her, but who knows? With us, I know I love you and I know you love me, so just the thought of something happening to where you leave me or I leave you has me in knots. When people look at you or try to holler at you, jealousy overcomes me. I don't want the temptation or anything. I just want us."

Her eyes are locked with mine as she breathes softly. Reaching out, she takes my hands and says, "Okay, this relationship can't soar if there is no trust. You have to trust me like I trust you. I don't think you're gonna run off on me with someone. I trust you. Give me that trust and let that jealousy go. No one is going to come between us."

Lacing my fingers with hers, I bring her knuckles to my lips and kiss each one. "I do trust you, Claire. I'm just so in love with you that the thought of losing you seriously fucks with me."

Her thumbs move along the back of my hands and her eyes never leave mine as she processes what I'm saying. I know that I can be completely and utterly honest with her. She wants that, and I like that we're talking about this. It will help, but something in her eyes says I'm not going to like what she's about to say.

"I love you, Jude, but maybe we need to take a step back, y'know?"

My brows come together as her thumbs still against my hands. "How does that make sense?"

"It doesn't, really! I'm just scared. I sorta feel like you're obsessed with me!"

Dropping her hands, I say, "Are you fucking kidding me? I tell you I love you, and you think I'm obsessed?"

She pauses and then her head cocks to the side. "Okay, maybe the wrong choice of words."

"You think?" I said in an offhand way that has her glaring at me.

"I was trying to say that we are so in this, committed and in love, that I don't want to walk on eggshells or make sure not to talk to someone 'cause it is going to piss you off. I want this to be good. I want us to be drama-free and fucking happy, Jude. I don't and I won't walk on eggshells. This is supposed to be easy."

Covering my face, I let out a long breath before taking another one in. "I shouldn't have said anything."

"No, you should. Communication is the key, Jude. But the thing is that we have to nip this in the bud. Are you going to cheat on me?"

I drop my hands and give her a look. "Fuck no."

"Good, 'cause I'm not either. No one holds a hockey stick to you, boo. You are it. You've left your mark on me. I'm yours, and we both know that. So let it go," she says, reaching for my hands. "Okay? We're good, right?"

Slowly I nod as I lace my fingers with hers. She's completely right, and while I've admitted that before, I'm not going to this time. Don't want her getting a big head, but seriously, I feel kind of stupid in a way. I know what we have, so why be jealous of anyone? I should be proud that my girl is hot and all mine, not want to freak out every time someone looks at her. I just don't want to lose her, and I won't. I have to trust that.

"Okay," I say since I know she's waiting for me to say it.

She smiles, running her fingers through the beard on my face before leaning toward me for a heart-stopping kiss. As we slowly kiss, my heart beats in double-time for her. It's so easy for me to love her; like she said, this is supposed to be easy and it is. I don't know what I was thinking trying to throw a roadblock in that. I've never been good at this though, but as she lays me down, lying across my chest, her legs tangling with mine, I know that I'm learning to be good at loving her. I'll probably never master the art of loving her since I'll make dumb decisions and stumble along the way, probably say the wrong thing at times, but the main thing is that I'll never stop loving her. I can't. As much as I want to be hard and manly, I know that I couldn't handle losing her, and I think that frightens me the most.

I just have to trust her.

And I do.

Rolling on my side, I wrap my arms around her, bringing her in close. She grins up at me after I kiss her nose and I say, "Now tell me something."

Her mouth pulls up at the side. "What do you want to hear?"

"Your past."

Her grins falls and her gaze diverts from mine. "Oh yeah, I did say I'd tell ya that, huh?"

"You did."

I don't dare say anything. I only watch as she bites hard into her lips as her brain works. It can't be that bad. I mean, yeah, she got around, who cares? But to her it must be horrible because I can feel her heartbeat against my chest.

Meeting my gaze, she says, "For as long as I could remember, my mom was a cracked-out stripper. She cleaned up for maybe three years when I was six, but then when I turned nine, she went right back to her old ways. We never had food. We moved all the time, and sometimes I had to sleep in a car. I went to school looking a hot damn mess, and I had to clean studios just for studio time with teachers."

Looking away again, she says, "For six years, my mom would bring home these sleazeballs, and I had to fight them off from trying to touch me and rape me while she was passed out in the living room. But when I turned fourteen, I didn't fight anymore. This guy, his name was Drew, he was maybe in his thirties, but he came in the room, drunk and stupid and was talking to me, telling me how pretty I was. When he made an advance on me, I let him and I ended up losing my virginity that night." Running her hands through her hair, she lets out a breath as she looks away.

"Why?" I ask and she shrugs her shoulders, still not meeting my gaze.

"I don't know. My mom didn't love me. I was a hassle to her and a quick way to get money off my uncle. When Phillip left for the NHL, leaving me with only her, I just didn't feel loved. I didn't feel special or anything. I felt hollow. So then this guy is here giving me attention without trying to rape me, and I thought he meant it but he didn't. He fucked me, hard, and left me to figure out why I was bleeding and why I was hurting so bad. But then he came back the next night and said he treasured me and I believed him, like the dumb girl I was, and I gave it up again. It felt so good, so amazing. I felt alive. So I didn't stop. I slept with anyone who wanted me, and to be honest with you, I don't know how I don't have an STD or how I didn't get pregnant."

She looks up at me but only for a second before looking away again. I don't know what to say, so I don't say anything. I instead wait for her to finish her story. Tracing the outlines of my tattoo, she continues, "My mom was found in a ditch, raped and murdered by someone. They still don't know who. I went to my crazy aunt who tried everything to fix me by the good Lord's standards, and when that didn't work, she sent me to rehab. Twice. I didn't want to live. I tried killing myself, but couldn't do it, and because of that, I decided to self-medicate with drugs and alcohol. I knew how I was going to end up. I was going to become my mom and then I would die. So before all that could happen, I decided to self-destruct since I didn't have the balls to kill myself outright."

"What made you change?" I ask when she pauses.

A slow grin comes across her face before she looks up at me. "Phillip."

I'm completely engrossed in her. Taking in a deep breath, I ask, "How?"

"He came and saved me. At the time, I thought he was ruining my life more, but I was completely wrong. He loved me so fiercely and helped me and pushed me to be a better person. Then Reese came along and gave me dance as my outlet and things just fell into place. I no longer think I'm going to end up a strung-out stripper dead in an alley. I may not know what I want, but I do want to be the best at whatever I choose."

Her story warms my heart. It really is a phoenix-type story. She burned to ashes but then rose from them. It's inspiring and only makes me love her more. I go to tell her that, but she says, "I know that it isn't your typical childhood story, but I'm not ashamed of it. I think it made me stronger. I just never wanted to tell you because no one knows but Reese and Phillip."

"I'm glad you told me," I say, squeezing her hands.

A grin pulls at her lips. "Not scared? Don't want to run the other way?"

I shake my head. "Nope, I admire you for your strength and power to overcome the shit that was dealt to you. You are inspiring, baby."

"Thanks," she says shyly as she looks away, a grin still gracing her lips.

"And I know what your next tattoo should be."

"What?" she asks, her fingers playing with the strings to my sweats.

When she looks up at me, I say, "A phoenix, because your story really defines just that."

"You're right."

I nod. "I know I am."

"Oh, hush," she says with a laugh. She then shakes her head as she says, "Wow, we really had a come-to-Jesus talk, huh?"

Reaching out, I take her sweet face in my hands, bringing her closer to me. "Yeah, and I have to say, I think I love you more."

Grinning, she leans her head to mine and says, "I couldn't agree more."

CHAPTER 32

Claire

Crawling slowly and very provocatively, I move to the end of the stage and then quickly spread my legs behind me in the splits. Running my hands down the lace of my top, I stop above my center before turning to my back, letting my legs fall open then shut and open again. Tens, twenties, and even hundreds rain on me as I circle my legs to the music of "Fever." Arching my back, I go to the tip of my toes and then bring myself to my feet, kicking the heels of my shoes against my ass as I walk toward the middle of the stage where my chair sits. With every step I take, a bill falls to the ground and I mentally count each one, adding it to my bank in my head.

I'm so close I can taste it.

Tonight is a good night. Lots of really important, *rich* people are here tonight, and they are throwing the cash like it's nothing to them. But it's everything to me. Taking the back of the chair, I shake my ass to the music, and the crowd claps and whistles in appreciation of what I'm doing. Straddling it, I lean back, letting my head brush the ground as I move my hands along my body, giving the boys a show. Sitting up, I turn around, stopping my legs in front before standing up just as the curtains go up. Behind me are four other dancers, and right on the beat of the music, we go into a hard-hitting dance routine that flaunts our bodies in the best way possible.

Slowly the girls head back up the stairs, posing in various styles as I go back to the end of the stage, my eyes never leaving the older man who has been giving me loads of money all night. Dropping into a squat, I run my hands along my thighs. His beady brown eyes darken as he stands, coming toward me. Ben, our security guy, stops between us, and the guy puts his hands up as I continue to shake and move. Opening his wallet, he takes out hundreds and waves them in front of Ben's face, but he doesn't care one bit about the money.

But I do. I want that money.

I pat Ben's shoulder and he steps to the side. I slowly move my body, biting my lips as I bend to the left, shaking my ass for him. He can't touch me. If he does, Ben will dismember him – but he can look. Running my fingers from my lips down my chest and between my legs, I give him a very seductive look, one that I know is my moneymaker, and he lays eight one hundred dollar bills at my feet, nodding his head, still holding a bunch of hundreds.

"Take something off, sweetheart. Let me get a–," he says, but before he can get the last word out, Ben places his hand on his chest.

"This is the burlesque side. The naked girls are on the other side," Ben yells.

The man shakes his head. "But I want her."

"She isn't yours to take," I hear Ben say and then he turns to me. "Go on."

I nod, blowing the man a kiss, and as I slowly walk backward trying to get some more money, I see the guy go to take back the money he laid on the stage. Ben is quick to act, and just as fast as the old guy reached for the money, his face ends up against it.

"And that's it for our beautiful Diamond. Let's hear it people, she'll be back out soon."

Turning, a grin comes on my face as the crowd hoots and hollers for me. Going through the curtains, I let out a long breath before pulling off my pin-curled, blond-haired wig. The wig is so itchy, I'm going to have to get another one, but I love this style. It is so pretty and very burlesque. As I wait for Tony, our money collector, I scratch my head and basically moan out from how good it feels. Pulling down the long black gloves that go up to my elbows, I tuck them into the bra of my lacy black outfit before stretching my arms. I'm sore and I'm tired, but I only have one more dance and then I'm done for the night. I haven't seen Ms. Prissy yet and I need to.

I'm gonna quit the stage.

I can't take it anymore. I feel like I'm lying, and I can't do that anymore. I love Jude too much. Ever since we lay in bed and basically opened the closet and aired it out, I know I can't do this. I should have told him then. He was so compassionate, so sweet and understanding. He thinks I'm strong and believes in the person I am, and I think that's why I didn't tell him. I couldn't taint what he thinks about me; I want him to continue thinking I hung the moon and stars. For that to happen, I have to quit. I have to let this go. Yes, it's hard because I am so good at it, but I just can't help but think that Jude will throw a fucking fit.

For the last two days, I've felt like I'm allowing some guy to change me, but sometimes you change for the right person. Reese doesn't do this anymore. Yeah, she'll choreograph stuff, but she hasn't been onstage since she was twenty-one, back when she didn't have someone to care if she danced for men.

I found that person early, and this isn't a job that a girlfriend or maybe even a wife should have, especially the other half to an NHL player. How would that look? What if people found out? How would Jude handle that? Yeah, he may be fine with me doing it, but what about when the world finds out? I don't know and that scares me. I can't lose him. I just can't. If something happens and the investors want to hire me, then I'll tell him about this. He'd have to be proud, right? He'd still believe in me, but then again, maybe he won't and everything will come crashing down on me.

Who knows? All I know is tonight will be my last performance.

Finally, Tony shows up with my bucket full of cash. "One thousand twenty-eight."

"Fabulous, thank you," I say, handing him a five out the bunch and then taking out four twenties for the girls who were onstage with me. Turning, I head to my station where all my stuff sits. I put my wig on a mannequin head and then kick off my sky-high heels, loving the way the tile cools my feet. Catching my reflection in the mirror, I smile. I love this outfit; it's my moneymaking outfit since it is the most revealing. The whole thing is black, the top a see-through lace, my nipples only being covered by a darker piece of lace. Ten strips of satin ribbon run along my stomach, connecting to satin panties that have to be held down with glue to stay in place. Let's just say, this outfit is gorgeous and may get me paid, but man, it's a bitch to take off.

Laying my bucket on the table, I stand in front of it and count each bill, making sure that Tony's count was accurate. He almost always is, but I still like to check. Bundling my money up, I open the safe I keep in my station and lock it up before dropping onto the bench. Combing my hair up with my fingers, I bundle it on the top of my head before reaching for my phone to check the time. It's a little past midnight and that surprises me because I usually have already seen Ms. Prissy by now.

Looking over at Ellen, I see that she's on her phone, a dreamy little grin on her face. "Have you seen Prissy?"

She shakes her head without looking up from the phone. "Nope."

"What are you doing?"

"Talking to my man."

My brow quirks up. "Your man?"

She looks over at me, nodding her head, her curls bouncing against her face. "Oh yeah, I've figured it out."

"Figured out what?"

Laying her phone down, she looks over at me like I'm beneath her. I'm not sure what the look is about, but before I can ask, she says, "That guys our age are dumb and nasty. Older is the way to go."

I scoff. "Oh, is that right?"

"Yes, Claire, you just don't know how amazing this man is. I am completely in love with him."

"You are?" I ask since Ellen hasn't been with anyone long enough to even like them.

She nods quickly. "Oh yeah, we've been dating for almost a month."

My point exactly, she goes from crab boy to older guy. Not that I tell her that. "And Claire! He's so rich and powerful!"

Bingo, ladies and gentlemen, that's why she loves him.

"Wow, that's wonderful," I say, holding in my laughter.

"He's amazing. He's actually one of the investors. He's from New York and only comes in on the weekends to see me."

Hearing the investor part, I look over at her, intrigued. She may not know how big of a deal it is to be dating someone like that, so I decide to remind her. "Well, make sure to keep him happy! We need him to consider us," I say with a wink.

But she glares, her eyes and demeanor acting as if she's the older, wiser one of us, when that couldn't be any further from the truth. Ellen is a dimwit. "It is more than the investor shit, Claire. This is true love!"

"Yes, it is," I say sarcastically, but she won't ever realize that. "I wish y'all the best."

She smiles sweetly before turning to pick her phone back up. Looking back at the mirror, I move my hair out of my face and wash off the makeup from my previous performance. I'm doing a softer song in my next set. It's something I've been working on, and I'm excited since this will be the first and last time I perform it.

It's for Jude.

I know it's dumb since he will never see it, but every time I hear the song, I think of him.

"There's Ms. Prissy," Ellen says suddenly.

Whipping my head around, I catch her going into her office. Standing up, I check the time and I have plenty of time to talk to her. Rushing to her office, I knock on the door and she looks up from her desk, her red hair falling into her face. She's wearing a black leather bodysuit today with matching whip. She must have been on the Rock Room side.

"Hey, Claire, you okay?" she asks, a grin growing on her face.

I bite my lip because I know by the end of this conversation that grin won't be there. "Yeah, can I talk to you?"

"Sure, baby, close the door," she says, closing a file as I do as she asks, then I fall into the seat in front of her desk.

"What's up?"

Moving my fingers together, I bite the inside of my cheek and take in a deep breath. She isn't going to like this one bit, but I have to remember the reason I'm doing this.

Jude.

"I'm quitting the stage," I say and watch as her face contorts in anger. "I still want to choreograph for you, but I mainly want to be backstage only. I can't be onstage anymore."

Nothing is said. Her eyes are locked on me, and I'm ready for her to start screaming. Surprising though, she doesn't.

"Why?" she asks, her voice sharp and to the point.

Swallowing loudly, I say, "Well, for two reasons, or maybe two people. I'm not sure how my uncle will react to this, and I have a boyfriend now. I'm pretty sure he doesn't want his girlfriend onstage."

"No one knows it's you. We make sure of that."

I nod. "I know, but *I* know and I feel like I'm lying to them."

"Who cares? Lock that shit up. You are my best dancer, my biggest moneymaker."

"I know, but I can't stay here for the rest of my life, Ms. Prissy. You knew this day would come."

"Yeah, I did," she snaps. "But not three weeks before the investors come. I need you."

"I will be here, backstage. I will still come and work with the girls and get them stage-ready. I'm not going to leave you hanging."

She starts to shake her head before I even finish my sentence. "No, I need you onstage. What do you want, more money?"

I shake my head. "No, I can't do it."

She eyes me and then leans on her forearms, looking me straight in the eye. "Yes, you can, and here's what I'm offering. Give me until the investors come. I won't take a cut of your tips, no station fee, nothing."

Holy crap, that's over a grand I'll be keeping. She must have known that would mess with my decision to leave because she goes on. "You will be strictly coming here, working, and leaving with every cent you make. On top of that, I'll pay you five hundred dollars more, in addition to the money I'm already paying you."

Fucking hell, I'll have way more money than I wanted to save. I'll be set.

"After the investors come and go, if you don't get hired, which, by the way… What happens if you do get hired?"

I shrug. "I'll have to tell them then, and pray that they'll support me."

She shakes her head, bored with me as she says, "Okay, whatever. After that, you can go and strictly be backstage. Don't turn this down; this is a good deal. I need you and you know that."

I nod. "I do, but it isn't about the money," I say, but I think we both know that is a complete lie. "I love them, and I don't want to lose either one of them."

Looking me square in the eyes, Ms. Prissy basically says what Reese said weeks ago. "If they love you, they will support you, no matter what." Clearing her throat, she says, "My parents did not support me at first when I opened this business, but when they saw how happy I was, they did. Some people are made for this, and I believe you are one of them. The investors are going to eat you up, you watch. I've been talking you up something crazy, and I bet your bottom dollar that they are going to offer you something you won't be able to refuse. I suggest you tell your loved ones now before you are forced to."

I look away and take in a deep breath before blowing it out my nose. "But I'm quitting."

She scoffs. "No, baby, you're not and you know it. We both know that money talks, and I just gave you the mother lode."

Not answering her, tears rush to my eyes because she's completely right. I need that money; it will set me up for the rest of my life. If things don't work out for me and Jude, not that I would expect to live off him, I'll need the money in the future. If they do work out for us and I get picked up by the investors, I can put this money in a trust fund for our little hockey-playing babies. The best hockey schools aren't cheap.

This money is my future.

I can't turn my back on it.

It's only for a few more weeks.

Everything will be fine.

"Okay," I say, meeting her gaze again.

"That's right, now off you go. You have a pole dance to get ready for," she says, waving me off. I go to stand and she says, "I believe in you, Claire. You have talent, talent no one can touch, and I know that these men who you love will come around once they know how much you love this and how good you are at it."

Not able to trust my voice since tears are threatening to fall, I nod and then leave the room. As I walk back to my station, a stray tear rolls down my cheek, but that's the only one I will allow to fall. I chose this life, and as much as I want to believe her words, I can't.

It doesn't matter, though. I need the money.

CHAPTER 33

⚔ JUDE

eaning against the doorframe, I knock twice on Claire's door and wait. We both have classes this morning, and I won't see her until it's time to pick her up to go to her uncle's. Since I got her something awesome, I can't wait that long to see her. When the door flies open, Claire grins at me and I smile back. She just woke up and is wearing my favorite pair of dance shorts and my Bullies sweatshirt I gave her the other night when she came over to stay the night. Her hair is in a tangled mess on her head, and her eyes are covered with black-framed glasses like the very first time I saw her.

Smiling, I say, "Are those real?"

"Yeah, for reading," she says as she goes up on her toes, kissing my lips.

"They are superhot. You should wear them to bed one time," I say with a wink.

She laughs as she pulls me through the door. "I'll keep that in mind."

"Do that," I say in a low voice as the door slams behind me. "Skylar here?"

She shakes her head as she goes to pack her books, obviously not noticing that I'm holding something behind my back. "Nope, she had classes early."

"Sucks for her."

"Sure does," she says, looking up at me. "Come over to walk me to class?"

I smile. "That and to give you something."

Her eyes light up. "Oooh! A present?"

"Yup," I say, bringing the bag out from behind my back. Taking the purple bag that was tied specially by me, she grins big as she asks, "Did you tie it for me?"

"How did you know?" I ask, a shy grin on my face.

"'Cause it is the most pitiful looking bow I've ever seen in my life," she says, her eyes full of love.

I laugh as I nod. "I did. I can tie skates but that bow was about the death of me."

She sends me a happy grin. "You did wonderful," she says before untying the bow and opening the bag. When her eyes meet mine again, a little awe in their blue depths, I smile. Looking down again, she pulls out the black and teal jersey with a big number 91 and Sinclair across the back. On the front is the Bullies emblem, a bull wearing the same jersey shooting a puck. Cuddling it to her chest, she grins at me. "This is amazing."

"Figured you could wear it to the game. I had the coach order me an extra."

"I'll wear it when I'm not dancing; I don't care what Rachael says."

"I don't either," I say with a laugh. "There is more in there."

Her eyes light up again and she reaches back into the bag, pulling out the black leather riding jacket I got her. It has pink stripes that match her helmet. "Oooh, this is badass."

I nod. "Yeah, now we'll match when we ride."

"Awesome, I love it."

"You can wear it tonight."

She looks up at me quickly. "Or we can drive my car or Jayden's."

"I'm the man – I drive. And Jayden needs his car tonight."

Letting out a breath, she lets the jacket fall onto the bed. "Okay, well, prepare yourself because Phillip is gonna flip and hate you if you are driving my car, but even more so if we ride your bike. But since I have a new jacket, we'll go that route."

"He'll love me," I say confidently. "We both love hockey, love the same girl, and we like riding. It's a match made in heaven."

She gives me a deadpan look and shakes her head. "If you weren't dating me that might be the case, but since you are, he instantly hates you. So just be ready for that."

Reaching for her, I pull her to my chest. "It will be fine. I'll charm him. Everyone loves me."

"Have you ever met a dad or uncle in this case?"

Shaking my head, I shrug. "Nope, can't be that hard."

"Yeah, keep thinking that, babe," she says as she laughs.

I know she's thinking the worst, but really this is going to be cake. He's a supercool dude. He can't hate me – I'm a cool dude!

Claire then kisses my jaw before turning out of my arms to take my sweatshirt off. When I see that she's bare-chested, I go to get me a quick grab but she smacks my hand away. "I don't have time. Do me a favor, grab me a sports bra out of that drawer real quick. I know if I walk past you, you'll attack me."

I laugh as I open the drawer because she is very right on that. Reaching in, I grab the first bra and throw it to her, but then something catches my eye. Reaching for the big hunk of cash that is wrapped in a roll with a rubber band holding it closed, I look at her. "Damn, babe, why do you have all this money in here?"

Looking up at me, her eyes wide, she pulls her bra over her sexy breasts and then shrugs. "It's my paycheck."

"Oh man, you make a lot. Perks of being the best damn dancer in the world, huh?"

She grins as she nods. "You know it. Tuck that back under my underwear; I must have just tossed it in there last night, not thinking. I was dead on my feet."

I do as she asks even though I want to open it and see how much is in there. It's huge, but the only bill I can see is a hundred. Since it would be rude to ask, I close the drawer and then say, "Make sure you put that in the bank."

"Okay, Dad," she teases and I give her a look.

"Ha-ha, just saying."

"I know, thank you, and I will. I'm gonna go out today actually," she says as she puts my jersey on. I like how it looks on her, so much so that I close the distance between us and hug her tightly to my chest, dusting her jaw with kisses. "Jude, I have to go."

"You can be a tad bit late," I say just as my mouth meets hers.

But we weren't late, we missed our first classes completely, but as I lay beside her, running my fingers lazily down her naked back, I can't find it in me to care.

Kissing her lips, I smile as she whispers, "Love you. I'll see you at five, right? You'll pick me up?"

I nod. "Yup, see you then," I say and then kiss her jaw again. "Love you, have fun at class."

She sends me a grin. "Thanks, hope that Skylar has notes for the one I missed!"

"It was worth it," I call as she walks away.

Looking back at me, she says, "Sure was, bye!"

"Bye, babe," I say, and once she goes inside, I turn to head to my own class.

Waving at some of my friends as I pass by, I know I'm going to be late, but I really don't care. I've never been much of a student. I try to study, but I don't try more than I have to. I make sure my grades are good, but I focus more on the ice. That's where I'm meant to be. If anything, I'll get the notes off someone in class.

Heading through the quad, I spot Rachael a few yards ahead of me. She's walking alone, and even though I'm late, this is the perfect time to talk to her. Running up toward her, I fall in step with her.

She glances over at me and rolls her eyes. "What?"

"You have class?"

She shakes her head. "Nope, but you do."

No, it's not creepy that she knows that. Ignoring that fact, I say, "Yeah, but I wanted to talk to you."

She lets out an annoyed breath and says, "Why?"

"'Cause we need to. I feel like I need to fix this."

She turns to face me and I stop, doing the same. "Are you going to love me?"

I shake my head, my face scrunching up. "No, I love Claire."

"Then you can't fix this, Jude. I've loved you since I was nine and you friend-zoned me, which was fine; I figured I'd get you one day. But then when I did, you still wouldn't be with me. I've constantly just followed along with you, waiting and hoping. And now, you're with someone and it hurts. You broke my heart."

A little taken aback, I hold my hands out. "I never meant to. I didn't know."

"Yeah, well, if you would have asked or cared more about the person you were fucking instead of just using them as a hole to get off in, then you would have known," she says, her eyes cutting me left and right.

"I never wanted anything more than sex, and you knew that from the start. This is not my fault."

"How is it not your fault?" she screeches.

"'Cause like I said, Rachael, I never made any promises to anyone. I never once promised anyone anything. Yes, I said if I started dating I'd call, but I never promised it. I went in telling you and anyone else I fucked that it was a one-time thing. Nothing more. You kept coming back for more, and I'll admit that you were a great lay, that's why I kept taking it, but I never once looked you in the eyes and promised that I would love you, or tell you to love me. So if this is anyone's fault, it's yours."

When her eyes start to fill with tears, I look away. I hate it when a girl cries. "Maybe you're right, but it doesn't ease the pain, Jude."

"I get that, and I'm sorry that you're hurting. You are a sweet person when you're not being a bitch, and you've been a good friend. I never meant to hurt you."

She shakes her head, roughly wiping away a tear that falls. "I just don't get how you can fuck everyone with no feelings, no cares in the world, but then one girl comes along, someone who isn't even that big of a deal, and you change. It baffles me."

"She may not be a big deal to you, but to me, she's everything. I love her."

"Whatever," she says, dismissing me.

"It isn't whatever, it's for real, and I'd like it if you'd stop giving her a hard time and trying to fuck with our relationship. Respect that I love her and be a friend. Don't be an asshole."

Still not looking at me, she shakes her head. "You should be with me."

This time I'm shaking my head. "No, Rachael, I'm meant to be with her, and as my friend, I hope that you remember that I love her and she is special to me, and you won't cause any more problems."

She doesn't say anything and I almost walk away since I don't know what else to say. But then she looks up at me, her lip wobbling, and she says, "I have to let you go completely, don't I? Nothing will ever happen?"

Taking ahold of her hands, I squeeze them, willing her to listen to me. I don't know any other way to tell this girl that nothing will ever happen. As much as it sucks to hurt her, I love Claire. She's it.

"I can *promise* you that nothing will ever happen between us ever again. I love her. Let me go, Rachael."

More tears fall and she wipes them away. "Fine, Jude."

"Thank you."

She doesn't say anything else; instead she turns and leaves without even a glance back at me. While I know she's still hurting, I like that this is fixed as much as it can be. She just needs time to get over me, and I hope that during that process, she won't fuck with Claire and me. If she does, I'm pretty sure I'm gonna have to cut her completely out of my life, and I don't want to do that. I enjoy her friendship; we've been friends since we were kids, but I will let that go for Claire.

⚜

"You're acting like a fucking girl, dude," Jayden calls from his bed, and I flip him the middle finger without looking at him as I pull clothes out of my closet.

"Shut up," I say, reaching for a shirt, then putting it back. "Her uncle hates me and I want to dress nice to try to impress him a tad bit."

"If he hates you, why does it matter?"

"'Cause I want him to like me, dumbass! I want her to marry me one day," I say, glaring at him.

Jayden shakes his head and looks down at his books. "You're weird."

Turning, I say, "Why?"

"'Cause Jude, this is your first girlfriend, and you're already thinking marriage?"

"I said one day, asshole. Open those ears."

"Whatever. I see it in your eyes. If you could, you'd do it today."

Maybe so, but there is no way I'm admitting that to this asshole. Reaching for a light blue collared shirt, I throw that on and look in the mirror to make sure it matches the charcoal pants I have on. Thankfully it does, but I look plain. Throwing on a black tie and then a black sweater, I push my sleeves up to my elbows and let out a breath. Moving my fingers through my hair, I wish I had gotten it cut. It's a little long and falls in my eyes, giving me a troublemaker look. Which I guess is right, but still I don't want Claire's uncle thinking that. I probably should have shaved too, but Claire loves my beard and so do I.

I guess this will have to do.

Turning, I look at Jayden with my arms out. "How does this look?"

Looking up at me, bored, he rolls his eyes before holding his hand out. "Gorgeous, darling. Simply breathtaking."

Throwing a pillow at him, I reach for my riding jacket and put it on as he laughs. I don't know why he's playing around when it obvious I'm nervous. I don't ever get nervous, so I really don't know what the hell my problem is. I got this. Phillip will love me before the night is over and everything will be fine. Instead, I am sitting here, freaking out, thinking that he's going to make Claire break up with me. Even though that won't happen since she's a grown-ass woman and she loves me, she still values his opinion, and I really don't want that to come between us. It will just be easier if he likes me, so fingers and toes crossed for that.

Reaching for the door, I go to leave but then Jayden says, "Don't worry, dude. He'll love you, and y'all will get married and have little Claires and Judes running around. Just don't call me to babysit."

A grin pulls at my lips as I shake my head. "I wouldn't leave my kids with you, so don't worry about that, but thanks."

We share a smile and I leave feeling a little bit better.

When I arrive at Claire's building, she's standing out front, wrapped tightly in her jacket. When she spots me, she puts out a thumb and hikes up her skirt, making me grin under my helmet. Pulling up beside her, I turn the bike off and say, "Hey, sweetie, wanna go for a ride on my bike?"

She gives me a seductively naughty grin and asks, "Will it be nice and long?"

"Yes, very long and satisfying."

"Mmm," she murmurs in a suggestive way. "Maybe a little hard too?"

"You dirty girl, come on," I say, not able to take it anymore. If we keep on, I know we won't make it to dinner. Putting her helmet on, she gets on behind me, wrapping her arms around me before kissing my shoulder.

"I missed you."

"I missed you more," I answer and then turn the bike on. Pulling out, I follow the directions my GPS tells us from my Bluetooth. It's a little bit of a long ride, but I don't mind it. I worry about Claire though, she's only wearing tights under her skirt, and I hope she isn't too cold. When we pull up to a big stone house, I stop my bike by the curb and turn the bike off since Siri is telling me I've reached my destination.

"You all right back there?" I ask as I remove my helmet, then my body off the bike.

She pulls hers off and shrugs her shoulders. "My legs are frozen. I forgot to put my sweats on when I was teasing you."

"Sorry about that," I say as she comes off the bike, handing me her helmet as she fixes her hair.

"It's my fault. Come on, we're late."

"Hold on," I say, reaching into my saddlebag for the flowers I got. "For Reese."

"That's so sweet. She'll love them. Gerbera daisies are her favorite," she says, her face beaming as we head to the house. I don't know what Gerbera daisies are, but I am glad that she will like the flowers. Reaching the door, Claire puts her hand on the handle and says, "I hope you still love me after this circus."

I laugh as I nod. "I will."

Letting out a long breath, she throws open the door and the first thing I see is a very big Phillip Anderson. He's huge on the ice but in person he's bigger, and with one look at him, I know I need to hit the gym some more or I'm going to get killed in the NHL. His blazing blue gaze locks on me and his brows meet as he glares.

"Hey, Jude," Reese says, and I feel horrible that I didn't see her standing beside Phillip. He takes up the whole room, though.

"Hey, Reese, these are for you," I say, handing her the flowers. "Thank you for having me."

"Oh, thank you, these are gorgeous," she says happily and I smile.

"Phillip–" Claire starts to say, but he interrupts her.

"What the hell are you wearing?"

She looks down at her jacket and then back up at him "My riding jacket."

His eyes cut back to me and he says, "So you ride a motorcycle?"

I smile. "I do, a sweet Star Bolt. Wanna go check it out?" I say, my voice cracking a bit.

Somehow he glares more and says, "No." He then looks at Claire. "I don't like him. At all."

With that, he turns, and Reese says, "He doesn't mean that."

Claire throws her hands up and chases after him as she yells, "But you haven't even given him a chance!"

Well, this is going to be fun.

CHAPTER 34

🩰 Claire

Phillip is being positively impossible!

"Phillip! I'm talking to you! Hello?!" I yell as I chase him through the halls of the home in which I spent my teenage years. I loved this house when it was just Phillip and me even though it was more a bachelor pad than a home, but I didn't care. I mean, I lived in a car for over a year; his house was beautiful to me, but once Reese moved in, it was like a home makeover show. She went to work, hiring people to make Phillip's house a home for our little family, and nothing has changed since I left.

As we make our way through the gourmet kitchen that Reese said we needed, I know he's heading to his man cave where he will sit and wallow in the news that I am dating. He's being so childish! He knows I date, he knows I have sex, I'm nineteen damn years old!

"Phillip, Phillip!" I yell just as he reaches the door. I rush to him, standing in his way, and he glares down at me.

"Move."

"No! We're talking about this! You didn't even give him a chance! He is great! Superawesome!" I plead, but Phillip doesn't look like he gives a shit at all.

"I don't care."

Just as I thought.

"Please," I say as he tries to reach for the door handle.

"No," he says firmly, getting his hand on the handle even though I'm pushing my hip into it.

"Phillip! That was just rude!" Reese yells, and he looks back at her.

"Stay out of this," he says just as I trap his hand between my hip and the wall, causing him to yell out.

"Damn it, Claire! That hurt!"

"Oh, hush and stop being a big baby! I want you to meet my boyfriend!"

"I met him and didn't like him!" he yells, his face red with anger.

"You didn't even give him a chance!" Reese and I both yell, and he glares even more.

"I don't want to get to know him. Now move! You and Reese can fuss over him, but I won't!"

"That's not fair!" I say, stomping my foot on the ground like a five-year-old. "Please, he really is special to me."

"If she cares for him, you should give him a chance!" Reese yells and Phillip cuts her a look that could kill. I don't think it scares her much because she gives him one right back.

"I don't care. Move," he says, trying to push me out of the way, but it's obvious he's not trying hard since I'm not moving much. He probably doesn't want to hurt me, but I don't think he realizes that he is by not giving Jude a chance.

"Please, Phillip," I basically whisper. "Please give him a chance," I say hoping that if I ask nicely enough and bat my eyes at him, it will work.

Looking at me, his eyes locking with mine, and I think I have him, but he says, "No."

He then pushes me hard to the side, knocking me out of the way, and he throws the door open without even giving me a side glance. As he steps through, I yell, "But Daddy, I love him!"

He pauses mid-step and looks over his shoulder at me as Jude goes, "I knew you were my little mermaid."

I hadn't realized he was there, and while I would love to grin at him since I am acting like a very dramatic Ariel, my eyes stay locked with Phillip's. Taking a deep breath in, I say, "I love him, Phillip, like, a lot. If you love me, then please give the guy I love a chance. He means a lot to me, and I think that you'd actually like him."

He doesn't say anything for a moment, only turns and places his hands on his hips. "You love him?"

I nod. "Yeah, I do."

He looks at Reese and she shrugs her shoulders. "She's right. If you love her, you have to give the guy she loves a chance, Phillip. It's only fair."

"I don't give a shit what's fair. The guy is a delinquent."

"Actually I'm not," Jude says then. "I'm really pretty awesome."

"And cocky obviously," Phillip says and I smile.

"Yes, very, but I love him," I say, hoping to God that he gives Jude a chance. Phillip means the world to me, and I can't have him not like Jude the way I do. I'm not saying he has to pick flowers and paint hearts with him, but I'd really like it if he would at least be in the same room with him.

Shaking his head, he asks, "How long have you been with this guy?"

"Almost a month," I answer.

"And you love him? Do you even know what love is?" he asks incredulously.

"Yeah, I do. I learned from you and Reese."

I knew that would get him, but maybe I'm wrong because he's still glaring at me. I'm holding my breath, my heart pounding, and I don't know how this is going to go. Taking in a deep breath, I let it out as Phillip starts to shake his head. Then his eyes cut to where Jude stands and Jude quickly stands up straighter, his hands coming out of his pockets and dangling to his sides awkwardly.

He wants Phillip to like him, and I find that incredibly sweet.

"Fine, what's your name again?" Phillip barks at him.

"Jude Sinclair."

Phillip steps up to him, holding out his hand. "I'd like to say it's nice to meet you, but I'm still on the fence about that."

"For fuck's sake," Reese mutters. "Can't be nice, can you?"

Jude takes his hand cautiously, and I don't blame him, before shaking it in a manly way. "It's great to meet you. I've followed your career since you started playing for the Assassins."

Dropping his hand, Phillip cocks his head to the side. "You like hockey? You aren't one of those froufrou dancer boys?"

Jude scoffs, "Heck no, I love hockey and I play too. I'm going into the draft next year."

"The NHL draft?"

Jude nods, the smug grin I love on his face, and pride warms my chest. Yup, that's my man going into the draft. "Yes, sir."

"No shit," Phillip says. "I'm impressed, but I still don't like you."

He then turns and heads to the living room without another word to any of us, and I swear I'm going to kill him. Jude looks at me, and I look at Reese. She shakes her head and then lets out a long breath.

"Yeah, I got nothing, honey. Your uncle can be such an ass," she says, heading after him.

I let out a breath as Jude comes to me, wrapping his arms around my waist. I'm so mad I could cry, but I don't have time for that. I have to figure out how to get Phillip to give him a chance. He was nice to another guy I went out with – well, I mean, as nice as he could be – but he's being downright rude to Jude, and I don't get that. Jude isn't a bad guy.

"That went great," he says, but I can see in his eyes that what Phillip said sort of hurt his feelings, and that makes me even madder.

I roll my eyes as anger eats me alive. "I don't get him. I'm sorry. He's so good to me, but when it comes to me dating, he can be such an ass."

"He's protective and probably hopes to scare me away. But you know what?" he asks and I look up, my eyes meeting his.

"What?"

"While I will admit that I'm scared out of my mind of him, I'm not going anywhere. He *will* like me."

A grin pulls at my lips. This is classic Jude: he isn't a giving-up kind of guy. That's something Phillip would like if he'd give Jude a chance!

"That's good to know. But why are you scared of him?"

"'Cause he's probably the only person who can take you away from me," he says so quietly I almost don't hear him. "I can't let that happen, so I'm going to make sure he can at least tolerate me."

"He can't take me away, Jude. I'm yours," I say with the hope of reassuring him.

But he's shaking his head before I even finish the sentence. "No, he can. I know that because I know how much he means to you. Don't worry, I'll grow on him."

He's probably right, but I don't want to accept that. I want to think that I'll be with Jude for the rest of my life, even if Phillip hates him.

"But he isn't even giving you a chance," I say, letting out a breath, my eyes itching with tears.

"Don't worry your pretty little head about it – it will work out."

Running my hands up his chest to his neck, I lace my fingers together and bring him down to where my lips almost touch his. Looking deep into his eyes, I smile and can't believe how much I love this guy. The fact that he'll face my uncle even though he's scared of him speaks volumes about him and also makes me feel like a complete asshole. I wasn't strong enough to say no to Ms. Prissy and the money she offered. Instead, I caved and now I'm continuing to lie to the person I love. While I know it's wrong, I just can't seem to tell him. I need the money, and hopefully I can get through this last month and after that quit and never look back. But sometimes when I get lost in his green eyes, I wonder what he would say if I told him. I wonder if he would love me enough to accept it.

Bringing his lips to mine, I close my eyes tightly and let the kiss show how much I love him. I'm about to deepen the kiss when I hear, "Yeah, you kissing her in my house isn't going to help me like you."

Parting, I find Phillip watching us, and of course, he's glaring.

"Sorry, sir," Jude says then, taking a good step away from me.

I roll my eyes and let out a breath as I stomp toward Phillip. "I am so mad at you," I say as I pass him.

"You'll thank me one day," he calls to me.

"The hell I will," I say, whipping around to look at him. "You claim to love me, that I mean the world to you, but you can't even give Jude a chance. That's screwed up."

"I do love you, Claire, more than anything in this world, but this guy is not it for you."

"How do you know? You haven't even talked to him!"

"'Cause he's dating you," he says like it answers all.

He's so frustrating! I want to strangle him!

"I love her," Jude says just as I'm about to say something. I look at him and Phillip does the same as Jude walks up beside me, lacing his fingers with mine. "And I know that means nothing to you. I know you see me as some punk kid off the street, but I am actually a good guy, and I love her so much. I don't ever want anything bad to happen to her. I would like nothing more than to have the opportunity to prove that to you."

I squeeze his hand, and he looks down at me as I smile. When I glance at Phillip, he's looking at us, shaking his head. I think he's going to say something amazing, like "Yes, Jude, I accept you," but instead he says, "Dinner is ready."

As he heads to the kitchen, I shake my head and say, "What an ass!"

Jude kisses my jaw and then whispers, "It's going to work out."

Pulling back, I meet his gaze. "I hope you're right."

"Aren't I always?"

He gives me a goofy grin and I laugh. "Sure," I say offhandedly and then pull him to the living room where we discard our jackets before heading to the dining room. Phillip is sitting at the head of the table, his phone out, as Reese brings out the food.

"Do you need help?" I ask and she shakes her head, sending me a grin.

"No, babe, I'm done. Y'all have a seat," she says.

Jude pulls out my seat for me, and I look to see if Phillip saw that, but whatever is on his phone must be very important. "Thank you," I say, giving him a wide grin as I sit down.

He squeezes my shoulder and then sits in the seat beside me which is also across from Phillip. When Reese is finally seated, Phillip says grace and then we dig in. Nothing is said as we all prepare our plates, but then Jude says, "I love breakfast for dinner. It's great, Reese."

She smiles proudly. "It's Claire's favorite meal."

Jude smiles back at her. "Yeah, we eat a lot of Waffle House."

I grin as I pour syrup all over my waffle before taking a huge bite. Looking up, I see that Phillip hasn't touched his food; he's staring across the table at Jude. I look at Jude, but he doesn't seem to notice. He's eating, not paying any attention. I kick Phillip under the table, and I glare when his gaze meets mine.

"What?"

"Stop staring," I mouth and his scowl deepens.

Leaving my gaze, he looks back at Jude and says, "So the draft?"

Jude looks up from his plate and nods. "Yes, I have four teams looking at me now."

"Must be pretty good then," Phillip says, cutting his waffle and sausage up before mixing them together and drenching them in syrup.

"I think so," Jude says.

"He's really good," I say. "Reminds me of you – he has a good game. You should come Friday, watch him play. I'm dancing too."

"Oh, that sounds like fun. Doesn't it, Phillip?" Reese says brightly.

He gives her a look and then shrugs. "I guess."

"We will be there," Reese says with a grin. "Remember we have the wedding rehearsal that morning, though." Both Phillip and I groan, and she says, "Oh, shut up, I told you it won't be bad. Take ten minutes, tops."

"I'll be there," I say, and Reese smiles at me before taking a bite of sausage.

"So what are you going to school for?" Phillip asks, looking straight at Jude.

He takes a swig of his orange juice and then says, "Sports medicine."

"Are you going to keep up with it once you get picked up?"

Jude shrugs. "Not sure yet. My mom wants me to."

"You should. I did, and I like the security I have in case something happens."

"Thanks for the advice. I'll consider it."

"You should," Phillip says and then he crosses his arms. "Your family lives here?"

"Yeah, about an hour from here. My brother goes to school with me. He plays too and then also our younger brother. My older sister is going to design school."

"How long have you played?"

"Since I was old enough to skate. My dad played."

"That's good. The NHL is no joke, though. So you need to be ready. Be strong, work hard."

Jude nods, and I can tell he's hanging on every word Phillip says. "I plan to."

Phillip nods and I thank the heavens above that he is actually talking to Jude. Yeah, it's something so impersonal like hockey, but then again, this is what they are: hockey players. I knew that would be the one thing to bring them together, and I trust that Phillip is giving him a chance. When I glance at Reese, she seems to be just as happy as I am, a grin sitting on her face. Reaching out, she takes his hand in hers, and when he glances at her, she smiles and mouths, "Thank you."

Phillip shrugs and then glances at me. I do the same, and he smiles before taking my hand in his. I never thought that another man could protect my heart the way Phillip has, but as I look from him to Jude, I know that my heart is safe with him.

After dinner, I figure that we should leave. Not only do I have to work tonight, but I want to leave on a good note, and so far things are good. Let's just hope they stay like that and hope that Phillip hasn't been pretending he likes Jude just to make me happy.

"Come back anytime, Jude. This was so much fun," Reese says, and I don't miss the look Phillip gives her.

"I'd love that. Thank you for having me. I look forward to the wedding this weekend," he says, and I smile as he places his hand on the small of my back. Holding his hand out to Phillip, he says, "Thanks for having me."

I hold my breath as I wait for Phillip to take it, and finally he does, shaking it as he says, "It wasn't that bad. I still don't like you, though."

I want to punch him dead in the throat, but before I can, Jude goes, "I'll grow on you, 'cause I'm not going anywhere."

Phillip's eyes become slits, and it's almost like he's challenging Jude. "We will see about that."

"I swear to God," Reese mutters and I roll my eyes.

"Yeah, we will," Jude says, pulling me close to him as Phillip continues to glare.

"And we thought the dinner went well," I say, pushing him out the door with only a wave to my uncle and aunt. I feel their gazes on us as we mount the bike, and when I glance up, I'm right, they're watching us. We wave and then we're off, heading back to campus. I lean my head against Jude's back as I let out a long breath. I don't know what Phillip's problem is, but I hope to God he gets over it and gives Jude a chance. I don't want to believe that he could break us up, but I think Jude is right. Phillip's opinion matters, but I know I can't live in a world without Jude. I know I can't live in one without Phillip either, so I'm gonna need him to pull his big boy pants on and like my boyfriend.

When we pull up to my dorm, my legs are frozen again but I don't mind it much. I love riding with Jude; I feel free when I'm on this bike with him. He takes off his helmet and then gets off before helping me. I take my helmet off as he leans against the bike, watching me.

"So that went well?" he asks and I laugh.

"As well as it could, I guess," I say, letting out a breath. "He's so damn overprotective, it's pathetic."

"It's nice 'cause you are worth it."

I smile and step between his legs, wrapping my arms loosely around his neck. "Why do you love me, Jude Sinclair?"

A grin pulls at his lips as he wraps his arms around my waist, resting his chin against my breast as he looks at me. "Because you are the most beautiful person, inside and out, that I've ever met."

My heart warms as I bring my hands up to cup his face. "Sometimes I feel like I'm not worth it."

"Well, I need to work a little harder then 'cause you should feel like the most important person in the world every moment of the day."

After I run my thumb along his bottom lip, my eyes lock with his. The words are there and I know I should say them, but how can I risk a love like this for something that isn't going to be a big deal in a month's time? Instead, I ask,

"You'll support me no matter what I do, right?"

His brows come together. "What do you mean?"

"Like whatever job I want."

He smiles. "You don't want to be a dancer anymore?"

"No, I do, but what if I can't find a job?"

"That's crazy. We both know you will, but yes, no matter what, I'll support you. You wanna work at Wendy's? I'm down, babe, as long as you are mine. I know that you'll always support me, so you have my support."

Letting out a long breath, I lean my head against his and whisper, "You're right. I will."

"Good," he says, and then his eyes meet mine. "Why? What's going on?"

I shake my head. "Nothing. I'm just thinking about the future."

He smiles. "The future is me and you, babe. The world is at our fingertips."

Or me alone.

I smile, not wanting to think that way. I lean into him, brushing my lips slowly along his before whispering, "You're right."

"I know, and I also know I love you, Claire."

Closing my eyes, I say, "I love you more."

"If you say so, baby."

As his lips meet mine, I don't know why his words and actions aren't making me feel better.

Because they should, shouldn't they?

CHAPTER 35

 Claire

I'm running late.

So fucking late that I'm embarrassed, but surely Mrs. Sinclair and Jude will understand that Reese's "ten minute" wedding rehearsal ran over. I swear! How hard is it? Erik and Phillip walk down, then the billions of Assassins kids go, then me, and then Reese and her dad. It isn't that hard! Jeez! Instead, Phillip and Erik are making jokes and chasing the kids down the aisle, Reese is throwing up because she's so damn nervous, and I'm standing there, yelling at everyone because I have a lunch date with Jude and his mom.

It was your typical Assassins wedding rehearsal.

I should have known better.

Pulling into the parking lot of Moss, a southern-cooking place, I shut the car off and pull down the visor to reapply my makeup and then do something with my mass of hair that looks stringy and icky. I had a late night, didn't get to shower, and then having Dimitri and Journey pull and yank on my hair didn't make it look any better. To top that all off, I drove with the windows down, so it's safe to say my hair is a freaking mess. I really should have planned this better. I am hopeless.

I'm reapplying my lipstick when I hear, "You're gorgeous."

I pause mid-swipe and look over to find my boyfriend watching me. He looks delectable in a pair of fading blue jeans and a gray shirt that reads "We are all freaks." On his head is a black beanie, and while I'm starting to develop an unhealthy obsession with beanies, I can't help but be completely turned on by the scruff on his face. My man grows the best beard.

Smiling, my shoulders fall and I say, "I'm a mess, I'm late, and I'm so embarrassed."

"Don't be. My mom likes you a lot and understands. Come on, let's not keep her waiting," he says and opens my car door. I look in the mirror, finishing another swipe before tucking the lipstick in my purse and taking his hand to get out. Pulling me to his chest, he presses his lips to mine, and I smile against his lips as we kiss. I've missed him. I didn't even get to see him yesterday; he had practice twice and I had work, dance team, and then the club at night. We're both so busy, but being pressed against his body like this, his lips on mine, makes the time apart bearable.

Lacing his fingers with mine, he pulls away and kisses my nose. "Come on."

I agree and we head inside as he wipes his mouth free of my lipstick. I see Mrs. Sinclair sitting in a booth, and a grin spreads across my face as she stands to hug me tightly. I don't know what it is about this woman, but I've liked her from the moment I met her. It's probably because Jude is so much like her.

Pulling back, she smiles at me and says, "I have to admit, I didn't expect to ever see you again."

I laugh as I nod. "Yeah, apparently no one did! Jayden bet Jude that he wouldn't last two weeks with me."

She tsks as she sets Jude with a look. He shrugs his shoulders. "It was an easy hundred bucks, Mom. I knew she was a keeper," he says, hugging me tightly before kissing my temple.

I smile, warmth spreading throughout me and then sit down, scooting over so he has room too. Sitting down beside me, he takes my hand in his and rests them against his thigh. I love how he has to touch me when he's near me. I know that his need for me is just as strong as my need is for him. It's very reassuring, not that I need reassurance. I know he loves me. More than he loves himself and that makes me giddy with happiness. Especially since I love him just as much, maybe even more.

"Sorry I'm late," I start, but she holds up her hand.

"Jude told me you had a wedding rehearsal. It's completely fine."

I let out a breath, my cheeks warming. "Yeah, tomorrow is my uncle and aunt's wedding. We're pretty excited, but it's a circus since Reese thinks she can do it all and be in the wedding. I think my uncle is going to hire a girl for tomorrow 'cause today was hell."

She laughs and Jude chuckles beside me. "So you'll be busy for the next couple days?" she asks and I nod.

"Yeah, I plan on sleeping all day Sunday."

"Sounds like a good idea to me," Jude says and we share a grin. I hope he knows that I very much want him to nap with me, and by the look in his eyes, I think he does.

"Jude, are you going with her tomorrow?"

Jude's eyes leave mine to meet his mom's. "Yeah. I'm her date."

"That's nice. Are they coming to the game tonight? To watch you dance?"

"Yup, and to watch Jude play," I say with a grin.

"Well, hopefully I'll run into them. I'd love to meet them."

"I'll try to make that happen. My uncle is being a jerk right now," I say, but as soon as the words leave my mouth, I wonder if it was a good idea to mention that.

"Why?" she asks like I knew she would.

I glance at Jude for help, but he's just grinning. Looking back at Mrs. Sinclair, I say, "He's crazy overprotective of me."

"And doesn't like me," Jude adds. "But that will change."

"Sure, it will," she says with a grin. "That's the thing with parents. In our eyes, no one is good enough for our babies."

Her eyes meet mine, and I know that she thinks that about me. That shocks me a bit because I thought she liked me, but maybe I was wrong. Maybe I was so caught up in my feelings for Jude that I didn't realize that his mom could see me as some tramp out to steal her son from her. While that hurts my feelings a bit, I know she's right. I'm nowhere near good enough for Jude, especially with the secret I'm carrying. Looking down, I wring my fingers together and let out a breath.

"As parents though," she says, and I look up to meet her gaze, "we have to trust what our children want. When Lucy brought Rick home, I wanted to gag. He was a creep."

"Yeah, he was," Jude agrees.

"But he was what she wanted, so we all put aside our thoughts and let her be. When it all came crashing down, we were there to catch her. That's what family does."

"I agree, but Phillip doesn't see it that way. He just hates anyone who wants to date me."

She laughs as she shakes her head. "That's a man for you, but it will get better," she says, almost like a promise, and it honestly makes me feel better. "You know, I thought I wasn't going to like you either. I figured the girl who bagged my Jude would be a train wreck. Since I threw every good girl his way and he didn't want anything to do with them."

"Wow, thanks, Mom," Jude says, and she reaches over to take his free hand, grinning at him.

"But I was wrong. I knew the moment I met you that you were right for my Jude. It was the way you looked at him. Like he was the flame and you were the moth. It's a beautiful sight to behold. So obviously, you weren't looking at her in front of Phillip the way you do when you're around me," she says and inside I turn to mush.

She likes me!

Jude laughs. "I couldn't look at her 'cause he scares the crap out of me. But don't worry, I'll stare at you all day tomorrow," he says, looking over at me.

"Oh, I bet that will go over great," I say, rolling my eyes.

We all laugh but then Mrs. Sinclair says, "The main thing is Phillip might be hard to deal with now, but once he sees that you aren't going anywhere, and that Claire trusts and loves you, then he'll let up. It's hard on us, but we have to trust the people we love." She then looks at me before saying, "Without trust, there is no relationship."

"Yeah, you're right," I say, my heart in my throat as I slowly nod.

I feel like a complete and utter hypocrite because I'm not being honest at all.

Lunch was awesome, even though I mostly tore myself apart and went back and forth about telling Jude about Ms. Prissy. I still don't know what to do and sometimes I get so tired of going around in circles. I wish I could just make a decision. Just tell him or don't and be done with it, but it isn't that easy. I wish I didn't care so much about the money. I wish I could trust that I can make it without it, but something inside me is programmed to make sure I have it. Make sure I'm protected.

Ugh, it's so frustrating, and I have no clue what to do, but I do know I love Jude's mom. She makes me feel like a part of the family, but in a way, I felt like something was wrong throughout the whole lunch. When I wasn't looking directly at her, I swore I caught her with a sad look, but once I looked up at her, she was grinning. I don't know what that was about, and I think even Jude caught on to it. I'm not sure when I will be able to ask him about it since, with the game and the wedding, we will both be so busy and then dog-tired afterward, but I know I need to ask. I care about his mom, and I don't want anything to upset her. If I'm doing something wrong, then I need to know.

"I rode with my mom. Can you take me back to the house?" Jude asks me once we're outside.

"Sure," I say as I pause in front of Mrs. Sinclair. "Thank you for inviting me to lunch. It was awesome."

She smiles as she wraps me up in a hug. "It really is a pleasure being around you, Claire," she says in almost a whisper. "I am really glad that Jude has found you. You make him a better person."

I pull back, meeting her gaze, and I smile. "We're better together."

"I couldn't say it better myself. He's lucky to have you," she says and I want to believe that, but all I see is the back of his head when I tell him about Ms. Prissy's.

"I think I'm the lucky one," I say, reaching out to pull him to me. He smiles as he wraps his arms around my shoulders, holding me close.

"She is," he says with a grin, and I laugh as his mom kisses his cheek.

"You kids be good and I'll see you two tonight," she says with a wave as she heads to her car.

We both say bye then get in my car to head back to campus. With the windows down, the music blaring, and my hand laced with Jude's, I feel like I'm in heaven, but still the thing with his mom is bugging me.

Turning the music down, I ask, "Is your mom okay?"

I feel his gaze on me as he asks, "Yeah, why?"

"I don't know, she seemed sad in a way, like she was faking her good mood. Is it me? Does she not like me?"

He scoffs. "She loves you, babe, but I did notice that too. I don't know. She told me before lunch that things with my dad are rocky."

"Oh, that's not good at all," I say, turning onto the road that will lead to campus.

"Nope, but in a way, I'm relieved. I kinda hope she wants a divorce or something. He doesn't treat her good."

"Yeah," I agree. "But I don't want her to be sad."

"Me neither, but I hope that once he's gone, she'll be happy."

"Yeah," I say as I let out a breath. "She's such a good person."

"The best," he agrees as I pull up next to his bike.

I look over at him and ask, "Will your dad be there tonight?"

He sighs before running his hands through his hair, knocking his beanie off his head. "Apparently, but Mom says he called this morning saying he might be late. He's coming in from New York. That's the problem lately; he's only home like once a week. It's pissing her off, hell, it's always pissed me off. Sometimes I think he's fucking around on her."

"No, surely not," I gasp as I can't imagine who could cheat on someone as amazing as Mrs. Sinclair.

"Yeah, I don't know, but if he is, Claire, I swear I'll kill him. That's the worst thing you can do to someone you love – lie and cheat like that. Just be truthful, you know?"

My heart is pounding against my chest as I slowly nod. "Yeah."

"Yeah, so I'm gonna go. I'm going to nap before heading to the rink," he says, leaning over to kiss my mouth in a lusty but quick way. He reaches for the door handle and is about to step out, and I know I should let him go, but his words play over and over in my head.

Just be truthful. Just be truthful. Just be truthful.

"Hey Jude," I say suddenly. He looks over at me with a grin on his face.

"Don't be afraid?" he asks and I smile.

"Yeah, but I want to tell you something."

"What?"

I take in a deep breath and say, "Have you heard of that burlesque club, Ms. Prissy's?"

He nods. "Yeah, I've been there a few times with the guys. Not since I started dating you, though!" he adds and I smile.

"You're silly," I say, looking for the courage to say what I need to say.

"Anyway, I…I…um… well, you see–"

"What? Why are you stuttering?"

I laugh, letting out a long breath, my heart pounding against my chest. "I work for her," I say and then meet his inquisitive gaze. "I choreograph the dances for the burlesque side and even the pole dancing. I'm doing like six numbers for some investors that are coming, and I'm hoping to land them."

"That's awesome, babe. I told you you're the best," he says with a grin. "Is that why you asked if I would support you in any job you chose?"

I nod. "Yeah, it's not the best kind of job, you know."

"How do you figure? You could choreograph, like, shows and stuff. That's amazing," he says, and it's what I want to hear. I want him to be supportive.

"Yeah, I could be picked up to run clubs and stuff. It's a huge opportunity."

He smiles. "That's wonderful, baby. I'm proud of you."

"So you'll support me?"

He laughs as he reaches for me, pulling me close. "Of course. It isn't like you're on the stage taking your clothes off, so no big deal. I'm excited for you. Make sure you let me know how that goes."

He kisses me again and then he's gone as I sit in my seat, completely stunned. The tears threaten to fall, and my heart feels like it's about to explode. I was truthful, but the only problem is I only told half the truth.

It isn't like you're on the stage taking your clothes off, so no big deal.

No big deal, but if I was, it would be a *huge* deal and probably would be the end of my relationship. I need to quit, I need to stop, but can I lose that money? Can I really let go of the opportunity of thousands to secure my future? I know the answer is no, but can I risk losing him?

No. I can't.

So what the fuck do I do?

There is really only one answer and that's to work my ass off, get the money, and then quit and never look back. I'm not completely lying to Jude anymore. I told him most of the truth; I just left out the part about me on the stage. What he doesn't know won't hurt him, and it's only for another month and then I'll be done. That can't be that bad…right?

But if so, then why does it feel like it is?

⚜

Standing in the dressing room outside of the rink, I hop on my tippy toes, warming my legs up. Pulling at the bottom of my uniform, I curse the dance gods above for the monstrosity I'm wearing. I mean, I guess it's sort of cute, but with an ass like mine, it's falling out the bottom. Even with my tights on, I feel like the bottoms are creeping up my ass, giving me the ultimate wedgie. I don't know if Rachael ordered me a smaller size – which I wouldn't put past her – or what, but if it actually fit, it would be cute. It's a one-piece shorts set that is solid black except for the sheer black lace that goes over a teal blue bra. Crystals stud every inch of it, and on the back are our names in crystals along with Bellevue Bullies.

Looking the mirror, I'm pleased with what I see. My hair is up in a high ponytail with a black and teal bow at the base. My makeup is done very dramatically, bright teal and a smoky black covering my eyes, making them seem bigger and brighter. Rachael may be a bitch, but the girl has some great skills at applying makeup. Pulling at my shorts, I turn and look around the room. All of us look so good, and I'm really excited for this performance. We have been training for weeks, and I'm ready for my family and the arena to see us kill the choreography I put together for us.

"All right, come together," I hear Rachael say.

I look around the room to find Skylar standing beside me. She grins at me and I return the grin before together we go to the circle, holding hands with our teammates. Rachael bows her head and we all do the same as she prays for a good performance and for each of us to be strong and safe throughout the performance. She then thanks the Lord above for all of us, and I have to admit it's nice. I like seeing this side of her; it makes her less of a raging bitch.

When she glances up, she says, "Now don't y'all get out there and fuck up."

But then she says things like that.

Rolling my eyes, I listen as she says, "Claire has worked hard on this dance and this is our debut to the whole school. Be on point, hit the marks, and rock that ice. This is our time to shine, and we're going to make everyone in the place drool. Make sure to stay on the gray tarp. I am not responsible if one of you dumbasses goes off it and slips on the ice."

Some giggle but stop when her eyes cut to them. "When we're here to cheer the boys on, you know not to talk to anyone. You stay in Bullies dance mode. No messing around. I don't care if your boyfriend is hollering at you, your family, your friends, or some random dude. It doesn't matter. You are working tonight. Remember our dances for the particular songs, and if you get lost, find Claire or me. I'll be behind the home team, and she'll be behind the away."

Everyone nods and then she glances at the clock before clapping her hands together. "Okay, let's go kill this," she says before heading to the door. As I follow behind her, my heart is pounding in my chest, but then the adrenaline takes over and I'm ready.

In a straight line, our hands on our hips, we strut to the ice on a teal carpet in perfect unison. As I walk, I see Phillip and Reese sitting across the ice behind the home team. Reese is waving like a maniac as Phillip stands with his arms crossed across his chest. When his gaze meets mine though, a small grin appears on his face, and like he always did when I competed, he gives me a thumbs-up.

At that moment, a calm comes over me because I got this. This is what I'm meant to do.

"And now, give it up, Bellevue, for your Bellevue Bullies' dance team!"

The crowd loses it as we take our spots. I wish Jude were here watching me, but I know he's in the back, prepping for the game. He promised he would watch the video later, and that's fine with me. I know, no matter what, he'll be proud of me.

When the music to "Animals" by Martin Garrix starts, the crowd gets louder. I've performed in packed dance competitions and even for a club full of grown men, but nothing can compare to the sound in this arena. It's almost hard to hear the music, but right on cue, we all start, killing the hell out of this dance. A smile so wide spreads across my face as we dance, all in perfect unison from what I can tell. I know Rachael and I are on point, moving as one to the music. Mouthing the words to the song, I move my body like it is part of the beat before jumping up into a split leap. Landing on my feet, I start to turn, over and over again until the music stops with a funny little noise, and I stop with my hands on my hips as the whole place goes nuts.

We just killed it.

Now it's Jude's turn.

CHAPTER 36

⚒ JUDE

Claire is mesmerizing.

That's all there is to it.

There are over nine girls I think on that damn team, and the only one I can watch is her.

After sneaking out to watch the girls hit the ice, I know that Coach will rip me a new one, but I had to catch a least a little bit of Claire's dance. When I found that Shane had left too, to watch Amy dance, I figured that Coach will be a little lenient about it since both of us came to watch. We aren't missing anything yet. Everyone usually just sits with their headphones on their ears, getting ready for the game. Maybe the way I get ready is to watch my baby tear the ice up.

And once she starts, that's exactly what she does.

It's downright unbelievable the way she moves. The music is hard-hitting and very techno, but she moves to it like it's a lullaby. I swear this is what she's meant to do for the rest of her gorgeous life. She's amazing and I swear she steals the show. I couldn't be prouder of her than I am right now, especially with the fact that my whole family is watching my girl make the dance floor her bitch.

As the song ends, she goes into a series of turns and then stops right on point with her hands on her hips and a grin on her succulent mouth. The crowd is deafening, and I find myself cheering along with them. Even Shane is hollering for them and that's probably how we got caught.

"What the hell are you two doing? You are supposed to be prepping for the game!" Coach Moss yells.

"Right, Coach, going now," Shane says, waddling in his big goalie equipment back to the locker room, but before I follow, I look out just in time to meet

Claire's gaze.

Her face breaks into a grin as her cheeks warm, and my heart explodes with love for this girl. "Great job, babe!" I yell out.

She blows me a kiss, and I am two seconds from catching it and tucking it in my girdle, since that is what a pussy does. Since my coach is standing beside me, I wave and turn to head back to the locker room, pride seeping out of my pores for my girl. I can't wait to get my hands on her so I can tell her and show her how proud of her I am.

After a very long speech from Coach, we start to file out for warm-ups. As we head down the tunnel, I hear the crowd getting louder, and when we hit the ice, everyone loses it. You could honestly confuse this with an NHL game. The Bullies' fans are hardcore and I like that. I like that hockey is so important to our college, to our community, especially in a football state like Tennessee.

Turning in circles, my skates cut into the ice as I dig in, picking up speed to warm up. We're playing our rivals, Vanderbilt, and we're ready to whoop some ass. As I make my second pass around, I spot my family, even my dad, sitting, watching as I play. Angie is sitting on Jase's shoulders, cheering me on, and I smile even though they can't see me through the cage of my helmet. I can't wait till I get in the NHL when I can start wearing visors instead of full cages. While I like to protect my pearly whites, I hate how I feel so trapped inside this thing.

Letting my gaze leave my family, I look around the crowd, finding Phillip and Reese next. He's watching me, and for some reason that makes me want to play better. He makes me nervous, and I want to be the best in his eyes. Letting out a breath, I turn again and this time I find Ralph with his family. He's not talking to his wife though; he's talking to some guy who is holding a clipboard.

A scout.

Adrenaline is coursing through me, my palms sweating in my gloves, and I know that I can't worry about impressing Phillip; I have to impress this scout. He's my future. He's Claire and my future. I can't fuck this up. I have to win, and I have to impress.

For Claire.

I want to give her the life she deserves, and the only way I can do that is by being signed by a great team. That's probably the only way Phillip will ever respect me, and since I want those two things more than I can breathe, I am going to play my heart out every single game I play.

Rounding around the goal, I take a puck and practice my puck handling as I continue making my circle. When I hit the blue line, I turn and take a shot, getting it right past Shane. He gives me a look that says I got lucky, but I know the truth – I'm the best out here. With a grin on my face, I turn around the goal again, and this time, I find Claire behind the visitor's bench, her hands on her hips, holding pom-poms. She looks hot as hell in her little Bullies uniform. It may be a little tight, but I'm not complaining at all.

Seeing her smiling face reiterates how important this game is as well as the rest of my college career. I have to make sure we're good. I have to give her everything she wants because not only does she deserve it, but I want to do it. I want to treat her like a princess, just like Jayden said.

When warm-ups are called, I go out to the blue line, lining up with my linemates, including Jayden. As a little girl sings the national anthem, I close my eyes and send a little prayer up to the heavens. I know I've got this, and as I line up for the puck drop, my opponent meets my gaze and I ask, "You ready to lose?"

"Fuck you," he sneers and I smile.

When the puck drops, I win it back for my defensemen and head up, waiting for them to pass me the puck. I look back to see Jayden with the puck, deking around a player before shooting it up to me. Hitting my blade, I dig in, going around one player, putting my hip into them as I turn, passing the puck to Martin. Pushing off the jerk, I head to the goal, blocking the goalie from being able to see. He pushes me in the back, but I stand strong, blocking him and waiting for the puck to come my way. Jayden gets the puck and lines up the shot, shooting hard, but a defenseman gets in the way, blocking it with his shin. Luckily though, it lands in front of me, and I quickly backhand it over the goalie's shoulder and into the back of the net.

My arms go up as the goalie pushes me away, and I skate toward my team, getting wrapped up in a tight hug as the crowd chants for us. Scoring used to be my ultimate high before being with Claire, and while it doesn't hold the same feeling that kissing Claire does, it still shakes me to the core. Skating toward the bench, my gaze catches Claire's and she's grinning from ear to ear, her arms up in the air, shaking the pom-poms.

That was for her.

Hell, everything I do is for her.

We won.

Three to zero.

Just like I knew we would. I had two of the goals, and while I wish I had scored all three, I'm just glad we shut them out. The locker room is jubilant, and we're ready to win the rest of the season. We will win the championship, and I will go into the draft a winner. That's my plan, and I hope that every game ends with me off to meet Claire.

After showering, I head out of the locker room with Jayden to find Claire waiting for me. Her face breaks into a grin, her eyes bright as she pushes off the wall. Like me, she wears Bullies sweats, but still has her makeup and hair done from earlier.

"Hey, gorgeous," I say, slinging my arm around her shoulders.

"Hey, hotshot, great game."

I smile. "Thanks, babe. That first goal was for you."

"Aw, really?"

"Yup, really, both of them were."

"Ugh, I can't stand you two," Jayden says, walking faster and away from us.

I laugh as her grin grows, her face turning a pretty pink. "I like that a lot, and you're just jealous, Jayden!"

He scoffs as he shakes his head, and I smile before meeting her gaze. "You killed it out there, baby."

"Thanks, it was a great performance, and seeing you there made it even better."

"Good, it was a pleasure watching you," I say before kissing her temple as we head out into the lobby.

I see Angie first; she's running to me, her arms out as she calls, "Ude! Ude!"

I drop my bag and pick her up, kissing her loudly on the cheek. "Hey, girlie! You like the game?"

She nods quickly and then reaches for Claire. She takes Angie, kissing her cheek and talking sweetly to her as the rest of my family reaches us. I don't hear them congratulating me and Jayden on a good game though, all I see is Claire loving my niece like she's her own. She's so good with kids, and it does something to my heart to see her with children.

"Hey, Claire. Wow, you are a great dancer," Mom says, and Claire grins at her.

"Thank you so much. It was a great performance, followed by an awesome game," she says as Angie wiggles down and runs to Lucy.

"Your backhand was a little sloppy," Dad says, and I meet his gaze, hating that he's here.

"It went in," I say with a shrug.

"Even an ugly goal is a goal," Claire says. She quickly adds, "But that goal wasn't ugly, Jude, I'm just saying."

I laugh. "Yeah, I know, babe."

"Oh, there are Phillip and Reese," Claire says suddenly. "Sorry, excuse me."

"I want to meet them, Claire," Mom says and Claire nods.

"Yes, ma'am, just a second!" she calls as she runs toward to Phillip, hugging him tightly.

"Why do you want to meet them?" Dad asks.

I pull my gaze from where Claire is hugging Reese now to see my dad with an annoyed look on his face, watching Claire with her family.

"Probably because she's important to me?" I ask.

"I'm surprised you're still with her," he says and I glare.

"I don't know why you even care," I say, and my mom places her hand on my chest.

"Not now, they are coming this way," she says, and I look over to find that Reese and Claire are coming toward us, pulling Phillip along. He doesn't look pleased at all.

"Reese, Phillip, this is Jude's mom and dad, Mr. and Mrs. Sinclair," she says with a grin. "And then his sister Lucy, her daughter Angie, Jace, and Jayden. Everyone, this is my uncle and aunt."

Everyone shakes hands, my brothers acting all awkward since he's an idol to us, but to my surprise, Phillip is really pleasant to my family. But when his gaze meets mine, I see the annoyance in his eyes. He doesn't want to meet my family at all. He wants me to go away.

Too bad I'm not.

"So, you don't like my son, I hear?" my mom asks, and Claire's mouth drops open. Mine doesn't though; I'm not shocked at all. My mom is a mother hen; everyone loves her people or she cuts them.

Phillip looks a bit taken aback but he recovers well, laughing as he shrugs his shoulders. "It's not that I don't like him—"

"I think your exact words were 'I don't like you,'" I say, and he cuts me a look that seriously scares the fuck out of me.

Trying to cover it with a laugh, he looks back at my mom. "You have to understand that I don't think anyone is good enough for her. I mean, do you like Claire?"

Mom smiles sweetly. "I do. She is a wonderful girl. You've done well."

Phillip's face reddens a bit as he says, "Thank you. She's special to us."

"I can see why. She dances like a dream."

"She does. We're very proud. And just to clarify, I think Jude is great," Reese says, sending me a grin.

I smile back, and when I glance at Claire, her face matches her hair.

"Thank you," Mom says with a polite grin. "And I do understand, but I also think that if Jude loves her, she has to be special. Maybe you can consider that?"

Reese chuckles beside Phillip, and he sends her a glare before nodding his head. "Yes, ma'am. I'll try."

"Good, I have a feeling it's serious between these two."

"Please, it's only been what, a month?" my dad asks.

"Almost," I say. "But when you know, you know."

My mom nods. "I agree and I believe in them," she says, reaching out and cupping my face.

"Thanks, Mom," I say as she drops her hand. I grin over at Claire and she grins back, lacing her fingers with mine.

"Let's hope for the best. But anyway, it was wonderful meeting you two. I hope to have you over for dinner one day. Congratulations on your wedding tomorrow," Mom says, holding her hand out to shake Reese's and Phillip's again.

"Of course, we would love that," Reese says.

"Thank you, it was great meeting you," Phillip says, but his face says he wishes he'd never come over here.

"It was. We will see y'all later. Jude, honey, great game. Call me tomorrow."

I agree and then kiss her and Lucy, thanking them all for coming. After saying bye to everyone, minus my dad, I meet back up with Claire, who is still standing with Phillip and Reese.

"That wasn't awkward," Claire says once I rejoin the group, a grin on her face.

"My mom is a little outspoken," I admit, wrapping an arm around her waist.

"You think?" Phillip says, shaking his head.

"She was right," Reese sings, and he gives her a dark look.

"You hush," he says forcefully, but when she gives him an even darker look, he kisses her quickly.

As he pulls back, she grins and Claire says, "Ugh, get a room."

"You hush," he says, pointing a finger at her, but then he points the finger at me. "And you, you need to roll your wrist on that backhand. It was a great goal, but it was a lucky one. Roll your wrist more and you'll have more control."

I nod. "Thank you. I will."

"Maybe you can show him some moves," Claire suggests.

He gives her a deadpan look before glancing over at me. "Maybe."

"I'd love that," I say, eager to get in the rink with him. I'd love to pick his brain, and maybe he'll like me a bit more.

"Yeah, so, we need to get out of here. Big day tomorrow," he says, wrapping his arms around Reese and holding her close to him.

"I know. I'm so excited," she says, grinning up at him.

"Me too, been waiting three years for this," he says then kisses her hard against the lips. It's a little awkward watching them kiss, and when I turn to look at Claire, she's looking down at the ground, shaking her head.

"Okay, you two lovebirds, we're leaving! See you bright and early!" she says and then takes my hand in hers, pulling me away as I laugh.

Once outside, the cold air hits me and I smile. I love the cold. It means that Christmas is coming, and that's my favorite holiday. Wrapping my arm around Claire's shoulder, we walk toward her car in silence, holding each other close. Leaning into me, she wraps her arms around my waist and I feel perfect like this. After I kiss the top of her head, she moves away from me to unlock her door.

Throwing her bag in, she turns and asks, "Have you heard that song 'Latch'?"

I shrug my shoulders. "Nope."

"It's our song," she declares, pulling her phone out. She has a different song for us every other day. I don't mean that it's a bother, but isn't a couple supposed to have only one?

"Is that right?" I ask, and she nods as she bends over, going into the car, giving me a spectacular view of her gorgeous ass. Before I can get me a handful of it though, music starts blaring from her car and she stands upright, coming toward me. It's a slow song, soft and sultry, and as she wraps her arms around my neck, resting her head on my chest, I hold her close to me as I listen to the words. The song is about finding that one person who you want to latch on to and never let go.

"Dance with me," she whispers and I oblige, slowly swaying to the meaningful music. I've never heard the song before, but it is amazing, and each word of it is how I feel about Claire. It *is* our song. She is completely right. Lacing her fingers behind my neck, she rests her chin on my chest, looking up at me, and my heart beats out of my chest as I get lost in her sweet blue eyes.

"I'm latched to you," I whisper and she nods.

"I know, and I won't let go," she says, bringing her hands to cup my face. "I love you."

"I love you more."

"Not possible," she says and then she brings her lips to mine.

And as my lips move with hers, I'm in what I consider to be utopia.

 PHILLIP

"She really loves him."

I glance up to meet my soon-to-be wife's eyes, and I know that she's right, but I don't want to accept it. We stand beside our car, watching as Claire and that bonehead hold each other, swaying to the music playing from her car. I want to go over there and scoop her up and steal her away, but I know she'd fight me away. She loves the guy. I want to imagine her single and a virgin till she's thirty, but I know that isn't true. She hasn't had it easy, and I wish I could undo those years of hell, but I can't. All I can do is pray and hope to God that nothing ever hurts her again.

And by the way she looks at that kid, I know he could be her biggest heartache.

"Something about that guy rubs me wrong. I don't know what it is. I mean, he seems like an all right kid, driven and ready for life, but I don't know," I say once we're in the car. I feel like a creeper watching Claire as she canoodles with that guy, but I can't bring myself to drive away.

"You're jealous," Reese says, and I whip my head to her.

"The hell I am!"

She laughs as she turns in her seat to face me. "Yes, you are, babe. She's your number one, your right-hand man, and you know that he's taking over."

"You're my number one too," I say, not only because it is true but because I don't want to admit that maybe she might be right.

"Oh, I know. Don't try to distract me with sweet stuff; I know the truth – I can read you like a book, Phillip."

I take her hands in mine, kissing her knuckles. "I know, but it scares me, you know," I say. I usually don't talk about my feelings, but I can say anything to Reese and she won't judge me one bit – she'll only love me. "I don't want anything to hurt her, and I think she's in too deep with this kid. He could hurt her, and then I swear to God, Reese, I'll kill him."

Leaning her head on my shoulder, she lets out a breath. "I know, baby, but we have to trust that she knows what she's doing. And if it all comes crashing down in a heap of hell, then you know what? We will be there to catch her and help mend her wounds."

"And then we kill him."

"You're damn right, we will," she says, and I laugh as I wrap my arms around her.

"I can't wait to marry you tomorrow," I whisper against her hair as I watch as Claire's hands cup that kid's face.

"Me neither. Are you sure you want to marry me?"

I scoff, tipping her chin up so she's facing me. "I've waited my whole life to hear you say 'I do' when the preacher asks if you want to be my wife, so yeah, I think I am sure."

Grinning up at me, she runs her fingers along the hair on my jaw and I'm breathless, getting lost in her brown eyes. "Good," she whispers. "'Cause I really don't want to be left at the altar."

"No worries, sweet cakes. I'll be the hot one in the tux."

"Good to know. I might have missed you," she teases. "Marry Erik or something."

"Cold day in hell, lady," I say sternly and she laughs.

As she cuddles into me, I kiss her temple and whisper how much I love her. She giggles, running her nose along my jaw, basically making me the happiest man in the world. When Claire kisses the schmuck, I cringe and look down to find Reese watching me.

"Don't worry about her," she says quietly. "I know it's hard, and I know you want to jump in and tell her to take it slow, but did we take it slow the first time we met?"

I chuckle as I shake my head. "No, we were at it like rabbits, which does not make me feel better, Reese."

She laughs as she shakes her head. "I meant that no, we didn't take it slow, but our love was real. You never know. It could be real for them."

"Or it could be a train wreck."

She nods slowly. "You're right, but let's hope she's found her true love."

"Why would we hope that?" I ask.

"Because we want her to be happy."

"You're right," I concede, and she smiles.

"I know, now make sure to remember that 'cause I'll be right this whole marriage."

I scoff and shake my head before glancing back at where Claire stands wrapped up tightly in that kid's arms. She's looking up at him like he is her world, and the smile on her face is indescribable. She's completely in love with him, and that scares the living shit out of me because, while I want her to be happy, I want her to be safe, and I don't know if giving her heart to this kid is the safe route.

Can I trust him?

CHAPTER 37

Claire

"You ready?" I ask as Phillip paces in the room across the hall from Reese. I should be in there helping Reese get ready, but she has her mom, Harper, and Piper fussing over her. I was completely dressed in my long blue dress that hugs every curve when something inside me told me to check on Phillip. I'm glad I did. He's sweating bullets and is white as a sheet.

"Yeah. I got this."

"Then why do you look like you're about to pass out?"

He cuts me a look and expels a long breath. "Because I'm nervous. What if she decides she doesn't want to do this and runs out? She's unpredictable! You know that."

I smile as I lace my fingers and lean on my elbows. "You're right, but I know she loves you and she wants this. I'm pretty sure she didn't put us through all this wedding crap to bail on ya."

"Yeah, true," he says, wiping his face for the tenth time with a towel. "You look beautiful, by the way," he says when he glances up at me. "So beautiful."

I smile, my face cheek warming with color as I shrug. "Thanks. Wait till you see Reese. She's stunning."

A goofy grin comes across his face. "I can't wait."

I love how much he loves her. His love for Reese is soul-deep and so beautiful. I'm lucky to be on the receiving end of his love too because Phillip loves hard and with all his heart.

He lets out another breath and says, "Aren't you supposed to be helping her get ready or something?"

"She has help. Figured I'd sit in here with you for a minute."

"Making sure I don't pass out?"

"Yeah, told you you're looking a little white."

He scoffs as he nods. "I didn't think I'd be this nervous."

"This is a huge deal. You finally got her to commit to only you."

He smiles. "She's always been mine, just hardheaded as all hell and didn't want to admit it."

"Very true," I agree and he smiles.

"You're a good kid, Claire. You know that?"

I grin as I squeeze my fingers together. "I was raised by the greatest parents in the world."

Closing the distance between us, he hugs me tightly, squeezing me so hard that I can't breathe. With his lips at my ear, he says, "I love you, Claire, so much, and I am so proud of you."

"I love you too, Phillip."

"And remember when we're in the Hunger Games, I'll die for you."

"Thanks," I say and then I start to laugh so hard it hurts, but I don't let him go. There was a time when I declared that I would kill him in the Hunger Games, but I think we both knew that wasn't true. I continue to hold him tight, fighting away the tears because I don't want to mess up the makeup that took forever to apply. I also know that if I start crying, he probably will too, and I can't handle his tears. I'll come undone, and I already don't think I'll be able to hold it together during the wedding. There is something about a man crying that guts me, so I'm going to pray that Phillip doesn't lose it.

Pulling away, he kisses my cheek and says, "You like that kid, don't you?"

I smile. "Yeah, I do."

He lets out a long breath, his eyes locked on mine. He's giving me that "I don't want to accept you have boobs" look, and I don't know what to make of it. "The main thing I have to remember is that I want you to be happy, and because of that, I'm gonna be nice to him."

A grin cracks across my face. "Oh, how sweet of you."

He sets me with a look. "But the moment he hurts you, Claire, he's dead."

I laugh again, nodding my head. "I wouldn't expect anything else."

"I hope it doesn't happen though," he admits.

"Me neither," I say, letting out a long breath. "I love him a lot."

"Just be careful, kiddo."

"I know," I say and a knock comes at the door.

Looking over at it, Phillip says, "Come in."

The door opens and in comes a man about the same height as Phillip. He looks a lot like Phillip – the same blue eyes, blond hair, and bone structure – but I have never seen him before. Looking at Phillip, confused, I'm about to ask who it is, but Phillip's face is white again, shocked.

"Miles? What are you doing here?" he says, letting me go and walking toward the man.

"Came for the wedding. Reese invited me."

"Oh shit, it's great to see you," he says and then they hug, awkwardly, I might add. "I'm so glad you could make it."

"Yeah, me too. I didn't know if I should come. My dad – our dad – wasn't too happy about it."

Our dad? What the hell?

"Phillip?" I ask, and they both look at me.

"Oh, um, Miles, this is my niece, Claire. She was my sister Rochelle's daughter," Phillip says, bringing me toward them. "Claire, this is my half brother, Miles."

Shocked, I meet his gaze and he gives me a half smile. "So are you my uncle?"

"No, he's my half brother. We have the same dad, not the same mom," Phillip says, a grimace on his face.

"Oh," I say, looking back at Miles.

"It's nice to meet you, nonetheless."

"You too," I say, shaking his hand. "This is weird."

They both laugh and I smile. "Yeah, a little, but I'm really glad you're here. Reese will be excited to meet you in person."

"Yeah, I mainly wanted to stop by before everything got started 'cause I know once you're married, everything else won't matter." He takes in a deep breath and then says, "I wanted to say that I'm sorry for the last few years."

"It's not your fault. Don't worry about it."

"Yeah, but still," Miles says, and I feel like I shouldn't be here.

"I'm gonna give y'all some privacy. I think Reese needs me," I say and they both look at me. I almost think they forgot I was in the room.

"Yeah, okay, I'll see you out there," Phillip says.

"Yeah, good luck," I say before kissing his cheek and then I escape from the weirdness of that situation.

Crossing the hall, I open the door and the first thing I see is the back of Reese, her dress falling ever so gorgeously down her body. Her hair is up in a very intricate hairdo, braids and curls all wrapped into one. Her eyes meet mine in the mirror, and she smiles. I smile back and come up beside her, leaning my head onto hers as we gaze into each other's eyes in the mirror. Unlike her hair, mine is down in one long braid, but with a bump at the top, giving it a very elegant look. Her makeup is done so softly, almost classic, like her dress.

And by the way, the dress is looking a little snug. Especially around the midsection. She's gained some weight, but I wouldn't dare tell her that. She's stressed out, and the way she deals with that is Ben & Jerry's, and who can blame her? I'm a whore for those two men too.

Putting her hand up on my cheek, her big diamond ring sparkles in the light, and she smiles as she whispers, "You're gorgeous, Claire."

"So are you."

"I don't look fat? My dress is tight," she says, her face dropping the grin from before. "I curse you Ben & Jerry!"

I laugh as I shake my head. "Not at all, you're gorgeous."

"Such a smart girl."

She winks at me, and I grin as I wrap my arms around her waist. I hear cameras going crazy, but I don't care about them. I'm mentally treasuring this moment with a woman whom I look up to and love.

"How's Phillip?" she asks.

"Good. His brother showed up, Miles?"

"Did he? Good," she says with a grin. "I was hoping he would."

"Yeah, it was weird," I inform her.

"Yeah, they have a strained relationship. Hopefully, his coming will mend it."

"Phillip seemed happy to see him," I point out.

"He loves Miles. I know it was important for him to be here."

"You're a good fiancée," I say with a grin, and she returns it.

"I try," she says with a wink. Standing up, she goes to the desk before turning to me with a little box in her hands. "I got you something."

I smile. "Oooh, what?"

She laughs as she hands it to me. It's a little blue box, and that means one thing – it's from Tiffany's. Opening it quickly, I'm suddenly fighting back tears when I see a necklace that holds a heart charm. The chain is silver and gorgeous, but the charm is a thing of beauty. It's made of diamonds, except for three colored stones that I know are Reese's, Phillip's, and my birthstones.

"Turn it around," she says, and I swallow as I do as she asks. On the back, it is engraved: *So you always have a piece of us with you. Love, Reese and Phillip.*

"Oh, Reese," I gasp, running my finger along the engraving. "It's amazing."

She takes it from my hands before putting it on me. Looking in the mirror, I take in the beauty of not only us but also the necklace as she wraps her arms around my waist.

"No matter what, Claire, we will always be here for you. We are your rock. We love you. I love you."

A small tear streams down my face, and I wipe it away quickly. "I love you. Thank you."

She kisses my cheek and leans her head on my shoulder. I hear a camera again, and I hope that shot came out. I want it, but just in case, I mentally lock this moment away.

"It's time, guys."

I turn to see that it's Reese's dad, Blake, and I smile. "Hey, Papa."

He smiles and says, "Hey, sweet girl, you look gorgeous."

"Thanks. You clean up nicely."

He laughs as he comes up beside us. "I try to for weddings."

Reese turns then, meeting her father's gaze. "You look stunning, baby – my last girl to get married."

Tears fill Reese's eyes as she nods. "I can't believe it."

"Me either, darling, come here."

I choke back the tears as they hug tightly, and I watch as he whispers something in Reese's ear. Sensing it is a private moment, I look away and suck in a deep breath. I wonder if Phillip and I will be a blubbering mess at my wedding. More than likely so. Not that I'm thinking of my own wedding – that's far away – but still, I can't wait for that moment. I used to see myself marrying a dancer, but now I have my eyes set on one hell of a sexy hockey player.

"Okay, it's time, Ms. Allen," Ginny, the wedding planner that Phillip hired yesterday, says. "Claire, you're first."

I grab my bouquet of blue irises and yellow Gerbera daisies and then hand Reese hers. Following Ginny down the halls, we come to a big black door and I know on the other side is my uncle, waiting for his bride. I look back at Reese and smile. Even with her eyes full of tears, she looks so beautiful, almost like she stepped out of a bridal magazine. Reaching out, she squeezes my shoulder and mouths that she loves me. I say the same back and then the doors open and I start out behind Harper's daughter Ally and Elli's daughters Shelli and Posey, as they throw little yellow flowers all over the aisle in their cute little blue dresses.

With a huge smile on my face, I walk slowly as all eyes land on me. Searching the packed room, I find Jude off to the side, sitting all alone with a great big grin on his face. My heart skips a beat at the desire that swirls in his green eyes. He looks dashing in a black tux jacket, a royal blue shirt underneath it with no tie. His hair is combed to the side, giving him a classic look, and I'm glad he is all mine. Giving him a grin that I hope he knows is just for him, I tear my gaze off him to make sure I don't run into anything and find that Phillip is watching me, a proud smile on his face. Stopping in my spot, I turn to look back at the doors I just walked through, waiting for Reese to come in. In the front row is the whole Allen family, minus her dad at the moment.

What kills me the most though is when I look over at the other side where Phillip and my family is supposed to sit, it's only full of hockey players. We don't have family. Only each other and Reese, and I guess Miles, but even he is sitting in the back, not in the front, supporting his brother. Swallowing the tears from the pain of not having anyone here to support him or even me, for that matter, I blink a few times. Thankfully though, I look down the aisle where the door opens and Reese appears on her father's arm, looking completely breathtaking.

I look over at Phillip, and the grin that is on his face lights up the whole room. He doesn't need anyone; he has Reese. That's all he needs. But to my surprise, he looks over at me, all the love in the world in his eyes as he jerks a thumb toward Reese.

"Hot, huh?"

I laugh along with everyone else; even Reese is laughing as she closes the distance between them. I watch, fighting the tears as Papa Blake gives Reese to Phillip, making him promise first that he will love her for the rest of his life. Of course, Phillip agrees, but unlike at the rehearsal where he brought Reese up to the altar, he pushes the birdcage veil up and cups her face, pressing his lips to hers. Everyone gasps and laughs but I didn't expect anything else. This is my uncle we're talking about.

"I didn't say you could do that yet," the preacher calls out as they part.

Phillip waves him off. "Do you see how gorgeous she is? I can't wait that long to kiss the love of my life," he says, his eyes locked on Reese's.

And that's when the tears fall.

Wiping them away, I watch as they come up to the altar and the wedding starts. It's all a blur, really. I'm a weeping mess, and I know I should pay attention to all the undying love talk, but all I can do is wipe my tears and thank God that these two found each other.

"Now, you two have written your own vows, yes?" the preacher asks and they both nod. "Then let's have at it, Reese?"

I can't see her face, but I know she has to be smiling because Phillip is smiling big enough for the both of them.

"I didn't want to love you when I first met you," she says, and I can hear the collective murmurs through the crowd, but I ignore them. "I was supposed to live my single life with no cares in the world, but then you came along and threw those plans out the window. Now that I have you, Phillip, I couldn't imagine life without you. You not only brought your love to me, you brought Claire, and made me the luckiest woman in the world."

Ugh, she's killing me. Tears fall in streams down my face and come faster than I can wipe.

"I love you, and I promise to love you for the rest of my life, no matter what. Good times and bad and all the times in between. It's me, you, Claire, and the gift that is growing within me for the rest of our lives."

Say what?!

I hear Elli holler something, even Harper and Piper are yelling, but I can only hear my heart beat in my ears. I'm pretty sure I heard her right because the whole room is in an uproar, but to be certain, I ask, "What did you say?"

And when they both look back at me, grinning, I know it's true. "You're pregnant?" I still ask, completely shocked.

"Yup," she says, her own tears flooding her beautiful face. "Surprise!"

Wiping my eyes, I take a shuddering breath as the news registers in my head.

Phillip and Reese are having a baby.

Holy crap. This is insane but at the same time so freaking wonderful. I've always thought they would have the most gorgeous kid ever, and now that is becoming a reality. I'm stunned, completely and utterly stunned. My favorite people are procreating. How amazing is that!

"Congratulations. Now, Phillip?" the preacher says, completely ignoring the fact that I'm freaking out over here.

"My turn? Awesome," he says and then looks deep into Reese's eyes. Usually they gag me with their corny love, but right now, I'm in awe of them. They are perfect for each other. "I couldn't live without you, Reese. I couldn't be the man I am without you. I couldn't be the father I am to Claire and the one I will be for our new baby without you. I couldn't be the hockey player I am without your support. That's all there is to it. I love you, you know that. I think you're hot, and I know I'll always think that 'cause you are by far the most gorgeous woman I've ever set eyes on. I promise to love you at your best and your worst 'cause you are mine. Now let's get this over with so I can kiss the hell out of you without the preacher yelling at me."

A grin pulls at my mouth, and I watch them exchange rings, Phillip being his goofy self. When it is time for them to kiss as husband and wife, I find myself not watching them, but watching Jude. He's smiling, his eyes locked on me, and for some reason, I think that this could be us one day.

And if that day is as perfect as this one has been, then I can't wait.

CHAPTER 38

JUDE

I am in a room full of hockey royalty.

Some of the greatest players came for Reese and Phillip's wedding, and while I want to get up and mingle with them, I can't seem to move, or talk, for that matter. I should appreciate the fact that I'm at such a prestigious wedding at the beautiful Belle Meade plantation about to see my hot-ass girlfriend at any moment, but all I can do is try to keep from freaking out because Shea Adler just sat right beside me. Giving him a sideways glance, I look away quickly before he catches me looking at him. Jayden and Jase met him once at an Assassins foundation thingy, but I was home with the flu and didn't get the chance. They said he's a really nice guy, but he is the captain of the Assassins. The greatest player in the NHL.

How do you talk to someone like that?

I know I need to get over that since I will be playing against him in no time, but I can't seem to do that at this particular second. Pulling my phone out, I know there's only a slim chance that Claire has her phone, but I text her anyway.

Me: I am sitting beside Shea Adler. #freakingout.

I wait a second and thankfully, a text comes through.

Claire: Lol! U dork! Say hi, he's supernice.
Me: No way, he's Shea Adler.
Claire: I know, he's my uncle.
Me: That's so weird!
Claire: Ur weird, talk to him or I'll introduce you in a few. I'm

about to be there.
Me: See u in a bit. You look really hot babe.
Claire: Thanks ☺
Me: I still get to peel that dress off right?
Claire: Definitely.

A grin comes across my face as I tuck my phone in my pocket. Leaning back in my seat, I take in my surroundings. It truly was a beautiful wedding, but the reception is really awesome. Lights hang from the ceiling; lots of blue flowers are in the middle of the tables with pops of yellow everywhere. As soon as I walked in and was directed to my seat, a beer was placed in my hand. I chugged the sucker, not only because I was worried they'd take it away from me, but because I'm nervous. I've never been around so many important people.

"Hey," Shea says unexpectedly from beside me. I look over, not sure he's talking to me, but then he says, "I'm Shea Adler. I don't think I've met you."

I take his hand and shake it as I say, "Jude Sinclair."

"Oh, Elli, this is the guy that's dating Claire."

Elli looks over at me and waves. "Yeah, Jude, hey, how are you?"

"Fine, thank you," I say and then look back at Shea.

Elli returns to talking to one of the ladies from the afternoon when I picked Claire up and Shea leans toward me, dropping his voice almost to a whisper before saying, "Yeah, don't hurt her. You do, you'll have a whole hockey team after you."

I think I just peed on myself.

Leaving me with wide eyes, he sits upright, and I look away just as the music starts.

I just got threatened by Shea Adler.

That is so fucking cool.

Yes, I am shaking in my boots, but come on, it's not every day that the captain of the Assassins threatens to kill you. As I look over at the door that is opening, Claire comes in on the arm of Erik Titov. She's grinning from ear to ear, looking completely stunning all done up. As my eyes lazily make a trail down her gorgeous body, I can't wait to get that dress off her. It's been days since I've been deep inside her, and I'm itching to get her naked. But I have to admit, she looks amazing fully clothed right now.

Heading in next are Reese and Phillip, looking so fucking happy they could star in a newlywed sitcom. They are disgustingly cute, but I bet that's what people think of Claire and me. As people cheer and holler for the bride and groom, my eyes go back to where my girl is standing to find that her eyes are locked on me. A sneaky little grin pulls at her lips, and I smile as she starts for me before dropping into my lap. I wrap my arms around her, kissing her red-painted lips.

"Hey, Jude," she says with a wink.

"Hey, gorgeous."

"I can't stay for long. I have to sit up there with them, but I couldn't stand to be away from you any longer," she says in a perfect rendition of a Southern belle.

Clearing my throat, I say in my best southern way, "Well, ma'am, I'm glad you came because I just can't live another second without your lips on mine."

"You're in luck, cowboy, 'cause I've been cravin' some kissin'," she says right before she presses her lips against mine.

Corny. Yes, we are. I don't think either of us cares, though. Holding her face in my hands, I kiss her long and hard, my dick coming to life in my pants and pressing against her ass. Grinning against my lips, she whispers, "Something is poking me."

I grin. "Yes, he misses you."

Her eyes darken as she runs her nose along mine. "I miss him."

I groan inwardly as she pulls away and says, "Shea, this is my boyfriend."

Shea looks over at us and smiles. "Yeah, I know. I already threatened to kill him if he hurts you."

Rolling her eyes, she looks at me. "I'm sorry, but did you know that the Nashville Assassins team is full of a bunch of overprotective crazies?"

"No, I didn't see that in the paper," I say and she smiles.

"Well, it needs to be there. Don't pay any attention to him. He's a big softy."

Shea gives me a look that says otherwise, but I don't think I should point that out.

"Okay, I gotta go do wedding crap. Can you believe they are pregnant?!"

I smile. "I'm guessing that's huge?"

She nods. "Oh yeah, Reese never wanted kids, so yeah, big, huge deal. I'm really excited!"

"I can tell. That's awesome, babe."

"Yeah, okay, I'm off. I'll come visit as I can. Everyone be nice," she calls out to the table of Assassins, but by the way they are looking at me, I'm pretty sure they won't be nice. Each guy is looking at me like I'm trying to steal her virtue, and all the women are looking at me like I'm a piece of cake.

It's superweird.

Why am I sitting here again?

I bet this was Phillip's doing, wanting to scare me. While he may be succeeding because I'm pretty sure Shea could squish me with one hand, I won't let anyone know. Sitting up a little straighter, I take a pull of the new beer I was given before digging into the dinner that was magically placed in front of me. No one really speaks to me through dinner except for Elli; she talks to me and is really nice while her husband glares at me like I stole the last cookie.

"You play hockey, don't you?" she asks and I nod.

"Yes, ma'am."

"For whom?" Shea asks, looking over at me. He has his daughter, Posey, I think is her name, sitting in his lap, sleeping against his chest.

"The Bellevue Bullies."

"Coach Moss?" he asks.

"Yup, you know him?"

"I do. I played for him when I was nine. Great guy, hard, you have a good coach," he says, meeting my gaze. "Don't waste the time you have with him. He is one of the greatest."

"Couldn't say it better myself. I went to Bellevue because of him."

"Good, you'll get better. Are you hoping to play for the NHL? Probably, huh? That's basically any player's dream," he says, and everyone laughs around the table, nodding in agreement. The more I'm around real-life hockey players, the more I know I need to bulk up. When you see them on TV, you think it's the pads, and while I have a great, strong body, it can be bigger, stronger. I need to get serious about it.

"I'm going into the draft this year," I say, and he raises an eyebrow.

"What's your name again?" he asks.

I take in a deep breath. "Jude Sinclair."

"I think I've heard about you. They think you'll go first round, top ten."

I nod, a proud smile on my face. "Yes, sir. That's the plan."

"That's awesome. I wish the best for you, but if you hurt Claire, you can kiss the draft goodbye," he says, tipping his beer to me.

"'Cause I'll be dead?" I ask.

He laughs as he nods. "Dead as a doornail. We're big dudes, which, by the way, you might want to put some more muscle on those shoulders. Those boards are hard."

"Duly noted, on both accounts. Claire is safe, I promise."

I smile as I lean back in my seat, looking over my shoulder to find Claire laughing at something Reese has said. She leans against her, Phillip reaching across Reese to point his finger at Claire. They all look like such a happy little family. It's an amazing thing to see, and sometimes I wish my family was like that. For that to happen though, my father would have to actually be a father, but I don't want to think about him or that right now. Not when my girlfriend is probably the most gorgeous girl in the world.

She's stunning in her blue gown, her hair so pretty, and I can't help but be breathless when I look at her. Shea talks about being thrown into the boards and how I need to bulk up because they hurt; he's completely right, but being in love with Claire is like being thrown up against them. She knocks the air out of me every time I look at her, and I can't believe how much I love her. Never in my life did I think this could happen, but man, am I glad I was wrong.

A sigh escapes my lips; I go to turn back around but Claire's eyes meet mine and a sweet grin comes over her face as she waves her fingers at me. A grin pulls at my lips as I cock my head toward the dance floor. A few people are dancing, and I need to be closer to her. I don't like how far apart we are. Thankfully, she nods and gets up, saying something to Reese and Phillip. I stand as well, pushing my chair in and then meeting her halfway.

"You are unbelievable, Claire," I say, taking her hand in mine.

A grin covers her sweet mouth as she cups our hands with her other hand. Leaning into me, she kisses my jaw before saying, "So are you."

Kissing her temple, I take her to the dance floor and wrap my arms around her waist, holding her close, praying that I don't ever have to let go. At least for the next couple songs, anyway. As we slowly sway to the crooning voice of Michael Buble, I cuddle my nose against her neck, taking in her soft, delicate smell. Running my lips up her neck to the spot beneath her ear, I say, "I love holding you like this."

Pulling back, I see that she's grinning, her eyes bright and intoxicating. Her lips press together in a pucker, and while I want nothing more than to kiss her, I can't seem to get over the fact that her lips are a work of art. "I love your lips," I say and she blushes.

"Good, kiss 'em."

Cupping her jaw, I shake my head. "I rather stare at them. I should get them tattooed on me when we go to get your tattoo."

She laughs, her eyes full of amusement. "'Cause that's not crazy!"

I shrug. "It's not."

Her grin falls. "Oh, you're serious?"

"Like a heart attack," I say and I am. I want a piece of her on me, and I think the idea is golden. May be a tad bit crazy like she said, but that's how I work.

"We'll see," she says, a grin pulling at her lips.

"I want them above my heart," I declare, and her cheeks warm with color.

She gives me a shocked look, her breathing hitching as she whispers, "That is incredibly romantic."

"I try, it comes in spurts," I say offhandedly and she laughs.

"You're actually super-romantic. It's nice. I've never felt this special in my life."

Locking my gaze with hers, I say, "Didn't I promise to always make you feel special?"

"You did," she says breathlessly, her eyes swimming with love.

"And I'll never break a promise, Claire."

Running her fingers through the hair on my jaw, she fixes her gaze on my lips and then she closes the distance, locking her mouth against mine. Slowly I kiss her, thoroughly, and with all the love and passion in my heart. I honestly dream of kissing this girl. Every second, I imagine her lips on mine, her body pressed to mine, and when it happens, I swear it takes me a while to recuperate from her. I love the feel of her heart against my chest, her lips so soft against mine, and the dreamy look on her face when we part for a breath.

It's all so perfect. It feels like it's meant to be.

Cupping her neck, I press my head to hers, sharing the same breath as we continue to move slowly to the music. Looking deep into her sparkling blue eyes, I know I don't have to tell her I love her. She has to see it, to feel it, because I know I do. Her love for me pours out of her in waves, and I can't believe I am on the receiving end of such a beautiful love.

Our love.

We dance for a little longer before Reese is pulling her away unexpectedly. "I'm sorry, Jude. We need her for a few pictures."

I smile. "That's fine. I'll go get a drink."

"I'll be back," Claire promises, and then she's off. I watch her for a moment; she laughs and jokes with the women who stand around her before they all pose for the photographer. With a grin still on my face, I head for the bar, getting myself a beer before leaning against it. I people watch as I wait for Claire to come find me.

"Enjoying yourself, Jude?"

Glancing to my left, I find Phillip standing beside me, his own beer in his hand. He's not looking at me, and if he hadn't have said my name, I wouldn't have known he was talking to me.

"I am. It's a beautiful wedding. Congratulations."

He nods, still not looking at me. "Thank you. I'm very blessed."

"You are," I agree and take a pull of my beer.

"Are you old enough to drink?"

I shake my head. "Nope, but they served it, so I took it."

He laughs. "I should probably say something."

I shrug my shoulders, taking another pull of my beer. The liquid has taken the edge off, and I'm not tipsy by any means, but I know this is my last one. I have to drive Claire home.

"Don't drink and drive, especially with Claire in the car."

"Wouldn't think of it," I say, hoping that he knows I am genuine.

Nothing is said for a moment and it isn't an awkward silence like I would expect with us; it's more of a relaxing one. Letting out a long breath, I watch as Claire talks animatedly with her aunts, and I smile when she does. She steals the show, even beside Reese, who is hands down the most gorgeous bride I've ever seen. Looking up, she catches me watching her, and I chuck my chin up at her. She sends me a grin before turning to look at Elli, the small smile still gracing her face.

"She really likes you."

I look up at Phillip. This time he is looking at me, his eyes stern, and his jaw taut. "I know, and I feel the same."

"Because she cares for you and I want her to be happy, I plan to be nicer to you."

"Good to know," I say, liking where this is going.

"But you don't deserve her. Not in the least."

Nodding my head, I look down at the ground, my heart in my throat. "I couldn't agree more, but who does, Phillip?" I ask, turning to face him. His eyes turn to slits as he glares, and he goes to say something, but I stop him and say, "No one deserves that girl because she is the most beautiful and unbelievable person I've ever met. She makes me want to be a better man. She has come along and completely changed the way I think, the way I want my life to be, all with one smile and one little snarky comment. So, yeah, I don't deserve her, but you best believe that now that I have her, I won't ever take her for granted. I'll love her until the day I die. I know you don't trust me, or even like me, but it doesn't matter. All that matters is who makes her happy, and I'm the man to do that."

He's still glaring, and I don't understand that. I thought that speech was a good one. I meant every single word, it came from my heart, but obviously he must think it was all lies.

"You think you got it all figured out, don't you? In only a month you think you are her forever?"

"I don't think – I know. She is my forever and I'm hers."

Shaking his head, he lets out a long breath. "I swear to God, you break her–"

"You'll break me. Yeah, you've said that, your friends have said that, but am I running for the hills? Did I run when she told me about her past, about the men, about her shitty life before she got to you? No, I'm here. You don't have to like me, Phillip, I get it, but you might want to accept I'm not going anywhere without her."

Looking away, he takes in a deep breath and then looks back at me, letting it out. "I should kick your ass."

I scoff. "Why?"

"'Cause you're a smug bastard, and I don't like the things you've said."

"You don't like that I'm basically latched on to that girl, and want to do everything in my power to make her happy?" I ask incredulously. "Shouldn't you be thankful?

He steps closer to me, and I want to step back, but I know that would show weakness. So I stay where I am, meeting his angry gaze. "No, I can't be because I know you tell her these things, these promises that have the chance to be empty. I know that she believes you and is probably planning her future around you, and when you decide that you don't want this, you're going to leave her in your dust. And who will be there to pick her up? Me. So no, I'm not thankful. I'm scared. She's had it rough. I can't handle you breaking her all over again, and you have the power to do that."

Taking in a deep breath, I look away and gather my thoughts before glancing back at him. "I know there is no telling you that I'm not going to do that. You've already made up your mind about me, and all I can do is prove to you that I'm not going to hurt her. I love her, Phillip. I can't stop that."

"Whoa, this looks intense."

Taking a step away from each other, we both look over to find Claire watching us. "Is everything okay?" she asks.

"Of course, just having a chat with Jude," Phillip answers.

She looks at me and I smile. "Yup, talking about how gorgeous you are," I say, bringing her in close and kissing the side of her mouth.

She giggles before looking up at me. "I don't believe either of you one bit."

"No worries, baby. Come on, let's go dance," I say, lacing my fingers with hers. Looking up at Phillip, I say, "Thanks for the talk. I got this."

I can see his fists clenching, but I ignore them as Claire leans into me, her eyes locking with mine. I kiss her nose as Phillip's words play over in my head. *She's had it rough. I can't handle you breaking her all over again, and you have the power to do that.*

I get what he's saying, but I wish he would realize that she has the power to do the same to me.

And still I love her.

More than words can define.

CHAPTER 39

 JUDE

Sitting on my bike, I watch as everyone leaves while I wait for Claire. While I wanted to peel that dress off her, it isn't suitable for the bike, so she's off changing.

The rest of the wedding reception was beautiful. Love was in the air and everyone seemed to have a good time. When Reese and Phillip drove off, heading for the airport, I held Claire as she cried. I haven't seen her cry anything but happy tears, but I sense that she felt a bit lost as she watched them drive away. They really are her rock, and I hope that one day she'll consider me as someone she can always rely on. A part of me thinks she does, but that doesn't mean that I don't want to work hard to make her realize that I'm here for her anytime she wants.

I'm always here for her.

Letting my head fall back, I look up at the clear night sky. It was a wonderful evening for a wedding; even though it is close to November, it's uncommonly warm. I don't think I'll ever understand Tennessee weather. It's supposed to be winter soon, but still, it feels like a warm fall night. I really want to get Claire back to my house. Jayden is out with a couple of friends, so I have the room to do whatever I please, but a part of me wants to go for a nice long ride. Maybe Claire will be game if she isn't too tired.

When she comes out the side door, she heads straight for me in a pair of jeans and a T-shirt. I don't see her in jeans very much, and when she wears them, I drink in every single inch of her. She really does have the best curves, but then again, I'm a little biased.

"It's nice out," she says as she reaches me, putting her backpack on.

"Yeah, do you wanna go for a ride?"

She shrugs. "Sure, I'd love to."

She takes her backpack back off and pulls out her sweatshirt, putting it on before closing the bag and putting it on her back. We both put on our helmets, and she climbs on as I start the bike. After she wraps her arms around me, I take off, the chill biting into my neck as we ride. I don't mind it though; I welcome it. As we ride out of the city, the lights disappear behind us, and then the blackness of the interstate is all I see. I figured we could ride up and down the interstate, but then I decide to go out by the woods by my mom's house. We have a creek out there and I think Claire would love it there. I worry a bit that my mom might hear my motorcycle, but that's only if she's outside, which she probably isn't with it being almost midnight. It takes about an hour to get out here, and when I pull down the dark road that leads to the spot where my brothers and I used to make forts, I smile. These were my stomping grounds, my childhood, and now I am bringing Claire here.

Slowing my motorcycle, I basically creep toward the creek. Not only to make sure my mom doesn't hear us, but because I don't want to kick the dirt up around us. Stopping in front of the creek, I turn the bike off and take off my helmet, looking over my shoulder at her. She already has her helmet off, a grin on her flushed face.

"This is deserted."

I laugh. "Yeah, I used to play out here when I was a kid. It's my spot."

"Awesome," she says, looking around at nothing but darkness. It's a little spooky, but we will be fine. Nothing is out here. I used to camp out here; the only thing that ever had us sprinting back to the house was a raccoon one time. Mean little shit, that raccoon was. "If we weren't together, I'd think you were bringing me out here to kill me off," she says with a teasing grin.

"You need to stop watching those murder shows," I say with a shake of my head. She giggles behind me. "But good thing we're together, huh?"

Her eyes darken in the moonlight, her hands slowly creeping up my thighs until they rest right where my dick is coming alive. With her lips close to my ear, she says, "True. Means we can hook up."

I scoff, lacing my fingers with hers, breathing a little faster. "We don't hook up. I take way more pride than that in sex with you."

She gives me a minxy little grin, and I decide that I need to change our position. Pronto. Standing up, I throw my helmet on the ground, reaching for hers next before doing the same thing with it. I lift her up off the bike, and she wraps her arms around my neck, her legs around my waist just as my mouth meets hers. I want to say I brought her out here to share this part of me, but the more I think about it, I think I brought her out here to give her the best sex of her life.

Holding her up, I straddle the bike, sitting down, holding her ass in my hands as I continue to devour her mouth. Her tongue teases my lips, wanting to deepen the kiss, and I'm one to give her anything she wants. Deepening the kiss, I squeeze her ass. My whole body burns with need as my legs ache from where I'm holding the bike up. My dick is pressing against the zipper of my slacks, begging for a release as she slowly rocks against it, driving me insane. Parting, I lift both her shirts off, leaving her in only a strapless bra, her breasts spilling over the top. Like a starved man, I trace the swells of her breasts with my tongue, her moans encouraging me as I get my fill of her delectable breasts.

My body is shaking with need and hers is too. Her fingers dig into my forearms as I peel the cups of her bra down. The cold air hits her and quickly her nipples are hard, screaming to be licked. Sucking each nipple in my mouth, swirling my tongue slowly and teasingly around her sweet, rosy peaks. I swear this girl makes me feel like it's my first time every time. I want to discover everything about her, treasure her, and make her scream my name. As I bite her nipple softly, she arches her body, her breasts pressing into my mouth, her nails breaking the skin of my arm. Crying out, her fingers leave my arms, going up into my hair, massaging my scalp, as I pay the same attention to her other breast. Closing my eyes, my body is taut as I try to worship this girl's body instead of giving in to my need and fucking the shit out of her.

Kissing down her ribs, I dip my tongue in her cute little belly button before flicking the button of her jeans open.

"This was your plan, huh? Take me out and do dirty things to me in the woods?" she gasps, her breasts rising and falling with each breath she takes.

"I think it was. Subliminally," I say, laying her back and pulling her jeans and panties down her legs and off and throwing them over my shoulder. Her glistening center is right there, her legs up in the air, so I do what any other man would do, I bury my face in her sweet pussy.

"Thank God for your subconscious," she groans out, her legs crossing behind my neck, my hands holding her behind her knees as I devastate her clit. Swirling my tongue around her clit, I lick her, pressing my whole tongue against her taut nub before quickly flicking the tip of my tongue against it. She cries out, her hands squeezing my hair, her body shaking under me from the torture my mouth is inflicting on her.

"Ah, stop," she cries.

"Huh?" I say against her dripping wet center, looking up at her.

"Keys or something is digging into my back," she says, sitting up. "I can't come 'cause it hurts," she complains. I reach behind her, pulling the keys out and dropping them on her jeans. I then take my sweatshirt off and lay it down to make it a little softer for her. Lying back, she says, "Oh, thank you. As you were."

I chuckle as I lift her legs back up and press my mouth inside her, finding her clit with my tongue. Flicking my tongue against her clit, I hold both her legs up, freeing my other hand so I can dip my fingers inside her. Her cries become louder, her body shaking, and soon she is screaming with her release, my name falling from her lips in a whimper. As she gasps for breath, I slowly lick along her lower lips, getting drunk off the taste of her release.

"Jude, please," she cries, her hands coming between her legs to keep me from licking any longer. "I can't take it."

"Yeah, you can," I say, pushing her hands away and devouring her some more. I can't get enough of it. She tastes so good, so sweet, and the crazy thing is, I used to not like doing this until I was between her legs. She's bare, and she honestly does have the sexiest pussy I've ever seen.

"Jude," she gasps, her back arching as I continue to devour her. "Please, oh God, I think, oh, oh, oh, oh fuck," she cries and then she comes undone again, this time jerking and flinching underneath my mouth.

I don't know why, but my dick thickens to the point of pain knowing I made her come twice. Grinning, I wipe my mouth with the back of my hand as I stand up, undoing my slacks as I take in the sight of my girl laid out on my bike, the moonlight kissing her skin, making it glow.

"Jesus," I mutter as I push my pants down, toeing out of my shoes before kicking them both to the side. Grabbing my dick in my hand, I squeeze him, hoping to calm him down, but it doesn't seem to work. I can see the wetness glistening on her skin between her legs, and just the sight has me coming out of my skin. Mounting the bike again, I lift her up, bringing her slowly down on my dick, inch by inch until I am fully in her. We both moan at the connection, her body squeezing mine as her arms hang loosely around my neck, her eyes locked with mine.

"You're beautiful," I whisper against her lips, my fingers squeezing her ass. "So fucking hot."

Nipping at my bottom lip, she begins to lift and lower herself onto me. I don't know what she's bracing her feet on, but soon I don't care. I am insensible – completely and utterly gone beneath her. She rides me like she was meant to, going the right speed, coming down just enough to tease but please me. My fingers are biting into her ass, my breathing unsteady, and my heart is surely about to come out of my fucking chest. I can feel her squeezing me, her body reaching its peak again; I can feel mine doing the same but I want to draw this out. I want this to last forever.

As I suck her neck, she cries out, squeezing me so tight that I can't take it. Stopping her hips, I lift her up and sit her on her ass before getting off.

"What the hell?" she cries. "I was coming."

"Shut up, bend over the bike," I demand, and when I see the look she gives me, I add, "Please."

She gives me a grin before doing as I ask. I squeeze my dick, watching as she bends over, bracing her hands on my bike. She wiggles her ass in the air for me, and everything inside me is white-hot. Directing my dick into her, I take ahold of her hips and I can't control myself. I slam into her, my fingers digging into her hips, my body slapping against hers, our moans and groans filling the air over and over again until my toes are curling in my socks, and then I come so hard that lights go off behind my eyes.

Gasping for breath, I let my head fall back as I pull in lungfuls of air. "Fucking hell, that was hot."

She can only nod, her body trembling with the aftershocks of her orgasm. "I can't even form words," she gasps. "Well, except those and these."

I chuckle as I run my hand down the middle of her back to her neck where I lift her, turning her face so I can bring my lips against hers. I kiss her softly but in a very dominating way. I don't mean to but I just want her. So bad. Even after blowing the biggest load of my life. Parting, I pull myself out of her and then she turns, wrapping her arms around me and meeting her lips to mine again. Parting, I look deep into her eyes, pushing pieces of hair out of her face that fell from our activities. She's so unbelievable beautiful and she is all mine.

"That was really good," she says, her lips moving lightly against mine. "You delivered very hot motorcycle sex."

My mouth pulls up at the side as I cup her jaw in my hands. "I aim to please."

"Oh, you hit the bull's-eye, buddy."

I nibble at her bottom lip as I admire her body in the moonlight. It's getting chilly; I know we should put on our clothes and get out of here, but I just can't bring myself to do it. I love her body, everything about it, and in the moonlight, it's even sexier.

Leaning against me, she closes her eyes and says, "I'm so tired. You wore me out."

I smile. "So you're saying we should get dressed and get out of here, huh?"

She giggles as she opens her eyes. "Yeah, I am."

"Okay, but I want to ask you something," I say, sliding my hands down her back to grip her ass.

"Yes?" she asks breathlessly, leaning into me, her sweet center teasing my dick.

"Tomorrow you said you want to lie around and sleep all day, right?"

She smiles. "Yeah, that's the plan."

"Well, here is my plan, and I hope you're game."

"Hit me with it," she says, her teeth nipping at my lip.

"A marathon of Disney movies with candy, popcorn, and soda. I have it all set up at my room for us."

Her face breaks into a grin as she cups my cheeks. "You know what I think?"

"What?" I ask.

"I think I just fell even more in love with you. I would love that."

"That was my plan," I say with a wink.

As she giggles, her grin so bright and happy, I can't think of a more rewarding feeling than I feel right now. I'm drunk with love for this girl, and to be honest, I don't ever want to sober up.

CHAPTER 40

 JUDE

I'm a little early, but I don't mind. I wasn't supposed to be here for another twenty minutes, but I'm sorta glad I came early. I love seeing my girl in her element. Bracing my forearm against the doorframe, I lean into the wall, watching through a window as Claire trains one of her dancers. The dancer doesn't look that much younger than Claire, but it's obvious that she looks up to my girl. Her eyes haven't left Claire's body since I took up my post against the wall, but neither have mine.

She is breathtaking.

The song that is playing is the one we danced to after my game, a little over week ago. "Latch" by Sam Smith. I've downloaded the song and listen to it on repeat when we're apart, which has been a lot lately. Tonight is the first night we actually get to have a date night, and I can't wait to just be enveloped by her awesomeness. We text constantly and see each other randomly throughout the day, but for the next twelve hours, she's mine.

"Megan, you have to pay attention. You're missing most of the song's key parts, and you have to have the emotion. You've been in love, right?" Claire asks. Her voice is muffled by the glass, but I can still hear what she's saying.

Megan nods. "Yeah. I have."

"Okay, channel that. This dance, this song is about having the soul-deep, amazing love that leaves you breathless and wanting more every second of the day. It's like when you're apart from that person, your heart is coming out of your chest, trying to find the person who causes it to race. It's almost like you are dancing for that person. You're doing great, technically, but you need the emotion for this song to work. I'm going to show you, full-out, okay? Watch me," she demands as she goes to the middle of the floor.

I'm not sure how she hasn't seen me yet, but I'm thankful for that. I want to watch her do this full-out because I feel like this is for me. Pulling out my phone, I go to my camera and push record as I wait for the music to start. And for the next minute and thirty-nine seconds, I'm completely speechless. Every emotion she described to Megan is brought to life by her body. It is honestly the most gorgeous thing I've seen in my entire life. It's not only her body that has me completely enraptured, it's her face, the way her eyes tell the story along with her body.

A small smile tugs at my mouth as she turns, letting her back arch before slowly pulling it up. When she is fully erect, her eyes meet mine, and a grin pulls at her lips before she waves at me. I hit the end button on my camera and wave back, my heart coming out of my chest for this girl. I want to go through the wall to close the distance between us. I want to hold her, tell her how much she means to me and how life is nothing without her. Because without her, I'm not complete.

Tucking my phone in my pocket, I listen as she says, "That's how you do it."

"Wow," Megan says, her face full of awe. "That was beautiful."

"Thank you. Now go home, practice, and when we meet up next week, I want that emotion."

Megan nods and I watch as they clean up before both coming out, grins on their face. When Megan's eyes meet mine, she giggles before sending a look at Claire. "So he's the reason for all that emotion?"

Claire's face fills with color before she wraps her arms around my waist. "Yup, he sure is."

I kiss her temple and hug her tightly as Megan says, "Cool, see y'all later."

"Bye, Megan," Claire calls as she cuddles into me tighter. Once I hear the door shut, she looks up at me. "I've been waiting all day to see you."

"Me too. All day, I've been watching the clock."

She hugs me tighter. "I'm sorry for this week. With Reese and Phillip gone, I had to take over the studio, and I'm so damn tired."

I hug her back, dusting her jaw with kisses. "I understand. I've been busy too."

"They come back tomorrow, though, so hopefully things will go back to normal."

"There is a normal with us?" I joke and she smiles.

"Very good point. You know what I mean," she says and I nod.

"I know. Come on, let's get out of here. We don't want to be late," I say as we start for the door.

Once there, Claire locks everything up and then we head toward her car. I had Jayden drop me off since it's a chilly night. I didn't want to freeze on my bike or subject Claire to that. Might be time to put the bike up; the weather is starting to stay cold instead of fluctuating like it had been doing. Taking the keys from Claire, I kiss her knuckles and she bats her eyelashes at me before she heads to the other side to get in.

Getting in, I adjust the seat and put my seat belt on as she says, "I still can't believe I let you talk me into this."

I grin over at her. "What better way to spend date night than in a tattoo parlor?"

"I can give you a lot of places we could spend date night, mainly my bed or yours, but tattoos it is."

I laugh. "You know you're excited."

She shrugs, but I can see the grin pulling at her lips. "Maybe."

I poke her in her side, making her giggle out loud before smacking my hand away. Flashing me a bright grin, she leans across the console and gives me a loud kiss on the cheek. "Okay, I lied. I'm excited."

"That's what I thought," I say before kissing her lips quickly and then carefully backing her car out of the parking lot. She's already nervous about Phillip finding out I drove her car, which makes me nervous, and for the next ten minutes, I'm driving like a great-grandma to the tattoo parlor.

"Oh my God! You are driving slower than molasses! What the hell?"

"Shh," I say, pulling very carefully into the parking lot. I hate that I drove this slow. This car was made for power, but no way am I going to test that tonight. Not until I am in good standing with Phillip will I attempt that. "I'm taking it easy."

"Taking it easy? Jeez, I'm driving home," she says, throwing the door open and getting out. I do the same and point my finger at her.

"The hell you are. I'm the man – I drive."

Putting her hands on her hips, she says, "Oh, I'm sorry. I thought I was riding with my great-aunt. A real man would put the pedal to the medal. You were driving so slow, I'm pretty sure we were passed by a slug."

Glaring, I say, "Take that back."

"No, it's the truth," she says, standing a little taller.

Taking a step toward her, I expect her to take a step back or even run from me, but I forget that Claire isn't like other girls. She doesn't back down from a fight, and man, that turns me on. Cupping my hand on the back of her head, I pull her against me, crashing my mouth against hers in hot need. Walking her back until we hit the wall, I deepen the kiss, my hand squeezing her hip as her fingers hook in the loops of my pants.

Parting only an inch, I say, "I drove slow because I don't want to give Phillip any more reasons to hate me."

Meeting my gaze with a lusty one, she smiles. "It doesn't matter what he thinks. All that matters is that I love you." My heart feels as if it is literally coming out of my chest as she cups my face. Looking deep in my eyes, she says, "Stop worrying about pleasing him. It isn't going to work. Just worry about us."

As much as I want Phillip to like me, I know she's right. He doesn't hate me as a person; he hates that I am important to Claire and what I could potentially do to her. As long as I do right by her, it doesn't matter what he thinks. She's all that matters. I just need to remember that. I think, too, that it has something to do with the fact that no one has ever hated me. I've always been liked at first meeting, and for once, someone doesn't like me, and that bothers me. I feel like we could get along great, but that's not the case. He cares more than anything about Claire and doesn't want any sort of pain to come her way. I get that; I just need to accept that he'll probably never like me.

But I know someone who will always like me, and I'm kissing her.

Nibbling on her bottom lip, I say, "I can do that."

"Good, now let's go do this," she says before pressing her lips to mine.

Parting, I wrap my arm around her shoulders and we head in. When my tattoo artist Mackie sees me, he stands from his chair, a grin on his face as he shakes my hand. "Jude, my man, nice to see ya, bro."

"Hey, Mackie," I say, my arm hanging loosely on Claire's shoulder. "This is my girl, Claire."

"Claire," he says, shaking her hand softly. "Wonderful to meet ya. You ready for this?"

She nods slowly. "As ready as I'll ever be."

"Awesome, come on over into my studio and check out what I have for you."

We follow him to his studio and then to his desk where the stencil for her tattoo lays. We have been sending him pictures and planning this tattoo all week. I'm excited to see what Mackie came up with, and like always, he does not disappoint.

"Oh wow," Claire gasps, leaning against the desk with her palms on it, taking in the beauty of the drawing.

"It's perfect," I say as my eyes roam along the paper. In the middle is a bright red phoenix; it's so bold and vibrant, almost real enough to come off the paper. Around it are big red and black blossoms, giving more depth to the picture. Underneath it, it says: "Ón luaithreach, a éirím"which is Gaelic for "From the ashes, I rise."

Nodding her head, she says, "Yeah, it is."

"Awesome!" Mackie says, and then he grabs a piece of paper before turning to Claire. "Now all I need is for you to kiss this."

Her brow rises before looking back at me. "Huh?"

"For my tattoo," I say with a grin, and I take out a tube of red lipstick I stole from her dance bag since I knew she would protest to this. Ever since I mentioned it at the wedding, she's been telling me I'm crazy for this, but I want it.

"I thought we decided against that?"

I shake my head. "No, that's not what we did. I'm ready for this."

"Jude. That's insane. We've only been together a little over a month! That's crazy, right, Mackie?" she says, turning to look at Mackie.

He shakes his head. "I work in a tattoo parlor in downtown Nashville. Him wanting your lips tattooed on his chest is nowhere near crazy."

She lets out a breath. "You're not helping." Turning to me, she says, "Jude, come on, let's wait. When we get married, we can get matching tattoos or something. It just seems so early to me."

Crossing my arms across my chest, I say, "You don't want me to have your lips on me?"

"I didn't say that. I'm saying let's wait."

"I want it now," I say and she glares.

"And I am asking you to wait. Why rush this?"

"'Cause I want to," I say and I'm not budging. I want this.

"Whatever," she says, shaking her head as she looks away, her face red with frustration. "I wish you would just stop being so headstrong and wait."

"I don't want to wait."

"Yeah! I get that," she says, letting out another long breath.

"Are we fighting?" I ask, even though I'm pretty sure I know the answer.

"No, I just think it's crazy."

"You're starting to hurt my feelings. I love the way your lips look. They're a work of art, Claire. Aren't they, Mackie?"

Mackie nods and Claire glares at him as he says, "Hottest lips ever."

"You are no help," she accuses again before holding her hands out in front of her. "While I think that's totally romantic and hot, Jude, I don't want you to regret this."

Taking her hands in mine, I pull her to me. "I can't regret something as beautiful as a tattoo of your lips. Even if for some insane reason we don't work out, I'll always have that piece of you. I want that. I want that constant reminder of the greatest love ever. Not that I'll ever forget us, but just something to remind me of you every time I look in the mirror."

Her eyes soften and I know I have her as Mackie says, "That's some deep shit, dude."

"And I mean every word," I say, cupping her jaw. "And now I'm gonna be an ass and say that if you love me, you'll support me on this."

"Oh, that's dirty," she says, her body molding against mine.

A triumphant grin takes over my face as I reach for the paper and hand it to her. "I never said I play nice. Now, pucker up, gorgeous."

Later that night, after six hours at the tattoo parlor followed by eating a platter full of sushi, we lie in my bed, both of us completely naked and spent. She rocked my world, and I'm pretty sure the whole house heard us going at it. I'll probably get shit for it tomorrow, but at this moment, in my love bed in the sky, I couldn't care less. I run my finger down her spine as she lies in the crook of my arm, her fingers tracing the sensitive skin where her bright red lips sit.

Looking up at me, she grins as she says, "I still can't believe you did this. It's crazy."

"Why?" I ask. "Don't you know my love for you is crazy?"

Her eyes brighten as she shakes her head slowly. "Crazy it is, for sure," she agrees as she nods. "But I have to admit, I love seeing them on you. It's kinda like you're mine."

"I am yours," I whisper against her jaw. Kissing her, I lift my head to admire her tattoo. Her arm is swollen but still the tattoo is flawless and looks amazing on her shoulder. "This is fucking awesome."

Looking at her arm, she smiles. "Yeah, Phillip and Reese loved it when I sent them the text."

"Awesome," I say just as she yawns. "Tired?"

"Yeah, but I don't want to go to sleep yet," she says, and I can see that she is fighting to keep her eyes open. "If I go to sleep, then tomorrow starts, and that means I won't see you for a couple days."

I nod and hate that. I have an away game Saturday, and the dance team doesn't travel with the team. She was going to drive up to Cincinnati for the game, but she has to work this weekend, so that idea was thrown out the window. As much as it sucks since I won't see her till Sunday afternoon, I understand. We both have busy lives, but unlike other people, we work to make sure we have time together. We aren't giving up. We love each other way too much for that.

Moving my fingers slowly against her jaw, I nod. "I know, baby, but you're tired. Go to sleep. I'll be here in the morning."

Her eyes drift closed as she leans against me, nuzzling her nose against my jaw.

"You know what the greatest thing about being with you is?" she whispers against my jaw.

"What?" I whisper back, reaching up to shut the lamp off.

Opening her eyes, she looks up at me. I can see her eyes in the light from the TV, and I swear, the only thing I see is love. "That I get to be your other half."

Running my nose against her, I say, "I agree; that is the best part."

"I love you," she says, her eyes closing again.

"I love you too. Now go to sleep," I whisper and soon her breathing becomes even, telling me that she's asleep. As I hold her, I watch as she sleeps, her little lips puckered and her long eyelashes kissing the tops of her cheeks. She's so beautiful, and every time I think that she is all mine, I almost can't believe it. How did a cocky asshole like me land the greatest girl in the world?

With a grin pulling at my lips, I reach for my phone off my desk and open my gallery to look at my pictures. Mostly there are pictures of Claire and me, kissing, snuggling and being us. I love these pictures and usually go through them a lot, but as she lies in my arms, there is only one thing I want to look at. Opening the video of her dancing from earlier today, I watch as she moves to the music, her eyes captivating me even from the little screen of my iPhone. After watching it twice, I close it and kiss her temple. She stirs only a little before snuggling deeper into my arms, her sexy, naked body pressed to mine. If she wasn't as tired as she is, I would have my way with her, but I know to let her be.

Since I'm not tired, I open my Facebook app and play around on there to kill time. When Claire suddenly rolls out of my arms and onto her side, I stare at the back of her head and the love for this girl seriously takes over my body. Like I said at the tattoo parlor, I really don't think I'll ever experience this kind of love again. She is it. She is mine, and I want to get on my knees and thank the Lord above for her. He gave me this gift, this treasure, and I don't think I can do anything else but protect her and love her.

I'm about to close my app and cuddle against her when Facebook's question catches my eyes.

What's on your mind?

Letting out a breath, I look back at Claire and then back at my screen.

And it doesn't take long to tell Facebook what I'm thinking about.

And it isn't a surprise, either.

It's the one person I never stop thinking about.

Claire.

||||||||||||||||||||||||||||||||||||||||||||||||||||||||||||||||||||||||||||||||||||||||||||||||||||||||||||||||||||||||||||||||

CHAPTER 41

||||||||||||||||||||||||||||||||||||||||||||||||||||||||||||||||||||||||||||||||||||||||||||||||||||||||||||||||||||||||||||||||

🩰 *Claire.*

This is *my beautiful girlfriend, Claire Anderson. Isn't she amazing? I've never seen something so beautiful or breathtaking than when my girlfriend dances. I'm not saying that she isn't beautiful and breathtaking when she's just standing in front of me, because hell yeah she is, but when she dances, I honestly can't move or form a sentence or thought. Before meeting Claire, I thought I had my life figured out, but man was I wrong. So damn wrong. I don't think anyone will ever understand the love I have for this beautiful girl and frankly, I don't give a shit. I love her. She has my heart and I am proud to be her boyfriend. I know I have hurt people and I am sorry for that. I never realized how much of a dick I was before until the most amazing person I've ever met loved me. I would never want to make her feel the way I made other girls feel and again, I am really sorry for that. Claire has completely changed me and made me the man I want to be. Everything I do is thoroughly thought out because I don't want to ever embarrass her or make her unhappy. I just want to be the man she deserves and that's my new plan. #MyGirlfriendIsBetterThanYours #LifeIsCompleteWithHer #WifeyMaterial*

As I stand in the middle of my dorm, I still can't believe Jude's post. He must have done it when I was sleeping, and I'm just now reading it after my second class of the day. My phone was dead when I woke up this morning, and when I finally charged it, I saw that I was tagged in a status by him. I never expected to find a video of me dancing to our song and then a beautiful status like this. When I see the wifey hashtag, my eyes start to fill with tears. He has changed so much. He's still cocky and a little full of himself, but for the most part, he's the most amazing, sweetest man I've ever met. He cares for people, would give the shirt off his back to a stranger, and most of all, he loves me something crazy.

Crazy.

Ha, that is the perfect word to describe this whirlwind of a love we have. It has been crazy and intense since the moment we met. I still remember everything about the moment when his eyes met mine while I was tearing down the dumbass flyers that Ellen was stapling to trees. The way his mouth pulled to the side, how he looked at me like I was it. Was it love at first sight? Maybe, hell, I don't know. All I know is that I'm completely in love with this guy. It's been fast, it's been crazy, but it's our love story, and it's the greatest in the history of love, in my opinion.

After clicking LIKE, I hit the comment link, and write:

> *Claire Anderson: Life is nothing without you, Jude. I love you. More than words. The greatest thing in the world is that we are growing together and together we can do anything. Love you. #MyBoyfriendIsAmazing #MakesMeCryHappyTears #HubbyMaterialForSure*

"What the hell is the matter?"

Looking over, I see that Skylar has entered the room. I didn't even hear her come in; I was too consumed with Jude's post.

"Jude," I breathe. "He tagged me in the most unbelievable status."

She smiles. "Yeah, I saw that sugary sweet shit. Did you see that almost half his female friends deleted him too?

Taken aback, I say, "Really?"

"Yeah, I was messing around with Matty, and he was telling me that he, Bryan, and Jayden were giving Jude shit for y'all making the house shake last night and then his girlie-ass status, and Jude was laughing 'cause almost everyone deleted him."

"Wow," I say with a grin. "That's a good thing, I guess, but whoa… Wait, you're messing around with Matt?"

She shrugs, her cheeks blushing with color as she says, "Yeah, it's no big deal. We've fucked a few times, but it's nothing. Honestly. We're more friends than anything."

"That's how it starts," I sing, opening a message to Jude. "Reese and Phillip were friends with benefits and now look."

She laughs. "No, they were in love from the start but tried to act like it wasn't anything."

Setting her with a look, I grin. "My point exactly."

"Oh, fuck off," she sneers before throwing a pillow at me. I dodge it with no problem and fall back on my bed, texting Jude.

> *Me: So u made me cry.*

Hey Jude: Happy tears?
Me: Of course. I don't think u know how much I love u.
Hey Jude: yeah I do. I see it in your eyes every time I see u.
Ugh. Swoon. Taking in a deep breath, I smile as I type back.
Me: Where are you at?
Hey Jude: In the locker room. About to shower and head to the house.
Me: Anything once you get there?
Hey Jude: Nope, probably a nap.
Me: I think I have a better idea.
Hey Jude: I'm intrigued.
With a sneaky grin, I type:
Me: Good, meet you there.
Hey Jude: I'll beat you.
Me: Challenged accepted.

Hopping up, I strip my clothes off quickly and find the sexiest piece of lingerie I have.

"Whoa, where is the fire?" Skylar asks as I put on a lacy black number.

Shooting her a grin, I put some sweats on over my lingerie and say, "I'm going to beat Jude back to the house, and then I'm going to blow his mind with this."

Skylar laughs as I slide my feet into my tennis shoes. "Y'all trip me out. Have fun."

"Oh, I will," I say with a wink and then I dash out the door.

I know I should drive my car, but traffic is going to be busy since everyone is out for lunch. Running like there are zombies chasing me, I dart across campus. People get out of my way and some shout to slow down, but I ignore them. I have somewhere to be. My chest is burning along with my legs, but I don't let up; I will beat Jude. Rounding the quad, I spot Jude coming out of the Bullies arena. He must have spotted me too because a huge grin comes across his face and then he's off too. Pushing hard, I want to cry from the pain, but there is no way in hell I'm going to let him beat me.

He's fast, though.

Superfast.

"Your legs are longer," I yell out as I dart for the front door.

"No excuses!" he yells back at me as he rounds the house, only a second behind me.

He jumps over the shrubs onto the porch just as I throw the door open and run downstairs. I can feel him right behind me, but I know I have this. The only problem is that I'm running so fast that I don't stop in time to open his door, and I run straight into the wall beside it with my shoulder. I feel pain but I ignore it, backtracking to the door. I go to throw it open, but Jude's hand meets the handle just as mine does. Next thing I know, we're in a hip-checking battle trying to open the door and enter it before the other. Grunts fill the hall until finally I kick him in the shin and he topples over, giving me the chance to throw the door open.

Holding my arms up in victory, I scream, "Oh, yeah! Winner!"

"Cheater! You kicked me!" he yells as he enters the room, his brows together in frustration, his face flushed.

"No excuses," I say with a devious grin.

He shoots me a grin as he shuts the door behind himself, locking it as his eyes darken to the color of emerald. I'm breathing hard, and I know I need to catch my breath, but I can't help myself. I pull my shirt off and then kick my shoes and pants off, standing in my very skimpy panties and bra.

Bracing himself against the door, he groans, "Fucking hell, Claire."

A grin pulls at my lips as I slowly walk toward him. With every step I take, a piece of his clothing hits the floor. His shirt, his pants, then his boxers, leaving him deliciously naked right as I close the distance between us. Reaching out, I wrap my arms around his neck, pulling him down for a soul-deep kiss. His body is so hard against mine. He has been hitting the gym like mad, and man, his body reflects that. As my hands move up his arms, his biceps, I can feel each muscle defined beneath my palms. My heart races as our kiss deepens, his hands resting against my ass. His dick is stiff against my belly and I want him. Need him

When I feel his fingers dance up my back, I break the kiss, gasping for breath as his lips dust along my jaw. I'm burning up everywhere. My whole body is singing for his as he unclasps my bra. The cups fall away from my breasts and land at our feet.

"I want to rip this off you," he whispers against my jaw, his fingers yanking at my underwear. "But it's so pretty." He then runs his fingers down the base of my spine before slowly pulling my panties down my tingling legs. I haven't run like that in a while, and while my legs are crying, they are soon a distant thought when Jude grabs my butt cheeks and buries his face between my legs. My legs buckle and I have to brace my hands against the door as I gasp for breath. Running his tongue slowly and teasingly against my sensitive lips, I bite into my bottom lip, holding in my scream as he tortures me. When he runs the tip of his tongue along where my lips meet, my heart pounds in my chest and then my legs start to shake from the want for him.

Finally, he parts my lips and flicks his tongue against my clit. Closing my eyes, I lean my face against the wall, biting into my fingers as he assaults my clit like it stole something from him. He's ruthless with his attack, his tongue moving fast then slow, in figure eights, and then just rough and hard against my bundle of nerves. When he slowly slides his fingers inside me and starts to fuck me with them, I can't hold it in anymore.

Loudly, I scream his name, my body tensing up under his glorious touch. Slamming my fist against the door, I start to move against his mouth, wanting and needing my release. Quickly, his fingers pound into me, his tongue going just as fast on my clit, and then I come. I come so fucking hard, I jerk against him, my body going completely taut.

He kisses my center and I squeeze my eyes shut as the aftershocks of my orgasm run through my body. I would have thought he would have given me a second, but I was completely wrong. Lifting me up, he wraps my legs around his waist, my face resting against the crook of his neck as he carries me to what I assume would be his bed. Again, I'm completely wrong. I hear a crash and then my back hits a hard surface. Before I can even see where I am or what the hell is digging into my back, Jude is inside me, pounding into me with unbending need. His fingers bite into my hips as he thrusts into me, my legs flopping in the air as his body slams into mine. As I look up at him, his face is flushed, sweat dripping down his arms, and fuck, he looks hot.

Reaching between my legs, he cups my pussy as he says, "You are so fucking hot, Claire. Fuck, baby. Come on me. Now."

I don't know what to say, so I do what he wants. Moving his hand away, I move my fingers into my wetness and start to finger myself, watching as he watches me. His fingers dig into my thighs as I move my fingers along my clit. His breathing is so fast, matching mine, and his eyes are dark with desire. For some reason watching him watch me has my body burning with lust. It doesn't take long for me to get off, not with all the stimulation that is going on, and as I hit my peak, a guttural growl leaves his mouth as he slams into me one last time, his body going rigid as his eyes fall closed.

Gasping for breath, I squeeze my legs around him, running my hands up his abs and chest until he opens his eyes, a grin tugging at his lips. He then leans down, taking my mouth with his as my body throbs for his. Leaning his forehead against mine, he whispers, "If every time you beat me I get to have mind-blowing sex like this, I fully accept being a loser." Then his eyes meet mine, his mouth pulling into a grin as he says, "Really though, being with you, I'm never losing."

"Wasn't I supposed to be proving my love to you?"

He smiles, his lips whispering against mine. "You don't have to prove anything, Claire. I know."

"So do I."

It's been a good night.

I think we're ready for the investors, but I'm still drilling these girls, making sure we're perfect. Ms. Prissy seems happy with everything, but I know there is room for improvement. She wants me to do a solo of sorts on the pole, but I haven't really thought anything up. I have my dance for Jude, but I really don't want to dance that unless he's here. Which will never happen, so I guess I'll just come up with something. It won't be hard.

By the time I'm done for the night, my feet are crying and my back is sore. I hit my back on the pole, and then while Jude was pounding into me, I found that I was lying on Jayden's stapler. I want to feel bad for having sex on his desk, but I can't find it in me to do so. I do know that I won't allow it to happen again, though. I respect Jayden and I want him to like me.

Leaning back in my chair, I rest my feet on my desk and let out a long breath. When I feel eyes on me, I look up to find Ms. Prissy standing beside my desk.

"Hey," I say, sitting up a little straighter. "I'm leaving in a bit, letting my feet air out."

She smiles before nodding. "You're fine. I'm going to be here for another few hours."

"Oh okay, is everything all right?"

She nods. "Sure, I wanted to talk to you about the investors."

"Oh, okay?"

She pulls Ellen's chair out and sits down. Today her catsuit is yellow, and to be honest, she really should stop wearing those things. Not that I'll tell her that.

Looking over at me, a smile sits on her lips and she says, "New York is very interested, as in, ready to sign you now. The only problem is that I don't think you should take anything until after that night. They aren't offering you enough. They're trying to lowball you, and I feel that Vegas could offer you more. I wanted to tell you, nonetheless."

I process what she's telling me and can't believe it. They are already offering me a job? They haven't even seen me wow the crowd yet. I mean, I'm not saying I don't give it my all every night, but I plan to kill the stage on the investors' night. I have come up with some awesome stuff, and I want them to see what I can do.

"No, thank you for telling me. I think I'll take your advice, but can I ask what they offered?"

She smiles. "Only a twenty-grand signing bonus, which is disrespectful."

Twenty grand sounds pretty damn good to me, though. "Oh?"

"Yeah, Claire, you are worth triple that, and I think that Vegas will be the one to give you an offer you can refuse. I'm telling you, you are going to do big things."

She then stands and I smile as I look up at her. "Thank you."

"No problem, baby," she says before reaching out and cupping my face in a motherly way. "I'm very proud of what you've come up with, and while I'll be sad to see you go, I will be there opening night, cheering you on."

"Thank you," I say.

We share a smile and then she's off, leaving me completely in shock that I was offered twenty grand for basically a shitty performance. If I give it my all, no telling what they'll come at me with. I'll be set for life and the excitement is eating me alive. I reach for my phone to text Jude, but I pause. I can't text him this late because I'm supposed to be sleeping. Man, I'm getting tangled in my lie and I need to just tell him the whole truth, but I know I won't. I'm already too far gone in this deceit; there is no reason to ever tell him, or Phillip. I'll just wait till I'm hired by a prestigious company, earning thousands to make up dances for burlesque dancers. Then I'll tell them. They can't be mad because I'll be doing something with it.

Right?

I just don't know. Standing up, I pack up my stuff and throw my jacket on over my sweatshirt. I always make sure to wear it out of the club in case a patron is outside. I don't want anyone knowing where I am, or even who I am. I spent the whole night changing outfits to make sure my arm was covered so no one could see my tattoo. I should have waited to get it, but oh well, I love it.

Bundled up in my jacket, I throw my money in my bag and head to security so they can walk me to my car in the back. Ben is happy to do it, thankfully, and walks out with me. We don't really talk much as we walk, mainly because I don't want to distract him from seeing anyone who is out to get me.

A little paranoid? Yeah, just a tad.

Pulling out my phone, I click Jude's name and type:

R u awake?

I watch the screen, waiting for his response. When he doesn't answer by the time we reach my car, I tuck my phone in my pocket. But when I look up, I am frozen in place. My stomach drops, my heart races, and everything inside me goes cold as I gasp for breath.

"Who's that guy in your car?" Ben asks, but I can't answer him.

I can only choke back the tears as Phillip slowly unfolds himself from my car, his eyes flashing with anger.

Swallowing loudly, I whisper, "My uncle."

CHAPTER 42

🩰 Claire

"So you're good?" Ben asks and Phillip's head tilts to the side, waiting for my answer.

One would probably assume I'd take the coward's way out and say no so that Ben could protect me from the wrath of Phillip, but that's not how I roll. I knew this was coming; I had to face the music someday, and today, or well, tonight is the night. While, yes, my body is shaking with fear, my heart feels as if it's coming out of my chest, my throat is thick with emotion, and I have no clue what I'm going to say to him, I know I have to stand here and take responsibility for what I have decided to keep to myself.

He loves me. Phillip will support me. I know this.

Taking in a deep breath, I say, "Yeah, I'm good."

Ben looks wary to leave me alone, but like I knew he would, he says, "Okay, have a good night. Holler if you need me."

"Thank you," I say, and I watch as he walks away. When the door to the club closes, I look back at Phillip. "What are you doing here?" I ask, and as soon as the words leave my mouth, I wish I had kept my mouth shut.

"What am I doing here? Well, let me tell you," he says, his voice sharp and so full of anger it scares me. "I came for a bachelor party with my friends, Claire. Since we aren't out for a quick peek as we're all married, we came here, and the night was going great until I saw my niece onstage opening her legs and wiggling her ass for the world to see! So the real question is, what the fuck are you doing here?"

"Working," I answer simply, my tears threatening to fall.

"You've got to be fucking kidding me, Claire. Working? Why? I will give you everything you need."

"I know you will and I hate that!" I say, meeting his gaze. "I don't want you to support me. I'm old enough to take care of myself. That's why I work at the studio, why I work here. I need the money. I need to know that I am going to be okay."

"Okay?" he yells. "Claire, I will always make sure you are okay! That is my job!"

"And it was my mom's job, and we see how she provided, right?" I snap back, and his face goes blank. As he takes a step toward me, I take one back, but he snatches me by my arms, pulling me to him.

"No, no, she fucking didn't, and I hope you aren't trying to throw that in my face."

I shake my arms free and take another step back. "No, I'm not, but you have to understand why. You have to know that I'm doing this to protect myself. You may love and support me now, but you can leave at any time – you have before – and if that happens again, I'll be secure. I'll be set for life."

Shaking his head, I watch as his eyes go hollow with despair. "You just can't let it go, can you? Yes, I left, and I have spent the last three years doing everything in the world to make up for it. I may have left you, but Claire, I never stopped loving you. I did everything I could to protect you from your mom, but she wouldn't allow me to do what was best for you. She used you as a free ride, and I didn't realize it till it was too late. Did I try hard enough? Probably not, but I was a kid, Claire. Let it go! I'm here now, and I'm not going anywhere!"

His voice echoes through the parking lot, and I'm sure that Ben will be out in no time. Looking deep in his eyes, I know what he says is true. I know he tried to get me when I was younger, but my mom did use me. She couldn't let go of me when I was the only reason Phillip sent her money. Instead, she subjected me to her life, abused me, and allowed men to use me. Looking down at the ground, I take in a deep breath, trying to calm my heart, but it is beating out of control.

"I'm sorry. I shouldn't have said that," I say, meeting his gaze. "I know I need to let it go and that it is all in the past, but surely you can understand why I do this."

"No, I'm sorry I can't. If you needed money, I'd give it to you."

"But you shouldn't have to. I don't take handouts. I work for what I want, and you know that. I've been like that since I could work."

"I get that, Claire, but this is not a career – this is slutty."

"No," I say, shaking my head. "It's beautiful and I love it. I love the beauty of it, the sexy tease of it. I have fun, and Phillip, I'm amazing at it. I choreograph all the dances and I get paid bank. I'm so good that they have investors coming to expand Ms. Prissy's all over the US. I could get hired to run a whole club. A place where they will do what I say and dance to my choreography. I know you may not see this as a career you want for me, but it is a promising one. I mean,

Reese did this for years and didn't stop until I got the job."

His eyes widen as he takes a step toward me. "Wait, does she know about this?"

Oh fuck.

Pressing my lips together, I look away, and when I don't answer, he yells, "She fucking does! Un-fucking-believable! Wait, did she get you the job here?"

"No," I say quickly. "Prissy approached me on her own."

"So you two have kept this from me?"

I bite down hard on my lip as I nod. "Yes, but only because I knew you wouldn't like it."

"Damn right, I wouldn't! I don't want my niece flaunting her ass across a stage for a bunch of horny men!"

"It's only temporary. I'm quitting as soon as the investors come and go. I want to be strictly backstage 'cause I knew that you wouldn't like it, and I know Jude won't either, but I love this. I really do. It's such a beautiful art, and I swear, Phillip, they all say I'm going to be something big. Don't you want me to live my dreams?"

"This isn't what I thought your dreams were. I thought you wanted to dance with famous people or choreograph their dances, not dance with your ass and tits out for a room full of horn dogs to hoot and holler at," he yells, his face still so red with anger. Even with only the light from the streetlamp, I can see that he's about to blow a gasket.

"This is my stepping stone. I started as just a dancer, but soon I became a choreographer, and now, I might even run my own club. Everyone has to start somewhere. This was my somewhere. I want the lights of the big stage, I want Vegas or New York, I want something huge and amazing, my name in lights. This is how I'm going to get there. You have to trust me. I know what I'm doing. I'm going to be rich for the rest of my life. You'll never have to worry about me again."

He goes quiet for a moment, eyeing me with such disdain in his eyes. Clearing his throat, he asks, "Is that all that matters to you, Claire? Having money? Me not having worry about you?"

I shake my head, confused by his question. "I want the security of it, and I don't want to be a burden to you anymore."

Looking away from me, he takes in a deep breath and then sets me with a look that chills me to the soul. "I don't know how you could ever think you are a burden. Claire, you are the light of my life. I love you, unconditionally, and I've tried to make sure that you have everything you need and more. And to be honest, I don't care what you want to do as long as you're happy. Do I want you dancing with your tits and ass out? No, I don't, but if you can honestly look me in the eye and say this is what you want, then by God, I'll support you. But what bothers me the most about all this is that you not only lied and hid this from me, but all you care about is the money. The security. How about instead of having the security of money, you try having the security of love? Because money will not keep you warm at night."

"Maybe not, but it will keep a roof over my head and food in my belly, something I went a long time without," I inform him. "And I know you've done everything and more, but I can't depend on anyone but myself."

"That's really lonely," Phillip says and then a tear rolls slowly down his cheek, leaving me breathless and feeling like I just kicked a hurt dog. "You've hurt me, Claire, and I don't admit that often, but you have. Completely gutted me, and honestly, I don't know how to look at you right now."

When a second tear rolls down his face, everything inside me goes cold. I don't like seeing Phillip cry and the only other time I have is when Reese broke up with him. Knowing that, I realize that I have really hurt him and that wasn't my intent. I just wanted to be secure.

Biting hard into my lip, I whisper, "I'm sorry."

"Don't be sorry for something you believe in," he says as he turns to head to his car. "If this is what you want, don't be sorry, be proud."

"I'm sorry I lied and hid this from you, hurt you," I say and he shrugs.

"Yeah, me too. I thought I had raised you a little better than that," he says, putting the last nail in my coffin. "And I know that I've wished for the kid to get hit by a bus, but save him the pain and tell him the truth if you haven't. You shouldn't lie to someone you love, because most of the time, they'll love you no matter what, as long as you are honest."

My lip starts to wobble and I swallow my sob before saying, "I love you, Phillip, I do. I just didn't think you'd support me."

He nods slowly, running his palm along his face. "Then obviously I did something wrong, and I'm sorry for that."

Dropping my bag, I rush to him, stopping him before he gets in the car. "You did nothing wrong, Phillip. I was scared and couldn't figure out how to tell you."

Looking down at me, his blue eyes swimming with tears, he says, "You just open your mouth and tell me. I'll love you unconditionally. I loved you when you were an inch away from being your mom, and I love you now. What made you think I wouldn't love you now?"

That did it. My tears fall in torrents as I gasp for breath and he says, "Now, I have to go. Be careful going home."

I can't talk. I just stand there, holding my stomach as it turns with nausea. I watch as he drives off and then realize that it's not safe for me to be out here on my own. Forcing myself to move, I grab my bag, and once I'm in the safe cocoon of my car, I cry so fucking hard that my body shakes. I never meant to hurt anyone.

I just wanted to be safe.

Secure.

But right now, I don't feel either of those things.

I just feel empty.

It's been five days since I heard from Phillip.

Reese called and told me that everything would be okay, but Phillip isn't talking to her either. He's furious with us both, and while I understand, I just want to hear his voice and know that he stills loves me. I've been a mess. My heart is hurting, and I don't know what to do to fix it. To top it off, Jude is acting weird. Or maybe I'm acting weird, I don't know. I just know that for the last five days I've felt completely alone.

Jude's been gone for an away game, so he hasn't been here to comfort me, not that I can tell him what is wrong anyway. Also, his texts have been very short. Like he's too busy to answer me or talk, and I know that he is, but still, I'm just in a shitty place. I probably need to be locked away until Phillip decides to talk to me and tell me that he still loves me even though I am a lying jerk.

Ugh. This sucks.

I've been lying in my bed all day. I skipped my classes, not in the mood to deal with them or anyone, for that matter. I know Jude's working out, or training, or practicing, I don't know, something hockey, but I reach for my phone and text him anyway. I need him to tell me he loves me. I need to know that someone cares about me.

> *Me: I miss u.*
> *Hey Jude: Miss u 2.*
> *Me: That's it?*
> *Hey Jude: Huh? What do u mean?*
> *Me: I mean u can't say something more?*
> *Hey Jude: What do u want me to say?*
> *Me: I don't fucking know, don't worry about it.*

Throwing my phone across the room, it ricochets with a thunk against the wall before landing on the floor. While it felt good to do that, I'm extremely glad that I have an Otterbox. Lying back, I close my eyes and let out a long breath. I can hear my phone go off with a text, and I know that Jude is probably confused and pissed, but I can't bring myself to get up and fix that. He's obviously too busy to worry about me.

Ugh, I'm being such a bitch.

Sitting up, I go get my phone and click it to see the text from him.

Hey Jude: Are you on your period? Do you need chocolate or something?
Oh no, he didn't.
Me: Where are you?
Hey Jude: At the house, why? I can run out for you.
Me: No need.

Tucking my phone in my pocket, I leave my dorm and head to my car. I know I need to stay home in my dorm and not go anywhere, but I'm looking for a fight. I need to feel something other than just fucking empty. Driving over to his house, I park beside Jayden's car and then slam my door as I stomp toward the front door. Before I can reach it though, the door opens and Jayden comes out with Jude behind him.

"My fucking period?! Seriously?" I yell, and Jayden's eyes widen before he steps to the side.

"She has to be talking to you," he says, and Jude's brows come together when he sees me.

"I was about to go out for you. Are you okay?"

"No!" I yell. "I've been texting you all day, and lately you've been distant, only one-word answers or 'You too'! What happened to telling me I was the moon and stars and all that cheesy shit that made me smile?"

Crossing his arms, he looks at me confused as he says, "Claire, I'm stupid busy right now. You know that. I'm bulking up, working hard on and off the ice. You're working just as hard as I am, but do I get mad when you don't answer my texts right away? No, I don't 'cause I understand."

"Whatever. Why don't you just admit you're getting tired of me?" I yell, and I wish I would just shut the fuck up and go home. I'm being a needy little brat and I know this, but I just need to feel loved.

"Oh shit," Jayden mutters and he turns, heading inside. "You're on your own, buddy."

Jude ignores him, his eyes locked on me as he takes a step toward me. He doesn't say anything for a long time; my breathing is labored, and my heart feels as if it is constricted in my chest. I'm fighting back the tears. I don't want to seem weak, needy, but I am just that. I'm basically screaming for attention right now because I fucked up and my uncle hates me. And here I go doing it again. I know Phillip doesn't hate me.

Looking away, I let out a breath, sucking one in as my eyes cloud with tears.

"Claire," he demands, and I look back up, meeting his heated gaze. "Fucking stop it right now and tell me what is really going on. This is all bullshit and you know it. Stop trying to pick a fight with me, and tell me what the hell is wrong."

I lose it. Tears fall in buckets and I sputter for breath, but within seconds, Jude has me in his arms, hugging me and holding me so close that I feel safe and secure, not completely empty. Kissing my jaw, he whispers, "Tell me what's wrong. What do I need to do to fix it?"

I shake my head, nuzzling my nose in his neck. "I just need you to hold me."

"I can do that," he promises, and he does just that. He holds me until my tears dry, until I'm able to breathe normally and I can look him in the eye. "What's wrong, baby?"

"I had a fight with Phillip and he hasn't spoken to me in five days," I say, not meeting his gaze.

"About what?"

I shake my head, shrugging my shoulders. This is when I need to tell him. I need to be honest because I don't want to hurt him the way I hurt Phillip. But how can I tell him with the way Phillip reacted? Phillip loves me and I know that soon he'll forgive me, but I don't know if Jude will. He'll be mad, he'll break up with me, and that will be it. I can't lose him.

But I can't lie anymore.

"He found out I work for Ms. Prissy and didn't like it one bit. Said that he didn't want me working in that environment."

Cupping my face, he says, "I mean, it isn't the ideal place, but you are living your dreams. You're choreographing numbers to be performed and getting paid good money. He'll come around, baby, don't worry."

"He's so mad at me."

"He'll come around; he loves you. He'll realize how important this is when you land that huge job, hopefully wherever I am, and he will be so proud. And then you guys will laugh about this fight. Don't worry."

"I just don't know," I whisper, and I feel like the grip on my heart just got a little tighter. Looking up into his loving, supporting eyes, I bite the inside of my cheek as the tears well up in my eyes, threatening to fall at any second.

The words are there.

Just tell him. Tell him. Don't hurt him too.

But won't I hurt him? I've already lied, I've already hidden stuff from him, so no matter what I do, I am going to hurt him. I can be a coward and wait and pray he never finds out, or I can have the balls to tell him.

Stroking his thumb along my jaw, he kisses the side of my mouth. "I know you're upset, and I know that you feel like this won't work out, but come on, you know it will. How could anyone be that mad at someone like you? You are smart and amazing, Claire. He would be crazy not support you and love you."

"You're right."

"I know, now kiss me, and don't pick fights with me just 'cause you're upset. Talk to me, I'm here for you, and I will help you through anything. All you have to do is tell me what you need. I love you."

My tears spill over and roll down my cheeks as I nod slowly. "I love you too. I'm sorry."

His mouth curves into a grin and then comes down on mine, kissing me so softly and so tenderly that my heart hurts more. With that kiss, I know that I'm going to continue to take the coward's way out.

And just pray that in the end I have the safety and security of Jude's love.

CHAPTER 43

Claire

Another day passes before I hear from Phillip. When I do, it's in the form of a text while I'm teaching a bunch of nine-year-olds.

Phillip: Hey, come over to the house once you close up the studio.

I don't bother answering him. Instead I find myself watching the clock, begging time to go faster. Once it is time, I close the studio and get in my car, driving home. Taking out my phone, I dial Jude's number and he answers on the fourth ring.

"Hey, babe," he says roughly into the phone. Glancing at the clock, I see that it is his workout time.

"Shit, sorry, I know you're working out."

"No biggie, what's up?"

"I'm heading home. Phillip finally texted me."

"See, told you. It's going to be fine. Do you want me to go with you?"

I smile, loving that he wants to be there for me. "I'm almost there, thank you, though."

"No problem. Call me when you leave."

"I will," I say. "I love you."

"Love you too, baby. Bye."

Smiling from the love that is bursting in my chest for him, I hang up my phone before I turn the music up and turn onto the street that Phillip's house is on. Pulling into the driveway, I shut off my car and head toward the door. I think about knocking but then curse myself for it.

He loves me and this is my home too.

Opening the door, I enter and shut it behind me. "Reese? Phillip?"

"We're in here," Reese calls from the kitchen.

Placing my keys in the basket, I head to the kitchen to find them both leaning against the kitchen island. Phillip doesn't look at me, but Reese does, and I can see in her eyes that this is all a mess. The tension in the room could be cut with a knife; it's so thick and honestly chokes me. I hate it. There shouldn't be tension. Our family is too solid for tension.

"Hey," I say, waving awkwardly.

"Hey," Reese says back, a small smile on her face. "Get everything closed up?"

I nod as I come to the island, matching their stances. "Yup, good classes tonight."

"Good," she says and then she reaches out, lacing her fingers with Phillip's. "Honey?" she asks. He looks up at her, and when he finally looks at me, the sadness in his eyes kills me. Gasping for breath, I look away like a coward, my heart beating hard in my chest. The room falls silent; the only noise is the tick of the clock. When I glance up, he's watching me and his eyes lock with mine.

"Don't you ever lie or hide anything from me again, do you understand me?"

Fighting back the tears, I nod. "I promise."

"I've thought long and hard about this, Claire, and I understand why you think you need the money. I could never imagine what you went through growing up, and I wish I could take all those years away and replace them with new ones, but I can't. All I can do is promise you that you don't need to ever worry about that again. I'll protect you, I'll make sure you are taken care of, and I will always make sure you are loved."

"I know, but I can't depend on you forever, Phillip."

He nods. "I get that, but that doesn't mean I won't be here when you need me. I'm not trying to tell you to quit or stop what you're doing. If this is what you want, then I support you a hundred percent, but I want you to want it because you love it, not because of the money."

I don't even have to think about it. "I want to choreograph shows for burlesque dancers, Phillip. I've been doing research ever since I was told about the investors, and I can make my own world of burlesque. Something sexy and mind-blowing, I would be in complete control. It will be *my* show. Ms. Prissy thinks I can do huge things, and I agree. I feel good about this, but I promise, next Thursday is the last day I'll be on the stage. I want you to be proud of me, and I know that seeing me in next to nothing dancing around won't make you proud."

"You're wrong; I am proud of you no matter what," he promises. "I would prefer you do it with clothes on, but if you want to strut your stuff across the stage, I'll look away and wait till you're done. But I will be front row, cheering you on. We're so proud of you, Claire, and we love you."

"I love you guys," I say, my voice breaking and tears welling up in my eyes. He brings me in close and I hug him tightly, my heart pounding against my chest. When he lets me go, Reese wraps her arms around me, her eyes misty with tears.

"I love you too," she whispers, and I hug her a little tighter.

"I love you," I say, closing my eyes tight as I hold her.

"So when is this investors' show?" Phillip asks as we part. "Thursday?"

I nod. "Yup, I'm performing twice but the whole show is choreographed by me."

"Awesome. Hey, Reese," he says and she smiles over at him.

"Yeah, babe?"

"Want to be my date Thursday to watch our girl be a star?"

She glances over at me, her face beaming with pride as she says, "Hell yeah, I do."

I squeal in happiness and soon I'm wrapped up in a group hug with my two favorite people. As I hug them, wrapped tightly in their love, my mind drifts to Jude, and I wonder if I could get him to come.

And I wonder if he'll still love me when I come onstage as Diamond.

Jude couldn't come even if I had the balls to ask. He has a game in Chattanooga, which sucks because I had to tell him I couldn't go, and I had to lie again.

"Can I ask you to blow off Phillip and Reese and have you not be mad?" he asks, pulling me in close. I'm standing between his legs as he leans against my car while we wait for them to finish loading the bus.

"I can't. We have plans, I'm sorry. Rain check?"

He smiles, hooking his fingers in my belt loops. "I guess. You're lucky I love you."

"Yeah, I am," I say, emotion tickling my throat. "Very lucky."

"Can I at least get some good-luck loving?" he says, his eyes dark with desire.

"What do you want?" I ask, waggling my eyebrows at him.

He laughs. "I want a piece of this ass," he says, taking two handfuls of my ass. "But we're leaving in a bit."

"Yeah, how about a good-luck kiss?" I ask, looking at him through my eyelashes.

"I love when you do that. You look so innocent and hot. Come here," he demands and then his mouth is crashing against mine. Roughly we kiss, his hand tangling in my hair as I take a fistful of his sweatshirt, bringing him closer, wanting to mold myself against him.

Parting only to breathe, I move my nose along his. I'm nervous about tonight. My heart is pounding and I know that it's going to be okay, but I still wish Jude would be there too. Opening my eyes, I say, "Tonight is that investor thing. Wish me luck."

"I didn't know that was tonight," he says, his brow coming up. "Why didn't you tell me?"

I shrug. "We've both been so busy; it's not a big deal."

His brows come together as he shakes his head. "Yes, it is. This is important. I would have skipped the game tonight, said I hurt my groin or something."

I roll my eyes. "No flipping way. It's fine. I promise."

He doesn't say anything for a moment, his eyes searching mine. "I'm a little hurt you didn't tell me," he admits, tucking his hands into my pants pockets.

Cupping his face, I smile. "I'm sorry. Don't be, okay?"

He runs his nose along mine and then nods. "Okay, I assume you're going up there?"

"Yeah, probably after I'm done with Reese and Phillip. We're all going together."

"So you told them?" he asks, his eyes meeting mine, and I can see how much this bothers him.

"I'm sorry, Jude, I swear. I should have told you – you're right. The only reason they know is 'cause I said I had to be done by nine to get down there."

Nipping at my lip, he nods. "Okay, I forgive you, but next time, tell me. I want to be there for everything. I want to support you."

My stomach churns a little as I nod. "I promise. I'm sorry."

"Okay, well, let me know how it goes. I probably won't be home till close to one."

"Sinclair! Let's go!" someone calls, and I look over to see that it was his coach. Meeting Jude's gaze, I lean against him, hugging him close. Needing to feel his body against mine.

"Call me after the game. The show doesn't start till ten. You'll be done by then, right?" I ask, dusting my lips against his.

"Yeah, I'll text you."

"Okay, I love you."

"I love you more," he says, pressing his lips to mine again. He kisses me once more and then on my knuckles before saying, "Good luck."

I smile. "You too."

He sends me a grin, and I watch as he tucks his headphones in his ears and then heads toward the bus. I wait till they pull out, blowing a kiss to Jude before I slump against my car, letting out a breath. It's all over after tonight. I won't ever have to lie again or ever feel like shit the way I do now. I know I have brought this on myself, but I can't wait till I never have to worry about it again. When I don't ever have to wear sky-high shoes and dance in a way that disrespects my uncle and my boyfriend. When I started this, I don't think

I really thought it through. I was too blinded by the money. I never wanted to be cold or hungry again. I just wanted to live with the knowledge of being safe. I didn't think I could hurt anyone, but now after the fight with Phillip, I know I can, and I never want anyone to feel the pain I felt for those six days not knowing what my uncle was thinking.

Now all I need is the love of my family and my man.

That's it.

Getting in my car, fighting back the tears, I head back to my dorm. I plan on sleeping since it's going to be a long night, but Jude has other plans, and for the next two hours we talk and bullshit around as he rides to Chattanooga.

> *Hey Jude: My dad is an asshole.*
> *Me: I could have told u that.*
> *Hey Jude: Yeah, he told my mom she couldn't drive to Chattanooga for our game. He's in New York so she isn't allowed to drive herself. Thankfully Lucy is going to drive her and Jace and Angie.*
> *Me: Wow, what a jerk. I would have driven her, but I'm a bad girlfriend.*
> *Hey Jude: Lol. Yeah u are. U naughty, naughty girl.*
> *I smile.*
> *Me: Stop, ur turning me on.*
> *Hey Jude: Oh yeah? Hmm. I like that it doesn't take much.*
> *Me: Ha. I bet ur hard just thinking about me being turned on.*
> *Hey Jude: Guilty.*

Holding my stomach, I laugh so hard as I roll over to my stomach, holding my phone as I text him.

> *Me: U r so horny!*
> *Hey Jude: Only for u.*

Closing my eyes, I cuddle into my pillow as I look at the screen, wishing it was him instead.

> *Me: I wish you were here, lying with me.*
> *Hey Jude: I wish I was too, but we'd be doing more than lying.*
> *I laugh as I roll my eyes.*
> *Me: Agreed.*
> *Hey Jude: ☺*
> *Me: I do miss you though. Like a lot.*
> *Hey Jude: I miss you more than that and then some.*

Me: I think we should have another Disney night.
Hey Jude: Okay, but I swear if you make me watch Frozen more than once, I will never watch with you again.
Me: You don't want to build a snowman?
Hey Jude: Shut up.
I can't type, I'm laughing so hard.
Me: #lolololololololololololololololololol
Hey Jude: #ImGoingToBlowUpURSnowman
Me: You wouldn't dare!
Hey Jude: Probably not. But no more Frozen.
Me: Okay, promise.
Hey Jude: Thank sweet baby Jesus.

Yawning through my smile, I giggle as I look up at the wall that is fully collaged with pictures of us together. Each one so quirky and full of love. There is one where he's biting my chin, my ear. Us making funny faces and cuddling. Us kissing and even a picture of us playing a little hockey in the front of the Bullies' house. He won't admit it to anyone, but I won that game. When my eyes set on the picture of us with Jayden and then one with his mom, my smile grows. When I get to the one of us with Phillip and Reese at their wedding, my eyes start to cloud with tears.

Looking back at the screen, I text.

Me: I love you. #SoMuchItHurts
Hey Jude: Nothing could ever come close to my love for you. #RealTalk
Me: I'm so glad you chased me all over campus. #HeyJude
Hey Jude: I'm so glad you weren't a butterface. #HotAllOver #MyBabyIsFine

Holding my phone to my chest, I lose it with laughter as my heart explodes in my chest.

God, I love him.

CHAPTER 44

✦Claire

Knowing I have to leave, I rush to the club and still I'm so late.

"Claire! You're late! Tonight is not the night to be late!" Prissy yells at me as I run by.

"I'm sorry. I overslept!" I call as I rush to my station. Quickly, I change in to the first costume, which is a skimpy little corset and even skimpier black lace panties. Throwing in my brown contacts, I do my makeup in record time. I make sure I look perfect before placing the long black lashes and the crystals underneath my eyes to complete my look. As I'm placing my long, straight, blond wig on, I see that I have a text from Phillip.

> *Phillip: We're here, front row. Don't shake your ass in my direction.*

For some reason that makes me laugh harder than it should. When my phone sounds again, I look down to see that it's from Jude.

> *Hey Jude: Good Luck, hope your dancers don't mess up. If they do, you can use my hockey stick to break their kneecaps. #JustKidding #kinda*

I smile as I paint on my bright red lipstick before puckering my lips and standing up to put my high heels on.

"Claire! Let's go!" Prissy yells.

"Coming!" I call and then I rush to where everyone is already standing, waiting on me. Standing in my spot behind the black curtain, I pose as everyone wishes me luck, and I do the same to them.

As the music to "Show Me How You Burlesque" starts, the dark black curtain rises, leaving me behind a black lace one with a light shining behind me. Slowly I move in a tantalizing way to the song, but as soon as it picks up in tempo, the curtain opens and I move quickly down the stairs, rotating my hips to the song as my mouth moves with the words. The place is packed something crazy, but the only people I see are my aunt and my uncle clapping along to the song. I can see Phillip shaking his head at my outfit, but a smile sits on his face as I'm joined by every dancer in the club onstage. Quickly we move to hard-hitting steps, enhancing the music on another level.

Snapping our fingers, I lip-synch as I move my body to the music, getting the club pumped before we go back into another sequence of dance moves. Turning, I bend over, shaking my ass, and over my shoulder I can see that Phillip is hiding his face. It cracks me up, but still I work the room like it's mine.

Which, in a way, it is.

As I strut off the stage, I see Ms. Prissy with a grin as big as Texas, and as I pass by, my fellow dancers smack my ass, saying, "Way to go, baby! Let's do this!"

Excited, I rush back to my station and get ready for my pole solo so that I can watch the rest of the show. Wearing a crystal-encrusted bra and panty set, I rub glitter lotion all over myself before making sure my wig is tight and secure on my head. I can't be hanging upside down and the sucker falls off my head. Heading to where Ms. Prissy is standing, I cross my arms and watch as the show goes off without a hitch. Everyone is performing amazingly and pride sizzles in my chest. With the lights and smoke and atmosphere, it makes my choreography look a billion times better.

"The investors are here?" I ask and she nods.

"Yup, sitting up in VIP. I tried to get them drunk, but they aren't drinking apparently. Bullshit. I'm hoping for a Ms. Prissy's in Vegas."

"Or a Ms. Diamond's," I say and laugh.

"Or a Ms. Diamond's," she agrees.

"Or maybe Prissy's Diamond's."

Looking at me like a mom would her child, she smiles. "Yes, that sounds amazing."

We share a long look and then both look out where Ellen is moving across the stage like a cat in heat. She's a wonderful dancer, but she's more slutty than burlesque. Some of the guys like it, but the older ones are sometimes offended. Not all the time, though. For the next hour, I watch as the girls kill the floor, giving the crowd exactly what they want. My pole solo is last, and when the floor lights come on so that the crew can install my pole, nervousness eats at my heart. This is just me and my pole. That's it.

When the music to "Cabaret" by Justin Timberlake starts, the lights flash once, and then I come out with a swagger that has everyone hollering for me. Reaching for my pole, I move myself against it before lifting my leg and using the pole as leverage as I lean back, my head almost touching the ground. Doing various poses and leg stretches, I finally get on the pole, spinning around it and giving the crowd a great show. The only thing that bothers me is that I'm pretty sure Phillip didn't watch a lick of the performance, but the crazy thing was he was the loudest to cheer for me.

He's so amazing.

As the song ends, the lights shut off and I slowly walk off the stage, stepping on all the money that has been left on the stage for me. Prissy grins at me as I pass by, and for the next few minutes, I count my money and lock it up before changing in to a pair of sweats. I leave my hair and makeup on since I know I'll be meeting with the investors in a matter of minutes. Picking up my phone, I see that Jude will be home in less than an hour, and I pray that I will be done here.

Looking up at the mirror, I take a long look at myself, and I don't like what I see. I want to take all this stuff off because it's not me. I sorta don't want to be Diamond anymore. As I take in the long, fake lashes, the dark makeup around my eyes, my lips done up to be bigger and fuller, my straight, blond wig, the dark brown eyes, I don't like it. I know that if I get a job as a burlesque choreographer, I'll have to be glamorous, but I can be me. I want to be Claire. I look around my area, and I'm not sad at all to pack up my things. Not one bit. I'll miss the people, I'll miss my friends, but I'm going to bigger and better things, with the love and respect of my family and Jude.

When Reese and Phillip come into my line of sight, I turn in my seat to grin at them.

"You were so good!" Reese says excitedly.

"Thanks!" I gush as I stand to hug them.

"Really good. Great job; it was amazing," Phillip says, and I beam with pride.

"Thanks, I'm really happy. Hopefully, the investors like me," I say, my hands fidgety at my sides.

"I know they will," Phillip assures me. His eyebrows pull together and he says, "I really don't like you as a blonde."

I laugh. "Hey, it's so no one knows it's me."

"I knew from first glance," he says and I smile. "I know that face."

"Me too, but that's 'cause we know and love you so much," Reese says with a loving grin.

"So what are you doing now?" Phillip asks.

"I'm waiting for the investors or Ms. Prissy or something. I'm ready to go. Jude should be back in town in a bit."

He nods. "Okay, well, Reese is supertired, so we're going to go. I'll wait up to hear from you."

I wave him off. "Don't. I'll call you guys in the morning."

"Are you sure?" he asks uncertainly. "I don't want to leave, but she's about to pass out."

"True, this baby is sucking my life away," Reese says, but she doesn't seem upset about it. "Don't be mad."

"Not at all. I don't know how long this is going to be, so don't worry about it. I'll call y'all in the morning."

"Okay," Phillip says, kissing my forehead. "Good job tonight."

"Thanks," I say as Reese hugs me tightly.

I say bye, watching as they head out the back door before falling back in my seat to wait. Crossing my legs, I only have to wait a few more minutes before Ms. Prissy is coming around the corner with three men. All three are in expensive suits, all looking very important and serious from what I see as they walk behind Ms. Prissy to me. Today, surprisingly, Ms. Prissy is wearing a pantsuit, one that isn't leather. Guess she really does want to impress. When she grins at me, I smile back as I stand.

"This is Diamond. She's the choreographer of most of the numbers you saw today. She's the one y'all want to see," she says as she glances back at them. Looking back at me, she says, "Diamond, honey, these fine men are our guests for the night."

With a bright grin, I say sweetly, "Nice to meet y'all."

Two of the men smile, but I can't see the third. When he does step into the light, time stops.

"Diamond, this is Don Jackson from Vegas, Bruce Phillips from Florida, and Mark Sinclair from New York."

Oh. My. God.

Mark Sinclair.

Jude's dad.

I stand there as the three men look me over, all with smiles on their faces, and when Mr. Sinclair's eyes linger on my naughty bits, my stomach churns with disgust. When his eyes meet mine, I look away but feel his gaze on me as I say, "Thank you for coming out. I hope you enjoyed the show."

I try to make my voice higher. I'm not sure if he remembers how I talk, but just in case, I make sure to alter it even more.

"I did, very much," Don says with a nod. "So much so that I want to offer you the opportunity of your life."

"Really?" I ask, my heart speeding up. I'm not sure if it's from the excitement of Don's deal or if it's from the fact that Mr. Sinclair has not stopped staring at me.

"Let's go into my office," Ms. Prissy suggests.

The next thing I know, I'm sitting behind Ms. Prissy's desk with the three men in front of me. Mr. Sinclair's eyes have yet to leave my face, and my palms are clammy from the nerves. As much as I want to know what these men have to offer, I want to get the hell out of here. I thought Mr. Sinclair was a lawyer; why the hell is he doing investor shit? Does Jude know? Does anyone know?

"I'll go first," Mr. Sinclair says, and I force myself to look him in the eyes. Surely he doesn't recognize me, but I can see him trying to place me in his mind. His eyes roam over each of my features as he says, "I think you've heard my deal, twenty-grand signing bonus, with an annual contract of seventy-five grand, and full management of Ms. Prissy's in New York."

When Bruce scoffs, Mr. Sinclair shoots him a dark look, but that doesn't derail him. Looking at me, Bruce says, "We want to sign you for three years, fifty-thousand dollar signing bonus, a hundred-grand yearly contract, and free rein at the Ms. Prissy's in Miami. We will give you lodging, a new car, and a clothing budget. You will be treated like the queen you are, Ms. Diamond."

Holy mother of God. I knew the New York deal was going to be crap, but I never expected the Florida deal to be so amazing.

My lips go to form the word yes, but before they can, Don says, "Ms. Diamond – by the way, is that your real name?"

"No, it–" Ms. Prissy goes to say, but I interrupt her.

"No, but I'd like to keep my real name to myself until we sign contracts," I say quickly, and I can feel Ms. Prissy's eyes on me. Ignoring her, I add, "If you don't mind."

"That's fine with me," he says with a grin. He's a good-looking man, young, late twenties, with short blond hair and blue eyes that shine bright in the dim light. "I can guarantee the deal I have for you will be ten times what these two are offering you. I don't want you to run a Ms. Prissy's, no offense," he says to Ms. Prissy before looking back at me. "But I want you for your own show. I work for Lights and Sounds Hotels, and we want you to headline a show for us."

"I'm not performing after tonight. I want to be strictly backstage."

He nods, not missing a beat. "That's fine and I can promise you that the deal I'll have for you is something you can't turn down. The only problem is I can't offer you the deal without my bosses. We've heard of you. I've sent them video of your work here, and they want to see it for themselves. They can come in ten days, and we're hoping instead of signing with someone else, you'll put on a showcase for us and give us a chance."

For some reason, I feel good about this guy.

"My deal will be on the table for five days," Bruce says suddenly.

I meet his gaze and say, "I'd like to wait to see what they offer me."

"I can't wait that long," Bruce says and then he stands. "So I'll bow out of this pissing match. Good luck to you."

"Thank you," I say and then he's gone.

"So I guess I'm out too. I can't wait two weeks," Mr. Sinclair says and then he stands. "Good luck to you both."

I don't say anything to him, and when he leaves, I let out the breath I've been holding, meeting Don's gaze as he says, "I promise you won't regret this."

"I hope you're right," I say. "Because I just watched one good offer walk away."

He nods and then sends me a wink. "Don't worry. You'll be swimming in money when we get you to Vegas. See you guys soon."

Shaking my hand and then Ms. Prissy's, he leaves after that and I take in a lungful of air. Biting into my lip, I replay everything that just happened.

"Did I do that right?" I ask, looking up at Ms. Prissy.

She nods. "I think you handled that beautifully."

"What if the Vegas deal sucks?"

"Then you say no, and you wait for the next deal. You'll be okay."

Nodding, I look away as my heart pounds against my chest like a drum. "Can I do this in two weeks, put together a whole show?" I ask, my stomach churning with fear. I've always disliked that fear. It has such a power to take you down, and I hate that. I want to be strong, confident in my decision, but that just happened so quickly. I turned down two offers, and now I'm putting all my eggs in one basket. Is it the right choice? I want to say yes, that I feel good about it, but I can't. I'm nervous as hell. Not only is this going to skyrocket my career, but I'll also be living my dreams.

"Yes, you can. I believe in you," she answers, and I let out another breath.

She's right and I'm going to rock the hell out of that show. With a grin on my face, I stand up. "Thank you."

"Anytime, darling," she says, hugging me tightly before I leave the room. Heading to my station, I decide to leave my stuff there since I'm obviously not done here. Looking around the room, I see that it is empty except for Ben leaning against the door. I'm pretty sure that Mr. Sinclair is gone, so I sit ready to take my contacts and wig off, but just as I go to do that, I hear Ellen say, "Sweetie, come meet my best friend, Claire!"

Best friend in the least, I think, but when I turn to see who she's talking to, I'm cold again. My heart starts to race, my body feels rigid and almost not like mine as my eyes go wide and I'm suddenly fighting for my next breath.

"Claire, I wanted to introduce you to my boyfriend, Marky."

Mr. Sinclair's eyes meet mine, and his head cocks to the side as if he is realizing who I am. I don't say anything; all I can do is look at him with nothing but horror and disgust on my face. Jude's dad is cheating on his mom with Ellen? A girl who is younger than his daughter? I disliked this man before. Now I absolutely hate him.

"Hello? Earth to Claire!" Ellen sings, and I look at her. A part of my heart breaks for her. She may be an idiot, but I know she would never sleep with a married man. She came from a broken home and told me before that she would never be a home-wrecker; now Mr. Sinclair has made her one.

Another reason to hate this man to the fiery depths of hell.

"Hey," I blurt out, my heart beating so fast as my chest burns with nausea. I have to call Jude; I have to tell him.

He's going to flip.

"Guess what? He just offered me this amazing deal in New York! I'm going to run a Ms. Prissy's if she allows me to!" Ellen says, but I can't even listen to her. My heart is breaking for Jude, his family, and the devastation this is going to cause. As much as I don't want to be the one to tell them, I know I have to. No one deserves to be cheated on, and I refuse to allow someone I care about to go on not knowing that her husband is a complete snake.

"Wonderful," I mutter and then very slowly, I remove my wig and pull out my braid, letting my red hair fall down my shoulders.

When I meet his gaze again, his eyes are narrowed with recognition and he says, "Ellen, sweetheart, can you go on out to my car and get my briefcase? Maybe we can catch Prissy real quick."

"Sure, baby," she says and then looks at me. "Hey, keep my man entertained for a second, but not in like a slutty way. That's not what I mean. You have a boyfriend. What am I saying?" she says in her ditzy way and then she's walking away, her hair bouncing with each step she takes.

Looking back at Mr. Sinclair, I growl, "You are the lowest piece of shit I've ever seen in my life."

"You listen to me, you little bitch," he snaps, taking a step toward me. "You keep your mouth shut or–"

"Or what? You can't do anything to me, and if you try, Ben will stop you," I say, nodding my head toward Ben. He comes off the wall, crossing his arms and narrowing his eyes. When Mr. Sinclair looks back at me, his face is red with anger.

"I won't let you ruin my family."

"You did that yourself."

He pauses, breathing heavily, and everything inside me tells me to run, but very slowly I lay my wig down and then pull my hair up in a messy bun, acting as if his presence doesn't bother me a bit.

"What do you want?" he then asks. "Money? I'll give you thousands. I'll give you the club, the clothing budget, car, house, anything. Just keep your mouth shut."

"I'd rather have nothing than keep something like this from the people I care for. How dare you hurt someone like Mrs. Sinclair? You are a horrible, sad man, and I'm sorry, but no amount of money is going to keep me from opening my mouth. I suggest you be honest before I do it for you."

I can see the desperation in his eyes and I don't understand it. Shaking my head, I ask, "Why? Why risk what you have?"

"What I have? I have nothing but a fucking burden on my hands. I have a wife who does nothing for me. Kids who are more a hassle than anything else and a granddaughter who drives me fucking nuts. Wanna know why I do it? I hate my life, I hate the people I'm supposed to love, I'm bored, I want out, and Ellen is my way out."

"Then leave, you disgusting rat," I say, shaking my head. "Stop putting everyone through hell."

"You are nothing but a stupid little girl. You don't know anything about this. So shut up and keep your mouth shut. I'll take care of it on my own time," he sneers, his eyes flashing with anger along with pure anguish.

"No way," I say, reaching for my jacket. "I won't let you lie to them any more than you have."

I go to pass him but he takes ahold of my arm and pleads, "I'll give you half a million."

I don't have time to answer him. Ben shoots by me faster than lightning and removes Mr. Sinclair's hand from my arm. Looking back at him, I slowly shake my head. Before I would have taken the money and I wouldn't have cared about anything else. That was before I found love, before I realized that my family and my boyfriend are worth more than anything in this world. Before when I was completely hollow and nothing but a scared girl with no options but to end up like her mother. I'm not that girl anymore. I have my dreams at my fingertips, a family who would die for me, and a man who would give me the world if I asked for it.

So as I look at Mr. Sinclair, I say the only thing that comes to mind.

"You don't deserve them, and they will be so much better off without you."

And then I leave, ignoring the names and the threats he's throwing my way because Mark Sinclair can't hurt me. He doesn't have that power over me, and the people he does have that power over deserve to know he is a piece of shit.

The only problem is I'm the one who has to tell them.

CHAPTER 45

JUDE

Claire: Where *are u?*

I smile because I was just about to text her. After kicking ass in Chattanooga, the guys and I decided to go to the Gilroy to hang out and wind down before heading to bed.

> Me: I was about to text u; wanna go to the Gilroy? I'm on my
> way there.
> Claire: I'll meet you there.

Awesome. I'm more than pleased that she's coming out. Ever since I left her earlier, she has clouded my thoughts and clogged all my senses. That is until a huge defenseman knocked me on my ass and then I woke up, remembering that I had a game to win. And that's what I did. We dominated, and really, it isn't fair how we basically murdered those boys. I mean, eight to zero is a little intense. I'm happy though, a win is a win, and we need it for the championship.

"Claire coming out?" Jayden asks as we pull into the parking lot of the Gilroy.

"Yeah," I answer, tucking my phone in my pocket as he stops. Getting out of the car, I look around to see if I see her, but I don't, so we head toward the door. Before I can reach it though, Jayden's phone rings.

"It's Dad," he says, his face scrunched together. "It's almost one in the morning. Why would he be calling me?"

"I don't know. Answer it," I say and he does.

Watching him, I listen since I can only hear his side of the conversation. "Hey, I'm sure she is. Lucy left before the bus pulled out. Maybe her phone is dead? Did you call Lucy? Yeah, I don't know."

When a hand slides into mine, I look over to find Claire, and I'm a little taken aback by what I see; she has more makeup on than I've ever seen on her before.

With my brow up, I say, "Hey."

I then lean over, kissing the side of her mouth since her lips are so red, I'm sure it will stain my mouth. I usually don't mind, but that stuff looks as if I'll need Clorox to get it off.

"Hey, I need to talk to you," she says, her eyes wide and her breathing labored.

Before I can answer, I hear Jayden says, "Yeah, she's with him. Why?"

Look back at Jayden, I make a face and he shrugs. Glancing back at Claire, I say, "Hold on, Jayden's on the phone with my dad."

"Um, okay," she says just as Jayden hangs up.

"Yeah, I don't know what the hell his problem is."

"What did he say?" I ask.

"He asked if Mom was home, and I said I'm sure she is, but he's bitching, saying she isn't answering her phone. He went on a tirade about that and then he asked about Claire," he says, looking over at her, pointing his phone at her. "So weird."

"That is weird."

"Yeah, he's on his way home, said he'll be there in a minute."

"I thought he was in New York?"

"Yeah, I don't know. I'm gonna text Lucy and let her know he's on another level and also check in, make sure they're good."

I nod. "Sounds good. He's an idiot," I say, shaking my head. "Oh well, I'll meet you inside."

"Okay. Hey, Claire," he says, and Claire smiles as she waves.

"Hey, Jayden," she says and then he heads inside, saying that he'll get me a beer.

"Can we go by my car? I don't want people hearing us," she says, but before I can agree or disagree, she heads toward her car and I follow. Something inside my stomach clenches because something isn't right. I don't know why I feel that way, but I do. She doesn't ever just walk away from me; she takes my hand or leans against me. Something is wrong and soon the hairs on my arms are standing at attention.

When we reach her car, she turns and I ask, "Why are you wearing so much makeup?"

She waves me off. "I just left the club. Remember the investors?"

"You wear that much makeup to meet some investors? It's caked on."

"I know. Just let it go okay? I need to tell you something," she says, flustered. "One of the investors was your dad."

My lip curls up. "Huh?"

"One of the investors planning to open a new burlesque club in New York was your dad," she says and something isn't clicking right.

"My dad is a lawyer for hockey players," I say. "Are you sure it was my dad?"

She nods. "Yeah, he threatened me," she says cautiously.

Shocked, I ask, "He did what?"

"Yeah, but it gets worse," she says, looking everywhere but at me.

"How?" I ask and somehow I think I know what is about to come out of her mouth.

"After I turned down his deal, I went to get my purse and he walked up with one of the dancers from the club. She informed me that he was her boyfriend. Then he sent her to go to the car, and when she was gone, he tried to buy me off so that I wouldn't tell you guys. When I said hell no, he threatened me but he never got his hands on me because the bodyguard stopped him."

I must not be processing what she's saying, but I know it's the truth. I've always thought my dad was fucking around on my mom. He's always such an ass to her and always gone and shit. For some reason though, my heart aches. It must be because my mom is going to be completely broken. She loves my dad for some fucked-up reason, and this isn't going to go well. Taking in a slow breath, I clench my hand into a fist, my nails biting into my palm as I let out the breath in a whoosh.

"Wow, I need to call my mom," I say almost like I'm in a trance.

"I'm sorry," she says, and I shake my head.

"It's not your fault," I answer, reaching for my phone in my pocket. When I hit the screen, I see that I have four text messages and five missed calls from Jace.

"Shit. Jace has been calling and texting me."

"I didn't hear your phone ring," she says and I nod.

"I had it on silent," I say and then I open his messages.

> *Littler Bro: Dude, shit is going down over here. Mom and Dad are screaming at each other and Lucy left with Angie cause she doesn't want her around this.*
> *Littler Bro: What the hell is wrong with your phone? I've called you five times.*
> *Littler Bro: Shit, Dad's cheating on Mom with some slut from a strip club. I didn't know that Claire is a stripper. She's the one who found him with someone.*
> *Littler Bro: Fuck, will you call me!*
> *I didn't know that Claire is a stripper.*

No. Surely I'm reading that wrong. Looking up, I see that Claire is looking down, messing with her nails. She's stiff, her shoulders back and tight and she's working her lip, something she does when she's nervous. My stomach turns and I feel like I might hurl everywhere.

No. No. Jace has to be wrong.

"Claire," I say and she looks up at me, but then back down.

"What?"

"Look at me," I demand, but she doesn't for a second.

Then slowly, she looks up at me and my heart starts to pound in my chest because something is very wrong here. "Why are your eyes brown?"

Her mouth opens, but nothing comes out. She then takes a deep breath in and says, "I go to the club in a disguise. I wear a blond wig and brown contacts when I'm there."

"Why?" I ask. "Because that doesn't seem right if you are only choreographing. You don't cake that much makeup on when you teach at the studio or when you do the dance team. Hell, even when you're on the ice, you don't have on that much makeup."

I wait, and when her eyes start to fill with tears, I know that Jace isn't wrong at all.

My girlfriend is a stripper.

Within seconds, my whole body is taut, burning with anger as I stare down at her, waiting for her to say something. Fucking anything, but all she's doing is staring at me, taking in deeps breaths, her chest rising and falling with each breath. Unable to take it any longer, I say, "Well?"

"What did Jace say?" she asks, and I shake my head.

"Fuck no. Don't let him tell me what you need to tell me."

Biting into her lip, a tear rolls down her face and I refuse to look away. I promised to myself that I would never make her cry unhappy tears, that I would have a life for us full of love and happiness, but all I feel right now is red-hot anger.

She's lied to me. She's hidden something from me, and that's not fucking okay.

Her lip wobbles, and she takes in a deep breath. "I work at Ms. Prissy's as a dancer."

And there it is. My blood boils under my skin as I slowly shake my head. "For how long?"

"Two years," she answers and everything stops.

"Two fucking years? And you never told me?" I say, my voice getting louder with each word.

"It didn't matter. It wasn't what I planned on doing my whole life. I just need the money."

"So you whored yourself out to get money and lied to me. Now it all makes sense," I say, a lump forming in my throat. "All those nights you came to my house, saying that you couldn't sleep. Lies. That day I found that money in your drawer, that wasn't from Reese. It was from where you took your clothes off for men."

"I don't take my clothes off," she cries. "I dance in panties and a bra."

"Don't fucking lie to me any more than you have," I sneer. "I've been to that place."

Her eyes fill with more tears as she nods. "I know, but you probably went to the Rock Room side. I work on the Burlesque side. I keep my clothes on. I do entice men for money, but they don't touch me or ever see me naked. It's not a big deal," she says, and I laugh but with no humor.

"So if it isn't a big deal then why didn't you tell me?" I ask, taking a step toward her. "If you weren't doing anything wrong, then why didn't you fucking tell me?"

Tears start to roll down her cheeks in waves, and something inside me just breaks. "I'm sorry, but you have to understand. I needed the money. I needed to know that I would always be safe and secure. I would never go hungry or have to sleep in a car to make it."

"What the fuck am I, Claire? I would never let that happen. I would work nine jobs just to make sure you are safe and happy! But no, you go and whore yourself out and lie to me," I insist. "I would do anything for you, and I have. I haven't lied to you or hurt you, and you've been lying to me our whole relationship!"

"You don't understand, Jude! I went through hell, and I promised that I would never depend on anyone again because the people I trusted and loved left me to fend for myself. I wouldn't eat for days; I had to sleep in a little section of the car because my mom would sprawl out, giving me no room. I had nothing. I had no one, and I thought money would be the way to fix that. I thought as long as I had money, then I wouldn't need anything else, but I realize that I was wrong. I need you and I need my family, but I let the fact that I was making so much money ruin that, and in the process I lied to the two men I love and need more than my next breath," she cries, big wet tears rolling down her cheeks and landing on her shirt.

As much as I want to gather her in my arms and tell her it's okay, I know it's not. I love this girl, I mean, I fucking do, but I refuse to be lied to. I refuse to be a doormat like my mother is. Claire has hurt me, honestly broken me. Like I feel as if she has carved my heart hollow and I just don't understand. How do you lie to someone you love? Looking away, I take in a deep breath, willing myself to breathe and not lose my shit. I want to scream; I want to yell and even shake her to make her see how much she's hurt me. That thought scares me to the core, but I know I'd never put a hand on her.

Looking up at me, her face full of black streaks from her makeup running, she whispers, "Jude, I'm so sorry."

"Sorry?" I scoff. "This isn't something that you can be sorry for because you knew you were wrong!" I yell, my own eyes filling with tears. "How did you look at me every night and day and hold this from me? You know how I feel about people looking at you, wanting you. You know how jealous I can get. I've learned to let it go because I trust you, but what am I supposed to think now? How am I ever supposed to trust you again?"

"I swear, I'm done, Jude. I only want to work backstage. I have a huge deal coming my way. I promise, I'll never get on that stage again if you say not to and–"

"Claire, stop!" I shout, make her cringe as she wipes her palms against her legs. "This is not okay. You know how I feel about you, how I love you more than anything in this world, and you just don't care. You don't fucking respect me. You lied and you sold yourself for money."

"I never sold myself!" she yells. "I danced. Something I love, and yes, I tried to seduce men with my body for money, but I promise, Jude, I swear, no one has ever touched me. I'm yours."

When she tries to grab for my hands, I move them out of her reach, shaking my head. "No, you're not, or you wouldn't have lied to me," I say, dying with each word that leaves my lips. "You're basically your mother. Better pick up the crack pipe since you have the stripper part down."

When her hand comes cracking against my face, I know I deserve that. As the sting of her hand burns my skin, my eyes don't leave hers. She's crying, sobbing as she looks up at me. I know I shouldn't have said that, but I want her to hurt the way I do. Childish, fuck yeah, it is, but I'm basically dying right now.

"How dare you, Jude? I know I'm wrong, and I know that I should have told you, but calling me names is uncalled for. I understand that you're upset, but what you just said to me is not fucking okay."

"Um, Jude."

Tearing my gaze from hers, I look to see my brother beside us, his face contorted in shock. Unable to speak, I just look at him until he finally says, "Some shit is going on at the house. We need to go."

I nod once and then turn to look at Claire. "We have nothing else to discuss. We are done."

"What?" she screeches, taking ahold of my arm but I shake it loose.

"Don't touch me," I warn and her eyes widen in shock.

"Don't do this. Give me time to explain and apologize," she begs, but I shake my head.

"I did that, and I can't do it. We're through, Claire. I'm disgusted with you. I can't even look at you," I sneer before starting for Jayden's car. His eyes are wide, but he walks with me as I ignore Claire's pleas.

"Jude, please! Stop, don't do this!" she cries but I shake my head.

"Leave me alone, Claire," I say, opening the door.

"If you get in that car and drive away without fixing this with me, then I swear to God, I'll never speak to you again."

Looking over my shoulder at her, I nod. "Good."

With that, I get in the car and slam the door shut. Jayden doesn't say anything; he just drives off, and I watch as she gets smaller and smaller in the side mirror. When I can't see her anymore, that's when I allow a tear to slowly roll down my cheek. When Jayden's hand squeezes my shoulder, I stiffen up and wipe it away quickly.

I only wish I could wipe away the pain in my chest.

Nothing is said as we drive out to my parents' home. Jayden doesn't remove his hand, and I appreciate the support. I need it, but I wish I could just be alone, lick my wounds, and prepare to wake up tomorrow knowing that the first thing I'm not going to do is text her. I told her we're through, but how do you completely let go of someone who is basically an extra appendage to you? How do you just stop loving someone? I know I have to, though. She lied to me, over and over again, about something she knew was wrong. That is the worst kind of lie, in my opinion.

Leaning my head back in the seat, exhaustion takes over, and I squeeze my eyes shut to keep from crying. I can't believe this has happened. In one night, two relationships were ruined because of lies and deceit. The person I thought to be the most beautiful, amazing, perfect woman in the world just ripped my heart out and broke it. Broke me.

Tears sting my eyes and I fight them away as I take in lungfuls of air.

How did this happen?

Why did it happen?

I don't have those answers, and when we pull up to my parents' house, all the lights are on, the front door open. But that's not what I see first. I see my dad throw a punch and hit Jace dead in the jaw.

"Fuck!" Jayden yells, and before the car even comes to a stop, I jump out, running full speed toward my dad and push him to the ground. Standing above him, I yell, "Get the fuck up!"

"Jude! No!" my mom cries from the porch.

"You son of a bitch, you broke my arm!" my dad yells from the ground, and a smirk replaces the line my lips were in.

"Good, get up so I can break your fucking face," I sneer. "You don't hurt my family and get away with it."

I feel Jayden flanking my left and then Jace on my right, but my eyes don't leave the man who is more a sperm donor than anything else.

"Boys, please!" my mom sobs, but all three of us ignore her. "Just leave, Mark, and don't come back."

"Shut the fuck up," he sneers at her, and I don't like that one bit.

I don't even realize I'm doing it until my fist connects with his nose. Falling forward, he holds his nose as my mom screams. "Don't talk to her like that."

"Get the fuck out of here," Jace says. "We don't want you here."

"I say we remove him," Jayden says, his eyes dark with anger.

"No, boys, please. Just go, Mark!" my mom says. I look back at her, seeing that her face is red, tears streaming down her face, but the main thing I see is that her shirt is balled up in the front, like someone took a fistful of it to get ahold of her.

Snapping my head toward my sperm donor, I say, "Did you grab her shirt?"

Before he can answer, Jace says, "Yeah, that's why I pushed him out the door. He tried to hit her."

Looking back at my father, I'm not sure how I'm going to control my body, but somehow I keep it together and say, "So not only did you threaten my girlfriend, you tried to hurt my mom?"

He scoffs. "That slut you're dating is just that. She's the reason this is happening."

Before I can defend Claire, though I'm not sure why when I just dumped her, Jace points at him. "No, this is happening because you are a cheating bastard," Jace says, shaking his head. "This is no one's fault but your own."

"Shut the fuck up, you little shit. You'll never be anything; you're too fucking entitled. You expect everything to be given to you. All of you do. None of you work for shit. Yeah, I cheated because I want out!"

"Then leave!" Jace yells and I can see his eyes misting with tears. "We don't want you here!"

"You little shit," he yells, and he tries to go at Jace, but I push him away, throwing Jace behind me.

"Do I have to hit you again?" I ask. "Maybe I should just on principle, but that would be disrespectful since my mother has asked me not to. I'm gonna give you two minutes to get the fuck off this land."

Glaring, he says, "You think you three are something, huh? Think you are going to make me leave? Cold day in hell! This is my house! All of you get out!"

Jayden nods. "Yeah, I know we can make you leave. Go."

"Yeah, go," Jace says from behind me, and I nod.

He glares at us, but I know all he sees are three big guys, ready and willing to beat the fuck out of him with years of pent-up anger and remorse. This man has never been a father. Yes, he gave me the gift of life and even the gift of hockey, but not once did he ever love me and nurture me. He was a constant pain in my ass, and I actually hope he doesn't get in the car and we have to remove him. I have anger coursing through my body, and a fight would help release some of it.

My father opens his mouth to say something, but he doesn't say it. Instead he just glares and then he turns to go to his BMW. Knowing that he's leaving, I turn and head toward my mother. She's leaning against the door, holding herself as she cries. As I wrap my arms around her, she lets go and basically throws all her weight on me. I take it and slowly lower us to the ground as she cries so hard into my shoulder. Stroking her back, I close my eyes and lean my head against hers.

"I loved him so much, Jude, even when he didn't deserve it. How could he do this?" she cries and I shrug.

"I don't know, Mom. I'm so sorry, but you don't deserve this."

"How will I make it? I don't work; I just take care of you kids. He makes all the money."

"We will figure it out together," I whisper, kissing her temple. "You are better off without him. I swear."

She starts to sob harder, and every tear that leaves her body hurts me. I don't want to see my mom cry, or anyone I love cry, for that matter. Squeezing my eyes tight, I hold her closer and soon tears are falling from my eyes onto her hair. I think she feels them because her arms come around me, and just like that, the roles are reversed, and she's comforting me like she has my whole entire life. Kissing my temple, she rocks me back and forth as I just lose it. I've never cried this hard in my life.

I cry for my mom, for the shit my family and I have endured from that asshole, but most of all I cry for my broken heart and for Claire's. We thought this was it. We thought we were going to be together forever, but the whole time she was lying. She wasn't being her whole self to me, and how does someone do that to someone they love?

I have no answers for anything.

I'm just empty.

CHAPTER 46

 *Claire*

My chest aches.

My eyes are all gummy and burning from where I have cried like a freaking baby for the last twenty minutes.

My nose is running like a faucet and my throat hurts from the sobs that have been ripping from me.

Along with all that, I just feel cold. Empty. Hollow. Meaningless.

Worthless. I feel fucking worthless.

Pulling into the driveway of my home, I park behind Phillip's truck and get out, running to the front door. The light is off because, of course, they don't expect company at one in the morning. Digging in my purse for my house keys, I curse myself for not just leaving them on my car key set. I always get nervous that if I lose my car keys I'll lose my house key, and then I won't be able to get into the house to get my car keys. I know; I'm crazy.

And I'm fucking stupid for lying to Jude.

Frustrated, I cry out, dropping to my knees and dumping my purse on the porch. I shouldn't be here. I mean, what are they going to do for me? I messed up, I ruined this, and now I have to figure out how to either A: fix it, or B: accept that Jude has every right to be mad at me and probably will never talk to me again.

"Oh, thank God!" I cry out, finding the house key that is on the Assassins key chain, but as I get up to open the door, leaving the contents of my purse behind, the door flies open and Phillip stands there in only a pair of shorts.

"Claire?"

I just stand there, tears dripping down my face, and I suck in a deep breath as my heart breaks all over again. Turning the porch light on, his eyes widen as he comes to me, stepping all over my stuff, but I don't care.

"Claire, what's wrong?" he asks, taking my shoulders in his hands. "Are you hurt?"

"He broke up with me," I whisper, looking up into his face.

"Phillip?" I hear Reese ask, and I don't know why, but I just break down. Crumpling against Phillip, he holds on to me as I cry so hard it hurts. Like, physically hurts. My body feels as if it has been hit by a Mack truck, my heart just feels numb, broken and everything just feels wrong. How did I let this happen? I knew that he could find out, but I thought he would listen to me, I thought he would understand.

Instead, he dumped me.

Picking me up, Phillip says, "That kid broke up with her."

"Oh no," Reese gasps as Phillip carries me into the house and into the living room. Once he lays me on the couch, Reese swoops in, bundling me in her arms, kissing my forehead. "Get her some water." She kisses my forehead, moving my hair out of my face, and says, "It's going to be okay, baby. Just breathe."

Gasping for breath, I bawl into her chest, wrapping my arms around her, needing her love and comfort. I know now why I came here because I needed this. I needed Reese to tell me it was going to be okay. For a long time, we don't move. Phillip walks around us, checking on me, and occasionally he rubs my back softly, asking me if I need anything. I say no because the thing I need won't have me. When I'm all cried out and empty of all emotion, I close my eyes and sleep takes me quickly.

The last thing I think of is Jude calling me my mother.

When I wake the next morning, I'm alone on the couch, covered with my favorite One Direction blanket. Reaching for my phone that I find laying on the table, I check to see if I have any messages. I don't. I check calls; there are none, so then I check Jude's Facebook, and he hasn't updated since yesterday. His last status says:

I love my girlfriend.

He then tagged me, and seeing those words, his profile picture of us kissing after one of his games, has my lip wobbling and my heart aching. I want to lie back down, cover myself with the blanket and just cry myself stupid, but then I feel like I need to wash my face. Sitting up, I look over to find Reese and Phillip at the kitchen island, watching me.

Looking away, embarrassed, I say, "Sorry for coming over so late."

"Nothing to be sorry for. You are always welcome here," Reese says. "I laid you out some towels and got you some old clothes if you want to go shower."

Nodding, I stand up and tuck my phone in my pocket. I don't look at them as I pass, heading to the bathroom and shutting the door behind me. Leaning against the door, a tear rolls down my face and I wipe it away before pulling out my phone. Clicking on my messages, I open a new text and type Jude's name.

Me: Hey... I miss u. A lot. And I'm really sorry.

Unlike every other time, he doesn't write back right away. When I get out of the shower after standing under the hot water for well over a half hour, I check and he still hasn't written back. Maybe he had a rough night with his mom or something and he's sleeping. When I look at the clock though, I see that it's two in the afternoon. Cringing, I shake away the thoughts that come. I refuse to think that he's moved on. He wouldn't do that. He loves me. We're just... Shit, he may love me, but that won't keep him from finding someone else to fuck his pain away.

Picking my phone back up after dressing, I type:

Me: Please, Jude. Just talk to me. We can work this out.
Me: I love you.
Me: I don't want to lose you.

When he still doesn't answer me, I slide down the door and curl up in a ball on the floor, hugging my legs as the tears drip from my eyes and wet the Hogwarts pants I'm wearing. Swallowing back the sob that wants to escape, I cry, rocking back and forth as I stare at my phone. Waiting. Just for a response. I need one. I need to know he still loves me. I need to know he still wants me.

Closing my eyes, I rest my head on my knees and cry until Reese comes knocking on the bathroom door. "Claire, honey, you've been in there a while. Can you come out?"

I love how she doesn't ask if I'm okay. I think she knows I'm devastated.

"Yeah," I answer, standing up and tucking my phone in my pocket. Opening the door, she waits for me on the other side, a small smile on her face as she looks me over. I'm waiting for her to ask what happened, but a part of me thinks she knows. I think she knows that my lies caught up with me and that Jude did exactly what I feared.

He left me.

Reaching out, she laces her fingers with mine and asks, "Hungry?"

I shake my head, but my stomach betrays me and rumbles. She smiles as she pulls me against her side and says, "Well, maybe you can eat just to make me feel better."

I shrug and lean my head against her shoulder as we make our way into the kitchen. Phillip is leaning against the counter, but that's not what holds my gaze. His bags are by the door, which means he's leaving. Looking up at him, I ask, "When do you leave?"

"Tonight," he answers. "But I have time to find that kid and kill him."

I'm not sure if he's being serious or trying to make me laugh, so I just shake my head, sitting down at the island in front of a huge plate of waffles covered in my favorite strawberry sauce.

"No, don't. It's my fault."

"What happened?" Reese asks, leaning her forearms on the island. "Did he find out about the club?"

Slowly I nod, my throat burning with emotion. "Yeah, he did, and it was bad," I say and then I tell them what happened. They don't say anything as I explain about his dad. I was sure that Phillip was going to lose his shit when I told him what Jude said about my being like my mom, but he surprises me and just listens.

"I mean, maybe I am, you know? Maybe I am just like her and I'm going to be alone and run through men thinking they're each the love of my life. I should have known better, but I just couldn't bring myself to tell him about the club. I knew that he wouldn't like it," I say, wiping away the few tears that have fallen.

Coming toward the island, Phillip says, "One: you aren't your mother, not in the least."

"He's right," Reese adds with a nod.

"And two: if he loves you, he'll come around. Just give him time to process. I needed time and we're fine."

"But you have to love me," I say, and he shakes his head.

"I know, but I didn't have to forgive you. It's not easy to forgive; you have to push aside your pride and believe that the person won't hurt you again. That's not an easy thing to do. Give him time."

"I just don't think he'll come around. You didn't see his eyes, they were hard, and my God, he was so upset."

"Of course he was, Claire. Not only did he find out you lied to him, but his dad was cheating on his mom. That's a lot to take in at once," Reese says. "Give him a few days, see what happens."

"Yeah," I say with a nod. "Maybe, but what do I do till then? I drove myself crazy when you didn't talk to me, and honestly, I don't know if I can handle it from Jude. I've talked to him every minute of every day. When we weren't together, we were texting. How do I just stop that?"

Reese reaches across the table, taking my hand in hers. "You have to be patient, just remember he is going through the same pain you are."

"Or he's sleeping with anything with tits," I supply, and she gives me a dry look.

"I doubt that. When you truly love someone, you don't get over them that quickly."

"That's the thing, though; how do I know he really loved me? I mean, he just ended it, didn't even try to understand my reasoning or even care that I was sorry."

Setting me with a look, Phillip says, "Do you really believe that he doesn't love you? I may not like the guy, but even I know that's crap, Claire. That kid worships the ground you walk on. You have him wrapped around your finger like a knot. He's mad, his pride hurts, and he is also dealing with the shit with his parents. He'll come around."

Before I can say anything, my phone signals a text. When I see that it's from Jude, I almost drop my phone trying to open it as my heart pounds in my chest. Opening the text thought, my heart falls into my stomach and dissolves away from the acid in my gut.

Hey Jude: You did lose me, stop texting me.

Looking up, I can't see Reese and Phillip because of the tears in my eyes. Laying my phone down, I shake my head as they roll down my face. "He said to stop texting him."

Reese makes a noise of distress and Phillip goes, "I can still kill him, Claire. Just say the word."

But I don't want to say the word; I just want Jude to come back to me.

⁂

It's been three days.

Three days of nothing from Jude. Not a single text, call, Facebook post, tweet, nothing. It's like he fell off the face of the earth. I haven't seen him on campus, I haven't heard anything, and it's honestly killing me. I just don't get it. How does someone disappear? And doesn't he miss me? I mean, I feel like my heart isn't even in my chest, that he took it. I can't concentrate on anything. Not school, not work, not even the damn showcase that I have to plan. I have to start teaching the girls this weekend, and I don't even think I'll have anything. Every time I go to work something up, I just imagine Jude walking away from me and I crumple in a pool of tears.

I need to see him. I need him to see me. Maybe that will help.

I head to the Bullies' house, my heart in my throat as I sweat bullets, but when I get there, Jude and Jayden aren't there.

"They haven't been back in a couple days. They had a family emergency," Matt says, leaning against the door. "Shouldn't you know that?"

"Yeah, I should," I say and then I turn to leave as my heart aches in my chest. Heading to the car, I get in and slam the door behind me. I'd head out to his mom's house, but I don't remember how to get there. I also wouldn't want to face his family when I know they know that I'm a liar.

I need to know that he's okay, though.

Opening my Facebook, I find Jayden's profile and message him.

Claire Anderson: Hey Jayden, I came by to the house to try to talk to Jude but you guys aren't here. They said it's a family emergency. I was just wanting to make sure that you all were okay.

Unlike his brother, Jayden answers me.

Jayden Sinclair: Hey, yeah, Mom isn't handling everything well. My dad is being a dick and keeps threatening to come by here. Since my sister has Angie here, we've decided to camp out till we can convince my mom to call the cops. She's being stubborn.
Claire Anderson: I'm sorry that this is all going on.
Jayden Sinclair: Yeah, it sucks. It will be over soon.
Claire Anderson: Yeah, very soon, I hope.

Biting into my lip, I take in a deep breath and type what I really want to know.

Claire Anderson: How is he?
Jayden Sinclair: Not good.

My eyes cloud with tears as I suck in a deep breath, letting it out in a whoosh.

Claire Anderson: He won't answer my calls, my texts, my anything. I can't get him to talk to me. I don't know what to do.
Jayden Sinclair: I don't know what to tell you to do. All I know is that he's hurting bad, and anytime anyone brings you up, he flips his lid but then I saw him watching the video on his Facebook. The one of you dancing, so I don't know. I don't know if it is his pride that won't let him talk to you or if it's the fact that he really doesn't want to be with you. I think it's the former though, if that's any help.
Claire Anderson: It does. Thank you. I really am sorry, for everything. For the pain your mom is going through and for Jude. I never meant to hurt him.
Jayden Sinclair: I try to believe that no one ever really wants to hurt the person they love. In my mom and dad's situation that statement isn't true but with you and Jude, I think it is. He loves you Claire, I know he does, you just have to figure out a way to reach him.

I read his message twice and then it's like a light bulb goes off above my head.

Claire Anderson: I think I know how.

An hour later I'm in the middle of the studio with Skylar standing in front of me with the camera.

"I can't believe you never told him," she says, adjusting the camera.

"I know I'm an idiot," I say, setting her with a look.

"You sure are, but I think this is going help him forgive you," she says, sending me a grin. "You look mighty cute too."

I smile as I look at myself in the mirror. I'm wearing Jude's jersey with a pair of blanket tights underneath it and teal booty shorts. My hair is down in curls, and I wear no makeup because I want this to be completely raw. I want him to watch this and know that I'm miserable without him.

Completely and utterly lost.

"I don't like the song. I think it should be something else." she says, and I roll my eyes.

"Skylar, I'm broken here. I want him to know that, and the words in the song are perfect."

"Whatever. I think you should do it to 'All of Me' by John Legend."

I nod. "While yes, that is an amazing song, it's not the right one for this moment."

"I think it is."

"Um, this is my 'please take me back' video. I hired you to videotape."

"Whoa, wait, you're paying me?"

"With ice cream," I say and she smiles. I wish I could smile back, but I just don't have it in me.

"Okay, let's do this," she says, taking the remote to the stereo and then setting up to where she isn't in the mirror but has a perfect shot of me. Heading to the middle of the floor, I turn with my back to her and my head tucked between my arms, my fingers dusting the back of my neck. I nod once and then the music starts to Adele's "Don't You Remember?"

When the piano starts, I slowly move my body to the sweet music, moving around so effortlessly, as if I am air. I make myself one with the music, the way I know Jude loves. As I spin on my toes, my arms in the air in the most elegant way, I know this has to work. Tears sting my eyes and I allow them to fall as I sing along with the song. Each word is everything I want to say to him because I know he has to remember that he loves me. I know he does, he just needs a little push, and this is the push to do it.

Turning, I look at the camera, tears streaming down my face, my eyes wide and full of love and hope that this will work. When Skylar drops the camera,

I close my eyes and wipe my tears free from my eyes. I try to pull it together. I don't want to break down in front of Skylar, but I can't stop this because if it doesn't work, I might die even more inside. Squatting to the ground, I hold my face in my hands as the tears fall in torrents out of my eyes.

"Oh, Claire," she whispers, wrapping her arms around me. "It's gonna work out. This will work. Come on, let's watch it and upload it."

Nodding, I take in a deep breath as we fall to our butts and watch the video. Of course, I'm my own worst critic and see where I could have done something better, but I feel that Jude will love this –that this might be the golden ticket to get him to talk to me. I mean, I just laid it all out there. I'm basically begging here and I thought I would never do that, that I would never beg for someone to love me. But for Jude, I'd do anything.

"It's perfect," she says and I nod.

"I agree. Here, let me upload it," I say, taking my phone from her and going to my Facebook. Opening a status, I type:

Jude Marshall Sinclair, I love you. More than words. I'm sorry.

I then tag him and upload the video. We don't talk as we watch it upload and then wait as it processes. When it's completely uploaded and I see it on my newsfeed, I wait. I know he has it set to where if you tag him, it text messages him. So as long as he has his phone, which he probably does, he has to have seen it, but I'm not getting anything. People are liking the video, even commenting that we're the cutest couple in the world but nothing from Jude.

"Maybe he doesn't have his phone?" Skylar asks after twenty minutes of staring at my phone.

"He always has his phone," I say, clicking on the status again, but this time I see that his name isn't tagged to my status anymore. "What the hell? Did I not tag him?"

"No, I saw it tagged," she says, looking over at my screen.

"Shit," I mutter and then click to tag him again, but when I do, I can't find his name. "What the hell?" I whisper and then I type his name up in the search bar. When I click on his name, I see why he wasn't tagged in my status and why I couldn't tag him.

He unfriended me.

He doesn't want me.

CHAPTER 47

 JUDE

I can't take it.

I don't make it through the video before I'm stopping it and closing my whole Facebook app down. The only problem is that everyone and their momma is commenting on the post, and it's a constant reminder of the love that I let go. Opening the app back up, I go to her profile and just stare at the picture of us together. We were so happy, and I was so unbelievably blind to what she was hiding, but it is by far my favorite picture of us. I even have it as my profile picture. My lips are so close to hers, and I'm whispering that I love her. She giggled and then she snapped the picture.

It is a picture of our love.

I want to go through my phone and delete everything, but I can't bring myself to do it. I know it's only been four days, but each day it gets harder and harder because everything reminds me of her. I want to call her, I want to answer her texts, I want to find her and just hold her. I want to forgive her, but all I see is my mother, balled up in her bed, crying. If Claire could hide this part of her, what would keep her from hiding anything else from me? How do I trust her? How do I forgive her?

I feel my tears stinging my eyes, so before I chicken out, I hit the unfriend button, and then without really thinking, I throw my phone across the hall. Falling into my pillows, I hide my face in them and allow myself to let it all go. As soon as I close my eyes though, I see her. I see her body moving to the music of the video in such an effortless way, a way I love because it's so beautiful. I see my jersey on her and something about her wearing that jersey always hits me straight in the gut. I see her eyes, flooded with tears, begging me to forgive her and to just hold her and tell her I love her. I can't, though. Biting the inside of my cheek to keep myself for sobbing out loud, I squeeze my eyes tight and beg for it all to go away.

The pain. I want it gone, but it doesn't subside. It only grows – completely taking over and making me feel like I have nothing. In a way, I don't. I don't have Claire. She was my everything, and now I'm just alone. I changed; I became the man who deserves a girl like her, and now I'm alone. Why is that fair? I did everything right. I never lied, cheated, I was brutally honest, and fucking hell, I love her with everything inside me. How could she fucking lie to me? Did she not trust me? Our love? What? Why didn't she tell me? I mean, yeah, I would have been a little mad and a little jealous, but we would have figured it out, but instead she lied. She hid a whole other part of herself because she knew it was wrong, and that makes me mad all over again.

꧁ ꧂

I feel almost lightheaded.

Like I'm high on something that gives me the shakes because I'm about to see her. It's been a full week since I've seen her in person. I still stalk her Facebook even though I deleted her, and I still look at our pictures more times then I'd like to admit. Tonight is a home game though, and I'm going to see her. Even if I'm not ready to. Dressed and ready to go, I stand in front of my locker, rocking side to side in my skates. I'm listening to a bunch of Ed Sheeran, which isn't what I usually listen to before games. He's all I've been listening to since I got in Jayden's car and we drove off. For some reason, I like his songs of love and getting drunk; they soothe me, almost.

Letting out a long breath, I look around at my teammates. Everyone is quiet, preparing for the game. I want it to be loud and distracting – anything to get my mind off what has happened in the last week. Since deleting Claire from my Facebook, somehow everyone knew and the girls are coming at me in droves. I don't even know how they got my number or why they think Facebooking me pictures of them in their undies is going to make me call them, but that doesn't stop them from doing just that. I want to delete everyone, hell, my whole Facebook. That is a great idea, so I'll do just that. Sitting down, I dig my phone out of my bag and deactivate my account. When it confirms that I'm no longer a member of Facebook, I feel a little better, but then I remember that I'm not with Claire and my mood turns sour once more.

Closing my eyes, I lean back in my locker and just wait. The game should be starting soon, and when my skates hit the ice, I think I'll forget everything. I'll forget that Claire lied to me, that my dad is a horrible excuse for a man, that my mom cries twenty-four seven, and that things may never be the same. I may live the rest of my life alone because if I can't be with her, I don't want anyone else. When my phone vibrates in my hand, I look down to see that it's a text from my mom.

> *Mom: Claire's uncle and aunt are here. They said hi to me and wished me well. That was nice.*
> *Me: Yeah, great.*
> *Why is she telling me this? I don't care...kinda.*
> *Mom: I thought so. I also saw Claire. Oh Jude, she looks completely heartbroken.*

That makes my heart hurt a little.

> *Me: She should be.*
> *Mom: Jude, don't be like that.*

Deciding I don't want to deal with my mom right now, I tuck my phone in my bag and close my eyes again. It doesn't take long before the coach comes in and does his speech about winning. I don't listen, though. All I think about is Claire looking heartbroken.

Thanks, Mom.

Letting out a long breath, I don't participate in the yelling of our school name, and I'm the first one out of the locker room. The anticipation of seeing her is killing me and has me on edge. I've done well hiding out and not having to see her. Yeah, I haven't gone to school in a week, and I may or may not have skipped out of practice early just to make sure she didn't see me, but I did that because I couldn't see her yet. Even now I know I can't see her, but it's inevitable. I'm going to, and I just have to pray I can get through it.

As I stand at the end of the tunnel waiting for my teammates, I wonder if she's nervous. If she's on edge and thinking of me? I wonder if she's going to try to talk to me, if she's going to ask me why I won't speak to her. What will I say? What will I do? She's had such an effect on me, and I really don't know how I'm going to handle being near her. So I'll hope she doesn't come up to me.

When it's time to go out on the ice, I take a running start, and when I hit the ice, I wait to feel good; I wait for everything to be better.

But it doesn't.

The first thing I do as I round the corner of the goal is I look for her. When I find her, she's staring right at me, and I swear there are tears in those baby blue eyes. She does look miserable, and it honestly guts me. Looking away quickly, I find a puck and start to play, trying so hard to get my head in the game. We need to win this; we're on a streak, and I'm not going to allow myself to fuck up because my heart is broken. But with every turn I take around the goal, I glance up to where she is standing, her pom-poms at her side and her eyes locked on me. She doesn't move the whole time I warm up, and when it's time to line up for the national anthem, for some reason I look back up at her, and she mouths what I believe to be "I love you."

That causes me to bite my lip hard as I look away. If it is this hard to be fifty feet away from her, how am I supposed to go the rest of my life sometimes bumping into her on campus? I still have seven months at this damn campus. How am I supposed to function when I can't even be in the same room with her without wanting to jump over sheets of glass and smother her with kisses? I know I could do it; I know I could get to her and take her in my arms and make her mine. She won't push me away. I know she loves me; she just said it. But what about a week from now? Will I sit there and accuse her of lying to me every chance I get? When she stays out late for whatever she's doing, will I believe what she tells me? I don't know the answer. Yes, I want her, more than I can describe, and God, yes, I still love her, but a relationship stands no chance without trust.

The game passes in a blur. I somehow score a goal, but I'm sure it's luck since I don't remember shooting the puck. When it goes in, the crowd loses it while I just stand there, staring at where the puck lays behind the goalie. This is supposed to mean something, this is supposed to be my drug of choice, but all I'm doing is standing here, feeling as if I'm not really here. When Jayden hugs me tight, saying good goal, I nod and turn to head to the bench.

"Get your fucking head in the game, Sinclair!" Coach Moss yells.

"I just scored!" I yell back as I sit down.

"You aren't even here!" he yells, and it always surprises me how he knows these things. Squirting Gatorade in my mouth, I lean against the boards and watch the rest of the game, refusing to allow myself to look back to where I know Claire stands. It's hard, but I manage.

When the game ends, I take my time and shower. When I'm standing at the mirror, I actually consider shaving the beard that Claire loves. I even reach for the razor, but I know it's out of spite, just to get rid of anything that reminds me of her. Then my eyes drift down to where her lips lay above my heart. I want to laugh. She told me not to do it, that it was too soon. Did she know that we would break up? Running my fingers along the lifelike tattoo, I feel tears sting my eyes. Letting out a breath, I walk away from my reflection with pain ripping me to shreds. I got the tattoo with the thought that it would remind me of the greatest love of my life, but all it does is remind me that I'm alone and without her.

Fuck, I was stupid, but I don't regret it. I just need to get over the pain.

Getting dressed, I see that most everyone is gone, probably out meeting their families. I know that my family, minus Dad, is waiting for me, but I don't want to leave the locker room. I know she's out there. She might even be waiting for me. To be sure though, I text Jayden.

Me: Is Claire out there?

It doesn't take long and Jayden answers.

Jayden: Yeah. She just talked to Mom and now is waiting by the door. You have no way of avoiding her.

I let out a long breath.

Me: Can you distract her?
Jayden: Lol. I would but I don't want to.
Me: Jerk.
Jayden: I think you might thank me one day.
Me: Highly doubt that.
Jayden: We will see huh? Stop being a pussy and come out.
Me: Fuck you.
Jayden: Love you too.

Fucking jerk. Grabbing my bag, I throw it up on my shoulder and head out of the locker room to the lobby. Before I even get out the door, I see her. She's leaning against the wall, her hands in the pockets of her sweats and her hair down, along her shoulders. When I'm fully out the door, she stands up, lacing her fingers together and coming to the middle the hall. I know I can go around her, completely ignore her, but for some dumbass reason, I stop in front of her.

Her lip wobbles, her eyes fill with tears, and I have to look away.

"I miss you," she whispers, but I don't say anything. I can't. There is a lump in my throat, my heart is fucking dead, and I don't know what to say. I don't know what to do. I need to just walk away.

"I love you, so much, and I'm really sorry," she says softly, her voice heavy with emotion. "I've thought about you every second of every day for the last week. I've texted, called, Facebooked you, everything, in the hopes that you'll talk to me. Give me a chance. I understand that you're hurt, and I know I was wrong, but I'm probably a second away from dropping to my knees and begging you to be in my life. I've never begged anyone, Jude, no one, but I will for you. Just say the word."

Still I don't say anything, and when I look up to meet her sorrowful gaze, something inside me cracks, and my own eyes itch with tears.

"Okay, one-way talking here. At least you're not walking away," she says softly, her hand cupping her throat. I tuck my hand that's not holding my bag in my pocket to keep from reaching out to cup her beautiful face, to wipe away the tears that are falling down her face. "I have a huge offer coming in from the investor in Vegas if my showcase goes well. I'd love for you to be there. I'm so nervous and so scared, and I know having you there will help. It's Wednesday at nine at Ms. Prissy's. I hope you'll come."

Looking away, I don't trust myself to say either yes or no. I want to support her, but I can't even think about doing that because this is what she was lying about. Can I even sit there and watch her move on that stage, knowing that she hid this from me? Looking back down at her, I suck in a deep breath and then I walk away without a word.

"I don't give up, Jude Sinclair," she yells suddenly, making me pause mid-step. Everyone turns, looking at us, and I'm frozen. I'm immediately taken back to the first day I met her, when she didn't want to give me her number or have anything to do with me. The day when I knew she was going to be the one to change me completely. How right I was.

"I love you," she says. "I won't give up."

I don't dare look back. Instead I finally will myself to move and head to where my family waits, but even then I don't stop. I keep going and once I'm outside, the cold hitting me in the face, I look up at the sky and gasp for breath. It's a stunning, clear night, big, beautiful stars in the sky, and that should calm me, but it just pisses me off. Stars remind me of Claire.

I'm about to look away but then a fucking shooting star shoots through the air. One would take that as a sign. Me? I flip it the middle finger.

CHAPTER 48

🏒 JUDE

"Jude?"

I look over my shoulder to find my mom standing behind me. "Hey, Mom, you ready?"

"Yeah, can you drive me home? I think Jayden wants to ride with Lucy and Jace to help with Angie."

Lie.

"Or you want to talk to me alone and told them they had to ride together?" I ask and she smiles.

"Just hush and drive me home," she says before turning and heading to Jayden's car.

I shake my head and follow after her. When we reach the car, she hands me the keys and I get in, starting it up as she buckles her seat belt.

"Seat belt, Jude Marshall."

I roll my eyes but do as she asks and off we go. She doesn't say anything like I expect her to. She just rides quietly, her hands laced together in her lap. Every time she takes in a deep breath or clears her throat, I know it's coming, but still nothing. I don't get it. I thought she wanted to talk to me?

Glancing over at her, I say, "Good game tonight?"

She shrugs. "Eh, kind of. Your head wasn't in the game."

"Yeah, it's been a rough couple days."

"Yeah," she agrees with a nod, and I wait. But nothing. That was the perfect opening! I basically gave it to her on a silver platter. I mean, I don't want to talk about Claire, or maybe I don't want to be the one to bring it up. It would be nice to ask what she thinks I should do, but I need some help here. I need her to pull it from me.

"I talked to Claire."

Okay, maybe I don't need it pulled from me.

"I saw," she says with a nod. I glance over at her, waiting for her to ask what happened, but she just sits there. What the hell?

Clearing my throat, I readjust in my seat and then say, "She apologized."

"That's good."

"And she says she still loves me and doesn't want to lose me. I didn't say anything, though. I just looked at her, and Mom, I swear it took everything not to lose it. I miss her."

"I know, sweetheart," she says, taking my hand in hers, clasping her other hand over it.

I suck in a deep breath. "I just don't know what to do. I mean, how do I trust her? You know, like, how do I know she won't ever lie to me again?"

"Do you think she will?" she asks as I pull onto our driveway. I take it slow and shrug my shoulders.

"I don't know. I mean, if you would have seen the way she looked at me, I don't think she would, but still it scares me. I don't want to become the way you were with Dad."

Her hand squeezes mine, and I know I shouldn't have said that. It is still very raw, the pain she's going through, but I have to be honest.

"Claire is not your dad, Jude. She didn't tell you about a job that she had. She wasn't sleeping with God and everyone," she says as I pull up in front of the house. "I think that she made a mistake. Maybe she was embarrassed by what she was doing and didn't think you'd stick around."

"I don't think she was embarrassed. I think she liked the money, but loved me and didn't want to lose me."

I look over at her, and she shrugs her shoulders. "You are the one in control here, honey. You can go back to her and make it work, or you can let her go. It's going to hurt either way. I made both of those choices, and I honestly can't tell you which one was easier. You have to decide what is best for you."

I sit for a long time, my thumb stroking her hand as I think. Lucy even pulls up with the rest of my family, but none of them looks at us, they just head inside. I'm glad since I'm not done talking to my mom. I nod, my heart thudding against my chest. Meeting her gaze, I ask, "What would you do?"

"I have no clue," she answers softly. "But I've been scorned too many times, and I'm bitter. I believe a relationship needs trust – it won't survive without it – but I also believe people make mistakes, and everyone deserves a second chance to make it better."

Biting the inside of my cheek, I look at the steering wheel, and I still have no clue what to do. While I agree that everyone deserves a second chance, I also agree that a relationship needs trust, and honestly, I don't know if I can trust her.

But I also don't know if I can let her go.

⁂

To say I've been miserable is the understatement of the year.

For the last four days, I've done nothing but play hockey and try to catch up on my work. Thank God for Jayden and Lucy, or I'd probably fail this semester. They not only helped me with school, but they tried to distract me. Jace, on the other hand, just yells at me and tells me to go find Claire and tell her that I forgive her. While I want to do that because I do miss her, I still can't come to terms with the fact she lied to me. Say I'm hardheaded or stubborn as hell, like my mom says, but I just don't know if I can do it.

If I can trust her.

But obviously, I'm willing to try.

When I pull into Ms. Prissy's, jealousy eats at my heart knowing that men have come in those doors to see my girlfriend move her body for them. Squeezing the steering wheel with my fingers, I park and then get out, slamming the door behind me. I'm a tad bit late, but I wanted it that way. I didn't want anyone to see me. I don't know who is going to be here, but I'm hoping to get in and out unseen. As my heart hammers against my chest, I open the door to the club and walk in.

I'm not entirely sure why I came. I'm not sure if it was to forgive her and live happily ever after or to feed my curiosity. I want to know what she has been doing in this club. I want to know why she lied, and maybe the answers are here. Or maybe I'm a glutton for punishment and just want to break my heart some more before I walk away for good. I don't know. All I know is I'm here, and a part of me wants to support her. Actually, a lot more than a part of me does. I want her to succeed, I want her to get all her hopes and dreams, and I just hope that I am a part of them. I need to figure this out. I need to decide what I want. It's been almost two weeks; I have to decide tonight. No more fucking around.

Walking to the desk since the doors are being guarded by two very large men, I pull out my wallet to pay as the girl goes, "Sorry, buddy, it's closed tonight."

"For a showcase, right? By Claire Anderson?"

"There is a showcase, but it's by Diamond."

Diamond? I assume that's her stage name, so I nod. "Yes, for that."

"Well, it's already started."

"Yeah, I know," I say, getting a little impatient with this girl. She's snotty and not making this any easier.

"Okay, are you like, on the list?"

I shrug. "Have no clue. My name is Jude Sinclair."

She looks up from the paper and nods. "You're number one on the list, and

I'm supposed to take you to the VIP area. I'm sorry for being so short with you, follow me."

Before I can decline that, she is coming out from behind the desk and walking through the doors the men were blocking. Once I'm inside, my eyes widen at what I see. A girl is using two ropes on the stage, dressed in minimal clothing, but her main parts are clothed as she moves and grinds her body against the wall, acting as if the ropes are holding her. It's very sexy and kinda hot, but it does nothing for me. I stop mid-step, taking in the risquéness of the club. Everything is white with gold accents, giving it a very classic, old-school feel. I totally expect men to be sitting around with cigars hanging from their lips as they throw dollars at the girls and make dirty drug deals, but to my surprise, all I see are men in suits, very intently paying attention to the girls.

When the hostess turns, she gives me a look that says come on, but I shake my head, dropping myself in the very back table that's in the shadows.

She comes back to me and says, "Hey, I need to take you up to the front."

"I'm good," I say, leaning back in the seat. She looks annoyed, but thankfully she walks away, leaving me to watch the show. A girl comes by and offers me a beer, which I gladly take. Probably gonna need it. Looking around the room, I like how it's so different from the Rock Room. Over there it's dark and kinda gives off a grungy feel, but here it's bright and almost feels like a cabana club from that dancing movie Claire made me watch. There is a massive gold chandelier that glitters hanging from the ceiling above the large stage. It's nice here and not like the Rock Room. Over there, people are drunk and throwing money at the girls like they're nothing but meat, but here, as I watch, I kinda feel like the guys are getting off but in a classy way.

If that even makes sense.

Do I like that Claire dances for them? Still fuck-to-the-hell no, but if she has to do it, thank God it's here. If it was over in the Rock Room, I'd probably get up and leave, to be honest. But it's not, so I'm going to sit back and see what happens. See how I feel once it's over and go from there. I've always trusted my gut when it comes to Claire, and I'm going to continue that.

When the girl leaves the stage, the maybe twenty people in here clap loudly, and I see a few guys lay some money on the bar, giving the girl a thumbs-up. I look at the people, trying to see if Reese and Phillip are here, but I don't see them. I think I may see Reese sitting beside some guy in a black suit, but I can't tell if it is her since I'm directly behind her. When the next song starts, within seconds, girls are everywhere, all wearing the same black lace outfit. My eyes go to each one, looking for Claire, but I don't see her. Then I remember that she's probably in disguise. But I know my girl, and I don't see her.

I'm not sure if I'm happy or sad about that, but I know I'm not interested in anything on that stage. Leaning back, I chug my beer and then ask for another before pulling out my phone. Signing in to Jayden's Facebook account since he's still friends with Claire, I go to her page – like I've done all day and every day since I deleted her – to see if she's updated her status. When I see that she updated about an hour ago, I click on it to read it.

> *Claire Anderson: My life is going to change tonight, I feel it in my gut. It may be the start of something new and exciting but it could possibly be the end of something else. While I want to be excited for my future, I can't when I don't have him beside me. #broken #IMissHim #HopeHeShowsUp #IDontWantToLiveWithoutHIm*

Chewing on the inside of my lip, I open the comments and read as all her friends say that if it is meant to be, it will work out, and all that stupid stuff that girls say to make the other girl feel better, when really they are just happy she's miserable like them. Taking in a deep breath, I read her status again, and I don't know how I feel. I miss her. So much. I love her, even though she lied to me. I know that, and I really don't want her to start something new without me. I want to be there with her. I want to be supportive and cheer on her endeavors. I just have to figure out if I can let it go. Since being on Facebook won't do that, I tuck my phone in my pocket and look out at the stage.

This time a girl is dancing solo with a chair. When I'm sure it is not Claire, I reach for my beer just as someone says, "I didn't think you were going to come."

I look over my shoulder to find Phillip standing behind me. I nod slowly and say, "Didn't think I was going to either."

"Is this seat taken?" he asks, pulling out a chair, and before I can answer, he lowers himself into it, leaving his forearms on the table and looking at me. "I'm glad you came. It will mean the world to her."

I shrug. "Yeah, don't tell her 'cause I'm not sure how I feel about this yet."

Phillip nods his head slowly, his eyes on his hands, and I'm not sure why he's here. "I wanted to talk to you about that."

"Why?" I ask, my brows coming together. "Shouldn't you be glad that we broke up? That there is a chance I'm no longer going to steal Claire away? I'm no longer a threat, so what is there to talk about?"

He glares and then says, "A lot actually. While I don't want you with her, and I don't want you to take her away from me, I know she loves you. And because she loves you, I have to give you the benefit of the doubt and trust that she's right about you."

"Yeah, that trust thing with Claire is a little iffy right now," I say, and I know he doesn't like that one bit.

"You know she lied to me too," he says and I meet his gaze, surprised by that. "But here is how I forgave her. I know it's different because you don't have to love her, but–"

"Yeah, I do," I say. "I do have to love her."

He nods with a grin growing on his face. "I thought you might say that. So let's just say we're in the same boat then, and this is how I've stayed afloat and not lost my mind," he pauses and lets out a breath before looking back at the stage. I don't know what he's thinking, but of course, I need to know how he forgave her. I didn't know that she had lied to both of us; I thought she told Phillip everything.

Looking back at me, he says, "I know I could just stop talking to her. Cut all ties and just do what is expected – make sure she's taken care of and safe. That was my plan at first because I couldn't get over that she'd lied to me. Me, her person, but she did. For a long time, and my wife was in on it too. You can just imagine how pissed I was."

I don't answer; I just nod as he goes on, "But then after five days, I sat there and thought, can I really let her go and never see her smiling face again or hear her tell me she loves me? The answer was no. I promised that I would love her and support her no matter what, and I've done a great job of that. Yeah, I'm hard on her about guys she dates, but she knows I love her. Do I like that she's on that stage? Hell no. I hate it and want to pull her off it, but she had it in her head that she has to have this security of money. She doesn't now, if you're wondering. She knows who she needs, where she finds her security – it just took trial and error to learn that."

I clear my throat since it is thick with emotion and say, "I understand that everyone makes mistakes, but how do I forgive her? How do I trust that she'll never hurt me again?"

"You just do," he answers simply. "I 'dated' Reese for months, and when she broke up with me, and then she wanted me back, I had that moment where I was like, do I take her back? Do I trust that she'll never hurt me again? I thought, can I live without her smile and the sound of her telling me she loves me? The answer was no again. Those two girls have me wrapped around their fingers, and yeah, they both messed up, but I forgave them because I love them."

Chewing on my lip, I let out a long breath. I'm not sure why, but I admit, "But I don't want to be my mom, forever forgiving my dad's mistakes."

"I understand that and I agree, but if they really love you, they won't make the same mistake twice."

Looking toward the stage, I take in a deep breath as another girl comes on and does some fan looking dance. Weird, but I need something to distract me because Phillip is killing me here. Every time I hear Claire's name, think of her sweet lips and loving eyes, a little piece of me breaks because I miss her so much. I'm so irritated with myself for falling so quickly and not seeing that she may have been holding back some things. Instead of questioning and being more sure of who I was falling for, I just fell. And for some reason, I don't regret any of it. I love Claire. With everything inside me. And I want her back.

"You've heard that song, 'Hey Jude,' right?" he asks suddenly, and I give him a dark look as he smiles. "Of course you have, but there is a part in the song that I think will help. You know the song, so correct me if I'm wrong, but I think it goes, 'Hey Jude, don't be afraid, you were meant to go out and get her.'" He waits for me to say something, but what the hell do I say to that? So I just stare at him as he grins like a fool, like he's the funniest guy in the world, and then he says, "I mean, it says it in the song; I think you should listen."

Scoffing, I roll my eyes as I direct them back to the stage. "I don't know."

Suddenly, his hand comes crashing against my shoulder and he says, "You do know."

Then I watch as he walks away, sitting beside the person I had assumed was Reese. Sitting down, he kisses her cheek, and I let out the breath I was holding. That guy makes me so nervous, but the surprising thing is he's the only one who's gotten through to me. I'm not sure why, but maybe I can trust her, maybe I can believe that this can work, that I can forgive her.

Glancing up at the stage since the room has gone dark, I watch as they set up a pole. Then the soft music starts and the curtain behind the pole opens to reveal Claire standing in all her gorgeous glory. She's wearing only one of my Bullies tees, her red hair shiny and down along her shoulders, with no makeup. It's not what I expected. I expected her to be all done up, ready for a show, but she looks so beautiful, so vulnerable.

And fuck, I miss her.

I've gotten her texts, her calls, her Facebook messages, but I've just ignored everything trying to figure out what I need to do. I've seen her around campus, but I don't think she's ever seen me. A part of me feels like she stopped looking, but then I realized that maybe she felt as empty as I do and was just going through the motions of life. Like I have. I mean, what is the point of trying to live a good life when it's not with your other half?

It's like lying, and I'm tired of lying.

CHAPTER 49

🩰 Claire

As I stand there, the lights warm my face and I look out into the audience. Searching for him.

My nerves are eating me alive, and I've never been nervous before, but the seven men that sit behind Reese and Phillip are the men who are going to decide my future in this business.

But I don't see him.

Biting into my lip to keep it from wobbling, I run my hands up my thighs, taking the edges of Jude's shirt and pulling it off, throwing it to the ground as Curtis Jarvis sings "Stay With Me." It's one of my favorite songs since Jude and I split up, if that's what you call it. I stand in only a black lace sports bra and matching boy shorts, not as Diamond either, as Claire. Claire Anderson, the girl who loves Jude Sinclair more than anything in this world, and this song is for him, but he isn't here to see it.

Slowly strutting forward, my fingers dance along the pole, imaging that it's Jude who I'm touching. Bending at my waist, I throw my leg up behind me, pressing my foot into the pole above my head. I hear clapping, but I ignore it because all I can think is that Jude didn't come, and that basically means we're through. That he doesn't want me.

Swallowing my tears, I drop my leg, turning my back to the pole and sliding down it till my butt hits the floor. Lifting my legs over my body, I wrap them around the pole and then lift my top half off the ground, arching my back up. I want to look graceful, I want to be pretty for everyone, but I just feel like giving up and accepting that I'll never truly be happy. Coming off the pole, I wrap one leg around it, spinning around the pole as my hair dusts the ground, running my hands down my body and then back up before climbing up the pole to do more tricks. But soon it's all second nature to me, and I wonder if everyone knows I'm not enjoying myself, that I'm not even trying.

That I'd rather be in my room, my face buried in my pillow, crying over Jude.

When I let go of the pole, stretching my arms above my head, holding myself with my thighs, I spin and spin and spin, the wind I'm making cooling my skin and the light blinding me. I'm used to it though, I've practiced this over a million times, it seems. Holding on to the pole, I open my legs and slide down the pole until my thighs touch the floor as I look out into the crowd. When my eyes meet Phillip's, and I see that pride is basically seeping out of his pores, I know I have to give this my all. He forgave me, he supports me, and I have to try for him.

Standing up, I kick my leg up, doing the splits on the pole as I drop my head back, my hands coming down my body into my hair as the singer sings his ass off. As I continue my tricks and wow the crowd, and hopefully the investors, I think that, yeah, we're through, and yes, it is going to suck really bad, but hey, I had the love of my life young. Do I regret my decisions? More than anything. But at least when I had the chance, I loved him with all my heart and soul. I gave one hundred percent to us, but I held back something that I know was wrong, and because of that, I learned my lesson. Everything in my life has been a learning curve, and when it is time for me to love again, and Lord knows when that will be, I'll love with all my heart and know never to lie to the person I love. I fucked up and I know this. I just have to accept that he's gone, but still, I can't give up a chance of a lifetime.

Dancing like this is the last dance I'll ever do, and I know everyone is impressed when the music ends and the lights dim. Phillip and Reese jump to their feet as they clap and Reese cries. Blowing a kiss to them, I watch as men lay money on the stage, and I smile a thanks to them even though I'm not thankful for it. I don't want the money, I want to see Jude, and I want him to wrap his arms around me and tell me he loves me.

That's my security, that's my safe haven…

That's what I need.

The show ends as I step offstage, and the first person I see is Ms. Prissy. She wraps her arms around me, hugging me tightly as she kisses my forehead. "Phenomenal."

"Thank you," I sigh, and I try to smile, but it's more of a grimace. It was my best pole dance, and I wish Jude were here. I wish he would have been sitting beside Phillip, cheering me on, but that isn't what's in my cards, and I'll learn to accept that. Someday.

"They'll be back in a few. Want to go change?"

"Yeah," I agree as I walk away, heading to my station. Ellen is sitting at her station on her phone, her things packed up, and it reminds me that I need to pack up my things. I throw on my Bullies sweats and I start to pack as I say, "So you're going through with it?"

She looks at me in the mirror and nods. "I love him."

"He's a liar and a cheat. You aren't making the right decision," I say, but I know it's no use. She's going to New York with Mr. Sinclair to run his club. Not only is the club going to suck, but they won't last. He's the dirt on the bottom of my shoe, and she doesn't deserve that. Plus she couldn't run anything. She doesn't have the smarts for it, as horrible as that sounds.

"I don't agree. We're happy, so he left his family for me. It's true love," she says, her eyes diverting to her phone.

I watch her for a long time, and I just shake my head. Taking in a deep breath, I want to call her a dumbass, tell her she's doing something so wrong and dirty, but who am I to judge?

Nodding my head, not in agreement, I say, "Good luck, Ellen."

She doesn't say anything to me, and I'm thankful for that. Quickly, I pack up my things just as Ms. Prissy calls me to her office.

As I pass by Ellen, she says, "Good luck to you too."

I send her a small smile, and that's all I can muster up for her. I can't believe that she would stay with someone like that, but it's not my problem. Mrs. Sinclair kicked him to the curb according to Jayden, so as long as she's done with him, I should be too. Especially since I'm not even dating her son anymore, and plus, I'm about to find out my future. I have bigger things to worry about than dealing with Ellen's bad choices.

Swallowing loudly, I go through the door to see that Ms. Prissy's office is full. Not only are the seven investors from Vegas there, but also the lawyer that Phillip hired, and Ms. Prissy, of course. Taking a deep breath, I put a smile on my face and decide that this is it; I have to let go of the past.

And that includes Jude.

⁂

An hour later I walk out of the office not really sure what just happened. My skin is tingling, my heart racing, and I feel breathless.

Did that really just happen?

Like a zombie, I walk to my station and grab my things before heading out to find Reese and Phillip. They said they would meet me in the parking lot, and that's where I find them, standing beside their car.

Phillip takes my box and asks, "So?"

"Tell us!" Reese giggles.

A smile covers my lips and tears rush to my eyes as I say, "I just signed a half a million dollar contract for three years to be the director and choreographer of Diamond Burlesque Revue in Las Vegas, Nevada."

"Oh shit!" Phillip yells, wrapping me up in his arms and hugging me. I feel Reese behind me, kissing my temple as they both hug me tightly. Tears rush down my cheeks as I hold on to the two people who have been my rock my whole life. When I told Reese that my life began when I came to them, I meant it. I came alive when I met Jude, but now that's all over. Knowing that makes the tears come faster, drenching Phillip's shirt. Kissing my cheek loudly, he says, "I'm so proud of you."

"Thank you," I cry as we part. Wiping my face, I take in a deep breath. "I can't believe it," I laugh. "Me in Vegas!"

They both beam at me. "We're so proud! When do you leave?" Reese asks.

"Around April," I say, letting out the deep breath I sucked in. I want to be happy. I want to know this is going to be the start of my new life, but I just feel empty. I miss Jude. I want him here, beside me, cheering me on. I want to know that he'll be there whenever I want to call him or need him. Swallowing a sob, I whisper, "I just wish Jude was here."

"I know, sweetheart," Reese says, running her thumb along my cheek, and we share a long, loving look.

"He was," Phillip says.

I whip my head toward him as I screech, "What?!"

"Yeah, I'm here."

I turn around, and I honestly feel like I'm going to pass out. Meeting Jude's green eyes, I'm breathless, and I swear my heart stops at the sight of him. I haven't seen him since the game and nothing has changed. He stills looks sad, his eyes dark and his beard growing thickly – which is so damn sexy, in my opinion. Taking in a breath, I whisper, "You came."

"I did," he says, his eyes locked to mine.

My whole body catches on fire, my heart clanking against my ribs, and I feel like a weight has been lifted off my chest. Breathing deeply, I say, "I'm so glad you did. Thank you."

He nods and his eyes cut to where Phillip and Reese are watching us. I look over at them with wide eyes that say "Get the hell out of here!"

Thankfully Reese catches on and pulls Phillip's arm. "Let's go. Claire, call us when you're done. We'll go celebrate."

"Huh?" Phillip says, confused. "I want to know what happens."

"No! Let's go," she urges, sending a grin at Jude. "So nice to see you, Jude."

"Nice seeing you, Reese," he says before looking down at the ground.

"I'm not going home, Claire. We're going to get barbecue," Phillip says, annoyed, and I give him a dark look.

"I'll meet you there," I say as they get into the car with only a wave from Reese. When they pull away, I look back over at Jude and say, "Maybe you would like to come?"

He looks up at me and shrugs. "Maybe."

Well, that's hopeful, right? I hope so because I don't think my heart can take any more. It is pounding hard against my ribs, my breath coming out in spurts, and I honestly don't know what is going to happen here. I don't know what to say, I don't know if I should move, I can't do anything but look deep into those emerald green eyes and hope to God I get the chance to look at them for the rest of my life.

"I miss you," he whispers, his lips moving ever so slowly, and I swear those words are music to my ears.

I don't even realize I'm crying again until the tears are running into my mouth. "I miss you, Jude. So damn much."

"I'm sorry," he says then. "I'm sorry for ignoring you and pulling away the way I have."

"I understand why you did," I say, my hands shaking at my sides.

"I'm scared, Claire," he says, his own eyes filling with tears, and it fucking kills me. "I'm scared that I'm going to trust you and then you'll break me again. I mean, I know this is probably not as big a deal as I'm making it, but I don't do lying. I've been one hundred percent honest with you. I never lied, and you held this part of you away from me? Is it 'cause you thought I wouldn't support you?"

I nod slowly. "I didn't think you'd want me if you knew I danced like this."

"Did you give me the chance, though?"

I shake my head, biting into my lips because he may very well miss me, and probably still loves me, but if he can't trust me, what is the point?

"No, I didn't," I whisper. "And I know that's wrong, but I couldn't lose you. I knew the dancing wasn't forever, I knew that it was just until I got the money I needed, and then I would quit. I had nothing, Jude, and I refused to live through that again. I don't ever want to go back to that life, where being alive didn't matter. A time when I didn't believe in anything." My throat is closed tight with emotion, and I have to look away to compose myself. "I thought I was going to be her; I thought I was going to be alone, no one loving me, and I couldn't do it. I knew that I had to work. I had to make sure that I never quit and did everything I could to secure my future. I thought I was on my own. I never believed in trusting someone, in being in love, but Jude, that all changed the moment I met you. You've opened my eyes, my heart, and now I know I don't need anything but the love of the people I love."

Chancing it, I take a step toward him, and thank God, he doesn't move. I then reach out, lacing my fingers with his, and I shake all over from the connection. I've been dreaming of touching him for the last two weeks, and to feel his warm, callused hands against mine causes the tears to almost choke me as I try to talk again. Taking in a deep breath, I clear my throat and very softly, I say, "Everyone makes mistakes, and I made the biggest one, but I promise you I will work my ass off to prove that I love you and that I will never lie to you or hurt you again. All I need is another chance. All I need is for you believe in me. I just need you to trust me again."

His eyes are swimming in tears as he looks into my eyes intensely. His chest is rising and falling very quickly, his lips parted as he breathes in and out. My stomach feels empty, fluttery even, and everything inside me is frozen waiting for him to respond. When his lips start to move, nothing comes out, and I squeeze his fingers, my heart stopping. Suddenly he brings me to him and then his lips are moving against mine. I sob against his lips, crumpling into his arms as he holds me close to him. Kissing my lips, the side of my mouth, my nose. A hysterical laugh leaves my lips, but when his lips meet mine again, I close my eyes tight, savoring this moment.

When we part, he cups my face, looking deep into my eyes and everything just feels perfect. Magical even. Wrapping my arms around his torso, I smile and he smiles back.

"I've dreamed of doing that every second I breathed."

I nod. "I've missed you so much."

He moves his nose along mine. "I've missed you way more."

As he moves his lips with mine, we hold each other as we kiss slowly, drawing out each kiss, making up for our time apart. Pulling back, I run my fingers through his beard and smile. "I'm so sorry."

"I forgive you," he whispers against my mouth.

I swear it's like Mount Rushmore just fell off my shoulders. Leaning into him, I kiss the side of his mouth and say, "Thank you."

Smiling, he says, "You're welcome, but really, I don't think there is any other option but to trust you. It was my pride that kept me from you. I couldn't let it go. I was worried that I would turn into my mom."

"I would never do that to you," I promise.

As he nods, his nose rubs against mine. "I know that now but it took me some time to realize that."

"What made you change your mind?"

Pinching my jaw between his thumb and forefinger, he says, "I had someone tell me that that I had to think about never seeing your smile or hearing you say I love you, and if I could go on without it, then I didn't need you. But if I couldn't, then I had to let you into my heart and then I could make it better."

"So they went all 'Hey Jude' on you?"

He nods. "To the fullest. It was kinda weird."

Running my hands up his back, I curl my hand along his shoulders and lean into him. "I'm glad they did, because we're way better together than we are apart."

Closing his eyes, he places his lips so close to mine and then whispers, "I couldn't agree more."

He then takes my lips with his, drawing the sweetest and hottest kisses out of me. I mold against him, cherishing every second his lips are on mine. Parting ever so slightly, he whispers, "I thought that I could let you go, and I thought that having yours lips tattooed on my chest would be a great reminder of our love, but all it did was make me realize that I don't want memories, I want us. I want to be with you for the rest of my life, Claire. When I watched you dance tonight, I knew I couldn't let my baby go to Vegas without knowing her man is right beside her, cheering her on."

"So you heard?" I ask, my lips curving in a grin.

"Oh yeah, and man, I'm so proud of you," he says with a beautiful grin on his face. Seeing it makes my heart hurt since I missed it so much. "The crazy thing is I trust you on that stage. If you want to dance, go ahead. You don't need to, but if you want to, I support you and I love you." My heart warms, my head feels fuzzy, and I can't believe the words that are coming out of his mouth. Smiling, he says, "It took losing you to know that. I had to grow a little more, and I think we needed those two weeks to realize that this wasn't some fast, crazy love, that this is real."

"It is real," I say through tears. "I knew that from the beginning."

"Yeah, I think so too."

"But I won't ever be on that stage. My contract is strictly to be a director and choreographer of the revue."

He lets out a breath and says, "Oh, thank God." I start to laugh and he smiles, holding me close to him. "I would have supported you, though."

"I know, and I'll always support you," I breathe, running my fingers through his hair. "I don't want to ever be apart, but there is a good chance we will be."

"I know, especially with you going off to Vegas and me going wherever, but Claire, you know that you're it for me, right?"

"I've always known that," I whisper, moving my thumb along his beard, my heart exploding for this guy. "And we will be fine."

"Of course we will because you're the one. You've always been the one."

I couldn't say it better myself. Wrapping my arms tighter around him, I go to goo when he hugs me back just as tightly. With his mouth so close to mine, he looks into my eyes and I want to cry I've missed him so much, but now I'll never have to miss him like that again. We may be apart in the future, but I'll always know that he's mine and I am his. We're going to fight and we're going to want to kill each other, but in the end, we will always love each other, and I can't wait to see what the future holds.

Getting lost in his gaze, I smile, running my thumb along his jaw. With a grin on his face, he kisses the side of my mouth and I suck in a deep breath, completely in awe of him. This is my boyfriend, my man, and I get to spend the rest of my days figuring out ways to show to him that he's mine, and I know he'll do the same.

"By the way," he says against my lips. "I love you."

I've never been one to believe words – I'm an action kind of girl – but when Jude's eyes meet mine and those three words leave his lips, I completely believe him.

So with a grin on my face, my head dizzy from the hit of love he just gave me, I whisper, "By the way, I love you too. So very much more."

"Just want I wanted to hear," he says with a wink.

"Glad I could please, but Jude, you'll need to get ready," I say, my eyes dancing with mischief.

"For?" he asks, his eyes darkening with lust.

"Not that!" I say, and he grins as he lifts me off my feet, kissing my lips. "Okay, maybe some of that, but for real, get ready for our life together."

Holding me close, his eyes bore into mine, and all I see is his love for me. I don't know how we made it those two weeks without each other, but I know we will never be apart like that again.

Kissing my nose, he says, "It's going to be amazing."

I couldn't agree more.

CHAPTER 50

 **JUDE**

Seven months later...

My whole body is shaking, my heart is louder than the crack of a puck on a hockey stick, and I still can't believe this is happening. This is my future. With my fingers laced tightly with Claire's, I glance over at her, thankful that she flew to Boston for the draft. I was worried she wouldn't able to make it, but she promised she would, and when I woke up this morning to her pounding on the door, I could have smothered her with kisses I was so happy to see her.

These past months have been unbelievably amazing. Claire moved out to Vegas early, after Christmas, and when I say we Skype more than anybody on the planet, I'm not kidding. It's constant. I sometimes just watch her tell people what to do and train dancers. We even sleep with Skype on, just so that if one of us wakes up, the other is there. I miss her constantly, but I'm thankful she has the weekends off and flies home to be with me. It's a lot on her, but she's doing the job beautifully and our love has never been stronger. Diamond Burlesque Revue opens in three weeks, and the buzz about the club is awesome. Claire is excited, which makes me excited, and with the club opening, I really didn't think she would be able to come, but she made it happen.

She is here for me.

When my mom squeezes my hand, I glance over at her and smile. She's a different person now, and I believe that my dad held her back. She went back to teaching, and I've never seen her so happy. My dad, who we now refer to as the dickhead, is holding off the divorce so he can avoid paying her alimony. It's a fucking headache, but one day she will be free of him. At first it was hard, though; she was extremely broke, and we thought we were going to lose the house, even with all of us working to help out. But then out of nowhere someone paid the house off, taking a huge financial burden off my mother since my dad left her with no money. To this day, my mom still tries to pay Claire back, but she won't take it. I think I fell in love with her all over again when I found out the check was from her. She told me it wasn't a big deal, but I think it was. I think it was extremely gracious of her.

She constantly amazes me.

Letting go of my mother's gaze, I look down at where everything is set up for the draft. All thirty teams are prepared. Their coaches, GMs, owners, everyone is down there deciding my fate. The first team is on their fifteen-minute time limit. I'm nervous and hoping I go first, but I don't know if I will. I feel like I'm going to throw up. I'm nervous as shit, but then I feel Claire's lips against my neck and a sense of calm washes over me.

"You are going to be fine," she whispers in my ear, and I nod.

"Thanks," I say and she smiles, kissing me again. "What if I don't get picked first?" I whisper in her ear.

She shrugs. "Then you'll get picked second."

I give her a look, and she smiles. "No matter what, I love you and I'm so proud of you."

"I love you."

I look back down to where the Los Angeles Kings are making their choice. They weren't supposed to go first, but they traded one of the top-scoring, senior forwards for the first-round pick. They love me from what my agent says, but they could pass me up for anyone, and that scares me. Did I not impress? I mean, I had a great season, we won the championship, and I know I'm the best, but am I good enough for first round?

"Stop shaking," she teases, and I send her a grin.

"I'm freaking out," I admit, and she shakes her head.

"You'll be–" she starts but then the announcer interrupts her.

"The Los Angeles Kings have made their pick." I squeeze her and Mom's hand as the announcer leans to the mic. "The Los Angeles Kings' first-round pick is Jude Sinclair of the University of Bellevue."

Holy fuck.

Jumping up, Claire cries out, pulling me up into her arms. Kissing me hard on the lips, her excitement is intoxicating and knocks me out of my paralyzing shock. Kissing her back, I say, "I love you."

"I love you!" she cries, her face flooded with tears. "I told you!"

"Yeah, you did," I say with a nod.

"Didn't I say I was always right?"

No way in hell am I going to agree with her, but I am going to kiss her because this moment marks the start of our future together. And what better way to start it than with a kiss from the most amazing girl in the world?

They always say that love is a fantasy, but with this girl, it's a reality.

✕ PHILLIP

I've tried so hard not to hate Claire's boyfriend, but it's getting harder by the second. I know I talked him into giving her another chance, but that was mainly for Claire, and now I regret that more than anything. Standing in the face-off circle with the smug little bastard who has already scored on us tonight, I glare, waiting for the puck to drop.

"You know you want to let me marry her."

"Fuck off, Sinclair," I sneer as the ref pushes me back, but Jude keeps on grinning.

"I'll take care of her, Phillip. Just say yes," he says and I swear I am going to beat the fuck out of this kid.

"Shut up," I say again, and he just keeps grinning. When the puck drops, he somehow beats me to it, making me feeling like a fucking grandpa, and passes it back to his defensemen as he flies past me.

Fast little shit. He's gotten bigger too.

I rush to catch up with him, but thankfully Adler is there, stopping Jude from getting past him.

Or so I think.

Somehow the little asshole dekes around him as the puck comes up, and the next thing you know, Odder is sprawled out on the ice and the puck is in the back of the net. He throws his arms up, and I glare as he hugs his teammates. I turn, heading to the bench, and I'm almost there when he skates up beside me. When he starts to sing to me about being rude, I can only glare at him because I've heard that song on the radio, and it's not the song I want my niece's boyfriend singing to me! And also, what fucking respectable hockey player sings on the ice?

"I'm gonna marry her anyway, no matter what you say," Jude says with a shrug.

"The fuck you are," I yell, and he just smiles.

"Who's gonna stop me?"

And for some fucking reason, say it's his smug attitude or the fact we're losing, but I drop my gloves and snatch him by the back of the jersey. He turns just in time for my fist to crack against the side of his face. He comes at me with a punch, getting me in the nose, and the next thing I know we're throwing and receiving punches back and forth. I have to give it to the kid too; he can hold his own, his punches hurt, and the little asshole has a hard-ass face. I know I'm going to get shit for this later, but surely no one expects me not to put this kid in his place.

Locking up, we fall to the ground, and as the refs part us, I say, "She's too young!"

"I love her! And she loves me! Let me marry her. I'll fight you over and over again until you let me," he says, and I can see in his eyes that he isn't backing down; he wants her.

"This isn't the place to do this, boys!" the ref says, and I can even hear my coach hollering at me, but I'm not done.

"You don't deserve her!"

"That again?" he says as they throw us in our own boxes. I then hear him yell, "I love her, Phillip. Say yes!"

"No. Shut up," I yell back, leaning back in the box, breathing hard. As the game restarts and Kings' fans yell how much I suck and I should go back to Nashville, I sit there and replay the last year. The little shit has been good to Claire. When she isn't flying home, he flies to her, and she does love him. He even came over and visited with Sawyer and Reese, just to check in on them since Claire and I couldn't. But I just can't get over the idea of my baby girl getting married. Maybe she'll say no, though?

No, she won't.

When our time is up, the doors open and I head out at the same time he does. I look over at him, and he's looking toward the bench, not paying me any mind. I know I'm not going to see him after the game since we're heading out to Vancouver.

Letting out a breath, I say, "Hey Jude."

He looks over at me, his eyes burning with anger as he says, "Don't be afraid?"

"No, dumbass. Why does it matter if I let you?"

He shrugs. "Because she loves you, and I want you to support us."

I think that over for a minute, and as I reach the bench, I say, "Go ahead, marry her. But know I'll kill you if you hurt her."

He pauses at the door and says, "Wouldn't think of it."

When a grin replaces his angry look, I know I did a good thing, and I'll probably get in less trouble with Reese since I said yes after kicking his ass.

Or so I think.

CHAPTER 51

Claire

"He still isn't sleeping?" I ask as I smile at Sawyer, giving him fishy lips. He's only six months old, but he knows who his sissy is, and soon a little toothless grin appears on his sweet, chubby face. He looks so much like Phillip, same eyes and shape to his face, but he has Reese's brown hair and dark skin tone. He's a doll and my favorite, of course.

She shakes her head. "Nope, he wants to sleep all day and party at night. He's killing me. I'm blaming Harper too; she spoils him."

I smile. Harper keeps him while Reese works at the studio since I'm gone now. "He's sweet, and she loves her nephew."

"Whatever. What time is it there? One?"

"Yeah," I nod as I lean back against my chair. The walls are vibrating with music, but one of the must-haves was soundproof walls so that when I needed to talk to my family I could. Thankfully my bosses were fine with that because they were crazy expensive, but then, I don't think they care. They love me and have been amazingly awesome. I mean, I'm living in a penthouse above the Lights and Sounds hotel, I drive a Mercedes, and I have a clothing allowance that would make Kim Kardashian piss her pants. I am set, and man, I love it here. I do wish that Jude was here a hundred percent of the time, but we both knew this was going to happen, that we would be apart. I do have the same problems that every director has, but I don't know many twenty-year-olds with this kind of job, a hot NHL boyfriend, and basically living a dream life. I am constantly waiting to wake up, but it still hasn't happened. I don't know what I did to deserve this amazing life, but I'm more than thankful for it.

Glancing at the clock, I glare. I don't know why Jude hasn't called me, he usually calls me an hour after his game, but it's almost been four hours, which is really weird.

"Did you see the game?"

"Yes, idiots," I say with a shake of my head.

Seeing my uncle and boyfriend fight shouldn't have been so shocking to me, but it was, and I plan on ripping both of them a new one. "Jude should be calling me anytime now. He's superlate, probably trying to ignore me, but when he does finally call me, I'll let him have it."

"Yeah, Phillip is ignoring me. Even sent me a text saying he knows I'm mad, but just give him a chance to explain. I can't believe he threw the first punch."

"It was obvious that Jude was taunting him. Figures the first time they play each other is the first time they fight. Been good the whole year, but as soon as they get on the ice, they want to be idiots."

"So dumb," she says with a shake of her head. She looks amazing and not like a momma that gets no sleep. Her eyes are bright, and I have to admit that motherhood looks amazing on her. Kissing Sawyer's cheek, she looks at the camera and waves his little hand. "Say, hi sissy, we miss you."

I smile, leaning on my hand. "I miss you guys. I'll be home for Thanksgiving."

"Good, we can't wait. Can we, buddy?" she asks Sawyer. He's just looking at the screen, trying to grab her phone. "Anyway, when do you get to see Jude?"

"I'm not sure. I was going to ask him tonight. I think this weekend he's going to fly up? I'm not sure. Things have been insane. I had to fire two girls 'cause they'd rather do blow than dance."

"More idiots," she says with a shake of her head.

"For sure," I sigh. "It's so annoying."

When my computer signals that I have another call coming in, I say, "Hey, let me let you go. Jude is calling."

"Okay, babe, talk to you later. Bye!"

"Bye! Love you, Sawyer! Love you too," I add quickly, and she laughs.

"We love you, bye!"

I smile as I switch over to Jude's call. When his beautiful face comes on the screen, I get a little breathless, like I always do. He's all smiles, but I notice right away that his right eye is almost swollen shut.

"You're an idiot," I say with a shake of my head.

"Wasn't my fault!" he says as he walks wherever he's going.

"Such a pretty face and you let him mess you up! And why the hell haven't you called me until now? It's been like four hours? Did you have to get right on the bus or something? Where are you? Why is it so loud?"

"'Cause I'm here to surprise you," he answers just as the door opens and he's standing there with a bouquet of red roses.

Squealing, I jump out of my chair and rush to him, wrapping my arms around him. Kissing his lips, I melt against him but then remember I'm mad at him. Pulling away, I smack him in the middle of the chest and he gives me a shocked look. "Jude! You can't fight my uncle!"

"Shh," he says as he grins, wrapping his arm around my waist and carrying me into the office. Kicking the door shut, he throws the bouquet down before holding me up with both hands and walking me to the desk. I know what he's about to do, and while I'm game for that since I haven't seen him in two weeks, I need to reiterate that he cannot fight my uncle. As his mouth meets mine, I sorta forget what I need to reiterate and get lost in the way his mouth moves against mine.

Things have been perfect between us. Even the fights we have over stupid crap are amazing because they are with him, and the make-up sex is unbelievable. Well, any sex is unbelievable, but still, I'm so freaking happy I could scream. Moving his hands up my corset, he kisses the tops of my breasts and says, "Fuck, you are hot in this thing."

"Thanks," I grin as he kisses up my neck to my jaw. "But seriously, Jude, no more fighting, promise me."

"I promise," he says roughly against my jaw.

Holding his face still, I pull back and ask, "Why were you fighting anyway?"

I feel his hands leave my body, and a second later he says, "Because of this."

He looks down and so do I to see the most stunning diamond ring. Gasping, I cover my mouth as my eyes fill with tears. Through my blurry eyes, I take in the rose gold band and the large diamond that is surrounded by little diamonds.

"Oh Jude," I gasp, and he smiles before dropping between my legs to his knees.

"I asked him if I could marry you. I've been asking since the day of the draft, and he has said no every time. Today, I decided I couldn't wait any more, not when I know my girl walks around looking this hot. I gotta put a ring on it, keep all the men away," he teases, and I laugh through my tears.

"Jude, there are no other men."

"I know there aren't," he says and all the laughter is gone as his eyes meet mine. "I want to marry you, Claire, and I finally have Phillip's permission. Took me getting my ass kicked, but hey, I'll do anything for the girl who, every time she looks in my eyes, makes me feel like I'm being slammed into the boards. I can't live my life without you because you are my other half. So what do you say? Wanna marry me?"

I'm nodding before the words fully leave his lips. "Of course I do!"

Sliding the ring on my finger, he grins widely at me before pressing his lips against mine and kissing the hell out of me. Smiling against my lips, he presses small kisses all over my mouth before pulling back to look into my eyes. Moving my fingers into his hair, I say, "So you've wanted to marry me since the draft?"

"I've wanted to marry you since I saw you in those geeky black glasses. I love you, Claire."

"I love you," I say, meeting my lips to his.

Pressing his head to mine, he locks his eyes with mine and I can't help but smile. I thought I was happy fifteen minutes ago, but right now I am ecstatic. I have the dream job, a healthy, beautiful family, and now a hot hockey-player fiancé. I'm living all my dreams because of the man who is staring into my eyes with a hunger that can't be touched, and while this would be a great moment to let him have his way with me on this desk, there is still one more thing that needs to be said.

"But still no fighting with your soon to be uncle-in-law."

I smile, expecting him to laugh with me, but his eyes stay serious as his mouth curves up just a tad. I love the little half smile he does. Hell, I love everything about this man and I will for the rest of my life.

Leaning into me, he whispers, "I don't have to fight anymore. I won the ultimate prize."

As my eyes swim with tears, I nod slowly because he's not the only one who won.

I did too.

THE END

A note from Toni Aleo

I hope that you enjoyed the spin off series from the Assassins. I was beyond excited to write Claire's book and what better way than to a spin off series! I love this book. It is probably one of my favorites, up there with Taking Shots. I enjoyed writing Claire's spunkiness and Jude's strength. Together they burned the pages but then at the end, I don't know about y'all but I was bawling. My heart was invested and I hope that yours was too, because that means I did my job. I thank you for reading this book and taking the time to spend with my characters. I hope they brought you a lot of enjoyment.

Without you, I wouldn't be in the business. I would probably be writing but just storing my books on a hard drive and living my life. I honestly can't thank you enough for the time you spend messaging me, emailing me and supporting me. Your love and support is so overwhelming but so much appreciated. I consider you a part of my family and believe me, I will never forget the reason why I spend hours away from my family and friends, the sleepless nights, the headaches from staring at the screen so long.

Its because of you.

So thank you.

Also I want to thank my family, Michael, Nick, Noey, Mikey and Alyssa: thank you for your undying love and support. Couldn't do this without you.

To my mom, who even in heaven is my biggest fan, I love you so much and miss you more than anything.

To my friends, Nortis, Bobbie, and Stacey: I know I get a little crazy around my deadlines, thank you for being so supportive and loving me even when I'm not there.

To Damaris: thanks for working so hard to make my books successful. Couldn't do it without you.

To Lisa: Thank you for coming in and editing the hell out of this book! You rock my love! And I am so thankful for our friendship.

To my beautiful amazing betas: Laurie, Lisa, Althea, Lisa, Mary, Susie, Lisa, Janette, Heather, and Kara: I couldn't write this book without you. Thank you.

To my family, thank you. I love you and can't thank you enough for being so supportive.

To Sommer: Thank you for a beautiful and amazing cover!

To Toski: Thank you for making this happen. I love this shot of Brandon and couldn't have it without you.

To Brandon: Thank you for being my model and also my friend.

To Elli: Thank you for bring me Brandon and becoming my friend.

To anyone else I missed, thank you. You will always be apart of my heart. All of you. Thank you.

Upcoming from Toni Aleo

A Very Hockey Holiday (Assassins 6.5)
Laces and Lace (Assassins 7)
Becoming the Whiskey Princess (Taking Risk Novel 2)
Clipped by Love (Bellevue 2)

And a brand new series is coming in 2015 from Toni Aleo
The Spring Grove Novels
Bring on the cowboys!

Make sure to check out these titles and more on Toni's website:
www.tonialeo.com

Or connect with Toni on Facebook, Twitter, Instagram and more!

Also make sure to join the mailing list for up to date news from the desk
of Toni Aleo: http://eepurl.com/u28FL

This paperback interior was designed and formatted by

www.emtippettsbookdesigns.com

Artisan interiors for discerning authors and publishers.

Made in the USA
Charleston, SC
17 January 2016